CONSUMING FIRE

ISABELLA MODRA

FOR THOSE WHO FAVOR FIRE.

ALSO BY ISABELLA MODRA

ROUGE
EMBERS & ICE

ACKNOWLEDGEMENTS

A lot of authors know how hard it is to close a trilogy. Some do it right, some fail miserably. It is because of the following people that I was able to conclude Hunter's story in what I believe to be a complete and enticing way… at least, until next time.

Phoebe – you're my favorite sister, and although you sometimes have weird things to say about the book, I love to hear them anyway. And you 'ship' Hunter and Will, which makes me happy.

Dad – you were the first to read this. Those tears you had at the very end meant I did something right.

My Wattpad fans – y'all think I'm famous or something but trust me, I would not have come this far without your support.

Aditi and John – without your input, Consuming Fire would still be a raw draft.

And most of all, my God – you created this blue planet, orbiting a ball of flames with a moon that moves the seas and you still had time to plant an idea in my head of a girl with red hair who plays with fire.

If anything consumes me more, it's the fire you ignite in me.

'THESE VIOLENT DELIGHTS HAVE
VIOLENT ENDS AND IN THEIR TRIUMPH
DIE, LIKE FIRE AND POWDER,
WHICH, AS THEY KISS,
CONSUME.'
- **WILLIAM SHAKESPEARE**

PROLOGUE

Though he knew the water would be terribly cold, Jack had to be brave. After all, his sister and his cousins were watching him. The lake that stretched before him glittered in colors of green and brown and blue, teasing him as the wind rippled across the surface and upset the water. The forest pines shadowed the shallow edges of the lake and the little picnic spot his family had worn through over the years. Their holiday spot.

Jack clung to the rope with all he was worth and turned his head once more to the shallows where Clare was waving at him and his older cousins Todd and Mike were laughing at his fear. Jack was never one to shy away from danger, and he'd swung the rope into the lake many times before. Yet this time his feet remained planted on the tree root, unwilling to jump. There was a deep fear swirling inside him that had never been there before. A dark fear.

Come on, he urged himself. *Don't chicken out. Clare will never let you live it down.*

So Jack took a deep breath in, clenched the rope tightly and kicked off the tree. He soared through the air with flailing legs and swung low over the surface with his toes dipping into the cool lake. It was colder than ice. But he couldn't turn back now, so Jack opened his mouth and shouted their famous jungle call before releasing the rope and landing in the lake with a splash even bigger than chubby Todd's.

Jack had been swimming in the family lake for as long as he could remember. He knew the waters; he swam so often in the summer when

1

they camped that he could open his eyes and wait, pretending he had drowned. Inside he chuckled to himself as he floated in silence, staring into the cold and murky waters that engulfed him.

Then suddenly, Jack saw something strange through the glare. It was a flash of red, about three feet away. Nothing was ever clear in the lake, but Jack did not doubt his own eyes. It could have been seaweed, or perhaps a fish of some sort, only it was bright red like a fire truck. Jack swam toward it with blind curiosity, but the moment he blinked, it had vanished.

Woosh!

Jack spun in the water as the red thing flashed like a bullet right past him. Now he was sure it was not a fish. It looked like hair. Red hair.

Scared and bewildered, Jack kicked to the surface. When he broke it and gulped in a lungful of air, he realized it was no longer daytime and his family had left. The moon was high above his head, stars twinkling down upon him. He shivered in the dark water and twisted, trying to understand what was happening. *I must be dreaming,* he thought.

Then he saw her. Through the rippling waters, near the other side of the lake with her head bobbing eerily above the surface as she stared at him, he saw a haunting face.

The girl with the red hair.

"Jack," she called to him in a soft and melodic voice, a mere whisper across the water.

"Who are you?" he shouted. "Where am I?"

"Jack," she called again. "I've come for you Jack."

She chuckled and then disappeared under the water.

Jack's heart threatened to leap out of his chest. He started swimming to the shore, his arms slashing at the water. Fear of what lurked in the black depths around him made him cough and splutter in panic. He had a strange and sudden feeling that he was about to die.

Before he had swum even a few meters, a hand closed around his ankle. Jack screamed for help, but the woods were empty and they watched his struggle in silence. The hand that held him burned through his skin, pulling him down, down beneath the surface where there was no air and no way to find the sun. There was nothing, only darkness.

Only darkness.

– PART 1 –

FROM ASHES TO FLAME

ONE

e was the greatest man I ever knew.

Those were the words Joshua repeated whenever she asked him, as an innocent little child, what her dad was like. She stopped asking after the years went by and the answer just confused her more. Hunter knew of people who searched their whole lives for the truth about their parents, never letting them go, *needing* to know who they were. But Joshua only said good things. Simple, humble things. And that was enough for her. Up until the day in the lab, that is.

As Hunter stood before the glass, her heart so crowded with emotions that it had no room to move in her chest, she remembered the day she visited her parent's graves after Joshua revealed how they actually died. She understood how different her life would be if she grew up with them, without powers, like a normal teenager. Joshua would only be a family friend and not the man who raised her. On that day, she accepted her fate and that she would never know her parents.

It had always been about her mother from then on. How she died giving birth to Hunter. How it was because of the combination of the chemical drug Feucotetanus and the volcanic substance called Ravenadium that she had her abilities. How her mother knew the truth about Joshua, about his experiments, about his demons. It was her mother's voice that calmed the fire in the warehouse so long ago.

He was the greatest man I ever knew.

But the man lying on the bed, a bed he'd been trapped in for nearly twenty years, could not possibly be her father.

Hunter looked up into Dr. Wolfe's cruel, oyster eyes. "That's not my father. He's dead. He died before I was born."

His chilling smile finally sent feeling back into her body and her heart lurched. "I'll prove it to you."

She was led with shaking hands out of the little black alcove that still smelled of gravy into the room itself. Hunter hesitated, not wanting to enter. The doctor left the door open. Two guards stood beside it, watching her, ready to take her back to imprisonment when given the order.

"He will be moved in the coming days to a more equipped station where my team of scientists will speed up the healing process."

That should have mattered to Hunter, but it didn't.

Dr. Wolfe sighed, as if she were a stupid child. "Come in, he won't bite."

Hunter swallowed nothing in her dry mouth and stepped inside. The man's physical appearance was enough to bring up the empty contents of her stomach. Burns covered every inch of his body. The room smelled of salves.

Dr. Wolfe passed her a file. It was hand-written and very old, containing information about the genetic studies performed on the patient before her. Even if it all made sense on paper, it did not make sense in her memory, nor in everything Joshua had told her about the night her father burned in the fire.

She looked down at the man, then back at the data, but could not comprehend it. Hunter watched the rise and fall of his chest under the blankets, at the flutter of his scarred eyelids, and realized she'd had enough. This was some new form of torture. The information was made up; this man was not the man who carried her DNA. This was a lie.

She stepped back. "I'd like to go back to my cell please."

"Wouldn't you like to hear how he survived?"

She shook her head. She was about to break, and she could not break in front of him. Not again.

"You're not happy to see your real father, Hunter?" he taunted her. "A man who would never hurt you the way Joshua-"

"Take. Me. Back."

6

The words were full of passion and anger, words of the fire in her core and not her grief. But Dr. Wolfe would not release her, and he left her no choice.

The only way he would send her back to her cell was if she deserved to go back there. Even worse, he would punish her for it. But she'd become used to punishment. Perhaps pain was better than being shown a lie claiming to be her only hope of family she had left in the world. Empty, physical torture was better than that.

Hunter found some joy in breaking the doctor's nose. It was a weak punch and it left her swaying into the guard's arms. If it were even possible, she'd become more fragile in the last few days of being imprisoned in the caves than all the weeks she spent above. She didn't fight back and slumped against the men, her vision swirling.

Blood dripped onto the floor from the doctor's wound. He stumbled back against the machine behind him, moaning through the hand clenched over his face.

Then suddenly, the man's heart rate monitor started to accelerate.

Hunter looked up. In that moment, his eyes opened and they met hers. It was like a cosmic explosion broke out inside her. The fire burst to life in a wonderful gust of warmth that spread through every inch of her tired, sunken body. The guards gasped and released her arms, for her skin had become so hot that she glowed again. And for the first time, the power restraint could not hold the fire in. Dr. Wolfe had a look of shock on his face that she'd never seen before, but at that moment, she didn't care.

Hunter stared into his eyes like staring into a mirror; a wonderful, ageless, golden mirror of the past.

Those eyes.

He *was* her father.

Two

If I have to stay in this hotel room for one more second," said Eli, "I'm going to eat all the pillows and hope I get fluff poisoning."

Joshua couldn't blame the kid, even though his moodiness was starting to grate on all of their nerves. Weeks had passed since they arrived in Seattle. *Weeks*. And all that time, it felt as if the FBI had sat around on their asses, twiddling their thumbs and waiting for more children to go missing.

"Just relax Eli," said Jenny in that perfect, calm-amidst-the-storm voice that made Joshua's heart flutter. But he had to admit; even she was beginning to look a little drained of her usual spark.

"Yeah right," Eli sighed and flopped back on the stiff hotel bed. "How can anyone relax when we're barricaded in by FBI agents and *no one* has rescued Hunter yet?"

Joshua couldn't agree more: relaxing was the very last thing on his to-do list. First and foremost, he needed to get to the cabin. It had been too long, and every day was another day Hunter was either still stuck in ICE, or out there running the risk of being captured again.

But the FBI were watching their every move. He was still under suspicion for kidnapping and attempted murder. They were right about him, of course, but it was circumstantial. And once he told them the truth about his powers... their trained eyes never left him.

"Joshua... have they told you anything?" asked Jenny as she sat by the open window with her feet propped up on the ledge, dressed in her habitual

8

ripped jeans and baggy sweater. Joshua loved that about her. "Because for law enforcement, they're very slow to react to the news that there are people with *superpowers*."

Joshua ran his hand over his jaw – conscious of how badly he needed to shave – and shook his head. He'd been wondering that too. Barry took the news somewhat lightly that Joshua had the ability to control ice. Once Barry had interrogated every inch of him – during which Joshua told him only the vital bits of information and not his entire life story – there had been nothing but routine questions, interviews with other FBI agents and then silence.

"I don't know," he said. "Every time I meet with Barry and his superior officer, Special Agent Fitzpatrick, they tell me nothing. It's like they're trying to make logical sense of it before they take it seriously."

"But this is big," said Eli. "I mean world-changing big. The existence of people with powers is something we read about in comics. If it leaks into the media, everyone's gonna explode. I think the FBI aren't telling anyone until they know for sure that not only do you have these abilities you claim to have, but that ICE exists too."

Joshua raised a hand and produced a beautiful swirl of light ice that danced above his palm. "I thought this was going to be proof enough."

"I mean *scientific* proof. These things only happen in movies. If I saw someone do what you do Joshua, I wouldn't believe it. I'd try to figure out how. Isn't that what you did?"

Joshua looked at Eli, and for the first time since this entire mess with him began, Joshua appreciated the kid for who he was: a very smart young man. He suddenly saw what Hunter had fallen in love with.

Love he had taken away.

"The FBI have strict protocol to follow," said Jenny as she moved over to the bed, distracting him. "They're not doing 'nothing'; they're just doing everything very thoroughly, by the books. Eli's right. If they make one mistake and the world finds out, it'll be chaos. People with powers like yours will be popping up all over the globe. And if the world finds out, Dr. Wolfe will know and he'll recede into an even deeper hole than he's already in. Then it will be impossible to find Hunter."

"I just need to know that she's out," said Joshua. He sat down on the bed beside Jenny and she softly rubbed his back. It was uncomfortably soothing.

Suddenly, there was a knock at the door. The three of them exchanged glances. Normally if the FBI needed them, they would call for Joshua to be taken to the field office located just across the street from their boutique motel.

Eli ran to the door and peered through the peep hole. "It's Barry and ... some other woman. Should I open it?"

"Yes," said Joshua, praying it was good news and not the food that fed the fear inside him.

Barry nodded to them somberly as he strolled in, followed by the only woman Joshua had ever come in contact with who made his skin prickle – and not in a good way. Her dark skin and bright, white eyes squinted at him in suspicion and brought more unsettling feeling into his rigid body.

"Everyone, this is Special Agent Fitzpatrick. Special Agent Fitzpatrick, this is-"

"I know who they are, Agent Sanders," Fitzpatrick snapped and Barry fell silent. She directed her attention to Joshua. "We have news."

His senses spiked and the tips of his fingers turned to ice as he slowly stood. *Don't let her be dead, please God, don't let her be dead ...*

"This ICE institution you claim to be responsible for the missing children does not exist," she said. "I've had every available operative scouring the mountain for the past two weeks, and there has been no sign of any life."

Joshua's heart dropped. "That's impossible. Unless they moved an entire underground operation, it will still be there in the mountains."

"Well it's not." She crossed her arms, a condescending look in her eyes. "You said you escaped nearly seventeen years ago, correct?" Fitzpatrick snorted a humorless laugh. "You have to be the dumbest human being I have ever known." With that, she clicked her hands at Barry and he withdrew a large map from behind him, which he laid out on Jenny's bed. The map was of the United States, and it was covered in geographical numbers and lines measuring the height of the mountains that surrounded it. There was a circle around a pass to the left of a mountain range called Gannett Peak in the state of Wyoming. "The directions you gave us led to the highest mountain in Wyoming. Because you told us that it was a two hour drive from this town–"

"I gave you the best I could," he snarled and stood to his feet. "I was lost, weak and carrying a two-year-old child in the middle of a snowstorm. I'm sorry if I didn't have the brain power or the technology to get you the exact coordinates. But for Christ's sake, if I could escape in a 4WD, surely you can find it in a freaking helicopter with satellite navigation and the entire force out searching for it!"

Fitzpatrick glared at him with such ferocity, Joshua felt as if he were being burned by her gaze. And only Hunter had the power to do that. Perhaps her own inadequacy fueled the anger inside of her. All Joshua had heard from her since his first meeting with her weeks ago was negativity and snappy comments. She looked exhausted, fed up and ready to throw in the towel with him.

That didn't mean she wasn't going to let him get the better of her.

Fitzpatrick raised a finger like a patronizing parent and walked slowly toward him. "Now you listen to me, *Snowflake*. The reason we have taken so long to track down your made-up institution is because it does not exist. We've sent in squadrons of trucks to scout the mountain range, questioned the local Indian reserve – who do not let anyone *near* the pass without strict permission – and we've done satellite scans of the area for any sign of technological activity. We found nothing. So by the sounds of it, your ICE institution has either gone out of business or else completely vanished." She was only a foot away from him, backed up against the wall, her finger against his chest and making him very anxious. "You sent us on a wild goose chase, Harrison, and I'd like to personally thank you for wasting my time and money, money that could be used to save lives and not for a fairytale rescue mission." With that, she snatched the map from the bed, causing Eli and Jenny to flinch.

Joshua's hopes were running thin. He recalled the drive through the whirling wind and snow to the nearest town – his first sign of the outside world in months – as being one of the most wonderful and terrifying moments of his life. It was night, it was cold and he knew nothing about where he was going, only that they were completely free. But there began the years of always looking over his shoulder, of trying to be strong for the baby girl whose life depended on his safety.

ICE existed. He knew that for certain. So how was Dr. Wolfe hiding it so well? *Maybe they moved.* Joshua had never considered it. It had been, after all, sixteen years since he escaped. Was it was possible Dr. Wolfe packed up when Joshua ran away, just in case he went to the authority and the secrets of ICE were revealed?

If that were so, then finding ICE was now next to impossible without the help of someone on the inside, or someone who had just recently escaped.

"Look, I'm sorry your search came up with nothing," he said. "But I'm not lying to you. And I know a way to prove it if you'll just let me leave the hotel for-"

"Not a chance," Fitzpatrick shook her head. "Not only have you wasted my time, but you've also managed to piss me off, Harrison. And not just me, but my superiors as well. While this vain attempt to hunt a madman was going on in Wyoming, I was sent to Washington to meet with the Secretary of Defense. He wants real proof of your so-called abduction."

Joshua raised a hand and shot a jet of ice at a vase of flowers that sat on the table beside the television. The vase cracked open and shattered everywhere, shards of ice spilling onto the prickly carpet. Fitzpatrick didn't gasp like most people would, but she did lose her composure, and for that, Joshua felt proud.

"Proof enough for you? Or how about the fact that you still have children going missing all over the world? And what about the unexplained money transfers?"

"It's all coincidental."

Joshua couldn't believe her. He was about to burst with frustration. "Then tell me you at least checked on the cabin? Was there anyone living there, any proof at all of what I told you?"

"We found nothing," Barry answered. "Your cabin had no records, no proof of life for years, registered under a name that doesn't even exist in our system. The records date way back. It's going to take us a long time to find the owner."

"Like we haven't heard that before," Eli muttered quietly.

A black cloud descended upon Joshua's vision. It couldn't be. Hunter was still in ICE? Did Dr. Rosenthal receive his message? Was he even alive?

Suddenly all hope of finding Hunter vanished from Joshua's mind, leaving him feeling hollow and colder than ice itself. The temptation to grab Fitzpatrick's gun from her holster and shoot a bullet through his head bloomed like the prospect of warmth and the end to all his suffering. It was absurd to know that suicide had even crossed his mind. He could not. Hunter needed him.

Fitzpatrick crossed her arms. "If we have no further leads, we'll have to close the missing children investigation. But I'm afraid that won't be it for you and your two friends here. You've been booked for an early flight tomorrow morning to DC. They want your DNA analyzed and further proof that your 'abilities' aren't just some hoax."

"You're serious?" Joshua looked at Barry, who was still inspecting the vase. He avoided all eyes.

"We all have to go?" asked Eli incredulously. "But I'm-"

"It's not a request," said Fitzpatrick in a tone as poisonous as sin. "You'll be escorted directly to the airport where the three of you and my team will take a direct flight to DC. That is my final word. You should be thankful we're not sending you to a prison, Harrison, or an *asylum*."

Jaw clenched, Fitzpatrick twisted rigidly and stalked to the door. Barry shot him an apologetic glance and hurried after his senior, locking them in behind him.

A thick silence descended upon the room. Jenny placed a gentle hand on his shoulder. The touch was electric, but it did nothing to soothe his mood. He shrugged away, feeling the anger of the Iceman surge inside him. In a sudden burst of fury, he raised both his hands and threw a shard of ice straight at the door, but it was too thick to penetrate. The ice shattered.

"That's it," said Eli and he leapt to his feet. "We're going. I don't care if we add another felony to our charges, we have to get out of here."

"And go where?" asked Jenny.

"To investigate the cabin ourselves."

Joshua shook his head. "No. I can't go through the disappointment again. They said it was empty."

"What if they're lying? Or what if they missed something? Come on Joshua, you know more about this house than they do."

"He could be right," said Jenny reassuringly. "What's the harm in checking?"

The harm is that my heart can't take losing her again, he thought.

"Joshua," said Jenny. "Listen to me. I know you feel like giving up right now. But if ICE is as real as you say it is, then we have to find it. We have to for the sake of whoever is trapped there. Even if we have to scour the mountain ourselves, we'll find it."

"That sounds fun," Eli snorted sarcastically.

"We've come too far to give up now."

Just her voice had the ability to melt the ice inside him. Even if he felt like hope had dissipated, Jenny could still bring sunshine back into his cold world. Joshua raised his head and gazed at her, giving her the smallest of smiles.

She turned to Eli. "How do you propose we get out of here?"

"I was hoping Joshua would have some input, since he's the one with the superpower."

Joshua ran a hand through his slightly damp, slicked-back hair. Again, he felt a spark of gratification for the two of them. He realized then that he could not have done any of this alone.

Maybe it was time he started making up for his mistakes, embodying someone who could be trusted and looked up to. Maybe this was his opportunity not only to set things right with Hunter and save her from Dr. Wolfe, but to become the man he always seemed to fall short of in his own mind.

Her father.

"You're right," he said. Both Eli and Jenny brightened. "No more relying on the government. We're finding them ourselves. Starting with the cabin." Smiles beamed across their faces as he grabbed his coat from the stand by the door. When he realized they weren't behind him, he shot a glance over his shoulder. "What are you waiting for?"

They snapped into action, grabbing everything they deemed necessary for an escape mission as Joshua summoned the dark and brittle ice from within and steeled himself for a fight.

THREE

The doctor mercifully decided not to punish Hunter, but instead ordered the guards to escort her back to her cell. She was so out of focus that she tripped twice down the stone steps, her bare feet so calloused that she hardly noticed the sharp rocks beneath them. There was no other sound but the shuffling of their footfalls and the occasional creak of a cell door far down the long corridor. The stench of cold cement, decay and loneliness hung in the air.

The golden glow of her father's eyes was still clear as day in Hunter's mind, lighting her way like the promise of hope. After that one glimpse, he fell back into whatever sleep he'd been trapped in. She wasn't even sure he re-gained consciousness, waving it off as some sort of paranormal reaction to her fire. A personal connection. A bond that only their blood shared.

But it was confirmed. She knew those eyes like her own because they *were* her own. Joshua always told her she had golden eyes just like her father. And now the doctor not only had Will to use against her, he had her long-lost father as bait as well.

It was impossible, but she was beginning to believe it.

As she marched through the caves in the tight grip of the guards, she tried to remember the story Joshua told her. The story in which her father burned to death the night she was conceived. The body was not found amidst the rubble. They presumed his body burned.

Did somebody cover it up?

Of course, she thought. *Dr. Wolfe did.* But how could he have possibly managed to rescue her father before it all began?

Hunter forgot about the present, escaping into a memory that was not her own and recalled Joshua's words again.

He was the greatest man I ever knew.

Suddenly, Hunter started to laugh.

The laughter bubbled from a deep and warm part of her, a part she thought had died in the Death Caves. Delirium wrapped its arms around her, or maybe it was just the guards, paranoid that she was going to try to run.

And at that moment, Hunter felt as if she could run. She felt invincible. The oppressive storm cloud that had suffocated her in the Death Caves blew away.

"What's so funny?" asked one of the guards.

Hunter gazed up at him, elatedly happy. "You don't know?"

He exchanged bemused looks with his co-worker, then turned back to Hunter. "Know what?"

Laughter slipped from her mouth again. And it grew. It was the kind of laughter that made hands reach from their cells, calling out to her, clawing for the same happiness that engulfed her.

Will shouted her name and at his voice she ripped her arms from the guards with a powerful force and started running.

The Men in White sprinted after her, shouting at the other prisoners, catching her just as she reached Will's door and grabbed his hand through the tiny iron bars of his cell. They'd not had contact for days, but all of a sudden, things were different. She was different.

There was hope again.

"He's alive!" she beamed, another giggle falling from her lips. She couldn't control herself.

"Who's alive?"

"My dad, Will. My dad is alive!"

"What?!"

"Get back!" One of the Men in White wrenched her from Will. But the guard's grip was shaky. He didn't know what to do. "I'm warning you, I'll-"

"What?" She whirled and the both of them stumbled back in shock. Her voice reverberated off the walls, almost as if it were amplified. "What will you do?!" Her smile was so wide that her jaw hurt, the muscles stretched for the first time in days. She looked back at Will and saw him smiling too, amazed at her energy and joy. His eyes burned like fire, and it took her only a second to realize that the glow was only a reflection of her own blazing eyes. She turned slowly back to the guards, flexing her wrists, feeling the burn from deep in her core.

The fire was coming to life again.

"There's nothing you can do. Not to me, or Will, or any of us! Not now, not ever. NOTHING!"

And from the palms of her hands came a luminescence that lit up the darkest corners of the Death Caves. Fire consumed her, slipping from her skin, dancing around her broken and bruised body, and the guards stood, gob-smacked, fearful and frozen, and the Death Caves filled with warmth for the first time in decades, and every hand protruded from the cells, desperate for heat, hungry for light, and Hunter put her head back and breathed in fire like the air of freedom. It washed away all her suffering and everything that buried her in darkness.

"He's alive," she whispered.

The guards finally remembered their authority and drew tasers from their holsters. They shot Hunter in the stomach and twice in her left thigh. She went down on the stone floor, not unconscious but unable to produce fire. The pain was too much. They dragged her across the filthy ground, one of them attaching a second bracelet to her wrist to stop the fire from growing stronger. Then they threw her into her cell.

She crouched in the dirt and darkness, the pain ebbing away into an uncomfortable sting. In the distance, she heard the Men in White ordering the other mutants to shut up, and then the corridor was silent.

"Hunter?" asked Will from his cell. "Want to explain what's going on? How do you suddenly have your abilities back? What do you mean, your father is alive?"

Hunter gripped her hair, feeling life course through her under the stinging after-bite of the tasers. But the fire had never felt so strong.

"I don't know how, but I *saw* him. I thought he died in the fire the night my mother got her power, the night I was conceived. But somehow Dr. Wolfe found him. He's been here all this time. Dr. Wolfe is healing him using some sort of salve he invented from your blood. He would have been on the brink of death when they found him, if not already dead. It seems impossible, I know. But he woke up and looked at me and even though I don't know how to believe it … I *know* it was him."

"What are you going to do now?"

She put her back against the scratchy wall of her cell and looked at her hands, watching the orange light course through her veins again. She couldn't push the fire out of her skin, but she could feel its strength revive.

"I don't know," she said. "How could we have been so defeated?"

"Hunter … do you really believe that your dad being alive is going to help us get out of here?"

"No." She shook her head and smiled. "It just gives me hope."

After a long moment of silence, Will said, "Want to know what I hope for?"

"What?"

"Paradise."

Hunter stared at the darkness. "After today," she said. "Anything is possible."

FOUR

Will knew his way around the Death Caves so well now that he didn't need the Men in White to escort him. When they came for him an hour later and opened his cell, he stretched and walked ahead of them. It was strange not living under fluorescent lights anymore, or lying in darkness rather than under anesthesia. His body was confused, not used to feeling the ache of a cell floor or lack of movement. He felt constantly ill. But at least he was no longer Dr. Wolfe's favorite guinea pig. Things were definitely different. Not necessarily better, but different nonetheless.

Hunter was sleeping, and he was grateful for that. She'd ask where they were taking him, and he'd have to lie again.

Hunter was filled with hope after seeing her father and Will was happy for her; she deserved some joy. But that changed nothing for either of them. In fact, if Will knew Dr. Wolfe – and by now he had a pretty good idea – bringing Leo back from the dead was a plan to make Hunter suffer even more than she already had.

The door of the morgue creaked open, revealing a dank room with the smell of ash lingering in the salty air. He walked straight past the cremation furnace and all of the little hatches where the bodies were stored before they were burned. It was just typical of the guards to make him see it every day, if only to remind him of how little time he had left.

Behind the morgue was a long room that the Men in White used as a dirty recreation area. Will was surprised when they first brought him there

19

over a week ago. He assumed they would have much nicer quarters above the cells where he used to live. Jamison said that this room – underground dungeon, more like – was allowed to get messy. Because after the humiliation of the escape and Alfie's attempt to destroy the Death Caves, the Men in White needed to feel powerful again.

Two guards ripped off his shirt and chained each of his wrists, raising his arms up on either side. He could hear other guards crawling out of the shadows around him, joking with each other and making bets as they usually did. The only light came from two trembling tubes above his head. The floor was covered in pools of murky water and the pipes were rusted to their core. It was almost as filthy as his new cell.

Hunter asked him every day what Dr. Wolfe did to torture him, and every day he lied to her. He told her that they fed him and showered him but did not operate, because the doctor had no need for Will anymore. Sixteen years in this place and he'd had his time under the microscope. He was only there to use as bait in case the doctor wanted something from Hunter. Dr. Wolfe had said so himself, and that was days ago. If Hunter knew where he was now, she'd go mad. The doctor passed him on like a broken toy for the guards to take out their testosterone and use him as a punching bag.

"How are we today Will?" asked Jamison as he wrapped dirty straps around his wrists.

Will glanced up and noticed that Jet was there again. He'd made his first appearance yesterday, but only stood in the background and observed the torture as guard after guard released their angry male instincts. It was mostly Jamison who threw the punches, perhaps as his way of dolling out revenge for what Chantal did to Steel. Apparently the guard didn't make it.

Jamison threw a right hook across Will's jaw. He wasn't paying attention, which didn't give him time to prepare for the pain. His gum split open and blood sprayed from his mouth. Another hit to the left side whipped his head back the other way and one of his teeth came loose. It didn't matter – it would be back in place after a few minutes.

The fact that he healed quickly often frustrated some of the guards. They liked to see blood, and when his wounds closed up so suddenly … they had to make new ones.

The perks of healing – you get to feel the pain all over again.

"I asked you a question," Jamison growled and then he hurled an uppercut into Will's chin. Will staggered back against the chains, feeling his upper and lower rows of teeth collide and throbs of sharp agony shot through his mouth. He hung weakly – it didn't take much to break him these days.

"I told you, kid," said Jamison. "He's basically as lifeless as a corpse."

"Still," said Jet as he strolled toward them. "It's fun, isn't it? You can thank me for suggesting him as your new project."

Will looked up through strips of hair and an agony-induced haze. Of course Jet thought of this. He was impressing Will more and more with his methods of cruelty.

"Well, it's not exactly a pay rise," snarled Jamison, "but it'll do."

Jet drew a knife from his sleeve and gave Will a long, measured look before slashing the blade across Will's chest, opening a deep cut along his ribs. Will groaned through his teeth. He hated knives. "You should really thank me, Will, for getting rid of Dr. Rosenthal for you. He won't be helping you and Hunter get out again."

Will no longer had the energy to be angry or even try to fight back, but he owed it to Dr. Rosenthal to be stronger than he felt. Since his hands were shackled, he decided a last resort, however petty, would be better than nothing. He gathered a mouthful of saliva and blood and spat directly into Jet's face with all the force he could muster.

"Go fuck yourself," he snarled.

Jet squeezed his eyes open, wiping strings of red from his cheeks. Chuckles started to bubble out of his mouth and he twisted the knife in his fingers so the silver flashed from the light above, taunting him.

"Oh, I am so very glad you did that. You've just freed up my afternoon for some much-needed physical therapy."

The knife dug into Will's stomach so deeply, he thought he felt it come out the other side. He gasped in air and choked on blood. Jet drew the knife out slowly so Will could feel the cold metal sliding against his internal organs. Once it was out and the blood poured from the wound, Jet didn't wait for it to heal before plunging the knife into the other side.

There was more stabbing and more beating and more jeering from the guards, but it was over for Will long before. In moments like these, he was so used to the feeling of agony that he trained himself to fall into a place in his mind that allowed him to escape reality.

It was usually with Fearne. Right then, just behind Jamison, he could see her watching the gruesome sight, wearing her dimpled smile. He thought about where she was at that moment, safe with the others on a train or a bus or in a small house on a hill, away from danger. He hoped she had moved on to a brand new life and forgotten him.

Will tried to focus on her and heard her melodic voice, singing to him a tune he'd heard before but could not remember. A Christmas song. It reminded him of Hannah his housekeeper and the way she used to sing so loudly during the holiday season. He listened to her sing and gazed into her loving eyes and didn't feel any pain. It was easier that way.

FIVE

There was something sinister about Joshua's powers that always gave Eli the heebie-jeebies. He felt his heart pound in his chest as Joshua threw open their hotel door.

Joshua drew the ice from within him and crafted it carefully into a dangerous weapon.

An FBI agent a few feet down the hall raised his gun. Joshua threw the icicle at his hand quicker than the agent could fire and the gun clattered to the floor. The other agent on guard ran to attack Joshua, his black trench-coat billowing around him. Joshua stood his guard, ice swirling around his hands.

It was like watching a ballerina dance in a snowstorm. Joshua's movements were both deadly and graceful. Joshua administered a sharp kick to the first agent's chest, bending low and swiping the other with his wrist. He threw a gust of ice at an agent running up the stairs at the end of the corridor and that agent went flying back against the wall, sinking to the floor. The two agents still standing fought Joshua with precise movement in the limited space, but Joshua was somehow more skilled. Eli made a mental note to ask Joshua who taught him martial arts, but for now, he and Jenny cowered in wonderment of their travelling companion as he formed another icicle and used it as a club. One took a hit to the gut, the other took a swipe across his jaw. Back and forth. Hit, hit, hit. In less than ten seconds, the agents were down and Eli had to snap his mouth shut before his tongue fell out.

Joshua turned back to them. Black strips of hair hung over his glacier-blue eyes. His veins were nearly white, throbbing under his skin. Eli had to admit that the man he knew as an awkward, lanky scientist suddenly looked scary-as-fuck.

Eli glanced at Jenny. She had a flushed look on her face.

"Let's move," said Joshua in a deep voice.

As Eli made to follow Jenny, he leaned in and whispered, "looks like the ice isn't the only thing that's wet."

Jenny scowled at him.

They managed to dodge the rest of the FBI agents, who had not been alerted to the fight upstairs. Joshua took them to the back streets, at which point Eli realized he was about to have a heart attack.

"Are you alright?" asked Jenny.

"Yeah," he said, bent over with his hands on his knees. "Thank God I don't have asthma anymore. I'd be dead."

The cab they caught smelled of pizza and leather boots. Eli sat squished between Jenny's small frame and Joshua's stiff, cold body, his heart pumping and his mind replaying the scene he'd just witnessed over and over again, hoping to permanently glue it there.

"That was … pretty much the most awesome thing I've ever seen." Eli gazed at Joshua and the blue glow that still throbbed beneath the skin of his pale arms.

"Thank you Eli," said Joshua as he rolled down his sleeves. There was an almost invisible smugness on his face. Clearly he enjoyed outsmarting the FBI and escaping the hotel they'd been trapped in for so long. Eli had to admit, it was wonderful to finally be free again, even if he was stuck being the third wheel for the second time. "I just hope we find something useful at the cabin, or we'll be in worse trouble than we're already in."

"It's okay," said Eli with surprising cheer. "I'm prepared for jail."

Joshua and Jenny chuckled, turning their eyes to the blinking city lights.

The drive to the secret cabin was long. They listened to the radio, watched the traffic pass by and the sun kiss the top of the buildings before disappearing from sight. It reminded him of being on the road again.

Eli hadn't been to Seattle for a long time, and he'd forgotten how serene it was. The outskirts were just as picturesque, but before he could truly appreciate it, darkness settled and all they could really see was the shadowed dirt road in front of them.

Eli was just starting to nod off, the bumpy path putting him in a kind of trance, when Joshua tensed and sat up. The three of them became alert, watching the road as the cab slowed down and turned left onto a small driveway. They were shaded by tall pines and everything but the path of the headlights was pitch-black.

All of a sudden, there was a house.

Eli's father owned a cabin in upstate New York. It was one of those summer holiday cabins, very movie-esque, something you'd expect a serial killer to target for a bit of *Friday the 13th* fun.

This cabin was exactly like that, only it seemed as if no one had lived in it for years. The tall walls with dark windows stretched two stories high, with a roof that disappeared into the low-hanging pines squeezed tightly against the edges. As the headlights of the taxi cab swept over the outside, Eli swore he spotted a face in the upstairs window.

Fear started to bubble inside of him as he remembered the Agents who had come so close to killing him and Jenny. Eli tried to remain composed, but a familiar feeling of helplessness overcame him.

The cabbie parked right up against the porch in the small clearing before the house and turned to them with an uncertain expression. "This place yours?"

Eli glanced at Joshua, but he was gazing at the cabin. In his eyes, Eli saw a whirl of memories, whether good or bad he could not tell.

"H-haven't been here in years," said Eli with a falsely confident smile and gave the cab driver a pat on the shoulder. "Thanks."

"No problem," he shrugged.

The three of them stepped out of the cab. Eli shivered in the light breeze, the smell of pines engulfing him. He would have felt better about the place if it was at least a little sunny, and maybe if he knew what was inside. Whoever lived there, they were excellent at hiding themselves from the FBI, and maybe they'd stay hidden from the three of them as well.

"You sure this is it?" asked Jenny as she took her usual place beside Joshua.

"I'm positive."

The cab rolled away, leaving them with a small amount of light from the porch. The trees bent and creaked around them. Eli stayed well back as Joshua moved up the steps to the front door. A spider web ruffled in the light breeze as it clung to the upper left frame of the door. The welcome mat was frayed and crooked and there was a black iron knocker on the door. Eli noticed a plank of wood nailed to the wall that read 'THE CABIN' in artistic writing. Nothing at all moved inside the house.

"Whatever's in there, we're here for you," whispered Jenny.

Eli could confidently agree with her.

Joshua swallowed then turned the handle.

Almost immediately, he leapt back in surprise as if the handle had given him an electric shock. At the same time, Eli swore he heard someone hiss from inside the house. *Oh shit,* he thought instantly, *it's inhabited by demons.*

"What was that?" asked Jenny.

"I don't know," said Joshua warily, "it just ... zapped me."

"T-try the doorbell," said Eli. He couldn't remember feeling so petrified since ... well, since he woke up from Cryonics. Perhaps he was starting to finally get in touch with his old, timid self. *Yay.*

Joshua glared at him.

"What? It's probably some kind of robbery-proof door."

"That's the stupidest thing I have ever heard." But Joshua rang the bell anyway.

Inside, there was a scuffle. Eli's heart pounded in his chest and he felt Joshua become instantly alert. It seemed he didn't expect anyone to be there.

"Hello?" he shouted. "Hello, is anyone in there!?"

Again, the inside of the house creaked and there were whispers from behind the door. Horrible, murderous thoughts came into Eli's mind. If it weren't for the ass-kicking Joshua gave the FBI agents earlier, Eli probably would have run away into the woods or had some kind of panic attack.

It was almost a relief when they heard a chain link being unlatched. Then the door itself swung inwards.

Before them stood an old woman with gray, frazzled hair dressed in a pink nightgown and velvet slippers. She wobbled unsteadily, peering up at them in confusion.

"Can I help you?"

Eli looked at Joshua, but Joshua didn't move. Eli elbowed him and watched as his eyes fill with tears of disappointment. He didn't know her, which meant that Hunter wasn't there and this was all a waste of time.

"Is there ... an Albert Rosenthal here?" asked Joshua.

"I don't know that name, I'm sorry." She stepped back into the shadows of her dark home. The door started to close behind her.

"Wait, please!" Joshua put his hand on the door and the woman froze. "I'm looking for a girl. She's about nineteen with cherry-red hair. She's supposed to be here. Her name is Hunter."

The old woman's frown deepened. Eli caught a glimpse of a figure inside the house that moved slowly, a silhouette slinking in the darkness. Chills went down his spine.

"Who are you?"

"I'm Joshua," he said. "Joshua Harrison. Hunter is my daughter."

Instantly, the old woman's face brightened in wonder. Her wrinkly old hands let go of the door and she stepped closer, looking up into Joshua's face as though he were her long-lost son coming back from the dead.

"*You're* Joshua?"

"Yes ... I am."

"*The* Joshua?"

"Uh ... yes?"

"Well," she puffed a sigh and threw open the door. "Butter my butt and call me a biscuit! Guys, it's *Joshua!*"

A loud "HA!" fell from Eli's mouth and Jenny almost did the same, covering her face with her hands. He'd never before heard that phrase, let alone coming from the mouth of an eighty-something-year-old woman.

Joshua looked as if she'd slapped him across the face. "Who are you?"

"Oh," the woman smiled. "I'm Zac. We've kind of been waiting for you."

Then, she started to quiver.

SIX

Hunter was summoned to Dr. Wolfe's company again later that day. Will wasn't in his cell when she passed. Perhaps he was in the shower or being fed. He seemed to be better treated in the loneliness of the Death Caves than in the cells above where he was operated on almost every day. Dr. Wolfe must've lost interest in him after all the drama.

When the doctor beckoned her inside his office, she was pleased to see a long strap over the bridge of his bruised nose. Dried blood flaked around the edges of it. She couldn't hide her smile.

"If I'd have known you'd get cocky," he growled, "I wouldn't have showed you your father."

"I hope I'm here because you're going to tell me how you found him."

"Firstly-" He handed her a black key to unlock her bracelets. "Remove those broken restraints and attach this one please."

Hunter reached for the new cuff – noting how much heavier and more sophisticated it was – and stared at him expectantly.

"Are you going to make me?"

He rolled his eyes, tired of their banter, and summoned a guard who stood near the door. Nodding, the guard unlocked the faulty silver bracelets she was so accustomed to and clipped the new one around her wrist. A blue light blinked on an uncomfortable tightness wrapped itself around her skin, numbing it. The bracelet felt like a block of ice. As an added restraint, the guard pulled her hands behind her and strapped them together with a sharp piece of plastic.

"Happy now?" She raised an eyebrow.

Dr. Wolfe muttered under his breath about protecting his nose and then relaxed in his chair. "I must say, Hunter, I never expected us to be here. Isn't it funny how we have such strong dreams, and even though they don't go the way we hoped-" he indicated to her as if she were some twist he didn't see coming, "-we still end up where we're supposed to, with our dreams laid out before us like a newborn child, more wonderful than we ever imagined."

"You dreamed of an empty institution, no family or friends of any kind, a reputation as a whack-job psycho and a broken nose?" Hunter shook her head. "That's a pretty sad little dream, Doc, but I won't judge."

Dr. Wolfe didn't laugh at all. In fact, he was mildly shocked. She was cracking jokes. Her confidence and her overall chipper attitude was beginning to make him wonder whether he still had the upper hand. She could see uncertainty in his eyes.

"When you saw your father, how did it make you feel?"

"What is this, a psych evaluation?" Hunter leaned forward. "I think it's pretty damn obvious that I felt a *little* excited to see my father."

"Yes." He nodded to her arms where a fading orange glow could still be seen pumping in her veins. "I noticed. Even with my restraints, you were able to produce fire. You also managed to wake your father up from his deep, medication-induced sleep. It was quite a show, my guards told me, down in the caves. Even now, I can see you would have the ability to burn right through those cuffs and walk out of this institution without a second thought."

Hunter frowned at him, testing the fire beneath the new power restraint. Strangely, Dr. Wolfe had more faith in her power than she did.

Dr. Wolfe stood and buttoned his lab coat. "The reason I showed you that your father is alive is to persuade you to reveal the location of the substance that controls you. If Feucotetanus combined with this substance has given you powers stronger than all the others ... imagine what I can accomplish if I have them both."

His words began to sink into her mind like a poisonous drug. Was it possible that her ability was more powerful than the rest of them because Ravenadium *and* Feucotetanus flowed from her core? Dr. Wolfe had to know that, or he wouldn't waste so much effort containing her. He wouldn't resurrect her father. He wouldn't keep Will alive.

He wants Ravenadium now more than ever.

"Why don't you just ask my father where it is? He knows the location better than anyone."

Something in Dr. Wolfe's eyes gave away that her father wouldn't be able to reveal that information. Or perhaps even talk at all.

"Your father is having trouble waking up, much less remembering. I am asking you."

"I'm not telling you where to find Ravenadium."

Dr. Wolfe looked at her as though she'd slapped him. "What did you say? Ravenadium?"

Hunter's heart leapt. But then she realized that giving the doctor the fake name she and Joshua had made up for the volcanic substance would not give him any clue as to where to find it.

"Yeah," she said. "Ravenadium."

He moved around his desk, standing over her with oyster eyes wide like a mad man's. "Where is it?"

Hunter chuckled deeply. "I'll never tell you where it is. You're going to have to kill me."

He drew back a hand and slapped it hard across her cheek. Hunter gasped, more from shock than from the pain. He'd never used violence with her – cruelty and malice were more his specialty – and the look in his eyes suggested he liked it.

"Do not forget–" he growled, snatching her chin and forcing her eyes to his, "-I am in control here. I hold your life, your father's life and William's life in my hands. I can have you disposed of at any minute."

Hunter let her eyes slowly open, gazing into the doctor's face, and felt as if things between them had changed. Violence was the doctor's last attempt to scare her. And though it worked at first, she was beginning to see how desperate he really was to keep control of the things he still held close. Jack was in a coma, he'd lost more than half of his test subjects, and her power was strengthening. He was going to lose this war before it had even begun.

A small yet noticeable smile appeared on her face and the doctor released her, looking startled.

"Go ahead," she challenged him. "Try. But then you won't ever get what it is you want most."

"And what might that be?"

"Power."

He sniffed arrogantly and clicked his fingers. Two guards entered and hoisted her to her feet. "Acquiring power does not depend on your cooperation. I have not lived this long and come this far by relying on others. I get things done myself. I *will* get things done. And I'm about to prove that to you."

"Where are we going?" She wrenched her elbow from the grip of the guards and followed him to the door.

Dr. Wolfe held the elevator doors open for her, keeping his cool exterior composed. As much as Hunter felt brave in standing up to him, she couldn't help but remember how many cards the doctor still held. She had a terrible feeling about where he was leading her.

They passed into the lower level; a much darker and less furnished corridor with single rooms on either side. Dr. Wolfe opened a door with a key-card and they stepped into a space similar to that in which they shared a roast dinner, though this room was brighter and with a window on either side. The left room was lit with a chair just like in a dentistry. Only there were no happy pictures and canisters of floss in the room.

A breath of air pushed itself from her mouth and her stomach rolled over. She knew what he was leading her to. It was either Will or her father, and if her father ever recovered he would be far more valuable because of his knowledge of Ravenadium. Will had no worth to him anymore.

As she predicted, a guard appeared through the opposite door with Will stumbling before him. The guard was Jamison. He swept his fist up and rammed it into Will's stomach, making Hunter shriek. They obviously couldn't hear her inside the room. Jamison forced Will into the chair, strapped his hands to the armrests and his feet to the padded legs. Then he turned and looked directly at Hunter with a wicked smirk on his filthy face and left Will alone.

Hunter hadn't seen Will away from the Death Caves in actual light since … however long they'd been trapped there. She guessed just over a week. She only just noticed that there were dried blood stains all over his white jumpsuit. He told her he was kept clean and showered.

There was no expression at all on his face. Whatever happiness she'd passed to him the day before when she released her powers had likely been diminished by whatever caused the canvas of blood across his body.

Will's head tipped to the side and then he looked right at Hunter. It was worse that he could see her through the glass. The defeat in his eyes was more than she could bear. *I will not watch this*, she thought. Hunter turned to the doctor. Hands being tied, she could only use her legs. She twisted her torso, raised her leg and threw a hard kick right into the doctor's stomach.

"Let him go!" she screamed. The guards pulled her back and she thrashed, knocking them up against the glass. The fire burned in fear, slipping between her fingers. The new and improved bracelet would do no good soon. The flexi-cuff snapped from the heat and the pressure and the guards fumbled with her free arms. "I swear Dr. Wolfe, I will burn-"

She felt a sting in her neck and the fire was flushed. Dr. Wolfe must've developed a formula just like Joshua's ice chair to freeze the fire. She felt instantly weak.

"This is what comes of your selfishness Hunter," said the doctor. One of the guards forced her to look at Will. Scientists were connecting tubes to his arms and strapping electrode pads to his bare chest. Her heart ached with guilt again. How many times had he been used and tortured on her behalf?

"I'm giving you one minute to tell me everything you know about where to find Ravenadium, otherwise very bad things will start happening to William."

"There's nothing you can do to him," she growled.

"Quite the contrary," said the doctor, "I've found Mikayla's blood has an interesting counter-reactor to powers. It has helped me a great deal in developing power restraints in recent years. I never would have been able to keep Jack down without her. The thing is ... Will cannot regenerate with Mikayla's formula in his system, or at least not for a few hours. With enough dosage, I can take away his powers and perform a whole manner of torture and he won't heal. Of course, it helps to have Mikayla around to keep the balance."

At that moment, Mikayla herself entered the room, followed by Jet. They both waved at Hunter cheerfully as they reached for a pair of plastic gloves on the bench.

Tears of anger burned in Hunter's eyes. She felt a powerful tug toward Will, as if the fire were begging her to give up what she knew. Dr. Wolfe would surely find out some other way. It wouldn't be worth Will's life.

Dr. Wolfe watched her closely. "Tell me where it is."

I can't, she thought. *Hundreds of people will die if Dr. Wolfe finds Ravenadium. Hundreds more will suffer.*

Hunter shook from head to toe. If these were the types of choices she had to make as a hero, she didn't want to be one. But Will would understand why she had to make this sacrifice, even though he held her heart in his hands, to save a world that did not know it needed saving. That's what heroes do.

"I'm so sorry," she said.

When he saw her mouth the words, Will turned away and stared straight ahead at Jet, who held a six-inch knife in his hand.

"Hmm," said the doctor. "I honestly thought you cared about him."

"I do," she snarled. "You have no idea."

"Well, neither does he now that you've sentenced him to die."

Do I have a choice? Is there no other way to save the man that I love?

Hunter had not yet thought that it was love between she and Will, but now it was more obvious than the messed up situation they were in. She loved him. She was about to lose another love right in front of her eyes.

"Please," she begged and thrashed in the grip of the guards, not caring how desperate and weak she looked. "I beg you Dr. Wolfe, *please* don't do this. You don't have to kill him."

"I'm afraid I-"

A knock at the door interrupted the doctor. The face in the window was a scientist Hunter had seen several times. Whatever he had to say was urgent enough to interrupt. Dr. Wolfe murmured to his guards to watch Hunter and left. Hunter turned back to Will and prayed he would look at her so she could see him one last time, to remember what it felt like to be lost in eyes so deep and tortured and loving.

But he wouldn't, because Will never showed weakness or fear. He would keep himself composed, stoic and brave until his last breath.

Jet twisted the knife in his fingers, waiting for the command, but it never came. Dr. Wolfe was in a bad mood when he returned minutes later.

"Well, it looks like we'll have to continue this conversation later. It will give you more time to reconsider your foolish decision."

"What's happening?" she asked him. The guards walked her to the door.

"I have some business to attend to. You're going back to your cell, where you won't have to watch William be executed."

"Executed?"

"Yes. I gave you the chance and you did not comply. We're not doing this dance again. It's over for Will."

"No," she breathed. "NO!"

Will looked up at her screams. The hopelessness in his eyes broke her heart in two, and even if he was not scared of death, he was scared to leave her.

"Say your goodbyes!" the doctor shouted so they both could hear.

Hunter said nothing. She couldn't bring herself to.

"Goodbye Hunter," he mouthed to her. "See you in paradise."

Tears burst from Hunter's eyes. "No no, please! I won't go through this again!" She fought in the grip of the guards, fought so hard that she twisted her wrist. But even through the pain, she could not escape them. When the guards hauled her to the elevator, Hunter fell to the floor and surrendered, so consumed with heartbreak that everything became numb. She cried silently and let the Men in White pick her up from the floor. Then they dragged her from the elevator and back into darkness.

SEVEN

Joshua hadn't seen anything as marvelous as Zac's transformation since Hunter first showed him her powers. The way his skin morphed and shaped into an entirely different person was enough to send his scientist mind reeling. From behind him, Joshua heard Eli mutter something like "Holy mother of Twinkies", and Jenny didn't speak at all.

Now, a young boy of about seventeen stood before them in a pink bathrobe and slippers. He had mousy brown hair and a pubescent complexion, looking like he may explode with excitement as he grinned goofily at them.

"So. You guys gonna come in or what?"

Hesitantly, Joshua followed Zac inside the cabin. It hadn't changed at all since he'd stayed there after escaping ICE. Still the same powerful scent of cinnamon, pine and old books. It made Joshua instantly sleepy, because he associated that smell with safety and comfort. The cabin itself was larger inside than it appeared outside, with multiple levels and a staircase on the right leading up to the bedrooms. Joshua remembered the kitchen on the left, the wide bench overlooking the living area where there were two fireplaces and too many Native American cushions on the sofas to the right. The living area was lined with five giant glass windows – one being a double door leading to the backyard where a windy path through the trees met the lake just down the way.

The day Joshua arrived at the cabin after two disorientating days of driving and a stressful night at a motel on the edge of the highway with a screaming baby was unforgettable. The cabin seemed like the most beautiful place in the world. Joshua remembered walking through the doors with Hunter asleep in his arms, lighting a fire in the fireplace and watching Hunter waddle up to the flames and wave her hand through them as though nothing about that were strange. And the house was empty and quiet and washed away every fear he had, because he knew it was safe. This cabin was where Joshua planned how he would live the rest of his life, and how he would raise Hunter. They sat out by the lake every day, even though he didn't like the sun. Joshua read some of the doctor's old books in his office upstairs. Simple things like listening to the cicadas chirp at night as Hunter fell asleep in his arms were a joy to remember.

This cabin was filled with memories, and now … it was filled with people.

Faces gazed at the three newcomers as Zac led them into the living room. Joshua's heart throbbed as his eyes swept over the crowd but did not find Hunter's. He felt weak at the knees, praying nothing had happened to her.

"Who are they, Zac?" asked a frail girl with dead-blond hair and ghost-like features. In fact, every one of them looked very hollow in the eyes and drained of energy. Joshua knew that look. They came from ICE.

"That's Joshua, Hunter's guardian," said a small girl of about eight. She had a dreamy air about her as her green eyes swept over him. "And that's Hunter's school teacher, Jenny, who really likes Joshua. The feeling is mutual."

Joshua's mouth fell open and he shot a glance at Jenny, whose entire face went red. *Telepathy,* Joshua guessed instantly. *It has to be.*

"And that's …" The girl gasped when she turned her compelling gaze to Eli. "Oh my goodness."

"What?" asked Zac, looking back and forth between the two. "Who is it Fearne?"

"That's Eli."

"Hunter's dead boyfriend?" asked the eldest girl.

"I thought that guy killed him." Zac waved a finger at Joshua, who felt a shiver slide over his body. Who were these kids and how did they know everything about him?

"Zac, remember when we talked about tact? Now is when you use it."

"Thank you Chantal," he spat.

"Joshua didn't kill him," said Fearne simply. "He just put them to sleep with his ice-"

"Woah woah *woah*!" Joshua raised both hands, ordering them to stop. He was already nervous not seeing Hunter in the crowd of hungry, cautious faces. He needed answers, not to be giving them. "First of all, don't you think it's a little rude to read someone's mind and then voice those secret thoughts to a room full of strangers?"

Fearne frowned slightly, trying to decide whether she liked having a parental figure tell her what to do or if there was a real reason behind him trying to protect his thoughts from her. Regardless, she said nothing more.

"Actually, we're all pretty close," said Zac. "It's *you* who's the stranger. And we don't particularly like strangers."

"Then why ask us inside?" Joshua shot back.

Zac's mouth closed.

"Where is Hunter?"

Their expressions alone gave him his answer. Jenny touched his shoulder in comfort. *No, it can't be.* Joshua ran his hand down his cheeks and over his mouth. He needed to remain calm.

"She was alive when we escaped, but … she's still in there," said Fearne.

"Tell me everything that happened."

"Wait." One of the quiet ones stood up, his skin so black he almost blended in with the windows behind him. He watched them cautiously, his expression giving nothing away. Then he turned his gaze to Fearne's.

"We can trust them, Mosi," said Fearne. "He is only looking to rescue Hunter and reunite her with Eli." She looked at Joshua directly, and in his mind he heard her voice. *"Am I right?"*

"I'm only here to find Hunter."

"Then we'll explain," said Fearne.

"Who'd like tea or coffee?" asked Chantal from the kitchen. With Jenny's assistance, she started pulling mugs from the shelves and setting the kettle on the stove.

Hands went up and the younger ones begged for hot chocolate. The others were taking their seats on the sofas, so Joshua followed hesitantly. Some of them looked comfortable – Zac, for instance, had the most easy-going air Joshua had ever seen – but the younger ones were wide eyed and hesitant. It seemed they had trouble trusting anyone with information about them. Joshua remembered what that was like in the first few months after escaping such a place as ICE.

While Jenny and Chantal handed around cups of tea and hot chocolate – Chantal even set down a jar of cookies for the younger ones – Joshua and Eli sat across from the fire with six others staring back at them. As they introduced themselves, explained their power and a little of their backstory in ICE, Joshua found he could not wonder of their incredible gifts and talents. None of them so much as mentioned Hunter. Something terrible had happened to her, he knew it.

"Why is Hunter still in ICE?" he asked.

"It was by her own choice," said Marcus. "She ran our entire escape, picking us up when we didn't believe in ourselves. We were getting so close to freedom, but then she turned around and said she had to go back and save the others-"

"What others?"

"Marcus, you can't skip ahead of yourself," scoffed Zac. "You have to *explain* things as you're going along. Trust me, I know how to tell a good story."

Marcus shot daggers at Zac and instantly, the lamp he was standing next to popped. Zac shrieked and leapt to his feet. The children laughed.

"What are the Death Caves?" asked Joshua impatiently, half-wishing there was a responsible adult he could talk to. "And the mutants, who are they?"

Zac went into great detail explaining the underground cells where Dr. Wolfe's test subjects were kept.

"It's also where he put our friend Alfie when he turned into a dinosaur and ate some of the Men in White."

Both Jenny and Eli stared at him in shock.

"Did you just say dinosaur?"

"I know," said Zac with a grin. "I've always wanted a dinosaur."

"And she also w-went back for Destructo," said Benji after not saying much the entire night.

"Sorry, who?"

"He's pretty much the most powerful guy we've seen at ICE so far – except we've never actually *seen* him," said Zac. "Dr. Wolfe keeps him pretty securely contained down in the caves. Hunter and Will saw him have a major freak out and nearly kill Dr. Wolfe. He turns into like the Hulk and starts making people explode and shit."

"Did he succeed?"

"No. Dr. Rosenthal shot him. He's apparently in a coma."

"And Hunter went back for him why?"

"Uh, because she's craz-" Zac shut his mouth as soon as he saw the murderous look on Joshua's face. "M-maybe she knew him."

At that very moment, Fearne raised a hand and put it over her mouth, staring at Joshua as though she'd suddenly come to a startling realization. "Of course. It's Jack."

"Who's Jack?" asked Marcus.

"Destructo. They know who he is."

"What?" Zac gaped.

Joshua's heart seemed to stop. *No, it can't be true.* "Are you saying Jack is this Destructo character? Dr. Wolfe's most powerful weapon is *Jack*?"

"Wait a minute," said Eli, standing up. "You're not talking about *Jack* Jack? As in *my* Jack?"

"I thought you were straight," Zac muttered with a frown.

"I *am* straight," Eli snapped back. "You're saying that Hunter went back for mutants she never knew, a dinosaur, and my best friend *Jack*?"

"Yes," said Fearne. The rest of them nodded, but uncertainly.

Eli ran his hands through his hair and started pacing the room. The silence was wrapping itself around Joshua's throat like the conclusion that, once again, he was to blame. Eli soon came to that conclusion too and advanced on Joshua.

"This is ALL your fault!"

"Hey calm down, bud," said Marcus.

"No." Eli slammed his hand on the kitchen bench and the dishes rattled. "No, I've had enough of everyone I know getting hurt because of *this guy!*" He thrust his finger at Joshua, anger building up inside of him.

"Should I calm him?" Chantal asked Fearne.

"No, let him get it out."

"Eli, I didn't hand Jack over to the Agents," said Joshua. "It happened when the Iceman-"

Eli let out a humorless laugh. "That's bullshit Joshua, stop blaming a fictional character for your mistakes!"

"Eli, that's enough," said Jenny firmly. "We can't point the finger of blame because it changes nothing."

"Try and stop me," he growled. "I'm done. I'm done with him and his mistakes and inability to see through that wall of denial telling him it's not his fault that everyone I care about gets hurt." With that, he stormed to the back doors and marched into the darkness outside.

Joshua turned to Jenny. "Should I go and talk to him?"

"I will. You find out how to get them out."

Grateful once again to have her in his life, Joshua watched her follow after Eli, the porch light coming on after the movement. He turned back to the group.

"I want to know if you've thought of any way to get Hunter back."

"And Will," said Fearne almost defensively.

"Yes, and Will."

"We aren't going back," said Marcus. "Hunter told us not to."

Of course she did. Joshua sighed and pinched the bridge of his nose. "Well, do you at least have an exact location of ICE so I can tell someone who *can* go there and rescue Hunter?"

They exchanged glances with each other.

"Who would you tell?" frowned Mosi.

Joshua tried shutting his thoughts off, but once again, the young girl saw them.

"The FBI," Fearne gaped. "You told the FBI about us?"

This brought uproar into the group of young people, and while Joshua tried to clarify that they would not be harmed, he was growing more and more hopeless.

EIGHT

In one last effort to grasp their attention, Joshua raised his hands and ice burst in sprays with the force of jets from his palms, not directly at any of them, but into the air, where the ice hit the ceiling and sprayed like rain upon the room. They were all speechless, looking up at the flakes of snow that settled around them.

"Look," he began in his most serious tone. "The FBI don't know a thing about you guys. They have been searching for answers to the mysteries of your disappearances for decades now, and when they found me, I was their first clue. They were suspicious that I had something to do with it all, so I told them my story. They tried to find ICE but came up with nothing."

"They came here," said Chantal. "I used my power to convince them that they found nothing. But we were so afraid, because Hunter told us this was the safest place to stay."

"We're leaving tomorrow," said Marcus. "If the FBI can find us, surely the Agents will too."

"You are all safer here than anywhere else in the world," said Joshua. "Trust me, I know. This was my safe house when I escaped ICE."

They were shocked, because clearly none of them knew Joshua had been imprisoned. He owed them the explanation, and when he finished, it seemed they were feeling more comfortable in the cabin than they were beforehand.

"I won't tell the FBI you're here. You can hide as long as you like. But sooner or later, you're going to have to help me."

After a moment of tense thinking, in which many questioning glances were made, Fearne spoke up.

"We'll help you."

"We will?" asked Zac.

"Of course. Hunter sacrificed her life for our freedom. We owe it to her. And we can't leave Will, or Alfie either."

"But we've talked about this," said Marcus. "We can't go back; it's too risky. Hunter and Will went back and they're still in there. Who knows what Dr. Wolfe is doing to them."

Joshua felt ice seal over his heart, making him angrier and more determined than ever. He turned to Ryo. "Can you teleport?"

The young girl kept her face composed, but her eyes did not lie. They were sparkling with fear. "I … I can, but I've never teleported to a place I haven't been before."

"What if you teleported into the labs?" suggested Chantal. "Could you walk down to the Death Caves and find Hunter?"

"But she could have been moved," said Marcus. "And what if Dr. Wolfe has her in surgery or something?"

"I need to know where I'm going," said Ryo. "It's too dangerous otherwise."

"Not if I train you," said Joshua.

They gazed at him.

Zac snorted. "What are you, some kind of Professor X?"

"No, but I'm a scientist."

"I thought you were a geologist," Chantal frowned.

"That *is* a science, dumbass," Marcus chuckled.

"I'm equipped with enough knowledge to analyze your powers and determine how to strengthen it and teach you to manipulate it to your own ability. I can show you, Ryo, how to envision your location and bend your body through space to get there."

"I may be able to find Hunter in her dreams," said Fearne. "That way we'll know if she's alone or if she's with Dr. Wolfe."

Joshua nodded. It was oddly exciting to have so many weapons sitting around him. Finally, he could make progress toward rescuing Hunter.

"But what about the FBI?" asked Chantal. "I mean, won't they be looking for you?"

Joshua knew there'd be a catch somewhere. The chances of them tracking his location back to the cabin were high, and if they discovered the children, it would make finding Hunter that much more difficult. It would leave him back where he was, sitting in the hotel room waiting for someone else to take action.

So how could he remain there without suspicion when he was supposed to be boarding a plane to DC in the morning?

"Uh," said Fearne hesitantly. "There could be a way to solve that." She glanced at Zac.

He stared back innocently, not catching on at first. And then his eyes widened.

"Are you kidding me? You want me to pretend to be *him?*"

"Yes, please take him away," said Marcus. "Give me at least a few days peace."

"Ha-ha," snapped Zac. "I'm a talented man, I know … but you are one odd duck Joshua."

"Zac, you'll be saving lives." Chantal turned her gaze to Zac's and from a distance, Joshua felt a pang of that compelling energy she gave off. It would be extremely difficult to say no. "Please do this for me?"

"Uh …" A line of drool started to seep from the corner of Zac's mouth. He quickly wiped it away, giving her his most charming smile. "Oh, alright. Just for you Chantal."

"Get a room you two," Marcus scoffed and the younger ones giggled.

Joshua put his hands together. "So it's settled. You'll go with Jenny and Eli to Washington-"

"And you will rescue Hunter and Willy," said Zac.

"Thank you." He nodded with his hands folded together as if in prayer. "Thank you."

Zac got to his feet, wiping his hands on his bathrobe. "Don't thank me just yet, most people get a little freaked out by this." He gazed at Joshua in deep thought. In just moments, his body was taller. His bones and muscles expanded and stretched against the fabric of the pink bathrobe. Before Joshua had time to gather his dignity, an exact replica of himself in a pink gown and slippers grinned goofily at him.

Joshua felt bile rise in his throat. "Urgh, please put some decent clothes on before you leave this cabin."

Zac-Joshua laughed. There was a chuckle from the back of the room, and that's when they noticed that Jenny and Eli had returned. Jenny was covering her mouth with her hand and staring at the two clones, amusement sparkling in her eyes.

"What?" both Joshuas said at the same time.

"I just think the color suits you Joshua."

She began to laugh, and then Imogen was laughing, and suddenly all around him, there was laughter. And despite it being directed at him, Joshua couldn't help but laugh too. It had been a very long time, and it felt more wonderful than knowing he was one step closer to finding Hunter. Because the laughter was a release, and to see Jenny laugh as well was something wonderful in itself.

They laughed for as long as they could, and then it was time to say goodbye. Joshua – the real one – shook Eli's hand, even though he didn't look him directly in the eye. But it wasn't time for forgiveness with Eli just yet. Then he turned to Jenny.

"You look after these kids, Joshua," she said in that commanding way that made her the wonderful, independent woman that he adored. "You're their guardian now."

"I'm not really, I'm just-"

She silenced him by forcing her lips to his. He was not yet used to surprise kisses. Jenny was such a passionate and spontaneous woman. Every moment such as this, Joshua cherished. He would miss her most of all.

"Protect Eli," he whispered against her cheek. "I can't lose him. But I can't lose you either. If anything happens, you run, okay? Don't risk your life for anyone."

She nodded. "Good luck. If you find Hunter ..." She thought carefully about her words and smiled. "*When* you find Hunter, I'm sure you'll know exactly what to do. I have faith in that."

Joshua tenderly ran his fingers down her cheek and over her chin, savoring the brightness in her deep, brown eyes and the smell of roses upon her skin.

Someone cleared their throat, and Joshua turned to see his mirror self making inappropriate thrusting motions.

"Zac ..." Chantal rolled her eyes.

"What? Oh come on, this isn't fifty shades of Joshua. Although-" he glanced down at his velvet dressing gown. "This is one shade I think quite suits your porcelain skin tone."

Joshua raised a hand and pointed it at Zac-Joshua. "Don't you dare make a fool of me. I swear, I'll shove an icicle through your heart."

"You'll do no such thing," snarled Chantal. She handed Zac a bag of clothes that they must have already had packed in preparation for leaving tomorrow. "You call us if anything happens, got it?"

Zac saluted her. "Yes ma'am. Well, bye everyone!"

Mutters of goodbye spread throughout the room. They made their way to the door of the cabin. Joshua worried that Zac would slip up in front of the FBI, or that he couldn't protect Jenny and Eli from the Agents if they ever attacked. And these nerves made the ice churn tensely inside him.

But their situation was nothing compared to Hunter's. And finding her brought him one step closer to Dr. Wolfe, where he would end this war.

He and the other children waved goodbye as Jenny, Eli and Zac stepped into the cab that had been called, chugging off into the thick darkness of the trees where they were gone from sight in moments, and the sinking feeling swelled inside him.

"They'll be okay," said Fearne who stood beside him on the porch. The others had gone back inside.

"How can you be sure?"

She smiled up at him with wise, innocent green eyes. "Trust me."

NINE

L ooks like it's just a party of three now."

Will grit his teeth so hard they hurt. He could feel the effects of Mikayla's blood in his veins, her presence making him a mortal man. It was strangely freeing. He used to wish he could give up his powers so he could have a normal life and not be imprisoned, but recently he'd come to appreciate the good things he once had: His family at ICE, his treasure Fearne, and Hunter and how hard he'd fallen for her.

A part of him was deeply hurt by how quickly she turned her back on him. If the roles were reversed, Will was sure he'd do anything he could to save her no matter the consequences. Perhaps that's what made Hunter a great hero. She made sacrifices for the good of others and not her own desires. He respected that.

Now he had to face the consequences.

"Go ahead," he snarled. "Kill me."

"Unfortunately, I'm not allowed to until the doc gives the orders. But it doesn't mean we can't have a little fun first."

Jet walked toward him and Will's heart thumped fast.

"Haven't you already had your fun with me?" asked Will.

Jet shook his head. "No, not at all. That was just a warm up. You know, I've always been curious about your power." He fingered the tip of the knife and then rested the cold blade against his arm. Will flinched. "If I sliced off your hand, threw it in that trash can over there, and then watched the blood pour from your stubbed wrist, would your hand grow completely back, or would I need to re-attach the old one?"

Will's stomach spun as it always did when he knew the pain was coming, but he said nothing, he did nothing. He'd felt it all before.

"Should we find out?"

Jet stepped up to Will's right side and curled his clammy fingers around Will's right wrist. Mikayla moved in front of Will and he couldn't help but notice that although she had a look of menace on her face, there was something hesitant in her eyes. "Bear with me a moment," said Jet. "I sort of need to take my time with this."

The knife gently rested on the surface of his skin. Will's breathing increased and he shut his mouth, ready for the pain, welcoming it, looking down at Jet and giving him his most fearless glare.

"Do it," he growled.

Jet chuckled. "Oh gladly."

He pressed down with the knife.

Will cried out through his teeth as the blade dug deep into his flesh, slicing through the tissue, eventually hitting the bone. With no antiseptic, Will felt everything. And it was torture.

"I'm sorry," said Jet seriously. "I'm actually really bad at this. I'm certainly no surgeon, that's for sure."

Will breathed sharply through his teeth, in and out, in and out. There was no escaping the pain – it was too strong for him to pull away and find his distraction. He had to take it. He threw his head back and screamed as Jet started sawing at the bone of his wrist. It was excruciating, so unbearable that Will's whole body pulled against the restraints. Maybe the knife wasn't as sharp as he imagined, or maybe time was just moving really, really slowly, for it felt as if the agony would never end.

"Usually I use my power to cause pain," Jet continued whilst sawing. Blood was pouring down Will's legs, making a puddle on the linoleum floor, spraying against Jet's clear apron. Through blurry vision, Will saw Mikayla put a hand over her mouth and dry-retch. "This is actually a lot more enjoyable."

The knife cut through the bone and must have hit a nerve at the same time, for Will felt the blinding slice of pain so strongly that his vision faded and he almost passed out. His head flopped to the side and he started to drift.

"Hey, stay with me!" Jet shouted in his ear. "I'm almost …done …"

A weight was suddenly lifted from Will's arm. Though he was still in agony, he knew his hand was gone. This was not the first time his limbs had been sawn from his body, but it was the first time he'd stayed awake through the entire process. Through the hazy images around him, Will looked down at his bloodied stub of an arm and the mess of sawed skin, flesh and blood that still spurted from the artery and waited. And waited. His eyes drooped shut. He managed to hear Jet laugh.

"Look at that, nothing's happening. That sucks."

Jet had to know that if he didn't get his powers back and heal soon, he would die.

A voice came through his consciousness. A sweet, small voice.

Stay, Will. Stay.

It had to be Fearne. He opened his eyes to find her, but everything was blurry. He fought hard against unconsciousness, but he couldn't much longer. The world was spinning away.

I can't, he thought. *I'm sorry.*

"Now you know what it's like to live as a mortal human being. We're going to have some fun, Will." Something slapped the side of his face and he flinched, realizing it was his own hand that Jet had thrown across his cheek. He wanted to be sick.

"You're disgusting," said Mikayla, but there was a smile in her tone.

"I am, right?" Jet laughed. "Come here, you."

The pain became too much for him. The last thing he remembered was hearing Jet and Mikayla cooing over each other before he let go and fell into unconsciousness, or death, he really didn't care.

TEN

"Have you travelled through time before Ryo?"

The girl looked at Joshua with blank eyes. They were all gathered in the living room just minutes after Jenny, Eli and Zac left. "Yes."

"And you can teleport as well, correct?"

Ryo gave a curt nod.

"Okay. When was the first time you travelled?"

"When I was nine."

"And did you practice travelling until you were captured?"

Ryo stared at Joshua for a long time. It was unnerving – he'd never met someone so young who could make him feel as if she knew something about him that no one else did. Ryo's face remained a mask of complete emotionlessness.

"Ryo?" said Fearne encouragingly. "You should tell him the truth. It could help him understand how to train you."

Ryo bit the corner of her lip and nodded. "Alright. When I first discovered what I could do, I was a young child. I didn't know of the consequences and I didn't tell anyone who could help me.

"I went back in time to save my father from an accident that took his life when I was eight. I was lucky not to get lost, but it worked and my family was happy and together again. Then … a week later my older sister was killed by one of my father's business associates because my father broke a deal he made with a wealthy colleague. My sister was perfectly healthy. She was engaged. In saving my father, I changed the course of life as it should have been. I killed my sister."

The room was left in bitter silence for Ryo's loss. Joshua didn't deal with sad stories very well. He looked down at the ground.

"Ryo, I'm so sorry," said Chantal with tears in her eyes. "I didn't know."

"Me neither," said Benji.

"It's okay," said Ryo. "I realized then that I was not granted this gift to change the fate of others, and I stopped time travelling completely. I forgot how. Dr. Wolfe couldn't make me do it either."

"That's probably a good thing," said Joshua. "Your ability is one of the most dangerous and useful powers there is. You can change the course of time and re-write history."

"But I won't. And I don't know how I can help you. Besides, you know nothing about my powers."

"Will this help?" asked Marcus from behind them. He handed Joshua an old manila folder creased at the edges. It was labelled '0544 Wasushi, Ryo'.

"Where did you get this?" asked Joshua as he flipped through the pages filled with hand-written notes and equations.

"In Dr. Rosenthal's office," he replied. "We've been looking in there since we arrived, trying to find answers. Instead we found copies of our files. But we don't understand them. Maybe you can."

Joshua nodded, his eyes wide as he skimmed through the information. The knowledge Dr. Rosenthal had acquired on Ryo would be a most valuable tool in training her, and in training all of them. Joshua's smile widened. This was the answer to understanding their abilities. This was also Dr. Wolfe's answer to complete power.

Joshua looked up at their young and innocent faces all eager for his help and ran a hand over his mouth. It wouldn't be easy, but it was going to work. It had to work.

"Okay." He took a deep breath in and exhaled. "I'm going to study these notes so that I can better understand you and your abilities. Tomorrow we'll start your training, Ryo. We'll begin by getting you to jump only a few feet, just enough to practice with. You won't need to go through time to get Hunter out, but you may need to go blindly."

"Not completely," said Fearne with a smile. "You'll have me to guide you."

"Exactly. And before we start tomorrow morning, Ryo, I need you to do something for me."

"What?"

"Go for a walk. Clear your mind. Try to forget what happened to your family and focus on the present. You're right; you were not granted this gift to change the fate of others. You were granted it to change your own. Will your fate be to survive? Or will it be to live the way you were created to live, and to use every talent to which you were entrusted?"

Ryo's black eyes sparkled as she nodded.

"That's deep man," said Marcus.

"It is," said Joshua. "And for everyone else ... I think it's time for bed."

Joshua pushed the door open and was met with the smell of books and leather and dust. The walls were lined with shelves filled with old volumes, a desk to his right and an armchair to his left. Thick velvet curtains draped over the giant window and a golden glow came from the lamps on the desk. From up so high, he remembered being able to see through the trees onto the glimmering lake.

Joshua took a seat in the antique armchair with fern-green leather upholstery and walnut-framed arm and leg rests. It had been a long time since he'd sat at this desk.

He flipped open Ryo's file and began to read.

Most of it he understood — the physics behind her ability to travel through space and time, the way her body was designed and such science matters as this — but there was always something in the back of his mind that wondered how. How was it possible?

When Joshua finished reading Ryo's file, he turned to the others. Regardless of his fatigue, hours went by as he focused the way he used to in his laboratory in New York, letting the information formulate answers in his mind. He suddenly found himself creating ways in which to enhance all of their abilities, just like he had with Hunter, to make them stronger and more confident with their powers. Dr. Wolfe would not have taught them that. They could use their powers to defend themselves.

And after a while, Joshua began to notice a strange pattern in the formulas. A connection that each of them had. He went back, analyzing them again, and soon found the answer he was looking for. It made Joshua's entire world freeze – literally – in time. He couldn't believe how oblivious he'd been to it before.

In every formula was the specific chemical substance Joshua knew as Ravenadium.

The reason his power and Hunter's power came to be was because of Ravenadium, but was it possible that Ravenadium had spread so far and wide that it gave other people powers, other people across the world?

What if Ravenadium isn't a rare substance at all, but something common, something every human has imbedded in their DNA?

Joshua was breathless. It was too unbelievable and there were too many theories to consider. He read on.

The spiral.

The word was written several times throughout the files. Joshua frowned, wondering what it meant.

At that moment, a knock on the door interrupted his brainstorming. The girl called Chantal stood in the doorway.

"I don't mean to interrupt," she said rather cautiously.

"Can't sleep?"

She shook her head.

Joshua patted the chair beside his and she sat down timidly, twisting a pinch of her hair.

"I'm curious … how did you say you discovered your powers again?"

Chantal lowered her head. "I uh … there was an accident. The only way I could explain it was to blame myself. Once I started trying it out, I realized it was real. I abused it, and I never questioned how."

"Can you relate it to anything in your life? Anything that would have connected you to the power of persuasion? A hypnotist, perhaps?"

Chantal shrugged. "Not that I can remember."

"Did you ever have a fever?"

"A fever?" she frowned. "What do you mean?"

Joshua shook his head. He didn't understand why their bodies fused an ability when they came in contact with Ravenadium and another substance – in his case, Feucotetanus – but when other people such as the homeless man Liz operated on could not handle the combination, it didn't add up. Or was there something specific in their bodies that made them susceptible to genetic mutation?

The spiral.

"Of course," he muttered.

Chantal picked up her file. "What have you found?"

"Something every scientist in the world would kill to discover. Look at this," he indicated to a printout of a microscopic image. "This is a genetic spiral, or the Double Helix as some people call it. What's supposed to happen is a continuous spiral, but what Dr. Rosenthal is saying here is that our spirals – or those of us that have abilities – were infected by something called a Retrovirus."

"A what?"

"It comes from an infection of a type of chemical or element. In my case … the element is ice."

Chantal looked at him with a less than understanding expression but didn't ask questions. Joshua was thankful. His mind couldn't comprehend what he had just discovered.

If my genetic spiral rejected this retrovirus that formed when I combined Ravenadium and ice and injected it into my system … would I have ended up like the homeless man on Liz's operating table? Is that why only a small percentage of the world has abilities like mine, like ours, because our bodies are immune to genetic malfunction?

"Well anyway," said Chantal with a sigh. "I think this science stuff is actually making me sleepy. I'm going to bed."

Joshua nodded. As Chantal slipped to the door, Joshua called to her.

"Hey Chantal?"

"Mhm?"

"I need to ask you a favor."

"Go ahead."

"Hunter is going to be in a very … emotional state when we bring her back," he said gently. "And the shock of seeing me may tip her over the edge. If she finds out that Eli and Jenny are alive, and that Zac has gone with them to DC to make the FBI happy and get them off our tail, I don't know what that could do to her mental stability. Not only that, but she'll be wanting to make plans to find Dr. Wolfe and get revenge. I don't want her to be frantic. I want her to rest for the time being."

Chantal's face fell slightly, but her eyes were calculating. "You want me to lie to her?"

"No. I want you to make her believe that she is safe here and that she needs to take a break before she plans a war. I know her, Chantal. She'll want to find Dr. Wolfe. You don't have to stop her from being angry with me – I deserve to take the blame."

Chantal looked at him sympathetically.

"Just make her own health a priority over revenge, if that makes sense."

"Why don't you ask Fearne? She knows the mind better than I do."

"Fearne will have Will to comfort. She doesn't need this on her shoulders." Chantal nodded in agreement. "Besides, I want to see your power in action."

Chantal paused, thinking to herself, and then she smiled. "I think that's wise. I'll do it."

"Thank you. Oh, and one more thing. We need to tell the others not to mention the fact that Eli and Jenny are alive to Hunter when she gets back."

"Again … are you sure?"

Joshua nodded. "She'll have enough to deal with when she returns. Goodnight."

"Goodnight," she said and left him to his studies.

ELEVEN

Eli had been on a private jet before with his father. Only once. His father wanted to show him what it was like to be privileged and rich, to get what you want quicker than others. It was a fun ride, he had to admit, but every other aspect made him wish the plane would take a nosedive into the North Atlantic Ocean.

This jet was different. For one, it was filled with FBI agents. Eli sat at the very back of the cabin next to the window with Zac-Joshua handcuffed to the aisle. When they returned to the hotel last night, the FBI were frantic and threatened to lock him up for good. Zac handled the situation with polite calm, winking at Eli every now and then. "I got this, watch," he'd say. Somehow, Eli trusted him.

Jenny was dozing off in front of them. She'd had no sleep last night without Joshua, and Eli knew it was because he'd always been there the entire journey to protect them at any cost. Though Eli still held a grudge against Joshua, he had to admit he felt empty without him, as though he'd forgotten to bring a suitcase with him.

Their flight was delayed for nearly the entire day for reasons Fitzpatrick did not care to inform them of, and then they were being loaded onto a stylish jet with a dozen FBI agents at sundown.

Fitzpatrick stood up the front of the cabin briefing her team on what was going down over the next twenty-four hours. Eli really didn't care where they were being led. To be honest, he didn't care much about anything anymore. Since this whole mess started, Eli felt as if he were just an accessory on Joshua's mission to get Hunter back. He was of no use to anyone. Nobody really cared where he went so long as he came back. It was Joshua they raved about. Joshua the crazy scientist. Joshua the amazing Iceman. Joshua who ruined his life and tried to kill him and then decided he was more valuable alive than dead and dragged him across the country to fix his volcanic mess.

Fucking Joshua.

Eli glared at the man beside him. Even though he knew it was some stranger, some kid with a power, he still hated him. His best friend Jack had been captured and was being used as some kind of mind-controlled weapon against Hunter and the others. It was too unbelievable to be real. *What's next? I bet my dad's psycho girlfriend Melissa has powers and she's working with Dr. Wolfe to take over the world and build an empire of black leather shoe robots.*

And I guess I should blame Joshua for that too. Fucking Joshua.

Suddenly, the fake Joshua looked up from his inspection of the in-flight menu and turned his gaze to Eli's.

"Seriously," Joshua sighed. "Who puts *grapes* on a pizza."

"Huh?"

"Look at this-" Eli didn't have a second to prepare before the laminated menu was shoved under his nose. Joshua tapped the pizza section furiously. "Whatever happened to good old-fashioned cheese pizzas? Has the world gone freaking insane?"

Eli looked at him in astonishment. "Joshua doesn't really talk like that."

"Why, coz he's got a stick up his ass?" Joshua shook his head and squirmed in his seat. "Maybe it's just these stupid suit pants, they're riding up in places you don't even want to – *oh.* Yeah, that feels weird."

Instantly, Eli wanted to laugh. Just watching him behave this way almost cheered up him. Almost. "Don't you get used to it after changing into so many people?"

At that moment, the FBI agents broke up from their debriefing. They spread out through the plane and took their seats. Eli watched the agents pass without taking a single glance at him.

Joshua shook his head. "Nah, I was the same fat kid for twelve years. I'm not used to it at all. This body isn't that bad though. It feels healthy."

"Aren't you afraid people will be able to tell it's not the real person?"

"Nope," said Joshua. "It's really easy to observe people's behavior before I change into them, and little clues about their body language, appearance and personality give things away. Watch."

Two FBI agents approached. Joshua turned to them and shook his cuffed wrist. "Excuse me?"

One of them stopped. "Yes?"

"I'd like to order this ridiculous grape pizza, and I'll have a scotch with extra ice." Joshua did this deep stare and raised one eyebrow suggestively. The agent frowned, not sure what he was implying. Eli rolled his eyes as the agent walked away.

"What the hell was that?"

"My Joshua impression."

He snorted. "You have a lot to learn about Joshua, buddy."

"Alright alright, I do a pretty good Cher impersonation. Want to hear it?"

Eli opened his mouth to say 'no', but Joshua raised his clenched fist, closed his eyes and began the chorus of *Believe*. Eli's mouth fell open. It was not only disturbing, it was surprisingly good.

When he finished, Eli rolled his eyes and told him to get some sleep. Joshua sighed dramatically and mumbled about waiting for his pizza. Eli nestled in and tried to close his eyes. The cabin lights dimmed and agents everywhere started to snooze or relax with a movie. Eli was just nodding off when something strange happened. He saw an agent drop a small piece of paper into Joshua's lap.

"This isn't my pizza," Joshua muttered and unfolded the note.

Oxygen masks on — you have fifteen seconds.

Inside the paper, a tiny key slipped out. A key to Joshua's handcuffs.

Eli's heart leapt. He had no time to question what it meant. Joshua looked at him again in surprise and some of the excitement he'd seen earlier flittered back into his pale eyes. Something was about to happen.

Eli leapt into action. He slid the note in the crack between the two chairs and shook Jenny's shoulder. She read it and her mouth fell open, on the verge of asking questions, but Eli didn't let her.

"Do it."

She nodded and opened up the pocket above her head. Joshua did the same.

Eli guessed it had already been eleven seconds. As he grabbed his own mask, he saw the same agent who had given them the note walk back through the cabin with a heavy-duty gas mask over his face. As he walked, he dropped something small and circular on the ground. The moment the object stopped rolling, it opened up and a gray gas started to seep from it.

All around him, there were coughing sounds. "What's happening?" an agent yelled. "I can't breathe," said another. Then they started to flop in their seats. Eli looked up through the dark, misty cabin room and saw the mystery agent standing at the head of the aisle with his hands behind his back, watching the silent chaos as all of the FBI agents fell asleep.

They waited. Jenny didn't move. Joshua gazed wide-eyed at the mysterious intruder. After at least forty more seconds, he removed his mask and strolled toward them.

"We don't have much time," he said in a thick British accent. In the dimness, Eli made out a young face with a close-trim beard and round eyes. He had curly black hair tucked behind his ears. There was a gun in the holster under his suit jacket. "I've managed to switch the cameras from the cockpit so they won't know what's happened. But we've got a two minute window of opportunity before they wake up."

"Wha …" Joshua gaped in wonderment. "Are you a wizard?"

He smirked down at them, flattered and amused. "Call me Barnes," he said. "Chevie Barnes. Now chop chop – we've got a plane to catch."

TWELVE

Hunter sat alone in her cell, thinking of nothing she hadn't thought of a thousand times already in her darkness. She heard horrible silence, endless and empty of Will. She didn't want to believe he was dead yet, not until she saw with her own eyes the way she saw Eli's body on the floor of room 23. So she waited.

The hardest part about waiting was not being able to see him. Usually when a person waits to hear if their loved one is alive or dead, they are in a hospital, free to visit and say a proper last goodbye. But there was no doctor there to deliver the news that Will would be alright. There was no way she could hold his hand and feel his warmth, or see his gaze upon hers with eyes that never let go of her heart. They had so much more to experience together, a relationship birthed in loneliness and a dark room with candles burning. It needed something else, something more to make it a love that could not be broken by pain or suffering. She wasn't ready to let go of Will the way she knew she had to let go of Eli. This death was different.

Amidst the silence, there came a scuffle outside her cell. Hunter frowned, wiping tears from her cheeks and listened to light footsteps. It sounded like a child.

"Who's there?" one of the mutants called through their cell, making her flinch in fright. Hunter closed her eyes, imagining hands reaching out between the bars. She'd heard this mutant's voice a few times before, but had never seen him. In her first few days imprisoned in the Death Caves, Hunter watched some of them be dragged from their cells: an older woman with ratted brown hair covered in rags; a skinny man hunched over and silent; a young woman with two heads like a Siamese twin. The girl in the white, tattered dress with the burns passed her once. Hunter probably looked almost exactly the same as her now – empty and sad.

"Hunter?" called a child's voice.

The sound of her name echoing in the darkness made all of her muscles freeze in place.

That voice sounds so familiar.

She crawled to her feet and wobbled across the dirt to the cell door. Through the window, she saw someone hurriedly peering inside each cell. She was a young girl with black hair and dark clothes. Her head turned to Hunter, and in the light, her pale face and sparkling eyes showed.

Ryo.

I'm dreaming, she thought instantly and her heart dropped into her stomach. Of course it wasn't real. Disappointed, Hunter closed her eyes and walked back to the wall of her cell.

"Hunter?" called Ryo again. "Are you in here?"

Ignore it. Ignore the hallucination and torture of Dr. Wolfe.

"Will? I'm here to rescue you!"

He's dead. He's gone.

Hunter sat down by the wall where her imprint was worn into the ground. She covered her ears and tried to block out Ryo's distant pleads for her, telling her she was there to be rescued, that there wasn't much time, that she'd gone through hell to get there, that Joshua trained her to-

Wait.

Joshua?

Hunter's eyes snapped open. She practically tripped to her door and thrust both her arms through the bars.

"Ryo!"

The girl came running to her. She grasped both of Hunter's hands and clenched them tight. The touch sent magnetic shocks through Hunter's body. It was real. She couldn't believe it was real. Ryo's face, so filled with relief, looked tired and worn, but that didn't matter. She'd come back for them.

"Thank God!" Ryo exclaimed. "I'm going to teleport you out of here."

Hunter wasn't sure she heard her correctly. Her mouth formed no words. She blinked over and over to try and make sense of Ryo's presence.

"What?"

In the distance, she heard an iron door creak open. Her body tensed out of habit, because she knew what that sound meant.

Ryo looked to her right. "Oh no, they're coming."

"Hey!" a guard shouted.

Ryo let go of Hunter's hands. There was a breath of air, and suddenly she was gone. Something grabbed her arm. She whirled and there was Ryo, inside her cell.

"I have to do it now before someone hears us. I wish I had more time to prepare you for this, but it's going to hurt. Please don't faint."

The footsteps were louder, and suddenly Dr. Wolfe's bald head appeared through the bars of her cell door. His eyes fell upon the both of them. He swore aloud and his keys shivered as he shoved them in the lock.

"Whatever happens-" Ryo yanked her arms and forced their gazes to meet. "Don't. Let. Go."

The cell door flung open. Hunter looked up as Dr. Wolfe lunged at her. She would never forget the look of panic and desperation on his face. His old, spindly fingers reached out for her, but he was too late.

And suddenly, he wasn't there anymore. A feeling not unlike the lurch of a plane passing through turbulence gripped her, and then her ears popped and she became light as air. She could feel nothing but Ryo's hands clenched tightly around her wrists. They were drowning in colors, blinking like fireworks, silently beautiful. It was the most freedom she'd ever felt in her life, until –

BANG!

Her body felt as though it had been squashed by a car. She was almost ripped from Ryo's arms as agony splintered through her body. It was nearly too much to bear. The colors disappeared and then a draft of warm and cold wind blew over her and she collided with gravity again.

Ryo let go.

She had landed on a wooden floor. If there was anything in her stomach at that moment, it would most likely be falling from her mouth with the way her body felt after teleporting.

She was inside, the air quite chilly but somehow refreshing. The smell of firewood and pine and old blankets and coffee brewing filled her lungs. Hunter let her eyes slide open.

The very first thing she saw was faces. Fearne. Chantal. Benji. Mosi. Marcus. Imogen. They gathered around her, their expressions anxious and relieved at the same time. They looked about to tackle her with hugs.

"How do you feel?" asked Ryo.

Hunter had no words.

"She's got all her limbs," said Marcus. "I think she's okay, unless she left her brain behind."

"Her brain is there," said Fearne with the biggest grin spread across her lips. "She's just in shock."

Hunter's mouth hung agape as she looked around. A very old, very beautiful cabin with a wooden staircase tipping up to their left and a border of giant glass windows surrounded her. The golden glow of the fireplaces made her feel instantly at home.

But Hunter didn't much care where she was. She looked again at the faces and felt her chest ache for the face she could not see.

"Will?" Her voice sounded unlike her own: Older, more pain-filled and mature. "Where is he?"

They shot glances at each other. A thick lump formed in her throat. She couldn't repeat the question; tears were starting to spill out of her eyes. *Oh God. Don't let it be true … he's not dead, he can't be …*

Then Mosi and Marcus shuffled aside and there, lying on a long futon with a thick, knitted rug strewn over him, was Will.

Hunter's weak legs carried her to him. She fell on the hard floor, grabbed his hand in hers and brushed the greasy, sweaty hair away from his eyes. She didn't care that the others were watching, that her body ached or that her eyes were drooping closed. All she cared about was that he was there, and alive.

"I'm so sorry," she murmured through sobs, resting her head on his arms. He smelled of blood and dirt but she wouldn't let him go. Not now, not ever. "I'm so s-sorry Will, it's all my fault, I should never have done this to you. Please be alright …"

"He'll be fine Hunter. He's just sleeping," said Fearne, her voice thick with concern. "Ryo brought him here an hour ago."

"He was in pretty bad shape, but he's healing. I found him in a surgery room and nearly got caught by a couple of guards," said Ryo. She looked pale and exhausted as she leant against the opposite sofa.

Mosi squeezed past Imogen, bent down on one knee and gently gripped her bracelet. She couldn't even feel the cold anymore, but as soon as he ripped it apart, the fire swirled inside her like a summer breeze. Mosi squeezed her hand and she met his deep, hypnotizing eyes. *Welcome home,* they said.

"How did ... you find us?" Hunter's eyes were falling closed. The warmth of the fire was putting her to sleep as she slumped against Will's body.

Ryo glanced at Fearne. "It was her. She connected me to your mind, and I was able to picture your location. I was trained to teleport by-"

"Me."

That voice.

A man appeared behind the others. He wore crinkled suit pants and a shirt to match the pale blue of his eyes. His normally slicked, black hair cascaded over his forehead.

He had changed, in every way physically and emotionally possible. He was not the Iceman she once knew, and he was not even the Joshua she grew up with. He was a wounded man, an open book and a reminder of the past that made her who she was.

Hunter remembered Dr. Rosenthal's words and wanted to say them. But ... Joshua killed Eli. She had not forgotten. And now he was there, with her closest friends. He could kill them. The Iceman could kill any one of them, and it would be her fault yet again.

Despite her limbs and muscles having shut down, Hunter summoned the energy to stand. The fire gave her renewed warmth. The others stepped back as a golden glow emitted from her.

"Joshua," she growled.

"Hunter, I'm so-"

Hunter screamed and the fire burst from her chest and surged for Joshua. He was expecting it and whipped up an ice shield, diminishing the fire with a hiss. If Hunter were stronger, she could have tried again, but with absolutely no food or water in her body and the impact of teleporting, she broke out in a sweat and slumped onto the sofa beside Will. Fire flamed from her fingers but did no more damage than a flickering candle. She glared at the man who had destroyed her life.

"Get away from us," she whispered.

Joshua didn't say anything, but instead he turned to Chantal and gave her a curt nod, his lip quivering.

The girl bent down over Hunter and whispered words into her mind that instantly doused the fire and her anger. But all Hunter heard was "Sleep."

THIRTEEN

D
r. Winston Wolfe was a complicated mind, as most men of
science are. He often found himself struck by an idea whilst
in the middle of something completely irrelevant to his
thoughts. For instance, he was once operating on a young
boy who had the power to glow as brightly as the sun. Dr. Wolfe couldn't
quite remember what had distracted him, but the human eye is almost just
as complex as the human mind. He made one little slip and the boy was
blind.

But that didn't matter now, because Sammy was dead.

Dr. Wolfe was in one of his deep-thought moods, so consumed that he
hardly noticed the chaos around him. The scientists in the lab were running
back and forth, trying to look hurried just like he'd asked. They barely
glanced at him.

Dr. Wolfe was thinking of one thing, and one thing only:

Power.

That morning, Hunter and Will escaped. He didn't know how it was
possible that Ryo found them again when the entire time he'd known her,
she hadn't once been able to teleport or travel in time. Nothing he ever did
could break her. Now suddenly she was teleporting into places she'd never
been before.

She had to have outside help, which meant that they survived. They had
all escaped.

"Dr. Wolfe!"

He halted in the middle of the corridor, frowning for a moment when he forgot where he was. Dr. Hosking came running up to him. She looked more distressed than he'd ever seen her.

"Yes?"

"The Agents have arrived."

Dr. Wolfe nodded and turned back to her. "Meeting room, now."

She nodded and scuttled back to the elevator. Dr. Wolfe wiped a hand over his bald head and stalked in the opposite direction. He threw open the meeting room door and went straight to the drinks table in the corner, pouring himself a glass of scotch, forgetting about the ice. He took a moment to collect himself before sitting down at the head of the long, black table and waited.

One glass later, they arrived.

Seven men in black suits swarmed into the room. Their numbers always changed depending on the type of mission, but when Dr. Wolfe wanted a possibly test subject 'handled', he only ever sent seven. They were all very qualified to collect quickly and efficiently without asking questions. Dr. Wolfe liked his Agents, especially when they brought back someone new and wonderful for him to explore. They did the job well, never faltering.

"Gentlemen," said Dr. Wolfe as he stood in greeting. "Welcome back."

They took seats at the long table but did not say a word. He didn't know their names; that was not how they worked. They had rankings.

"Alpha," he greeted the head of the table – a man with a strong neck and jawline, obvious build beneath his suit and dark, terrorizing eyes. He was a killer, and Dr. Wolfe's most trusted employee. "Any news?"

Alpha leaned forward on the table, regarding his fellow Agents. "We used every resource you gave us, Dr. Wolfe. But we found no path to the children."

Dr. Wolfe's lip twitched and he entwined his fingers together, resting his elbows on the cool table. "No path? No path at all?"

Alpha said nothing, his eye contact never faltering.

Dr. Wolfe couldn't take it anymore. He slammed his fists down on the desk. None of the men flinched.

"There were eight of them, and they walked through the mountains on FOOT! How did you not find them?"

"Dr. Wolfe, they stole a jeep. They disappeared on another road, and when we tracked them to town, they'd taken another vehicle. They're smart.

Not to mention they knew we'd be following them. They used their powers to get away."

"Oh please," he snorted. "They don't know how to take care of themselves any more than they can drive a car."

"With all due respect, sir, I think you've underestimated those kids. They learned from the last time we took them, and now they're working together. They're gone. We're still following up some leads, but it's gonna take some time. Is there anything else-"

"Yes, there is." Dr. Wolfe got to his feet and started pacing the room. "I have only one week left until the army arrives. Then we will put our plan into action. But I cannot run the risk of a bunch of misfit kids sitting out there, waiting for me to reveal myself, *especially* when they know exactly how to find me!" His voice grew to a yell and the men looked uncomfortably at their hands or the opposite walls. But not Alpha. He remained focused and unafraid.

"We'll find them Dr. Wolfe. But we need more assistance."

"I realize that," he sighed again. "Follow your leads, get back to me if you find anything. And please take Jet and Mikayla – those two have been grinding on my nerves. I need them out of my sight. And take the mutants with you as well."

This time, Alpha frowned. "Sir?"

"My mutants. They're a little out of control, but I've found a way to target their rage. I only have a dozen of them left. I've managed to install in them a mind control simulation using one of the formulas I've developed. They only want to find the children, and I've programed them to listen to your commands."

"Understood."

"In the meantime …" Dr. Wolfe felt a pang in his heart as he said, "We will be leaving this institution. I will send word of our new coordinates. It is no longer safe for us here."

"Yes sir. Is there a priority?"

Dr. Wolfe thought only for a few seconds before his immediate answer came to mind. "I want the Iceman, alive. I am certain he is with them. If you can get Hunter, that will also work. She is Joshua's weakness. I need her alive."

"Consider it done."

"And one last thing." The doctor took a deep breath before handing Alpha a black box the length of a pen. "Your target is Fearne. She was once my greatest weapon, and is now my greatest threat. This is the only way to stop her from stopping me. Use it at your discretion."

Alpha took the box. "Yes sir."

"It won't be long now before Jack will wake. And when he does, we will unite with the Chinese army to destroy this country. I don't need any kind of hero getting in my way." He turned to the Agents. "Kill them."

FOURTEEN

No. Freaking. Way!" Zac-Joshua's eyes widened to the size of tomatoes and his face lit up with glee. "Chevie Pulicover!"

Chevie frowned. "How do you know that name, Iceman."

"No it's me, it's Zac!" With that, Joshua disappeared and instead a chubby boy in a tight shirt and suit pants sat beside Eli. "Remember me?"

Chevie straightened up and crossed his arms. "Huh, yeah I remember you. You were that fat kid from ICE who used to annoy the shit out of everyone."

Zac smiled proudly. "The one and only."

"What the hell are you doing on this plane?" Zac opened his mouth to answer, but Chevie whipped up a hand and silenced him. "Wait, never mind, it's not important. What is important is that we get the hell off this plane. Oh, and it's not Pulicover anymore. It's Barnes."

"Uh, how do you expect to get off this plane?" asked Jenny.

At that moment, the jet rocked and quaked through a quick burst of turbulence. The four of them gripped their seats tightly.

"That's our ride now." Chevie lifted his finger to his ear and listened, as if through an earpiece. Eli stared, not knowing what to do. He kept looking at Jenny for help, since Zac was only sitting there in awe. The plane tipped again.

"Our *ride?*" asked Eli as he glanced down at his feet. He was really sweating now.

"That's right. We can't be on this jet forever. And those agents will wake up eventually. I want to be gone by then."

"Where are we going?" asked Jenny.

Chevie gave her a dazzling smile and leaned so close to her, Eli thought he was going to kiss her, but he only unclipped her seatbelt. "You'll have to trust me, love."

Jenny didn't like the way he spoke to her at all and wrenched her arm away. "Give me one good reason why I should."

The stare between them was so heated, Eli almost expected something out of the ordinary to happen. Perhaps Jenny would slap him for calling her 'love' – which Joshua never would.

Either way, Chevie's wide, dimpled smile stretched and he straightened up.

"Do you have a sense of adventure, Miss Smart?"

Jenny's mouth dropped open. Eli, too, was shocked he knew her name. "Y-yes," she stuttered defensively.

"Then I implore you," he purred, "to trust me."

"Uh, guys?" Zac was glancing behind Chevie at the unconscious agents who were beginning to stir. "Should we ...?"

"Yes!" Chevie ran to the back of the plane. There were cubicle bathrooms on either side and a bank of cupboards full of utensils and food trays. "Hurry up!"

Zac followed without hesitation. Eli and Jenny looked at each other, listening to Chevie bang about and yell at Zac to help him open up a hatch. Before Eli could even comprehend how in God's name they were opening the hatch without the jet being torn apart, Jenny grabbed his shoulder.

"What would Joshua do?"

Eli shrugged. "Kill him?"

Jenny bit her lip and then decided they had no other choice. "Come on. If Zac leaves, we'll be stuck with the FBI."

"But if we go, we'll be screwed when they find us."

Jenny grabbed her backpack from the overhead carrier and managed to smile down at him. "What else is new?"

A sudden jolt rocked the plane and alarms blared inside the cabin. Agents all around them started to stir dizzily awake. Eli and Jenny snuck into the back wing where they were being shaken by the turbulence.

A hatch lay open on the floor. There was obviously another aircraft attached to this one, or the cabin pressure would not have allowed the hatch to open. Zac was being lowered from the jet into the unknown. Eli's heart pounded as he peered down the hole. There was darkness everywhere. He felt ill.

"What's down there?" Eli shouted.

"Freedom!" Chevie shouted back with glee. He held out his hand for Jenny. She hesitated before taking it, and was quickly lowered down after Zac. "You're next, Akerman!"

"How did you-"

A bullet whizzed past Eli's ear and he ducked down into the hole Chevie was urging him into. His feet slipped on a ladder made of cold steel. The FBI were still firing at them. He heard nothing but the howl of wind until his feet made contact with ground and then Chevie was scampering down the ladder after him. A door slammed shut over their heads. Pressure valves sealed it. Their new plane dipped away from the FBI jet. Then, there was silence.

Eli looked around. They were in a dimly lit tunnel rather like the opening of a submarine, only far more high-tech. It was quiet, the sound of the engine far in the background.

"Barry and Fitzpatrick are going to kill us," Zac muttered to Eli as they stood awkwardly beside Chevie.

Brushing his fingers through his hair, Chevie clapped his hands together and grinned at them. "Alright, let's head down to the cockpit and I'll introduce you all to the rest of the gang."

"What gang?" asked Zac. The excitement in his voice was buoyant and renewed.

Chevie smirked crookedly back at them. "Follow me."

Zac looked at Eli and Jenny through narrowed eyes as if he were trying desperately to figure out whether he did know what Chevie was on about, but followed him anyway.

Chevie led them down a cylindrical corridor over steel floors that clanked every time they took a step. When they came to a titanium door, Chevie punched in a code and the steel slid aside to reveal a small tube elevator. They all squeezed in like sardines and dropped down to the floor below.

"Oh. My. God." Eli gazed in shock at the space before them. Plush seats lined both walls, a shining runway down the center that led to a raised cockpit with two large, red chairs facing a dashboard and a giant window. Along the back were extra-large, heavy-duty crates marked with coded words Eli couldn't decipher for the life of him. To his right was a separate alcove with a large coffee machine and a refrigerator. Everything inside the jet looked lush and expensive, as though it was used to fly the President himself.

"This is the coolest plane ever," said Eli.

"Thank you," said Chevie. "I designed it myself."

"You designed it?" Zac gaped. "What are you, a super-genius?"

Chevie gave him another dazzling smile filled with secrets. "Something like that."

On their left were two people, leaning against the wall talking closely. One was an older man dressed in black with a badass Wolverine-meets-Crocodile-Dundee vibe under messy brown hair, thick eyebrows and a structured jaw. The woman he was speaking closely with wore similar tight attire with a leather jacket and fingerless gloves. She had wild hair flowing down to her elbows and her brown eyes were thin and cat-like.

"Guys, I'd like you to meet Ace and Illya Monroe, from Australia."

"G'day!" said Zac and Eli cringed when Ace and Illya gave him a stone-cold glare.

"They run a rehab for people like you Zac with special abilities," said Chevie.

"Really?"

"Are you serious?" asked Jenny.

"Yep. They joined our team last year to help us find you guys."

Chevie stalked to the cockpit of the plane. Ace and Illya nodded their greeting to Eli and the other two, but continued to talk in hushed tones.

"And this is our lovely young pilot, Miss Amelia Grace Mackintosh."

Eli looked away from Ace and Illya and came face to face with a young girl probably no older than him. She had brown hair cut short in a concave bob. Her eyes were wide and bright with small features. She reminded Eli of a beautifully hypnotic deer. Eli felt his knees go weak at the sight of her, but he brushed it off as being dehydrated or … stressed.

"Hi," said Amelia.

"You're a chick," said Zac in awe.

Amelia frowned at him. "You're observant."

"I mean you're … you're driving a plane!"

"Again," she smiled and turned back to face the sky and the clouds whooshing past them in the darkness. "Very observant."

"Were you named after Amelia Earhart?" asked Jenny.

"As a matter of fact, I was." Amelia flipped a switch on the dashboard and released the wheel in front of her. "I've been studying aviation since I was eleven years old. But flying planes isn't my superpower."

"What is?" Zac asked eagerly.

She turned to him and said very seriously, "I make the most amazing lemon cheesecake known to man."

Jenny and Eli chuckled at the look of disappointment on Zac's face, and then Amelia was laughing too and it almost took Eli's breath away.

A tray of sandwiches was shoved in Eli's face and he jumped and turned to see Chevie's blinding smile and well-kept teeth again. He could immediately tell this guy was going to get on his nerves.

"Sandwich?"

"Thanks." Eli took one.

"Come over here and we'll let our good pilot get back to flying us home."

As Chevie led them to a few seats against the wall, Eli found he couldn't take his eyes away from the back of Amelia's head.

"Where is home exactly?" asked Jenny as she took a sandwich herself and sat down. Eli suddenly felt very important, as though he were in some kind of military plane about to embark on a high-priority mission or something. It seemed he wasn't the only one getting jittery. Zac himself was inspecting the straps on his seat and pulling things he probably shouldn't, muttering to himself about how much Marcus would be jealous of this.

"Let me start from – Hey, Zac don't touch that!"

Zac froze with his fingers clasped around a strap that was probably attached to a parachute. Slowly, he pulled his hand away. "Sorry," he muttered. Eli smiled.

"Alright," said Chevie. "I owe you an explanation. First of all, maybe a little history about yours truly?"

The three of them stared.

"Great enthusiasm guys." Chevie pulled up a crate and sat down in front of them.

"I know your history," said Zac smugly. "You were imprisoned at ICE."

"He was?" asked Jenny.

"Yep. Chevie Pulicover was a legend. Tried to escape a record total of eight times. How far did you get Chev?"

"The sewers," he said in a nonchalant manner, but Eli could tell he was proud of his efforts. "I also broke the record for longest time spent in Solitary."

"Uh-uh," Zac smiled. "I crushed your record. I spent nineteen days in Solitary."

Chevie's eyebrows shot up. "How'd you ever make it out?"

"Well you see, I enjoy being by myself. I ended up getting pretty weird and imagining a bunch of carrots—"

"Can we please get back to the topic?" Jenny interrupted. Eli snickered at the look of disappointment on Zac's face.

"My dad helped me escape ICE," Chevie replied. It was the first time Eli had seen him look somber, the memory both wonderful and horrible. "He worked at ICE as a guard, but he was different from the others."

"Who was he?"

"Alistair."

Zac nodded. "Yeah, I remember him. He was nice. They said he got fired for something, but we never found out what."

"When I was imprisoned," said Chevie, "he didn't know it was me at first until he saw the tests. It had been like nine years since my mother and I saw him. I didn't care at first – he abandoned us and I couldn't really call him a father. Then … he changed. He knew he had to get me out, to start acting responsible for me. He risked his life to help me escape and …"

"He died?" asked Zac.

Jenny scowled. "Show some sensitivity, Zac."

"It's okay," Chevie smiled, paying especially close attention to Jenny. Eli wondered what Joshua would do if he saw the way they were looking at each other. Chevie was much better looking than Joshua, and less creepy, and charming and friendly and … altogether a great person. Jenny could fall for him easily.

"When I was free I sort of went about living my life. I was selfish, trying to live back the years I'd lost. But in the back of my mind I remembered my dad, and I remembered every other poor soul trapped in ICE. I decided I needed to do something about it. That's when I formed the SSS."

"The what?"

"The Secret Society of Superheroes," he said proudly.

Eli felt like laughing. Zac actually did.

"What a lame name, you couldn't have been more inventive?"

"What would you suggest?" Chevie snapped.

"Uh …" Zac's face turned pink with how hard he was trying to think. "Justice for … uh …"

"Keep going," Jenny said to Chevie.

"It's not as lame as you think, Zackie. The society has been standing for almost five years now. Those who joined the cause are mostly normal people who have seen extraordinary things or are devoted to finding individuals who do extraordinary things themselves. People like us with abilities. It's a mix of both."

"What does this society do?" asked Jenny.

"We protect each other. The normal people help hide us, and we practice using our powers to find more people so they don't tell the world and so that people like Dr. Wolfe and his Agents don't find them."

"But why don't you do something about ICE?" Eli crossed his arms and sniffed. "I find it hard to believe that such an organization could completely ignore the torture going on for so long, especially when you know exactly what they were doing to the kids."

Chevie's face fell and he glanced at his clasped hands between his legs. Eli couldn't help but notice that a head was peering up over the chair and he locked eyes with the girl in the pilot seat. She quickly slipped back down, out of sight.

"Same reason anyone who escaped never went back. I was scared," he said simply. "Sure, I had the motivation, but I lacked the courage. It wasn't until a few weeks ago when I was almost taken by the Agents again that I realized it was time to stop living in fear and start fighting. I summoned our top representatives and we formulated a plan to rescue you and take down ICE."

"How did you know where we'd be?"

"We got wind of you through the FBI. We have an insider source that told us a man named Joshua Harrison was speaking out about people with powers. Now I realize that he wasn't exactly shouting it to the world, but he might as well have. I went in to investigate and discovered that the FBI was also trying to hunt down ICE. I had to get you out of there to find out what was going on."

"You hijacked an FBI plane to ask us some questions?" Eli gaped.

"Would you rather still be on that plane about to be locked in the Pentagon while they test Zac?"

Zac's face went white. "They were going to test me?" He shot a glare at Eli and Jenny. "Did you know about this?"

"Of course not," Jenny lied.

"As I said," continued Chevie, "the SSS is a safe zone for people with abilities and people who believe in them. We're not an army and we're not heroes ourselves. Just a family who protect each other."

They sat in appreciative silence until Chevie looked at them and winked.

"You three have a lot to learn. I suggest you buckle up, we should be landing soon. Unless you have any more questions?"

Eli wanted to open his mouth, but Zac beat him to it.

"If an African elephant moves to America, does it become an African-American elephant?" he asked with his hand raised.

Chevie, Jenny and Eli looked at him, dumbfounded.

"Uh, any *important* questions?" asked Chevie again.

They shook their heads and settled into silence. As they grew closer to landing, Eli held on to his seatbelt and gazed out at the wide expanse of sky where he could just see the top of a dark, dusty mountain.

FIFTEEN

Hunter awoke to a creaking sound she instantly presumed was a guard coming to collect her from her cell. Her eyes were sticky and her body ached, but her mind snapped to life as if she were being jolted by an electric shock.

But she was not in a cell anymore. She was in a strange, other-worldly place. And then it all came back to her and she remembered; she was free.

The cabin was colored silver and blue, embers long burned out in the fire at her feet. Her neck had cramped up from lying on the sofa. In the distance, an owl was hooting.

There was no one in the room. They must've all moved upstairs to bed. Only Will remained, lying on the other sofa, still deeply unconscious. Muscles aching, Hunter slipped off the sofa and crawled along the floorboards toward him.

His eyelids fluttered softly in sleep, his breath going in and out. She was so close, she could see the outline of the scar along the edge of his jaw, indented in the rough stubble littered with dirt. Almost subconsciously, she traced her fingers over his cheek and curled her hand around his.

"No matter what happens," she whispered, "I won't ever let him hurt you again. I *promise*."

She wasn't sure how long she sat there, but soon an urge to go outside moved her to the porch. Her bare feet took her through the glass doors and down the wooden steps to a path that led through the trees.

The air was warm but the wind chilled her. She filled her senses with clean air and freedom, ignoring the smell of the Death Caves still on her worn jumpsuit. Her limbs ached as she walked down the gravel path and soon came to a glittering lake.

It was beautiful and calm, billions of stars blinking down at her and the black expanse of space spread further than her eyes could see. She never saw a sky like this in New York. But it was nearing dawn and the sky would brighten soon.

The smile on her face faded when she saw a figure walking slowly across the shore, his back to her, his hands in his pockets. Her heart started to pound and she thought *Men in White* and *Agent*. But then he turned onto the short boardwalk just a little further and came to a stop at the end of the deck where he sat down on the edge and dipped his feet into the water. She knew even from a distance that it was Joshua.

A strange calmness overcame her. She should *hate* him. The last time they spoke – aside from just hours ago when she nearly set him alight – he was kneeling before her in the warehouse, a broken and confused man who could not control his power.

But she was not angry, and she could not explain why. Every time she tried to work herself up, a buzz of comfort washed over her and the anger dissipated. She gave herself a few more minutes to calm her beating heart – almost turning back to the cabin to avoid talking to him – before she finally went to the boardwalk. When her footsteps announced her presence, he turned and his pale eyes caught hers.

Joshua flinched, obviously expecting her to shoot a ball of flames at him.

"Hello Hunter," he said.

She sat down beside him, rolling up the filthy cuffs of her jumpsuit and dipping her toes into the chilly water. It was refreshing and soothing and cold all at once.

They sat in silence for a few moments, each of them not knowing what to say. Hunter couldn't tame her own thoughts. Looking at him now, she could tell he was a different man. She wanted to know what had changed him.

In the back of her mind, she still yearned to be angry with him. But she had been through so much more horror, and had taken him for granted all her life. He deserved some form of forgiveness.

"I don't know where to start," said Joshua. He looked out at the lake, clenching his jaw to keep it from quivering. "I don't know how to tell you I'm sorry, more sorry than I can express in words."

Hunter took a deep breath in and a deep breath out. When she felt brave enough, she spoke.

"I know. I can see that."

"I can't let it go. The things I've done … I can't escape them."

"I know what you were going through," she said. "I didn't back then, because it used to be all about me and how I wanted to use my powers and how I over exaggerated and thought I had the ability to be a hero. It was like this … consuming fire that took over my emotions, and the same happened to you with the ice."

Joshua nodded but said nothing.

"Weirdly enough, I found my peace with the fire after the warehouse. I didn't realize how much of a vice it became until I couldn't use it as a weapon when I needed it most. Now it's consuming, but … it's like it *knows* me. We're one soul combined. Does that make sense?"

The tips of Joshua's fingers crackled and turned white. Hunter frowned at him.

"What's wrong?"

"Nothing." He shoved them in his pocket. "I just don't like the thought of what happened to you in there. And I blame myself for it."

She sighed. "I hated you for killing Eli and Miss Smart. I hated you so much that I nearly lost my mind. And that caused me to let my guard down and I got captured and I went through hell and I blamed you for it."

He lowered his head and nodded dejectedly.

"But I know what it's like to make huge mistakes; I've made them too. So I have forgiven you. I may not love you like I used to, but I forgive you. Can you accept that?"

Again – and after some hesitation – he nodded. His next words were drowning in gratitude. "Thank you, Hunter. That's all I need."

Despite their past, despite all the secrets they still had buried inside them, Hunter found some peace in sitting on the deck with Joshua. The world stretched before them, freedom in their wake. If she tried hard enough, she could pretend that they were completely alone, that the past few years had never happened, that they were camping in a remote location with nothing on their minds but serenity, and that all was well with them.

Fire and ice sat together on the lake as the sun breached the horizon, torment and heartbreak behind them. And it was bliss.

– PART 2 –
THE CABIN

SIXTEEN

The SSS jet slowed to a hover over mountains of orange and brown earth beneath a black, star-lit sky. Whirlwinds of dust blew across the peaks. Then everything was dark and the jet touched down inside a concrete carrier. Amelia powered off the plane and Eli followed the others as they unclipped their seat belts and stepped onto the platform.

"Is this your base?" asked Zac.

"It's more of a … secret compound. We're located just a few hours outside of Vegas."

"Sick," Zac grinned.

"There's a few more people I want to introduce you to so … follow me."

Eli stepped in line behind Jenny, casting a glance back at Amelia as she stood by the dashboard, flicking switches and running through checks. He sighed, wishing she was showing them around instead of Prince Charming.

Chevie led them down a ramp into the aircraft bunker – a giant room built of hard steel rusty in some places but strong and firm. Quickly, they marched through the bunker to a large circular door that opened at Chevie's command. Directly before them was an elevator with only one button: up.

"This elevator leads to the main area of the compound," said Chevie. It was a sturdy elevator that shot up quicker than Eli could handle. When it opened, there was a double door on the right and left. Chevie led them through the right door and before Eli could blink, he was following the others into a low-roofed space filled with more people than he imagined there to be in this organization. It looked like some sort of military control room, with rows of computer hubs to his left and a large round table covered in maps to the right. *What is this, S.H.I.E.L.D headquarters?*

Chevie marched them around the outer platform, down the flight of three stairs to the main control unit on the other side of the room. Eli saw at least five giant panels along the wall, suggesting some sort of shield against outer light. He wished there was more natural fluorescence than the bright tubes above their heads. Eli couldn't stop staring at all the people dressed in everyday clothes – minus the few soldiers wearing military uniforms – all busy doing things he couldn't even guess. He felt as if they'd come to the wrong place, and it made him nervous.

While Chevie strolled up to a man with his back turned, Eli whispered subtly to Jenny. "Does this all seem a little strange to you?"

"Better than being at the Pentagon with the FBI though, right?"

"I dunno … I'm getting a kind of Area 51 vibe."

Jenny was about to whisper back when Chevie turned.

"This is our commanding officer, weapons specialist and tactical advisor, Captain John Mackintosh of the Special Forces. Retired, of course."

Captain Mackintosh was a man of around fifty with a broad chest, thick gray hair and hard-set lines around his eyes and mouth. He didn't smile, but appraised the three of them carefully.

"So … you're the three who've been spilling all your secrets to the FBI, eh?"

Eli bit his lip and looked at Zac, who seemed particularly interested in watching a radar screen emit green signals on the control panel.

"Actually, sir, it wasn't necessarily our fault," said Jenny timidly.

"Oh, it wasn't?" Captain Mackintosh peered at each of them in turn. "Where's the scientist, Joshua Harrison?"

"Uh …" said Zac.

"It's a long story," said Jenny. "But I think you owe us an explanation first. Now that we're here, what are we supposed to do?" She crossed her arms, determined to show them no intimidation. Eli wished he were as brave.

Captain Mackintosh chuckled deeply. "Fair enough, Miss…?"

"Smart. Jenny Smart."

"Miss Smart, yes. Mr. Barnes, would you care to explain to our guests why they are welcome inside our compound? I have some work to do."

"With pleasure, Captain." Chevie turned his attention to the three of them. "Perhaps a little tour first?"

They nodded eagerly.

Chevie gestured to the wide expanse of space. "Most of the people you'll come to meet in this compound are supporters of superheroes. We don't reject anyone who comes to live in this society, whether they have powers or they simply want to help people who do." Chevie raised his hand and pointed to the hub of computers where Eli spotted a group of young people furiously typing away on computers. "For example, these guys look exactly like your typical nerds who work for top-secret companies and do all the smart shit. And that's exactly what they are. Hackers, or 'nerds' as some people call them."

Zac snorted a laugh. Eli glared at him, catching a warning look from Jenny.

"By that I mean they're superhero fans. Like others here, I found them through the internet and decided to make use of their technology skills. They're sworn to secrecy of course, but it means they get to hang out with real people with superpowers like … yours truly." He pointed proudly to himself and then swung his arm out dramatically to the left side of the room where there was a table of maps and men and women dressed in smart suits and work attire were hurrying back and forth behind it. "Then we have the power planners – those who do the searching for more of us and run the missions. Right now, Captain Mackintosh has been holding a search for the Agents."

"You're hunting the Agents?" Zac gaped. "How?"

"We were able to track them down through our communications system. Turns out they're ex-special agents who do freelance work for Dr. Wolfe. We've been watching them since they left ICE several days ago."

"Where are they going?" asked Eli.

"Not sure yet, we're working on it. We're also following the FBI to Washington to see what they're up to next. We had to get you guys out of there of course, because once the FBI get their hands on us … there'll be an epidemic. It's bad enough they know we exist."

"Why is it bad?" asked Jenny. "I mean they protect our country, they can help us find Dr. Wolfe and get rid of him."

Chevie raised an eyebrow at her. "If they could do that, why have they not done it already?"

Jenny's shoulders slumped. *He's right,* Eli thought, *the FBI are useless and they're going to continue chasing their own tails until someone points them in the right direction.*

"Now, there's more to show the three of you but … it's getting late. I've organized some rooms on the upstairs level, so you can clean yourselves up and hit the sack. We'll have more of a debriefing tomorrow."

"That sounds great," said Jenny with relief. "I really need a shower."

"Showers are provided," said Chevie. "I'll show you-"

"I can take them Chev." Eli turned at the wonderful voice that he remembered from the jet. Amelia stood behind them wearing a white lab coat and clutching an iPad in her hands. "You probably need a break yourself," she smiled.

"Thanks gorgeous," said Chevie and he hurried away with a wink at Jenny.

"Follow me," said Amelia.

Eli practically sprinted to her side, Jenny and Zac behind him. "Do you live here?"

"Yup," said Amelia. "My father, the Captain, lets me work for the SSS – I'm a mechanical engineer and a biologist."

"And you're … how old?" asked Eli.

"Twenty-two. I'm advanced for my age though."

Eli felt his heart flutter. *She's hot and she's a nerd. Holy shit, I'm out of my league.*

They marched down a narrow corridor with fluorescent lights along the cement walls. Amelia led them to the left where a black arrow pointed to the 'C Ward'. All along the walls were rooms with heavily sealed doors. It was all very institutionalized, only more … military inspired.

"This room is yours Jenny," said Amelia and handed her the key to '39'. "There's a phone on your door if you need anything, dial 2. Yours is '38' across the hall Zac and Eli, you're in … '41'." Eli took the key from her and turned to his door.

This is the weirdest vacation ever.

"I'll see you at breakfast in the morning."

"S-sounds … uh …"

Amelia waited patiently for Eli to finish his sentence with an amused glimmer in her eyes. She tucked her hair behind her ear and Eli felt his heart somersault.

"He thinks you're hot," said Zac.

Eli glared at him.

"What?" Zac's eyes drifted down. "Seriously, your dingle-berry is showing."

"Okay, thank you Zac!" Eli put his hand over his crotch and saw Amelia blush.

Zac was chuckling as he closed his door behind him.

"I'll see you tomorrow," said Amelia and she walked gracefully away.

"Uh, g-goodnight Amelia," he said as he picked his pride up off the floor and went to bed.

SEVENTEEN

Will squinted at the strange flare of colors he awoke to. It wasn't fluorescence or torchlight. The bed he lay on wasn't a bed at all, but some sort of couch. He could hear strange noises in the distance outside; birds taking flight and wind rustling through the trees. The house he was in looked cluttered, made of wood and filled with worldly possessions. Normal things like kitchen utensils, books, armchairs and fireplaces. Will was so shocked at what surrounded him that it was at least a minute before he realized he was not in the Death Caves anymore. He was not even in ICE.

He was free.

Will had no idea how he got there. The last thing he remembered was passing out after Jet had sawed off his wrist. He didn't need to look down to know it had healed.

Getting shakily to his feet, Will walked toward the wall of windows that faced a forest of lush, green trees. The smell of it filled his nostrils. The sun flickered across his body. With quivering hands, he opened the door and walked outside into the first break of day he had seen in a very long time.

Tears spilled out of his eyes. If he had some other way to express the overwhelming joy he felt inside, he would have done it. The fresh air was glorious. The enriching smell of morning washed over his body like the happiness that flowed through him. It was almost too much. He dizzily sat down on the steps of the porch, staring into the trees, noticing the glimmer of water between the scattered trunks. He shook from head to toe, a mixture of happiness and fear waging war inside him. Eventually he summoned the energy and stood, tripping down the path, feeling the rich dirt between his filthy toes. He couldn't get enough of the smell.

Stretching his hands out, Will was surprised at the feeling of the rough tree trunks as they scraped across his skin. He stumbled out of the clearing and came face to face with a giant lake that glimmered in the morning sun. A couple of birds swooped down from the blinding sky above him and touched the surface of the water, then playfully danced in the air around the shore. Will laughed at them.

Soon his eyes spotted a large plank of wood extended out across the water. There were two people sitting on it. They hadn't seen him. Will recognized Hunter's red hair instantly and something in his stomach lurched. He was unsure whether he was glad to see her or not. But that was something else to think about.

The moment of utter bliss was over, and now it was time to get answers. Will spun around and looked at the house he'd just woken up in. Concealed in the trees, it was clearly some kind of cabin. Perhaps this was the safe house that Dr. Rosenthal had offered them. That must mean …

Fearne.

Will ran back to the house. Before he could make it, however, he felt his insides curl and suddenly he was leaning against a tree and vomiting. He couldn't remember eating last, but something was coming up. His vision blurred, but he didn't care. He was free and that's all that mattered.

When Will opened the door to the cabin, he saw that there were people in the kitchen. A girl with radiant golden hair in a jumper and denim shorts. It looked like Chantal, but not the Chantal he knew. Beside her was a boy in an oversized T-shirt that read 'I'M NERDY AND I KNOW IT'. Again, it looked a bit like Benji, but a more confident, mature Benji. They were both holding cooking utensils, frozen in his gaze.

And there, sitting on a kitchen stool on the other side of the bench, was Fearne. Like the other two, she was not dirty or shaven or anywhere near as hollow as she used to be. She had never looked happier than when she slipped off the stool and came running into his arms.

Will's heart practically exploded with ecstasy. He tried not to hold her too tight against him, but he couldn't help it. She was so small and light, wrapped around him. Her hair had brightened and grown out a little and she smelled like fresh soap and old clothes. His body shook with sobs as he buried his face in her hair and kissed her neck.

"I was so worried about you," he murmured.

"Don't be silly," she said. "We're safe here. Welcome to the cabin."

"How did I get here?" he asked as he pulled away.

"Ryo rescued you and Hunter last night," said Chantal. "Are you hungry?"

"I think he needs a shower first," said Fearne and she screwed her tiny nose up and laughed. "You stink."

Will's smile tipped to the side. "Of course I smell – you've all probably scrubbed yourselves clean of ICE by now."

"Come on," said Chantal. "We'll fix breakfast while you have a shower. I'll show you where everything is."

Gratefully, Will followed Chantal to the stairs.

EIGHTEEN

Hunter decided to cook breakfast for everyone that morning – since she and Joshua had spent the first few hours of dawn watching the sun rise over the treetops and not saying much at all – but when they went back inside, breakfast was already being prepared. She found Chantal, Benji, Fearne and Imogen fixing a continental breakfast to welcome she and Will home.

Chantal offered to show her where she could shower, and she gratefully complied. "Will's in there, but I think he just stepped out," she said as they climbed up the steep stairs to the upper level. Hunter swallowed, not sure whether she was ready to face Will. When Chantal took her into the second bedroom – complete with a chest of drawers, two single beds and an old desk with a simple lamp on top – she showed her the stash of clothes at their disposal. Hunter was amazed at how prepared Dr. Rosenthal was for their arrival.

Hunter meandered from the bedroom across the hall to the bathroom. She was so lost in tired thought that she jumped in fright as the bathroom door swung open before she could turn the handle and she bumped straight into Will's bare chest.

"Oh, shit-"

Will's long, wet hair hung over his eyes and dripped water down his muscled pecks. Her cheeks went instantly red when she saw the v-line leading below where the towel was wrapped around his waist. His doe-brown eyes caused her stomach to knot up and her knees to go weak. She was so distracted by how different he looked already that she found herself breathless. He didn't have dirt on his face. Not even a 5 o'clock shadow lined his square jaw. And though he still looked tired and beaten, there was a certain strength in the way he held himself. A renewed strength.

Taking advantage of the fact that he couldn't run away from her while she stood in the doorway, Hunter threw her arms around his neck. A puff of air escaped his lips. His skin was warm from the shower and he smelled like soap. It occurred to her that she had not yet showered and he was basically naked, but it only mattered that he was still alive and with her.

"No more suffering," she whispered against his collarbone, feeling strands of damp hair stick to her cheek. "I promise."

For a moment he stood there. That told her he was still mad, still hurt that she'd sentenced him to die. She understood that. But if she could find it in her to forgive Joshua for the way he hurt her, surely Will could as well.

One hand came to rest between her shoulder blades, the other pressed lightly against her hair, and she let her eyes close in relief. The touch sent the fire into a frenzy inside her, and for different reasons.

Hunter pulled back. "Are you okay?"

Will smiled down at her, but it was a reserved smile. She knew before he spoke that he was lying. "Couldn't be better. I'm uh … going to go put some clothes on."

"Uh, sure," she mumbled, blushing again. He held the towel as he crossed to the opposite room.

No sooner had he gone did Hunter feel a pang of emptiness. Would she ever want to let him out of her sight again?

After a rather strange and short shower, Hunter dried herself and changed without looking in the mirror for fear of scarring herself at how ghostly she must look. Then she went back downstairs to join the others.

Being in this place with those she'd met in ICE was a strange experience. They were all dressed in normal clothing. The sunlight and acceptance of freedom changed the way they acted. Benji laughed and talked more. Chantal actually managed to find make-up and had never looked more radiant. She even admitted Marcus scrubbed up nicely after a shave and a good haircut.

As they all sat down for breakfast – all except Joshua, whom she imagined was too afraid to face Will just yet – Hunter and Will asked them all to explain their escape and what had changed over the past week.

It was apparently easy for them to get to where they were. There was a bit of a hike through the mountain, and once they found a main road, Chantal forced a man to drive them to the nearest town and buy them food. Fearne then wiped his memory. They avoided speaking to anyone before they were sure the Agents hadn't followed them.

Everything they'd done since arriving at the cabin was mostly taking walks and exploring the cabin and venturing to the local store five minutes from the house to buy food and necessities with some of the cash they found in a jar in the pantry. When she asked how they got there, they explained that Dr. Rosenthal had an old car in the garage that Marcus knew how to drive from his days of playing *Grand Theft Auto*. At that, Hunter almost laughed. There was no way he learned to drive from a video game. There was more to that lie than he admitted.

Tomorrow was Benji's birthday and they'd already decided to bake a cake and have a party. It was such a simple thing, but it made them so happy.

The food they cooked up was more wonderful than her hot shower. She didn't want to appear ravenous in front of the younger ones, but it was all she could do not to shovel the entire table into her mouth. Will – having not eaten anything but gray goo for sixteen years – looked as though he was in some kind of trance. He ate slowly, not finishing his meal, and then disappeared to the bathroom shortly after.

The younger ones had found an old board-game and – while Chantal and Hunter cleared the table and washed the dishes – the younger ones sat down beside the fireplace to play, laughing and arguing like a normal family. Hunter couldn't keep the smile off her face.

"You feeling okay?" asked Chantal as she piled plates and cups onto the drying rack.

"Yeah," she said. She wasn't sure how she felt just yet. It was all so overwhelming.

"Don't worry, it'll all sink in after a day or two. I remember I couldn't get over how green and colorful everything was until I spent my second day staring into the toilet bowl at my green and colorful vomit." Hunter cringed. "That's when I had to step back and remind myself to take it easy."

"I'm more worried about Will. It'll be a while before he's used to it."

As she spoke, Will came back downstairs. His face was flushed and his eyes were bloodshot. Chantal offered him a cup of coffee but he declined, flopping down on the sofa beside Mosi to watch the children play.

When Hunter and Chantal were finishing cleaning the kitchen, she glanced out the window and saw Joshua walking back inside. Will turned his head and instantly, his eyes went dark.

"Guys? Who is that?"

They turned just as Joshua entered with a cautious smile on his face.

"Uh …" said Hunter, having forgotten that Will was the only person who hadn't met her guardian yet. She dropped the dishcloth and walked around the kitchen bench to stand beside Will.

Joshua and Will met eyes. It was clear they both recognized each other. Joshua's shoulders slumped – this was another person he needed to beg forgiveness from. But Will didn't look like he wanted to forgive Joshua as quickly as Hunter did.

"You," he said.

"William. It's … it's good to see you."

The tension in the room was almost unbearable. Hunter kept very still beside Will, afraid that if she moved, he'd explode.

"Really?" he breathed a bitter laugh. "I'm sorry, I can't say the same for you."

Joshua looked at Hunter as if for help, but Hunter was torn. Though Joshua had suffered enough these past few months over what he'd done to her, she wondered now if he ever felt any remorse for leaving Will behind.

"I understand you hate me for–"

"You could have taken me with you," he said through gritted teeth, advancing on Joshua, who took a step back.

"Will-"

He threw out a hand to her. "Let me say this, Hunter. I've been dying to after he walked away from me and took you with him. It was worse than any torture I'd ever endured. And then you go and *kill* Hunter's teacher and her boyfriend and torture her friend in front of her." Will looked at Joshua with so much disgust that for a moment, Hunter wanted to defend Joshua. But she knew Will was right. "I don't know how Hunter did it, but I can't forgive you yet."

Will stormed past Joshua, knocking against his shoulder and sending him staggering back, then went out the door.

Hunter didn't comfort Joshua, even though he looked like he needed it desperately. Some part of her wondered if the anger that came from Will was also reserved for her, but he was too nice to release it to her face.

"Well that was awkward," said Marcus loud enough for everyone to hear. "Whose turn is it?"

The others jumped back into their game. Joshua gave her a look of bitter hurt and then walked to the staircase where he would most likely go to Dr. Rosenthal's study, and Hunter was left wondering who to run after.

Fortunately, Mosi provided her with a distraction. He separated himself from watching the game and came and met with her in the kitchen.

"Hunter?"

She turned away from the window and looked up at him. "Yeah?"

"We found this on the day we arrived here." He handed her a crinkled envelope with her name on it. "We think Dr. Rosenthal left it for you."

Nodding, Hunter took the letter. "Thank you."

"Is that the letter?" asked Benji. The others peered over the sofa like little meercats eagerly watching her.

"Can you read it to us?" asked Imogen.

Hunter wasn't sure she could. The doctor's last words to her in ICE were to have hope, but did he know he was about to be killed by his oldest friend? The same friend who beat him and had him locked up in the Death Caves? His voice, his advice, the last look he gave her came after he wrote this letter. What if things had changed?

But the others didn't know that. They had a right to hear. She tore open the envelope.

"It says, '*Dear Hunter. If you found this letter it means I did everything right and you arrived safely at my house. I only hope that the others were able to escape with you and no one was hurt.*'" She glanced up at their sad faces as they remembered those they left behind, but she forced herself to keep going. "'*I've had to hurry through this letter to get it to you on time, so excuse me if it is rushed. Things have gotten out of my control lately. It's a miracle I was able to cause the distraction. I can assure you, however, that the following steps have been carefully arranged prior to our escape plan. Please take each one very seriously, as all your safety is imperative not only to me, but to the future of the world.*

'*Firstly, you will need to dispose of the transport you acquired along the way. I assume you found ways to steal a car, but you must get rid of it, or the Agents may find a way to track you.*'"

"Check," said Marcus.

"*There is a car in the garage if you need it. Secondly, I have hidden necessities in the safe in my office. Marcus can help you unlock it. And I know he is with you, because otherwise you would have had no way of entering the house without disarming the alarm system. I have set it up to stop anyone from entering through any door or window without permission from inside.*"

"Oh yeah," scoffed Marcus. "It was a piece of cake getting in here."

"Pft!" spat Chantal. "Except when you screamed like a girl at the black cat that ran out of the house."

Marcus huffed and ignored her.

"*To add to that, please ensure you all stay within the house unless you need food, and do not speak to anyone who may come by.*"

They all looked sheepishly at Joshua who stood on the staircase.

"That was a good call you guys," said Hunter reassuringly.

They mumbled in agreement.

"*There is also cash in the cookie jar in the pantry and more money in the safe to get you started-*"

"What safe?" exclaimed Marcus. "How did we not know this?!"

"Relax, we don't need to go shopping for a couple more days now," said Chantal.

"*I must warn you to stay well away from the authorities-*"

"Yeah Joshua," snapped Benji.

A few of them laughed. Joshua sighed good-naturedly, and for a moment Hunter wondered when he'd become so child-friendly.

"Uh … *Lastly, I will be contacting you within a week on the phone I have left in the safe. If you do not hear from me within that time, please assume that I have been reprimanded for my efforts in helping you escape. Do not worry about me; it is more important for you all to survive. My sacrifice was necessary for you to stop Dr. Wolfe from his plans. Please do not let my downfall be in vein.*

I say this with great confidence, Hunter, for these may very well be the last words you hear from me. I understand you may not be able to stop the others from leaving. They will want to see their families. But you must all face your future as heroes in this world. You are not just children anymore; you are warriors. If I am truly dead, then there is something big coming that will put millions of lives in danger, and you are the only ones who can stop it. Dr. Wolfe must be terminated. The fate of the world depends on it.

I am so very proud of you Hunter, you and the rest. I wish you all the best for the future, and when it is all over, please … keep my cabin. Use it as a sanctuary and a place of peace. It is about time you rested.

Sincerely yours,

Dr. Albert Rosenthal.

P.S.-" Hunter read the last sentence, the words catching in her throat before she could speak them. The others stared, hanging on her every word, but she could not read it aloud.

"P.S what?" asked Ryo. She flicked her leg out from under her and stamped her foot on the floor. "P.S *what* Hunter?"

She looked up at their faces and then looked at Joshua as he stood on the bottom stair with his arms folded and an expectant look. A sob rose in her throat. "*P.S, there was a message from Joshua left on the phone in the safe. He has been trying to find you. He begged me to get you out. Remember what I said: Forgive him.*" Hunter folded the letter over and sat back on the sofa.

There was a moment of awkward silence, then Marcus cleared his throat. "We'd better go find this safe guys. Anyone coming?"

Everyone but Joshua fled the room and hurried upstairs. When they were gone, he approached her cautiously.

"I wouldn't say it if I didn't mean it," said Hunter before he could question her and folded the letter carefully.

Joshua said nothing.

"It's over. The past is behind us now. We have bigger things to worry about."

Joshua looked startled. "Like what?"

Hunter held the letter in her hands, feeling the weight of what Dr. Rosenthal had asked of them, of her. But there was something in the back of her mind that told her to forget it, that it wasn't as important as healing her relationship with Joshua and Will, and healing herself as well. It was that same feeling that compelled her to forgive him.

"It doesn't matter," she sighed. "He's dead. Dr. Wolfe killed him."

Joshua ran a hand over his face and sat down on the sofa next to her. "Hunter, what exactly happened to you while you were in the Death Caves? Ryo said you looked … I just want to know if you're okay."

Hunter stared at him. There had always been lies between them both – Joshua keeping secrets about her parents and her powers, Hunter going to school and seeing Eli behind his back – and it lead to so much pain and heartbreak that there was no use in doing it anymore. But for some reason, Hunter couldn't bring herself to admit how damaging the last week in ICE had been, and how she wasn't sure she could ever be the same person again. The world was darker. And the only thing that brightened her ever so slightly was seeing her father alive again. The fire responded, breaking through the chains.

Joshua would want to know that Leo was alive, but Hunter didn't want to tell him. He'd only want to find Dr. Wolfe faster, to start a war again. And she was tired of war, tired of fighting. Just for a moment, she wanted peace.

"In time," she nodded, "I think I'll be okay."

NINETEEN

he pain was unbearable. The smoke suffocated his lungs, the burning feeling of fire on his skin worse than anything he'd ever endured. Jack wanted to scream in agony, but he couldn't open his mouth.

He didn't want to, either. The pain was worth it for what he could see in his mind.

In the middle of the bright, burning flames that surrounded him, Jack saw a figure. She was beautiful, a goddess, encased in flames. She looked like a superhero from his comic books. Her eyes were pure white, her hair twisted in fiery swirls. In the fire she reached out for him and called his name softly, urging him to join her. He did, not because it was Hunter – though he would follow her in a heartbeat if she asked – but because the flames were painful but warm. And after what felt like forever in the darkness, in the agony and in the cold arms of death, he needed warmth again.

Jack reached for Hunter, his fingers stretching, seeing the golden, loving glow in her eyes, but then suddenly he was wrenched back into the black hole that clutched his body tightly and squeezed it.

Let me go! he screamed in his mind.

But the darkness would not let go. Not now. Not ever.

The darkness hit him with memories to remind him of what he'd lost. He saw his mother and father the day they left for their trip to France. It was the last time he saw them before they were killed. He remembered waving at them from their old apartment in Brooklyn, holding Clare's hand.

The darkness stabbed him in the back and he yelped in pain.

He saw the time he won his first soccer match for the team. Eli was there, cheering him on, and of course Clare was there too, always so supportive of him.

Again, agony sliced through his heart as if a sword had been thrust through his chest.

He saw the first time the darkness came through. It was something so simple and small. He yelled at Clare for spending all of their rent on clothes, and their television exploded. Not just exploded, it *im*ploded. The television looked like it had been crushed by a ton of bricks. Clare never put the pieces together, but he had his suspicions.

BAM. Jack screamed internally as a force like a truck knocked him to his back, even though he was weightless in this hellish nightmare.

He saw Hunter, in the library. He remembered watching her study through the book case. He wasn't there to borrow textbooks, he wasn't even there to take Clare home. She could have caught the subway. Really, he was there for Hunter.

Yes, Jack loved Hunter. He loved her the moment Eli introduced them in the cafeteria. Even before then, he knew she was special. His life changed that night when he saw her walk into the laboratory, and prom both brought them together and broke them apart.

The darkness let him see Hunter's face just one last time before it swallowed that memory too, and he was left in complete darkness. All was silent, except for a voice.

I am all you have, Jack, it whispered. *I am all you need.*

It was easy not to fight the darkness, so he didn't.

TWENTY

His hand was closing around her throat, squeezing, tightening, taking away her breath with every beat of her heart. Hunter stared up into those oyster-gray eyes, feeling his cold breath ripple over her skin like a breeze over an iceberg.

The chill. The isolation. The darkness. It suffocated her, pushing her deeper into the caves of death where nothing could save her.

"You will never leave this place ..." the doctor whispered.

Hunter squirmed and shook her head violently.

"You will never speak to anyone but myself for the rest of your life ..."

No!

"... You and William will listen to each other scream in pain and misery ..."

Please, stop!

"... Every day and every night until you take your very ... last-"

"NO!"

Hunter bolted upright in bed, her chest heaving, morning sun beaming down on her through the window and the crinkle of the pine trees. She squinted, wiping her hair away from her eyes and off her sweaty forehead. She looked around at the quaint cabin room and the empty bed that Imogen and Fearne shared beside her and tried to relax.

It was just a dream.

But the dreams hadn't stopped. Ever since she was rescued only four days ago, Hunter had put on a brave face for everyone around her and tried to relax, not thinking at all about ICE and Dr. Wolfe. But it didn't stop the fear from seeping through the cracks.

Hunter flipped her bed sheets over and walked to the bedroom door. From there, she could hear someone in the bathroom and the sounds of retching. Hunter's stomach churned – she had heard that sound too often lately.

She knocked on the door and it swung inward to reveal Will, leaning over the toilet bowl, his face pale and his eyes sunken. He could hardly keep any food down.

"Want some water?" she asked.

Will shook his head as he leaned over and puke poured from his mouth again. Wincing, she went to leave him alone when she caught her reflection in the bathroom mirror and stopped.

She looked ghostly. Hunter hadn't really glanced at herself closely since she was rescued, and of course there were no mirrors in ICE. She used to have such vibrant red hair when her fire was strong, coursing through her veins, and her eyes glowed like the sun. But now everything about her was gaunt and dull and with hardly any light at all.

"We'll get better soon," croaked Will.

She looked down and caught him watching her.

"I hope so."

"So do I," he moaned.

Hunter turned away from the bathroom and went downstairs.

"Is that Will throwing up again?" asked Chantal from the kitchen. Hunter glanced outside where the younger ones were playing by the lake. Joshua sat on the sofa reading a book and there was music from outside: A classic *Queen* album that had apparently become their favorite. Such normal, trivial things.

"Yeah," Hunter sighed as she poured herself some ready-made coffee. "I'm worried."

"He'll heal," said Joshua from the sofa. "His stomach just has to get used to the real food. He lived on artificial nutrients and chemicals for his entire life, not to mention the lack of surgery lately. His body needs a proper routine."

"He's right," said Chantal. "It happened to most of us. Took about a week to get used to it."

Hunter went to sit down by the window with her coffee. Her heart still thumped from waking up heaving. She stared out the window, feeling restless, as though she were missing something.

"You okay, Hunter?" asked Chantal. She met eyes with Joshua and something was said between them. It made Hunter suspicious.

"I'm just thinking. Will Ryo go back for Alfie and Jack?"

Joshua shook his head. "We couldn't find Alfie – Fearne has been trying. And Jack hasn't woken up from the coma yet, which makes it impossible to teleport him."

"Okay ..." She sipped her coffee, her mind buzzing. There was just something there, something bothering her that she couldn't escape.

That was when Joshua sighed and stood up. "Come with me, I need to show you something."

Hunter followed him upstairs to Dr. Rosenthal's office. Joshua motioned to the chairs in front of the desk and they both sat down, staring at files with their names on them.

"Woah. What are these?" She reached forward and opened Mosi's, skimming over the background information. "Is this Dr. Rosenthal's research on us?"

"Some of it is. Hunter ... I haven't been completely honest with you lately."

She stared at him. "What?"

"I read through this just before we rescued you and discovered something shocking about Ravenadium."

Hunter swallowed. *I know something shocking about Ravenadium too: Dr. Wolfe wants its location to take over the world.*

"What is it?"

"Basically, Dr. Rosenthal believes that each of you – each of *us* – received our powers through the combination of a specific chemical and Ravenadium."

"That's impossible," Hunter shook her head. "Ravenadium comes from a volcano, a volcano that only you and my dad know the location to."

"I know it doesn't add up, and I have no idea how Ravenadium spread as far as Australia, but I've been reading through the doctor's research and ... Ravenadium is present in all of them."

Snatching a file, Hunter searched for answers in the documentation and lab reports.

"I don't understand. Dr. Wolfe knew that it was a living substance, but he could not find the origin. How is it so hard for one man with so many resources to find something that can apparently be found all over the world?"

Joshua shrugged. "Perhaps it's not a volcano, specifically, that Ravenadium comes from. Perhaps it's everywhere, we just can't see it. Or maybe the volcano is like … the motherboard or the Queen Bee. It's the home of Ravenadium."

Hunter looked at Joshua seriously. "You may be onto something."

"In any case, these notes actually prove that when combined with another chemical, Ravenadium produces powers. Look-" Joshua pulled out Zac's file and flipped to the second page of a DNA report. "Zac was from California. His family lived in an area where a particularly rare species of Chameleon were found over two decades ago. According to the doctor's notes … it's possible Zac was somehow affected by a combination of Ravenadium and a chemical-based formula for Chameleon chromosomes designed to clone, or 'mirror', DNA. Now while it's not possible for scientists to use this formula to create Zac's powers, when combined with Ravenadium-"

"*Poof,* he transforms. Dr. Rosenthal figured out a story behind *everyone's* powers?"

"Looks like. I also discovered something else extraordinary. You remember when I told you about the homeless man who passed Feucotetanus onto your mother that night?"

She nodded.

"I was trying to figure out why he didn't develop powers."

"Maybe he didn't have Ravenadium in his blood."

"Possibly," he said. "But then I started looking through the files again and found something else. Our genetic spirals are open-ended, Hunter."

She tried to think back to biology class, but she was too tired. "So … what does that mean?"

"It means that we develop powers because of this unique gene structure, and people with a closed double helix cannot. If they are subjected to certain chemicals and Ravenadium combined … their bodies can't handle it."

"So they die?"

"In some cases … yes. Feucotetanus was fatal to the homeless man. Your mother must've had an open genetic spiral, just as you do, and just as I do."

Hunter nodded slowly, letting this new development sink in. As much as she didn't want to admit it, Joshua had impressed her greatly.

"Although this doesn't stop Ravenadium from being an incredibly lethal weapon in the wrong hands, it does give us more insight into the stone's ability to create powers."

With this new information in mind, Hunter and Joshua spent the rest of the afternoon talking about Ravenadium, as if they were back in their apartment kitchen discussing her powers while making salad. It felt natural again, yet this time – despite him having killed the love of her life – Hunter respected Joshua. She valued his relationship.

Most of all, she was happy to see him happy and in control of his own demons. Perhaps, with these new findings, it would be an easier burden to bear knowing that everyone they lived with had their own fire inside of them, pushing for control.

"What happened to you?" she asked in the midst of his sentence. "You're not the same Joshua I used to know."

He smiled at her. "You're not the same Hunter. I guess we both grew up when we grew apart."

Without thinking, she folded her arms around his neck and hugged him. Even more surprisingly, Joshua hugged her back. The two of them wrapped in an embrace was strangely calm and non-explosive. Like everything was right in the world again.

TWENTY-ONE

Jenny followed the signs that led to the cafeteria and entered a room with a low roof and rows of tables. Several were occupied by strangers sitting together eating, laughing and chattering away. She would get the occasional smile from someone, and it made her feel welcome. Jenny spotted Zac, Chevie, Eli and Amelia already halfway through their meals and joined them after collecting her own breakfast.

"Hey Jenny! Amelia was just telling us," said Eli with so much enthusiasm, she wondered where the real Eli had gone, "that she and her dad went to Indonesia a few months ago to find this rare flower that-"

"It's a Rafflesia, or 'Corpse Flower'."

"Y-yes, that," he grinned. "And while they were there, they met this woman who could speak like almost *every* language ..."

Eli went on about Amelia and the Captain's adventures, but Jenny was preoccupied with thoughts of Joshua. It was easy for Eli to forget him, to come out in his element and finally start speaking for himself again. But Jenny felt like a piece of her had been ripped away when they left Joshua behind.

Apparently it was more obvious than she thought.

"You okay?" Chevie whispered to her under the cover of Zac's raucous laughter when Eli nearly toppled off his chair trying to help Amelia carry her tray of food and went bright red from embarrassment.

"Yeah," she replied too fast for it to be true. "I'm fine."

"Well you haven't touched your food." Chevie leaned closer to her and slipped her plate under her nose. "Mmm, looks good doesn't it?"

She didn't glance at him and gently pushed the plate away. "I'm a little preoccupied."

Chevie opened his mouth to answer when someone called his name from the doorway.

They all turned at the table to see a man who looked like your average Joe with a crew-cut and circular glasses. He reminded Jenny of a teacher she used to date.

"There's something you need to see. All of you."

Jenny's eyebrows shot up as Chevie raced to the door, the rest of them following.

"What is it Mark?" asked Chevie as they jogged down the corridor. Zac shoved past Jenny, carrying his breakfast tray and slopping gravy over the floor.

"We're getting a live broadcast directly from the government," said Mark.

The communications room was filled with more people than before, all of them buzzing around as a news report was being played on a large screen over the table with the map. Jenny could see Captain Mackintosh pointing at a virtual tracking system on the layout of the table.

Mark and Chevie approached the Captain at the table of maps. On the right side was a tall, thin boy of Asian origin with red streaks in his black hair. He wore layered clothing under a long trench coat, making him look like he was from the *Matrix*. Beside him were the Australian's, Ace and Illya, talking quietly together.

"What's going on?" asked Chevie.

"We're hearing this live from Parliament. It's bad," said Mark.

Everyone turned to the giant screen and the room grew to a hush.

"People of America."

Jenny, Eli and Zac gaped at the screen. A little bit of sauce spilled onto Zac's shirt from his open mouth.

"Barry?" said Eli.

"Shh!" snapped the Captain.

Jenny gazed in shock at Barry on a podium before the American flag, flashes from cameras blinking in his eyes. The caption at the bottom of the screen read 'BREAKING NEWS'. Jenny felt as if her heart would leap out of her chest. "I come to you today with an announcement straight from the

Pentagon. We have been informed that our country has been harboring people with altered DNA who have abilities beyond human reckoning. These people may not know they are different; they could be harmless, but they could also be dangerous. We are sending out a nationwide call: If you yourselves are aware of or know of someone who has experienced symptoms of altered DNA, please come forward to your local police station and we will ensure that no harm will come to you. We do not want a war. We do not want to isolate you. We just want to understand what is happening to our kind and offer our protection.

"In other news, we are on a hunt for this man-" An image of Dr. Wolfe appeared on the screen. "He goes by the name of Dr. Winston Wolfe. He *is* dangerous, and we must find him. Please contact your local crime division or authority with any information on this man. Thank you, and God bless America."

The screen went black and all through the communications room, whispers and mumbles of confusion and panic erupted.

"A nationwide call?" Zac gaped. "Turn ourselves in like criminals? What the hell is this?"

"They can't do that, it's unlawful!" Eli exclaimed.

"They're scared of us," said Chevie.

"Yeah, because you pretty much assaulted a plane of FBI agents," said Jenny. "We were going with them peacefully to show them that we mean no harm!"

"By we, you mean me," said Zac.

"This is insane, now the whole world is going to know about people with superpowers," said Jenny with a shake of her head.

"You're right," said Eli. "For a top secret agency, they're not subtle at all."

The young Asian boy began talking in a sharp Korean accent.

"No, there's nothing we can do," Mark answered him.

"Who are you guys anyway?" asked Zac.

"My name is Mark," said the man. "I'm a certified doctor and I've been living here with my wife for five years now. We lost our daughter to this ICE institution you and Chevie came from and we've been trying to get her back ever since."

"Your daughter, eh?" said Zac with one eyebrow raised.

"Yes. Our son died just after Imogen was born. She is all we have."

"Immi is your daughter?"

Jenny's heart broke at the look of wonder in Mark's eyes. "Y … you know her?"

"Of course!" said Zac cheerfully. "She's the cutest little ginger I've ever seen."

Mark blinked through tears in his eyes and leaned closer to Zac. "Where is she now?"

"She's safe," said Zac. "I can't tell you anything more."

Mark glanced at the Captain, but he held up a hand and the conversation was done. Mark didn't appear to think so, but he held his tongue.

"And who are you?" Zac asked the Asian boy.

"Mi-Kyung Wasushee," said Mark. "He doesn't speak English."

Zac peered at Mark through narrowed eyes. "Makka-Wakka-Sushi?"

"No," said Mark, "it's Mi-Kyung Wasu-"

"I'm sorry, all I hear is Sushi," Zac shrugged and glanced at Eli and Jenny. "Is anyone else hearing Sushi?"

Eli tried to hold back a fit of laughter, probably afraid of the murderous look on Mi-Kyung's face. He muttered something again to Mark, and Jenny was sure it contained several swear words.

"Call him Yung," said Mark with a smirk.

"Be careful though," said Chevie with a smile on his face, pretending he was discussing something else. "If he gets too mad, he goes major kung-fu on people."

"I could take him," said Zac as he appraised Yung.

"I don't think so. Martial arts is his superpower."

"What?" Eli and Zac gaped.

Chevie nodded.

"Do you guys have superpowers?" Eli asked Ace and Illya, who were silently watching.

"I can transform into animals," said Illya. "Ace doesn't have a power."

"Aw, mate!" said Zac in an Aussie accent. "Ya lucked out!"

A menacing glare appeared on Ace's rugged face and immediately, Zac's grin fell.

"Sorry," he muttered.

"Back to the topic," grumbled the Captain impatiently, "Now we have a major global crisis on our hands. The FBI are hunting us down."

"I don't think they're 'hunting us down'. They're asking us to turn ourselves in, hoping one of us will know where Wolfe is," said Chevie.

"They won't come here though, will they?" asked Mark.

"No," said the Captain. "To the outside world, we are merely a fan group."

"Yeah," said Zac, "and none of my friends would come out of hiding for the FBI. They don't even have cable in-"

Jenny elbowed him to keep quiet. She didn't want these people knowing about the others at the cabin, especially when Joshua might not have rescued Hunter yet.

"I think I have a way to know what the FBI are up to."

"We're already monitoring their systems, Chevie," said the Captain. "It's as far as we can go."

"Not quite. We have Zac."

Zac's eyebrows shot up. "What do you mean – ohh. You want me to spy on the FBI?"

"Are you crazy-"

"I'll do it." He grinned proudly and turned to Jenny. "Relax, I'm a professional."

"The FBI know my face after the attack," said Chevie. "My identity has been compromised. Plus, we lost our inside man when the FBI made all the cuts. Only Zac can do it. Captain? Thoughts?"

Their leader paused for a quick moment before sighing and giving the nod of approval. "Get the techs to pull up an agent's file. I want intel on this man, and I want a detailed analysis of your plan of action. Only send him in if it's for something important."

"Yes sir," he grinned.

Zac's face suddenly went very pale.

"Are you sure you can do this?" Jenny asked him. "This is a pretty risky mission."

Zac adjusted his pants and lifted his chin up. "I'll do anything to keep the others safe. We're not just battling an evil scientist anymore; we're battling to keep our secret a secret. No one can know, right?"

"Right," said Chevie. "Now follow me."

TWENTY-TWO

Eli said he went walking to clear his head, but truthfully, he went in search of Amelia. She was the only reason he kept himself sane in this weird compound. Sure, he'd only met her yesterday, but everything had changed since then. No longer did he feel like the third wheel with Jenny and Joshua, or the useless tag along, or the one who was never noticed because he didn't have special powers.

The SSS compound was buzzing after the announcement, but Eli paid no attention. To be honest, he didn't care that Zac was about to jump head-on into FBI central to spy on the law. He didn't even care that they hadn't heard from Joshua as to whether Hunter had been rescued yet or not. He'd never met Hunter. Why *should* he care?

Eli stopped to ask a woman where the greenhouse was – because apparently that would be where Amelia spent most of her time – and she pointed down the end of the corridor, telling him to take the second door and go down. Eli happily followed her directions. As he passed a door with a reasonably clear reflection, he made sure his hair was neat and brushed back. Then he found the door marked 'GREENHOUSE' and went inside.

The greenhouse was much bigger than he imagined. It was in a sort of cave, a very large cave. The walls made of rich, red dirt stretched over his head where, far above, there was a crevice in the roof letting sunlight beam down. That was where the plants thrived the most, all bending toward the light as if desperate for its warmth. There was a tree in the center, roots growing long and thick out of the dirt and branches stretched over the rest of the plants surrounding it. On his left and right were rows of different plant life. Several men and women in containment suits were watering and fertilizing them. Eli strained his neck and saw her small figure and short-cropped hair near the tree. He started toward her when someone stepped in front of him.

"What are you doing here?" asked a thin man with a white chemical suit and a pair of secateurs in his hand.

"Uh, I ... I'm here to help Amelia."

"Well you need to gear up," he said. "Follow me."

He led Eli to a separate shed on the right where there were plastic containment suits, helmets, gloves and shoes. The man helped him find his size and suit up. After thanking him, Eli hurried to Amelia, careful not to trip over his own clumsy feet.

Amelia stood over a beautiful bed of tulips, her sleeves rolled up and her hair tucked behind her ears. She wore a suit just like Eli and was using a strange device to scan the flowers before noting down numbers on a checklist. Eli cleared his throat as he approached and when she looked up, he caught his breath. The sun flittered through the tree canopy and brightened her hair and her eyes. It had been a long time since he'd had an asthma attack, and he wasn't about to start now in front of a beautiful girl.

"H ... um." He scratched the back of his neck, wracking his brain for words. "I ... that's a ... a very cool tree."

Amelia's lip twitched in a smile as she turned to the tree and looked back at him. "It is."

Eli wanted to kick himself. "Uh ... why exactly do you have a greenhouse down here?"

Amelia dropped her clipboard. "When my father brought me here, there wasn't much for me to do. I had a tutor, and someone who specialized in aviation taught me everything there is to know about aircrafts. But I didn't have anything that was ... mine." She started toward the tree and Eli quickly followed. "I found this tree here, and I couldn't understand how it grew in such a dark, empty place. But once the sun shines down on it, everything in the room seems to brighten and becomes filled with life. Something about the nutrients in the soil here causes things to grow rapidly. I decided to start a greenhouse."

Amelia and Eli arrived at the base of the giant tree. She bent down and sat herself on one of the roots, patting beside her for Eli to sit. He nearly tripped in his haste to sit down.

"What is this tree?" he asked.

"It's an Arizona White Oak. They don't normally grow this big, but I believe if you give something enough love and attention, it'll try hard to mature."

Eli smiled slightly. "I wish my dad could hear that. I'm surprised I'm not a midget with the amount of love and attention he gave me."

Amelia peered at him. "Is that why you're so insecure and unsure of yourself?"

For a moment, Eli felt as if she'd slapped him. "Uh ... no, I mean-"

"Obviously you grew up not being appreciated. That's why you feel like no one cares about you, right?"

Eli felt as if Amelia could see right through him, and even if they'd just met, he found himself spilling everything to her. About his past and the animal rights movement he was once involved in, about his mother abandoning him for a new life, about living with Joshua and Jenny and always feeling useless and worth nothing.

"Sometimes I wish I had superpowers just so I'd get noticed."

Amelia bent down and picked up a leaf from the white oak, twirling it in her delicate fingers. "This oak was here alone when our compound was built several years ago. It should have been half the size it is now, but instead it grows bigger every day. Why would it try so hard when there was no one around to impress?"

Eli shrugged.

"Because it doesn't care what anyone else thinks – what matters is how it views itself. It's going to grow into the best tree that it can be, and that's what makes it special."

She moved her hand to his and gently opened his fingers, placing the leaf in his palm.

"It doesn't matter if you don't have a superpower, Eli. It's just a label. It doesn't make you who you are."

"Who do you think I am?" he asked, conscious of her hand still holding his. The intensity around them sizzled and all he could see was the glow in her eyes.

"I-"

"Amelia!"

The both of them jumped, Eli nearly slipping from the roots in fright as the Captain marched at them. Amelia sprang apart from him and ran to her father.

Eli couldn't hear them talking, but he could see in their gestures that the Captain didn't like him associating with her. Amelia glanced back at Eli, gave him a sad wave and walked away. Eli waved back but stopped himself when the Captain gave him a 'stay away from my daughter' glare and followed her out of the greenhouse.

Sighing, he looked down at the oak leaf in his hand and committed Amelia's words into his unstable memory. Not only because he admired her and thought she was the most beautiful girl he'd ever seen, but because she was right.

TWENTY-THREE

One evening, Joshua asked Fearne if she could try to contact Jenny in her dreams. Joshua hadn't heard from her at all and he worried every day that something horrible had happened and she was in trouble with the FBI. Fearne agreed to try, and while Joshua waited on her bed, Fearne went into a deep unconsciousness to find Jenny.

It seemed like only a minute before suddenly, Fearne started having some sort of seizure. Her body twitched, making it look like she was being possessed. A line of blood dripped from her nose and Joshua didn't know what else to do but call for help.

Will, Hunter and Mosi came running. The rest weren't far behind.

Will panicked, shaking Fearne. "What the hell happened?!"

"She was ... I asked her to find Jenny in her dreams and she was-"

"You did *what*?"

Will looked at him murderously. Fearne stopped twisting and lay still, asleep. The heat in the room was so great that Mosi started pushing the others back into the corridor.

"She doesn't normally do this," said Hunter. "What *really* happened?"

"That's all that happened, I swear it."

"Bullshit," said Will. "She's damaged enough already and you had to selfishly put her life on the line-"

"Enough, Will!" Hunter snapped.

He turned to her and glared. "You don't understand what's happening to her. Remember when we were escaping from ICE and she started frying Jet's mind with her abilities? It had the same effect as this."

"What are you saying?"

"Her power is too dangerous. It's taking over her mind and weakening her at the same time. She can't use it like that, unless it's an emergency. Which this clearly *isn't*."

Joshua stared at Fearne in shock. Why had the young girl not told her that her power was taking control of her? And not in a way the Iceman manipulates his own mind, but in a dark and demonic way that cannot be stopped.

"I'm sorry Will," said Joshua.

"Just leave."

Without looking at either of them, Joshua stormed from the room. If he couldn't find Jenny then he could at least try and find a way to help Fearne stop her power from taking over her mind.

As Joshua stalked from the room and into Dr. Rosenthal's office, he started worrying about Jenny. If Fearne couldn't reach her, did that mean something had gone wrong? Was she safe? Was she alive? It was like being separated from Hunter all over again.

Joshua thought he could find answers in the doctor's study – some kind of training technique to help Fearne stay in control of her mind power – but a part of him wasn't motivated. He decided to go outside and spend time with the younger ones, who were stretching out in the sun by the lake. It was a beautiful day – a rare one in this cold month. Despite Joshua not doing well in sunlight, he enjoyed listening to them laugh.

"Have you guys seen the sunscreen?" asked Benji, who had only just recovered from severe sunburn after falling asleep by the lake on his first day.

"You used it all," said Marcus. "What did you do, eat it?"

"Hey. Skin cancer never takes a holiday," he said.

"I hope Fearne will be okay," Chantal moaned as she wrapped her arms around her knees. Joshua could see how much Chantal cared about her family, how she fit the motherly role to perfection.

"She will," Imogen nodded firmly. "She's braver than all of us."

"Will said it happened before, at ICE?" asked Joshua.

"This dickhead Jet tried to stop us from escaping," said Chantal. "He killed one of the younger boys, and Fearne lost her shit. I'd never seen her like that before. She nearly blew his head open."

Joshua's stomach squirmed. It was hard to imagine someone as gentle and kind as Fearne killing another human with her mind. Then again, he did horrible things with his power when he was angry or tried to protect someone. This was just further proof that Ravenadium flowed in all of their veins and not just his and Hunter's.

Which explained how Jack so easily turned to the dark side.

But if there was a way to cure his and Hunter's demon, there was a way to cure Fearne's. And he had to find it. If not for Fearne, then at least to mend things between he and Will.

As Joshua headed back into the cabin and up the stairs to the office, he heard the sounds of Hunter and Will shouting in Fearne's bedroom. He stopped at the top of the staircase and listened.

"-did everything I could, but I had no other choice."

"I know that," said Will. "I'm not angry that you almost got me killed, okay, I'm angry at myself. I feel useless. All I'm ever good at is sacrificing myself."

"But that's what heroes do. "

"Hunter, I'm sick of watching everyone I care about get hurt and not being able to do a thing about it. That's *not* what heroes do."

"Then we find a way. We'll get stronger again, learn to fight. Mosi and Marcus can teach us. I'll help you heal."

There was a pause. Joshua bit his lip, waiting.

"Just please do me a favor and talk to Joshua. I know you think it's his fault but ... bad luck follows him around."

"Yeah," Will sighed. "That seems to be his excuse for everything."

Hurt stabbed Joshua in the heart and he walked across the hallway into Dr. Rosenthal's office. He sat down and put his head in his hands. Will was right. Everything seemed to be his fault. If he wanted to help Fearne, it would be best just to leave her alone.

TWENTY-FOUR

For the first time in his life, Zac felt truly lost. He sat alone on a plush armchair in a room he'd come to like very much since arriving at the SSS – they called it the Lair. It was used as a common area for the 'fans' to watch movies and play video games and talk about the latest trailer releases and who their favorite super-villain was. Sometimes they even had debates. Zac went there to get away from reality, but today was different. Somehow, he felt the distance between he and the cabin grow a hundred times more. Even though he was surrounded by more powered people – the identities of which he didn't know yet – he missed his family too much to really care.

He watched a group of large, geek-looking guys in their twenties and three very unattractive women discuss one of the new *X-Men* movies in comparison to the comics with complete disinterest. There was a Bon Jovi song Zac remembered from his childhood playing in the background. Suddenly, it didn't matter anymore. Being funny or optimistic didn't make a difference.

"Hey."

Zac looked up from his trance and saw a girl of maybe twenty-five with straight blond hair layered with colors of pink and purple, looking like a goth Barbie-doll.

"Zac, right?" she asked. "The shape-shifter?"

He nodded. "Hi."

"I'm Ella," she said. "Well, my parents named me Barbarella … you know, after the space cadet played by Jane Fonda?"

Zac shook his head.

"Yeah, of course you don't. Anyway, call me Ella."

"Hi."

Ella chewed pink bubble gum and waited for him to speak. He found he didn't have it in him.

"I'm from Vancouver," she said and sat down on the edge of his chair. He leant away uncomfortably. "Where are you from?"

"California."

"Oh yeah, there's a few here from California. I met a lot of these guys online, before I came here with my mom and dad. I'm a blogger and a writer. My parents run the Fanclub meetings here, and they're also avid illustrators and graphic designers."

"They sound awesome."

"Yeah, they're pretty weird though. So I've seen you down here a couple of times. Have you met anyone yet?"

"Uh no. I'm not used to making friends." *Not when I'm a complete loner, at least.*

"Well, I know some people who are dying to meet you." Her blue eyes glimmered and she nodded at the group sitting around the table. When Zac looked back at them, they hurriedly lowered their heads and pretended not to be paying attention. A part of Zac felt proud.

"So you've come to ask if I'd join you?"

"Only if you want to," she shrugged. "I can understand why you wouldn't, you're pretty famous around here."

Zac's eyebrows shot up. "R-really?"

Ella chewed her gum for a few more seconds before jumping to her feet and smoothing down her mini-skirt. "Come on, I'll introduce you. We're like a great big nerd family here." Ella pushed him by the back toward the table of eager people with their comics and their coffee spread out around them.

"Everyone," said Ella. "This is Zac."

He lifted a hand and waved.

"Dude, you have one of the *best* powers," said a loud guy with a weirdly shaped beard and a T-shirt that said 'SORRY LADIES, I'M IN THE NIGHT'S WATCH'.

"That's Peetee," said Ella. "No power."

Again, Zac waved.

"Hey, come sit down," said another girl and Ella shoved him to the end of the table. She had huge, fat dreadlocks wrapped up in hippy scarves. "I'm Dakota, I came up with *Ironman* before Marvel did."

"What the hell Dakota?" shouted Peetee. "We've had this discussion before, you did *not* come up with Ironman. He made his first appearance in *Tales of Suspense* issue 39 in 1963 before you were even born!"

"I mean the movie adaptation, dingus," said Dakota.

"Hey, Zac?"

Zac looked to his left where a boy with a beanie peered at him curiously. "What's your *real* form?"

"John, that's not-"

"Well," said Peetee, "he could be like Mystique and have several different true forms."

Despite priding himself in having a world of knowledge compared to his ICE companions, Zac didn't feel weird at all saying, "Who's Mystique?"

They went on to explain that Zac was similar to a character from the *X-Men* movies, which they decided to have a marathon of that night to give him a bit of a modern-day hero education. It excited Zac – a movie about a character with his power sounded awesome.

"Can I meet some more of you first?" he asked almost shyly. "Does anyone have powers?"

Many of their faces fell, as if this were the thing they were most embarrassed about. Zac felt guilty for humiliating them so suddenly.

"I mean, not that you guys aren't cool, but-"

"It's okay Zac," Ella smiled. "We're pretty lucky to even be around you."

"Yeah," said another guy with orange hair and freckles. "If I wasn't here, I'd be working at my local comic book store. Here, I get to actually *live* my comics."

"You said it Andy." Peetee and Andy fist bumped.

"If you're wondering who the people with powers are," said Ella in a softer voice so only those at the table could hear, "It's them."

Zac followed her inclined head to a sofa in the back corner of the room that faced a smaller television than the main one. There was a girl sitting with her legs up on another boy's lap, twisting her thick hair around her fingers while he played an X-box with agro enthusiasm. From what Zac could see, they looked to be in their late twenties, with dark skin and heavy clothing as if they lived in the jungle.

"Who are they?"

"Zokani and Koko. Got here about six months ago when Chev found them online. They're from somewhere in Peru, but they look and act like they haven't been in civilization for ten years. We haven't had many Impossibles show up—"

"Many what?"

"Impossibles," said Ella with a smirk. "That's what we've called you guys."

"Since 'mutants' is already taken," Peetee said with a snicker.

Zac let the word ring in his mind, trying to see if it would stick. To be honest, he couldn't think of anything better.

"The Impossibles," he said slowly.

"Anyway," said Ella, "those Impossibles who are still out there must have heard rumors about you guys getting captured. People here tend to gossip a bit online."

"I'd say that's a good thing," said Zac. "If they're afraid, they'll be more careful."

"They don't know that they're pretty safe here," said Peetee. "But I guess Zokani and Koko were bored or something."

"What can they do?"

Peetee blew a long breath out of his nose and said, "Zokani can fly. I've only ever seen him do it once though. And Koko can turn invisible."

Zac nodded, impressed. They were extremely useful powers. Feeling more confident than he had all day, Zac decided to put on his big-boy pants and introduce himself.

As he stood up, they all looked at him frantically.

"Where are you going?" asked Dakota.

"To ... meet these guys."

Everyone at the table looked positively terrified and did not move from their seats. Zac almost laughed, except when he realized that half an hour ago, that was him sitting alone on an armchair too afraid to talk to strangers.

As Zac approached the back of the sofa, Koko looked up from her dreaded brown hair and gave him a death stare. Zac gave her a nervous wave and felt instantly like he was intruding on someone's territory.

"Heeey," he said lamely and Zokani paused the Xbox game, twisting in his seat. "I'm Zac. I thought I'd say hi to a couple of fellow Impossibles, so … hi."

The two of them continued to glare.

Maybe they don't know what Impossibles are yet.

"So I hear you guys are from Peru? Was it hot there?"

Koko's smile tipped to the side and she and Zokani started to snicker, either at his naïve comment or his stupidity.

"Look," said Koko in a thick accent, "We're not here to make friends."

Her eyes were so intense that Zac felt color creep into his cheeks. "Uh, sorry. Just thought we should at least introduce ourselves. I've been locked up in a psychotic torture institution for most of my life, so making friends with people like me is kind of a big deal."

As Zac turned to walk away feeling more embarrassed than he had in a while, Zokani called him back.

"Wait."

"Zokani …"

"Give him a break, Ko," Zokani scolded her. "He's been through more than we have."

The girl snorted and Zac gave her a sheepish shrug.

Then, Zokani held out his hand. "Pleased to meet you Zac."

Zac hesitantly shook the extended hand, noticing how tough his skin was. Some of the excitement built up again, but Zac had to restrain himself from prying and begging them to show him their powers. This wasn't the place for that.

"Well uh … I guess I'll see you around?"

Zokani nodded and turned back to his game. Koko crossed her arms and avoided eye contact, but Zac was satisfied. *Day one and I've already made friends with a bunch of geeks and two hostile natives with powers.*

This place is awesome.

TWENTY-FIVE

It was a strange and wonderful thing, to be free. Different to the freedom of slavery or of expressing your own beliefs. Freedom always seemed to Will like a dream that would never come true. Like the existence of aliens or giant marshmallow monsters.

Impossible.

He couldn't remember life before ICE. The first time he walked outside the cabin after Ryo rescued him was a surreal experience. He'd never forget the vast expanse of space across the lake or the endless sky above the tops of the trees. It was the most beautiful thing he'd ever seen.

It had been five days since he and Hunter were rescued. Five days of fresh air, good food and no surgery or torture or medicine or cruelty.

Five days of freedom.

But Will could not get used to it. He saw the way the others so easily blended into the world around them, how comfortable and happy they were. Why did he not feel the same way? Why did he constantly tense himself every time someone used the word 'doctor' or 'Men in White', or when he heard the sounds of knives in the kitchen?

The fear was still a plague in his life.

What had happened with Fearne hurt him the most. His worry for her was so deep that it pained him.

Everything around him was green and radiant and wonderful, but Will only paid attention to Hunter. The way her red hair flowed in the wind that rushed through them as they ran hypnotized him. The way she smiled when she threw blissful glances back at him and her golden eyes flashed in the sun. And how melodic her laugh was.

"Keep up, slow poke!" Hunter yelled and ducked under a low-hanging branch. She pushed harder, but that only made Will more distracted.

Hunter helped him get back into a routine of eating and regularly exercising. And he loved it: The smell of morning air and the moisture around him or the cool breeze on his face. He especially loved when the sun set through the trees and the sky was full of pink and orange.

He could definitely get used to this.

After a twenty minute run, Will's lungs were about to collapse. He yelled for Hunter to stop.

"Just up here, I see the edge of the cliff!"

Will jogged through the last few trees to a clearing where, just like she'd said, they stood over the edge of the hillside. To their left, they could see the lake a few miles away where the cabin was. Far on their right was the local town where Mosi and Chantal had just yesterday ventured out to go grocery shopping. Everywhere else was sunlight and clouds and woods and sloping mountains. It was coming close to twilight – Will's favorite time of day.

Hunter sat herself down on a flat rock, heaving. Will flopped beside her.

"You're getting … faster," she said.

"Soon I'll … beat you home."

Hunter huffed. "Yeah right."

Will looked at her, clamping a hand against the stitch in his side, distracting himself with the purity of her pale skin and the way the fire glowed in her hair. He'd never seen her so alive.

"Hey there's … there's something I've been meaning to tell you since we got rescued."

Squinting through the sunset light, Hunter sighed. "If it's about what happened at ICE again, I'm-"

"It's not, okay, we've already been through that." Will looked into her worried eyes, not wanting to give her any more reason to feel guilty than she already had. "Besides, you did the best you could under the circumstances. I've forgiven you."

"I wish I did more," she said. "Maybe my father would still be alive."

"I don't think you should worry about him. I'm sure the doctor is keeping him around just in case."

"I keep praying he will." She stretched out her arms. "What did you want to tell me?"

That I'm falling for you.

He couldn't bring himself to say those words out loud. They terrified him. He'd never felt anything like this, let alone been in love. He wasn't ready to publish his feelings.

"Later, it's not important."

"Okay. Have you spoken to Joshua yet?"

Will looked away. "No."

"Not at all?"

Will put his hands between his knees. "I know it's unfair for me to still hate him after what he did to you and how you got over it easily. But it's hard. I can't look at him without remembering the day he took you and walked away from me. I would have had a different life, a better life."

"I know I shouldn't be defending him after the things he did, but … what if he *did* take you? Would he be able to protect both of us from the Agents? If he was caught again, all three of us would have grown up in there."

Will stared at the fiery orange ball falling between two mountains in the distance, even if it hurt his eyes. Hunter shimmied closer to him and the electricity of her body leaning against his was different to the hours they spent lying in the guard's quarters at ICE. Now, they were free to remain there as long as they liked, free to be with each other even. The prospect excited and scared him.

"I'm sorry, I just … I need more time than you."

Hunter slipped her hand into his, their fingers intertwining.

"Good thing we have all the time in the world."

Will stared down at their hands. It was strange how something so simple could petrify him. Without knowing why, he pulled his hand away from hers and stuck both of them in the pockets of his hoodie. He looked away, a lump of guilt forming in his throat. It wasn't the first time she'd held his hand. There had been multiple connections in ICE. But they were all for comfort, nothing more.

This new relationship development scared him.

"Are you okay?" she asked.

"Yeah. Let's ... let's head back. I'm starving and I want to check on Fearne."

It was a lie, but despite the hurt in her eyes, it got her moving. As the sun disappeared like sand in an hourglass, they turned their backs on the view and ran home.

Will knocked on Fearne's bedroom door and quietly closed it behind him. She was propped up in bed with her lamp on, reading by herself. Chantal had helped him clean the blood away from her face, and she slept until midday the next day.

"How are you feeling?" he asked as he sat down on the edge of her bed.

"I feel fine," she replied. There were shadows beneath her eyes, but they still glowed in the lamplight. "What about you? There's something bothering you."

Rolling his eyes, Will sighed. "I may as well tell you, you can probably read my mind."

"It's a little fuzzy these days," she replied. "But I don't have to be a mind reader to see that it's Hunter."

He stared at his clasped hands. "I guess I'm afraid. I've never felt like this for anyone. And I don't know where to start."

Fearne picked up her book and pointed to the cover. "You should probably read this then. It's about Snow White who is poisoned by an evil witch, and Prince Charming's kiss wakes her up. It's true love."

Will scoffed. He'd read enough books with the younger ones to see a recurring theme in these fairytales. Their love was perfect. No curse could break it. No height or depth, no heaven or hell, not even death itself could take them away from each other. But was it real? Where did that kind of love exist?

"You're adorable," he said and kissed her lightly on her forehead. "Feel better, okay?"

"Will?"

He turned back after standing up.

"I know it seems hard to forgive Joshua, but you can't blame him for all the pain you've been through."

"I don't. I blame Dr. Wolfe."

"No," she said. "You blame your father."

Will blinked in surprise. He'd lived with Fearne long enough to know that sometimes she saw things clearer than even he did. "My father?" He hadn't thought about his father at all in a long time. So much had happened that he forgot all about him.

"It's not in your thoughts, but it's in your heart. You can't move on and start a new life. Let go of the blame."

Will stared into her eyes, into the pools of wisdom that were a light in his troubled world as a child. What would he do without her?

"I'll give it my best shot," he smiled. Then he tucked her in and went back downstairs.

"I really *really* want a pizza you guys," said Ryo as she lay stretched across Benji on the sofa. "Can't we get a pizza?"

"Why would we do that when we have plenty of food here?" asked Chantal as she washed dishes with Joshua in the kitchen. Hunter was upstairs showering and Mosi and Marcus were on the porch boxing with each other.

Ryo continued to moan about how hungry she was and Chantal suggested a piece of fruit. Will poured himself a glass of water while thinking of a way to approach Joshua.

Fortunately, the opportunity presented itself.

"Can I have a word?"

Will choked on his water at the voice that came from right behind him. He wiped his chin, nodded and followed Joshua outside where the night was dark and the only light came from the porch.

"I just want to ask your forgiveness, Will, for anything I might've done to hurt you. I understand that-"

Will held up a hand and Joshua stopped talking. Just the way he spoke made Will want to throw up.

"I hate you for what you did, to me and to Hunter. But I'm not going to let it affect the way we act around the others. I'll pretend that things have been fixed and I'll find my own way to get over it. But ... as much as I should forgive you, there's something stopping me. It's personal."

Joshua put his hands in his pockets, frowning. "Okay ... I guess that's all I can ask for. Thank you."

Will nodded and stormed back inside. One day he would bring himself to move past it, but forgiveness was one mountain Will had never been able to pass. Fearne was right – it was his father to blame for everything. It was his father he truly had to forgive.

TWENTY-SIX

It was easy getting into the FBI building undetected. All it took was a little tranquilizer in the neck of an agent coming out of the subway station next to the building. He had an FBI badge under his coat. Zac dragged him into a safe room in the basement, set himself plenty of time to be in and out, and then he entered; suit, badge and all.

The timing was perfect. A board meeting was about to take place upstairs in one of the briefing rooms with some of the top agents in the capitol. Zac buzzed with excitement.

He loved when playing the role of a real person went so well. Sometimes people just handed him clues to someone's character. Often they were small things that put people in their stereotype boxes.

The character he played today was far too easy to read. Things like a cheeky smile from two female agents as they passed and a fist-bump from a guy carrying donuts told Zac that Agent Lewis 'Mad Dog' Carpenter – the name he was referred to – was a popular guy in the Bureau. Sometimes when he changed, he felt as if he could do anything, be anything.

He made it to the briefing room with no questions asked and took a seat in the middle. He ventured a guess that Agent Carpenter was not high enough to be with the big boys, but not low enough to mingle with the common agents. His fist-bump buddy sat next to him, mentioning something about a bomb going off later when Special Agent Fitzpatrick finds out there's no more hazelnut coffee in the shop downstairs. Even though he couldn't give a fuck, Zac laughed anyway.

When the meeting began, Zac didn't pay attention to who all the official men and women were. He knew Barry and Fitzpatrick from the plane. They both looked a little stressed. But his mind only retained the simple things, so he focused instead on the FBI's strategy.

The FBI's main objective was to find Dr. Wolfe, but after turning up empty in Wyoming, they started searching the surrounding areas. Marcus's security system for ICE that Dr. Wolfe forced him to develop must've been working, for apparently the communications signal was sending the agents and their tech team all over the state.

"You okay, Mad Dog?"

Zac nodded, pulled at the collar of his shirt and gave his friend a smile. He wasn't sure why he was sweating so much. "It's hotter than a Victoria's Secret model in here."

Fist-bump buddy chuckled.

No one had come forward with information on 'altered DNA' human beings. Those at the SSS who were called the 'fans' had reported an increase in number of users on the website that formed their compound. Some admitted to seeing supernatural things occur, others claimed to have a 'superpower'. Some of these people actually showed up at the SSS and decided to join, because they wanted help but didn't feel up to revealing themselves to the Feds. Their numbers had almost doubled over the past few days, and the SSS was becoming more overcrowded by the minute.

After the meeting, Zac had exactly one hour to get out of the building before the real Mad Dog woke up. He mentioned something to his mate about taking a dump and hurried with his head down to the ground floor.

Just as he was crossing the lobby to the exit, he walked straight into a woman with beautiful blond hair in a cream pencil skirt and a pale pink blouse holding a cup of coffee that spilled all over her front.

"Oh, I am so sorry ma'am," he said in the tone he imagined Mad Dog would use to seduce women. "Let me buy you another cup of coffee, or maybe a new shirt?"

The woman smiled, her cheeks filling with color. "It's fine, it's laundry day anyway. Could you hold this for me?" she asked and handed him her bag.

"Uh, sure."

She started removing her gray cardigan, carefully holding her hair up as she did. Her blouse was *very* see-through. "It's a little busy here today, huh?"

"B-big board meeting upstairs," he replied.

"It's about the hunt, right? For Dr. Winston Wolfe?"

Zac nodded. "I'm not supposed to reveal that kind of information," he said. Though, he wondered whether Lewis Carpenter actually would reveal it under the pressure of such a beautiful woman as she slowly brushed her fingers through her hair.

"You can tell me, you know. I'm good at keeping secrets."

He laughed nervously. "Well it's no secret that Wolfe is hiding out. The FBI don't have a location though. If you ask me, they're on a wild goose-chase."

"Really? What about these people with special abilities?" she asked as he handed her the purse. "Would you say they're dangerous?"

"Some of them are," he said. "The good guys, though, they're the heroes. They're going to stop Wolfe. There's this one guy called Zac - he can shape shift. He's the most attractive one of all of them."

"He's a shape shifter. Of course he's attractive."

Zac almost re-butted, but something caught his eye. The lobby of the FBI building was swarming with people, but somehow he managed to see them standing outside on the street. They wore suits, dark glasses and there was just enough of them for him to jump immediately to conclusions.

Zac's heart leapt into his chest.

Holy fuckballs. The Agents are here.

"Are you okay?" asked the woman.

"Fl ... psh ..." Words weren't forming. His eyes darted around, looking for an escape. Even though he was in a disguise, he was positive they were there to catch him. Somehow, they knew who he was. "I have to go."

"But-"

He started walking to the door, and as he turned he shouted back at her. "You have a smoking body, by the way!"

Several people in the building turned to glare at him. The woman only blushed.

Zac turned back to the door and moved stealthily through the crowd. The Agents were looking around. If anything, they were more suspicious than he was. Seven suits coming out of a tinted, black van? If that didn't scream terrorist or highly organized bank robbery, nothing did.

When Zac passed through the revolving doors, he knew for sure that they didn't recognize him. They seemed to be waiting for someone else. Perhaps they were chasing a lead with the FBI and had no idea he was there. Zac stood idly by the door for a moment and spotted a man and a woman having a smoke nearby. He sidled up to them, glancing back over his shoulder. Excitement bubbled up inside of him. He hadn't been this close to the Agents since they caught him. And they had no idea who he was.

Evil bastards. I should bomb them.

"Hey, can I bum a smoke guys?" he asked.

The woman gave him a lighter and he shoved the cigarette in his mouth. He'd never smoked before, but it seemed like the time to start. Besides, it wasn't his body he was infecting. Kind of.

Through the busy street and a haze of smoke, he watched the Agents. He observed their actions, their glances inside the building, the way they spoke closely with the driver and then in their earpieces. Crazy, wild ideas were flowing through his mind. He knew that this was suicidal, but he couldn't help it. It was about time they had the upper hand with these dick-wipes.

"Thanks guys, see you inside?" he said to the other agents.

They muttered in agreement. Zac shoved one hand in the pocket of his trench coat and started walking toward the van. As he passed, he waited for the perfect moment and then, he tripped.

His cigarette went flying into the first Agent he came in contact with.

"Whoops!"

The Agent caught him, if only to stop Zac from knocking him over. Mad Dog was a pretty buff guy, which is partly what gave Zac his confidence. The Agent gripped him with strong hands and grunted before shoving him away.

"Oh shit, I'm so sorry pal," Zac said as he straightened himself. There was ash on the Agent's black suit. Zac slapped at it, but the Agent backed away.

"What's going on?" asked one of them.

"I really didn't mean to-"

"It's fine," said the Agent whose suit he'd nearly burnt a hole in. "Don't worry."

"You wouldn't believe it, but that's the second time I've been clumsy today!" Zac laughed theatrically. "I mean I am just the biggest klutz. If they gave an award to the clumsiest person in the world-" He raised his hand and grinned, "-I would win it."

They all gazed at him in stoic bafflement.

Zac glanced down at the van and gasped. "Oh, no way! Are those special edition rims? Those are sick!" He stepped down from the curb and only just managed to touch the wheel of the van when the door opened and the last Agent stepped out. Zac backed up with his hands in the air. "Sorry, didn't mean to pry. I'm a car enthusiast," he added, looking each of them in the eye. Suddenly he realized he was talking to lethal minions of Dr. Wolfe who kidnap kids. *I'm literally insane.* "M-my girlfriend hates cars, but I love them. I'm gonna go get a hotdog." Then, without another word, he walked off.

Zac only looked back over his shoulder when he was two streets away from the building and the Agents. He saw no sign of a black van following him. He breathed out the air he'd been holding in and pulled his cell phone out of his pocket.

Chevie picked up after two rings. "Zac? How'd you go?"

"Peachy," said Zac. "I just put a tracking device on the Agent's death-mobile."

"You did what?"

"I know," he said, "I'm amazing. Now could you please start tracking them immediately to make sure they're not hunting me down?" He glanced over his shoulder again. *Still not being followed.*

"No problem. Nice work Zac! Are you ready to be picked up?"

"Not just yet," he said and cracked his neck to the side. "I'm gonna get a hotdog, then you can come."

TWENTY-SEVEN

Her hair was all that Jack really remembered when he woke up. A flash of red in the darkness, even a glimpse of golden eyes and then everything was black and dangerous. That's what his life had become lately; darkness.

But he saw her again, and not just in his dreams, but in reality. In the prison after he lost control and the glass cage burst into a thousand pieces. He saw red hair and he knew it was Hunter. It was a blurry memory, but he clung to it. Did she get captured too? Or was she there to save him? Jack was a mess that day and he could have blown apart every brain in that room if he wanted to. But Hunter was there. He couldn't hurt her.

Then he felt the impact of the bullet in the center of his back. Pain sliced through him from head to toe, but it only lasted a second before … that was it. Back to darkness.

When Jack woke up, he was thinking of Hunter.

Voices mumbled around him. Someone spoke the doctor's name. "Get Dr. Wolfe, now!" they ordered. Jack felt heavier than lead and cold and hot at the same time. His eyes peeled apart, sticky and heavy. Most of his body was still numb, pain hovering on the fringe of his conscience, ready to jump in when he moved. So he remained still and looked around.

He was in a giant room, the space wasted by how empty it felt. He lay on a hospital bed, a heart rate monitor beside him and chemicals pumped into his arms. Everything felt gluggy. Bright light beamed down on him from above.

134

A scientist was jabbering on to another, checking his vitals and pressing buttons on the machines that surrounded him. The sounds of voices throbbed and echoed in his head. The light flew away and he saw stars. When his senses cleared, he tried moving his feet and flexing his wrists. One of the scientists gasped and after that came a sharp pain in his arm. He was soon drowsy again.

"Hello Jack."

The voice belonged to Dr. Wolfe, he was sure of it. Jack didn't care about the pain and clenched every muscle in his body, but an unknown force stopped him from getting up. He struggled against it, as if his body were too heavy for him.

"What have you done to me?" Jack croaked. His tongue felt fat and a line of dribble rolled down the side of his face.

"Sedated you," was the reply. "Your body has healed, so I don't want to take any chances. You wouldn't want to be shot again, would you?"

Jack didn't move.

"You've been in a coma for some time now," said the doctor as he wiped the drool from his mouth with a white handkerchief. "I was beginning to wonder if you'd ever wake up. Let me explain what you've missed out on. The man who shot you is dead. I had him executed. Many of the other subjects like yourself have escaped. There are only a handful of you left. I have sent my Agents to kill the others."

Jack wanted to ask about Hunter, but he was afraid that if the doctor knew of his connection to her, it would give him motivation to use her as bait.

"Because of this unfortunate incident, we have been forced to move our preparations for the coming war backwards. We have also had to re-locate our base. That was made difficult thanks to the FBI watching our every move, but we managed to escape with you right under their noses, thanks to a certain techno and his security system. And now that you are awake, we can begin."

"I'm not participating in any war. You may as well kill me."

"I would never kill you, Jack. You're far too valuable."

"Then how do you propose to use me if I won't cooperate?"

"Oh," he chuckled. "You'll cooperate. See, Jack, I have a way of making people do as I ask them to. I have connections, I have plenty of money and resources, but I also have something that not many people claim to possess."

Jack couldn't resist. "Bad breath?"

Dr. Wolfe chuckled humorlessly. "No Jack. I have no fear."

"Nobody is without fear."

When the doctor laughed, it was low and hair-raising, making Jack doubt his statement instantly. The man was terrifying, more terrifying than any character in his comic books. Not because he had a superpower or wore an impenetrable suit or looked at all frightening – even though at times he did. Dr. Wolfe was scary because he was unpredictable and psychotic, and right now Jack was helpless before him.

"I'm sure you know fear very well Jack."

He glared up at the doctor. "I knew fear when I discovered what I could do. And then I had no one to turn to when I needed safety. No one I could trust."

Dr. Wolfe's face went suddenly slack. "Of course. Someone they trust …"

"What?" Jack mumbled. The doctor ignored him, stepping down off the platform they were on and reaching into his pocket. Jack strained against the sedation but could not move his body. He only heard the doctor.

"Alpha? Good news: I know where they're hiding. How fast can you get to Seattle?"

Jack lay there waiting, wondering what the doctor had done with Hunter. He heard the phone beep and seconds later, Dr. Wolfe was back within his sight, leaning over the bed.

"You may as well join me, Jack. There's no one who will rescue you."

Hunter, Jack thought, and it made the doctor's words less heart-wrenching. *If she was there in that room, and she saw me, then I know she was there to rescue me.*

"You're wrong about that, Dr. Wolfe."

Jack thought he sounded confident, that just saying the words would make him feel better. But there was a look of utter certainty in the doctor's glimmering, oyster eyes that shattered his confidence completely.

"Oh Jack. You don't realize, do you? She got out."

Jack's heart slowed as he looked up at the doctor and hoped he was referring to some other 'she'. "Who?"

"Hunter. She was taken in a few weeks after you. And not even three months later, she led the others in an escape. She took nine mutants with her. But she didn't take you. She didn't so much as try, not even after she saw you in that tank. She was too afraid of the monster you've become."

"You're lying," he said though clenched teeth.

"I wish I wasn't. But it's true." He leaned closer so Jack could feel the chilling, dead breath on his face as he sneered each word. "Hunter. Left. You. Alone."

Time slowed to the beat of his heart. Jack gazed up at the doctor, and those words echoed again and again in his mind like slow, repetitive torture.

Hunter left you alone. She left you. She turned her back and walked away.

You are nothing to her.

Jack didn't think the darkness could crush his soul any more, but suddenly, there was an explosion inside him. It came down upon his heart like a wrecking ball, as if a switch had been flicked in his mind. His emotions shut down. His pain dissipated. And his soul, the good part of him that made him a hero not a villain, was sucked away by the blackness so fast, he couldn't catch it.

By the expression on the doctor's face, he had seen the transformation. And then Dr. Wolfe was smiling wider than he ever had, enriching glee and malice sparkling in his eyes.

"Hunter could not see how marvelous you are," said Dr. Wolfe in awe. "How strong you've become. I have been waiting for this side of you to come out. Do you feel different?"

"You're not speaking to Jack anymore," he replied. His voice was deep, emotionless and fearless. It was the voice of darkness.

TWENTY-EIGHT

It was a calm night outside when they decided to have a campfire at the cabin. Mosi collected the firewood – quietly tearing down a nearby pine tree – and Hunter lit the fire. They sat on logs by the lake, curled up with each other, a group of lost kids sharing stories and laughing beneath a clear night sky.

It was too perfect for Hunter. The voice in her head kept trying to tell her something was about to go wrong, and it wasn't the fire. Hunter stared into the flames, willing herself to push through the barrier of whatever was blocking the familiar voice she hadn't heard since she was rescued. The voice of reason and wisdom. The fire burned, at first a small flicker, and as it began to build, the voice started to rise and suddenly there were names in her head.

Dr. Rosenthal.

Alfie.

Sammy.

Leo.

Jack.

People she'd already lost and those she was about to lose. She couldn't sit around toasting marshmallows when every second they wasted was another second Dr. Wolfe came closer to bringing Jack back and finding Ravenadium.

Whatever had been compelling her to remain ignorant had suddenly been suffocated by the fire, and she was hit with the familiar urge to take action.

"I think it's time we talk about ICE," she said loudly.

"What do you mean?" asked Chantal, who sat beside Joshua with a knitted blanket wrapped around her. Ryo, Fearne, Benji and Imogen all huddled together on the opposite side, and Mosi sat back from the fire with a thoughtful look on his face. Hunter could see Will standing on the edge of the lake, skipping stones with his back to them.

"I mean ... about Dr. Wolfe. And how we should probably start forming a plan to kill him."

"I'm not going back," said Benji. "Nuh-uh."

"Me neither," said Chantal. "Let the FBI catch him, that's their job."

"Guys, Hunter is right," said Marcus.

Hunter caught Joshua's fierce glance in her direction but she ignored it. "As much as I understand you're comfortable here and you feel safe, we need to put an end to this. Just like Dr. Rosenthal said in his letter: we're not just children anymore, we're warriors. Dr. Wolfe needs to be stopped. He has Jack, he has Alfie, he has Jet and Mikayla, not to mention a small army on his hands. He could take us all now if he wanted to. And he's going to stop at nothing until he has all the power in the world." She looked directly at Joshua. "Plus he knows where to get it."

"Hunter, don't-"

"No, they deserve to know Joshua."

"Know what?" asked Marcus.

Joshua sighed. "She's talking about what our powers are made of. Ravenadium."

Marcus cleared his throat. "Come again?"

Hunter explained, from the very beginning. She didn't mention the location, of course, but instead opened up about her past and the transformation her life had taken just a year ago. She finished with Dr. Rosenthal's findings and his warnings about Dr. Wolfe.

"So you see? If Dr. Wolfe gets his hands on this stuff, the world is over."

They all gazed at her in shock, letting the truth of her words sink in. And then suddenly, questions were being hurled at her like bullets.

"How did it get to Australia?" asked Benji.

"This is what you were going on about?" Chantal yelled at Joshua. "So what chemical is mine made out of, some kind of vampire compulsion juice?"

"How do you *make* time travel?" asked Ryo.

"I bet mine came from like an electrical explosion and this Ravenadium stuff was inside the computer," Marcus said thoughtfully. "Or maybe it was eels. I did touch an eel once."

"But how did-"

"Why didn't you tell-"

"It makes no sense that-"

"Hey, hey!" yelled Joshua. "We don't know the intimate details, but tomorrow I promise you I will look over your files and consult with you individually. Hunter isn't the expert, I am."

Hunter snorted, but didn't argue; he could have this moment of glory and she could comfortably leave the science up to him.

"The point we're trying to make," said Joshua, "is that Ravenadium can create monsters in the hands of someone like Dr. Wolfe if they have an open genetic spiral, which is why-" He looked directly at Hunter, struggling to speak for a moment, and then shook his head and gave in, "Hunter is right. We need to stop him. He already has enough ammunition to take us down. I'm surprised he hasn't already made a move."

Hunter watched Joshua talk, wondering whether the doctor already had. Again, her thoughts turned to Jack and if he'd woken up yet. But then her attention was soon on Will still throwing rocks a short distance away and realized that what she first needed to do was fix things with him.

He needs to be a part of this. He's as much a member of this band of rebels as I am.

Hunter slipped away from the warmth of the fire and walked over to Will with her hands in the pockets of her sweater.

"Hey."

"Hey," he said in a soft voice.

She picked up a rock and tried skipping it across the surface of the lake, but her skills were about as good as a stuffed teddy bear when it came to the art of rock-throwing. She smiled up at him and blushed.

He flicked his wrist and the stone hopped three times before landing in the black lake.

"I hate you," she grumbled.

Will smirked down at her. "It's not rocket science, you just-"

"It's okay, I'm not training for the rock-skipping Olympics."

He shrugged.

Hunter clenched her fists and went for it. "Look, about the other day on the mountain, I didn't-"

"Hunter." He turned and put a hand on her shoulder. She looked up into his shadowed face, feeling protected. If only she could be reassured that he'd never leave her or that nothing would ever come between them, she could live with the tension. "I know what you're going to say. But first let me tell you that … I really do like you."

Her heart fluttered in excitement. "Yeah?"

"Yeah," he smiled. "A lot. But … I'm not ready for this yet."

Just like that, her buzz was killed. Not just killed, slaughtered gruesomely. She bit her lip and nodded, stepping back.

"Sure. I understand, you need some time."

His brow creased in a sexy, please-don't-hate-me kind of way.

"Seriously, it's *fine*," she lied. "Now what do you think about going after Dr. Wolfe?"

Will looked at the lake in thought. "I don't ever want to go back there. But you're right – we have to honor Dr. Rosenthal's wishes and take him down. No one deserves to go through the hell I did."

"Exactly," she said. "What should we do?"

"I think-"

Will was just about to throw another stone when he froze, slowly lowering his arm. His gaze was focused on the lake, a frown forming across his forehead.

"What is it?"

Will stepped closer to the shore. "Do you see that?"

Hunter tried to match his eye line, scanning the surface of the lake and the opposite shore. The line of trees was dark and distant, but empty. "See what?"

"There," he raised his arm and pointed. "In the trees? I think there's someone watching us."

Hunter's stomach flipped nervously. Laughter roared from the others around the campfire; they didn't notice anything.

"Will, I don't …"

They watched the trees for a few more seconds before Will sighed. "I must be imagining things."

"It's okay," she said and squeezed his shoulder. "I know what it's like to be paranoid."

"Are you still having the nightmares?"

She nodded. "I think I'll sleep better once we don't have a world threat on our hands."

"Maybe."

"Hey. We'll get through this."

"Then what?"

"What do you mean?"

"You don't think about the future?"

"I'm too preoccupied."

Will skipped another stone. "It distracts me. I think about going back to London."

"To see your family?"

"Well … not exactly. Mostly to see the place I was supposed to grow up in. I may need to get a job too, one day."

Hunter found herself grinning.

"What?"

"I don't think I can see you in a business suit," she chuckled.

"Well maybe I'll be a musician. Or an actor." He made an attempted smolder that was actually incredibly sexy, but Hunter was too busy laughing to notice. He laughed with her and shoved her lightly on the shoulder.

Their moment of warm joking shattered when suddenly, Fearne started to seize again. Will and Hunter ran back to the fire, falling down beside Fearne whose eyes were rolling back into her head.

"What happened?" shouted Will.

"I dunno," said Benji, "she just collapsed. I think she's having a vision or something."

Will slid his arms around Fearne and shook her, tapping lightly at her cheek. "Fearne? Wake up!"

A moment later, her eyes fluttered open. "It's … the Agents …"

Hunter's head shot up. She looked at the edge of the lake where Will thought he saw someone in the shadows. But now it was not just a girl that she saw, but a whole swarm of people. Figures were starting to bleed from the trees.

Men in black suits.

Hunched mutants in shabby, dirty rags.

A young girl in a bright, white dress. She raised her arms and waved at Hunter, who realized she knew exactly who she was: the burnt girl from the Death Caves.

Fearne gasped and her eyes slipped back into her skull again. In a deep, demonic voice, she whispered, "They're here."

– PART 3 –

THE FALLEN HEROES

TWENTY-NINE

ll at once, they were being attacked.

Joshua leapt from the log and stared through the smoke of the blazing fire at the men in black suits he remembered from the night he was taken. It was a long time ago, but he still recalled the terror that charged through him, the cold of the ice as it tried to protect him and the bite of the taser that sent him into unconsciousness.

Baby Hunter's screams tore through him.

They emerged from around the lake, sprinting at them, shooting electric bullets from their guns. The others with them looked exactly like the people he remembered from ICE, only ragged, psychotic-looking, edgy and angry as if they wanted blood to be shed.

The children huddled together around the fire, screaming "what do we do?!" and "let's get out of here!" and "to the garage!" but they were surrounded. The Agents and the mutants were coming from everywhere.

Joshua found Hunter's eyes. It was too late for them to run. By now there would be Agents at the front of the house, ready to catch them. They were outnumbered and unprepared.

"Stand and fight," said Joshua.

"Ow!" They all looked at Marcus, who clenched his right bicep. He'd been hit by one of the bullets. Immediately the group gathered into a circle, facing the mutants and the Agents, Imogen protecting them from the bullets with a shield. From the looks of shock on the young one's faces, they didn't expect them to be real. When Marcus pulled his hand away, his arm was sparking.

"They're electric bullets!" he shouted. "You can't get hit, it'll knock you out!"

The electric bullets zapped against Imogen's force field as the others gazed through the shimmering wall in horror.

Joshua's attention was diverted to the cabin through the trees, and at once he felt afraid.

Ravenadium is in there. If the Agents search the house, they'll surely find it. Dr. Wolfe will get his hands on it. Escape, said the Iceman. *Grab the briefcase and run. For the sake of them all.*

Time slowed and Joshua waited.

"What do we do?" screamed Chantal.

"On my count," he said, "Imogen, you need to blast your shield at the Agents. It'll stun them."

The Agents were close, still firing. It seemed like there were two mutants to each Agent, with the mutants closing in first. In fifteen seconds, they'd be on top of them.

"I can do it," said Imogen as she concentrated.

"Marcus, attack the left side with your energy. Use the fire. Hunter, attack the right. Benji, take out the back mutants. Mosi, try and shake the ground and rock them off balance. The rest of you need to run back to the cabin."

They nodded, no time to argue. Joshua summoned the ice, ready for a fight, itching to release some of the tension that had been building inside him over the past week.

"On three. One."

The blue bullets peppered the shield and it was like bright fireworks all around them.

"Two."

Imogen started to scream from the effort.

Get ready, Iceman.

"Three!"

The shield blasted from them, the force so great it not only knocked the Agents backwards, it pushed the tide into the lake and a wave rose up, roaring, ready to fall down on all of them. Joshua became distracted by it and threw up his hands, directing a blast of ice toward the wave and freezing it just before it fell on top of them. He looked back and saw

Hunter pull the blaze of the fire out of the enclosed circle, lift it above their heads like a giant serpent and throw it at several Agents sprinting at them. They screamed and dove for the lake. Marcus did as he asked and drove electric currents at the Agents, his bolts passing through Hunter's fire and exploding. Several of them were blown back and did not get up.

It was mayhem, beautiful mayhem, and for a moment Joshua was caught in wonder at the fight around him. He'd never seen anything more amazing. The night he and Hunter battled in the warehouse was poetic and meaningful, but this was unorganized and yet synchronized at the same time.

He could hear the *zing* of the bullets as they shot past him. Imogen was trying to block too many shields at once as the Agents targeted her. She lost focus for a second and was hit in the leg. The one that shot her came at her body with his gun raised, ready to end her. Joshua sprinted at the Agent and threw himself on his back. They smashed against the ground, grappling for a weapon. Joshua wrapped his arm around the Agent's neck in a headlock and twisted until he heard the crack. The Agent didn't have time to fight.

When he threw the body to the ground and crawled to Imogen's body, he saw that she was still alive, just badly wounded and unconscious. He was baffled that the bullets could do so much damage. *Dr. Wolfe doesn't want to take us back to ICE. He just wants us dead.*

With this new revelation, Joshua forced himself to focus. A large male mutant was charging at him from the trees, arms outstretched. He let out a warrior cry, and then two more arms peeled from his sides. Joshua froze for only a second before reminding himself that they weren't human anymore. In a flash, he had formed a stake of ice and launched it through the man's heart.

Something awakened in Joshua. An unsettling feeling that came from his core. It was slippery and cold and it was the essence of the Iceman that he hadn't felt since the warehouse.

No. Stay in control.

A bullet whizzed straight past his ear and nearly hit him. He turned to see the culprit – an Agent – ready to fire at his head. He didn't have time to defend himself. But suddenly, another Agent shouted "Stop! Don't kill him!" and the Agent lowered his gun.

Joshua blanked. An Agent was telling him *not* to go for the kill shot? Why?

The Agent who saved him raised his weapon and pointed it at Joshua's lower body. Then it made sense. It was okay for the others to die, but Joshua knew where Ravenadium was. Dr. Wolfe wanted him alive.

Smiling, Joshua created a shield of ice as bullets were fired at his legs. When the Agent ran out of ammo and went to drop his magazine, Joshua threw the shield like a Frisbee. The Agent was too slow to react and the thin sheet of ice sliced his head clean off.

Joshua saw Will scoop up Imogen's unconscious body and duck through the trees, but as he did, a mutant dove from out of nowhere and stabbed a knife into Will's leg. He and Imogen went rolling on the ground.

"WILL!" Hunter screamed.

"Hunter, duck!"

She dropped and Joshua bent his arm back and launched an icicle into the chest of the mutant who stabbed Will. He collapsed with a thud.

"Enough, *enough!*" someone shouted from the back.

Suddenly, Joshua felt the ice squirm inside him. He looked down at his hands and tried to freeze them, but it wouldn't work. He could no longer use his powers.

What's happening to me?

"Mikayla," Hunter growled.

Their group re-formed. Marcus, Mosi, Benji, Hunter and Ryo were still by the campfire. Chantal had taken Will, Fearne and Imogen inside. They faced the group of five Agents and a dozen mutants, staggered on the shore and in the tree line.

From the back, two people emerged. One was a girl of Hunter's age with a small body and a vicious demeanor, the other a tall boy with black hair and demonic eyes, slimy-looking and evil.

"Jet," said Marcus through his teeth.

"Hello brother!" Jet proclaimed, throwing up his hands. "Miss me?"

"What are you doing here?" Hunter growled. "Is Dr. Wolfe sending you to do his dirty work now?"

"That's right," he replied proudly. "Though I believe you already know why we're here Hunter."

"To take us back?"

"Not quite. You have something very valuable."

Joshua thought of Ravenadium. Hunter turned and met his eyes.

"I won't let you take any of us back to ICE," she said. "Not this time."

"Oh Hunter. The only thing I'll be taking back to ICE," he smiled sadistically, "is your dead body."

THIRTY

W ill could feel the knife in his leg, but he had no desire to pull it out. That would slow him down. Besides, Chantal and Fearne were weakened as well and could not carry Imogen to safety faster than him, even with a six-inch buried in his leg.

The forest path around them was dark, his vision affected by the haze of pain over his eyes. Chantal urged them to hurry, but Will could hardly walk let alone carry little Immi. Fearne was right beside him, trying to channel peace into his mind. But it didn't stop him from worrying about leaving the others behind.

They reached the porch and Chantal threw open the back door. Inside, the house was silent and sinister. Will lowered Imogen into the armchair chair.

"Help me lock the doors Fearne," said Chantal.

Fearne nodded, running to the back door while Chantal ran to the front. Will grit his teeth and ripped the knife from his thigh, growling from the sting. It had been a week since he'd felt any kind of brutal pain, and it burned.

When he looked up, a shadow slipped past the kitchen window.

He froze, listening. There was a shuffle of footsteps.

"Fearne," he whispered. The girl whipped around.

There was a squeal of fright from the front entryway and, next minute, an Agent appeared holding Chantal in front of him, his hand wrapped around her chest and the other over her mouth so she couldn't persuade him to release her. Her eyes were wide with fear as she begged him for help.

"Drop the knife," he said to Will.

He obeyed.

"Hello Fearne," the Agent said. "My name is Alpha."

"I know who you are," she said. "And I know what you're doing here."

Will watched them make eye contact for more than ten seconds and knew she was hiding something from him.

"Fearne," he said under his breath. "Make him go away, change his mind."

"I can't read his mind," she said. Something about her tone told Will she was lying. Even though Fearne was one of the best liars he'd met, he knew her better than anyone.

"We have no intention of going back," Will said to Alpha. "Let Chantal go."

The Agent pushed Chantal down the stairs into the living room, keeping a firm grip on her. She squirmed in his arms but stopped the moment Alpha brought out a long blade and rested the tip against her side.

"I don't want to be violent with you. But I don't care that you're all mutants – I do my job and I get it done properly. There'll be no hiccups."

At that moment, two more Agents appeared from behind Alpha. They were Chinese, tough-looking and emotionless. Will looked behind him in panic. *Where are the others?*

"We can do this the easy way or the hard way."

"Whatever way you chose will be the last thing you ever do," said Will.

"Very well."

Instantly, the blade went into Chantal's hip.

She screamed.

"No!" Fearne shrieked. "I'll do it, please don't hurt her!"

Will's heart was beating erratically in his chest. He didn't expect the Agent to be so cruel. Then again, he was Dr. Wolfe's employee. Of course he'd have no mercy.

You idiot, you could have gotten her killed.

Tears of pain rolled down Chantal's cheeks as she slumped in Alpha's arms.

"We'll swap," said Alpha. "Fearne for Chantal. An even trade. And no tricks, or this knife will be going across her throat next."

Fearne released Will's hand.

"No-"

"Will." She turned and looked up at him. Her eyes, though young and wide, were strangely calm. "I have to do this. Tell Hunter I'm sorry. Tell the others I'm sorry. Keep fighting, but let me go with them."

"I can't!" Will struggled for her hand. "Fearne, please don't-"

"Time is ticking," shouted Alpha. Chantal slipped in his arms, blood dripping down her side.

Fearne gazed up into his face and smiled. "I love you Will," she said.

Final words wouldn't come. His chin quivered. He couldn't bear the torture of watching his closest friend and the most beautiful little girl he'd ever known walk back into the arms of the men who worked for Dr. Wolfe.

But he had no choice.

Fearne moved toward the Agents. When they were only feet away, Alpha released Chantal and shoved her at Will, who leapt forward and caught her limp body before she hit the floor. She was completely unconscious. Fearne was taken by one of the other Agents and did not so much as squirm.

"Well done Will," said Alpha. "That had to have been hard."

"Fuck you," he spat.

There was a sudden commotion from the front of the cabin. Three shots were fired and everyone inside froze in shock until a second later, the Agents leapt into action. Clearly they didn't expect anyone to be surprising them from behind. Alpha turned to his fellow Agents and handed one of them a box he'd pulled from his pocket. Will tried to see what it was but he was straining to hold Chantal up without hurting her. Blood was pouring from her wound, and only his hands could stop it. Fearne watched the exchange wordlessly. *Why isn't she fighting back?*

"It's too late to risk it, take her out," Alpha ordered.

The Agent ripped a silver syringe from the black box he was given.

"No!" Will shouted, but he wasn't quick enough.

Through tears, he saw the point of the needle go into Fearne's neck. Just for a split second, she met his gaze and let it happen. She let them poison her.

Fearne slumped in the arms of an Agent.

They were already pulling out their weapons, preparing for the intruders coming through the front door.

"What the hell did you do?!" he yelled.

"Not important," said Alpha. "Dr. Wolfe wants-"

"Dr. Wolfe wants what?" a voice spoke from behind Alpha, and suddenly, there he was.

Dr. Wolfe.

Will had never felt such a shock of emotional rage in his entire life. The man who turned his world upside down was standing in the entryway of the cabin, his hands behind his back in an over-confident pose, glaring at Alpha.

"Sir, you said you wanted Joshua, so-"

"Whatever the fuck I said," he growled. "I take it back."

There was a shriek from somewhere near the lake and a fiery explosion erupted through the trees. Will had to get back outside to warn them all, to tell them to run. If Dr. Wolfe was there, God knows what he had in store for them.

"What are your orders, sir?" asked Alpha.

Dr. Wolfe pulled his hands from behind him and produced a shotgun longer than Will's arm. Alpha stumbled back against the wall, his mouth agape.

"I want you to say hello to my little friend," said Dr. Wolfe.

Then he blew an apple-sized hole in Alpha's the chest.

The two Agents behind him raised their own weapons, but before they could fire, a blade appeared in both their chests and they fell, dead on the floor.

Dr. Wolfe turned to Will, who was stunned as he knelt on the floor with Chantal still in his arms. Suddenly, Dr. Wolfe started laughing.

Clearly I'm missing something, thought Will.

Then Dr. Wolfe was morphing, shrinking and quivering into Zac. Will breathed a sigh of relief. At the same time, people were stalking through the door. A man in his thirties with rugged, handsome looks and a woman in all leather, followed by a curly-haired man who grinned with a bizarre kind of glee and a young Chinese boy who could not be more serious-looking charged into the room. Then came a man and a woman of Brazilian culture, clad in warrior attire and ready for a fight.

Zac turned to the rugged man and raised his hand as if for a high-five. "Wasn't that the best line ever!? Huh!?"

When no high-five was given, Zac turned back to Will. His usual joker grin faded when he saw Chantal. He ran to Will's side and started panicking, gently taking her from Will's arms and rubbing her cheek.

"We need to get outside," said the curly-haired man as Will scrambled to see if Fearne was alright. Whatever they had injected her with did not kill her – a pulse still beat beneath her skin. Perhaps it was only a tranquilizer so they could take her back to Dr. Wolfe without fear of their minds being hijacked. He thanked God for watching over them and scooped her up into his arms.

"Who the hell are these guys?" he asked.

"Oh right," said Zac. "Willy, this is Ace, Illya, Chevie and Yung. And that's Koko and Zokani. No time to explain anything else." A second later he was quivering into Alpha as a disguise. "It's time to end this. Take Fearne and Chantal outside – there's a car waiting to transport you to the jet."

"The jet?" Will gaped.

"Yes, and get Chantal there quick. She's losing blood." He clicked his hand and the rugged man bent down and gently pulled Chantal into his arms. "Hurry, Ace."

"I'm on it."

"But-"

"We'll go help the others," the woman in leather said fiercely to him. "Go with Ace and get yourselves to safety."

Nodding, Will hoisted Fearne onto one side of his body and lifted Imogen on the other. His leg had already healed. He followed Ace to the door. When he looked back on the dark cabin – his sanctuary and his first real home – he saw Zac and his team run through the back door to the lake and prayed they were enough to defend the others against the dozens of Agents and mutants.

THIRTY-ONE

Everywhere around her, Hunter could see Agents. The last time she came in contact with them, they were dragging her body into the back of a van. But here, she had a reason to fight. She had people depending on her. Her blood pumped in her chest.

I won't let them win.

But they were powerless, thanks to Mikayla. And now they weren't just up for ransom. The Agents were prepared to kill them all.

The fire snaked through her skin. To her left, the dying embers of the campfire sparked in agreement. Mikayla's power was strong –

But she was stronger. She just had to keep them talking.

"What's in this for you, Jet?" she shouted at him.

"Uh, entertainment?" he shrugged. Then he laughed and waved a hand at her. "No really, I'm just excited to see your new little hideaway. So this is where you guys escaped to? This is the wonderful safe-zone Dr. Rosenthal recommended? Did he tell you we'd never find it or some bullshit like that?"

Hunter pursed her lips and looked at the others. For a moment she let Jet get to her. Dr. Rosenthal said this was the safest place for them, and still the Agents found it.

That's when she realized that nowhere was safe. Not when Dr. Wolfe was still breathing.

"Okay Jet. We give up," she said.

There were gasps of protest from the others.

"Hunter-"

"It's okay, Joshua," she said. "He's right; there's nowhere else for us to go. We can't escape the Agents." She pointed at the men circling them. "Or these mutants. There's too many of them."

Grinning, Jet and Mikayla leaned toward them as if they were simply going to turn themselves in. But Hunter would not go down without a fight. The Agents took her once before, outnumbered her, caught her off guard. She had her powers then as well.

But she was broken and alone. She'd lost Eli. She'd lost everything. Now she was healing and surrounded by people who cared for her. Friends she called her family. And though Mikayla might have blocked her powers, she had not taken them away. If Hunter could summon the fire from the Death Caves with an entrapment around her wrist, she could certainly bring forth the flame inside her.

I'm here, the fire whispered. *Use me.*

"Guys," said Hunter with a sigh as she turned to the group. "There's nothing more we can do. Well – except this."

Quicker than they could blink, Hunter dropped to the ground, wrenched a tree branch from the dying fire behind her, spun back and launched the branch straight at Mikayla like a shot-put ball. As she did, a surge of energy exploded in her core and the fire burst through her arms to the tips of her fingers, setting the tree branch alight just as it left her hands.

"DUCK!" she yelled.

The Agents opened fire on them.

The flaming torch flew at Mikayla and Jet, but using his telekinesis, Jet was able to stop the branch mid-air. He let it drop on the shore of the lake, looked down at Mikayla and saw her cowering by his side.

With their powers free, the fight resumed. Hunter was angrier than ever, the fire burning bright and exploding the trees where several of the mutants were fleeing toward. The ground rumbled as Mosi buried Agents in the dirt. Marcus was fighting hand-to-hand combat, and once he got his fingers around a taser, he used it to direct current at three mutants at a time. For a moment, it looked like they were winning.

And for a moment, Hunter was distracted by this revelation.

"Hunter!" someone screamed at her.

Almost in slow motion, Hunter whirled around and saw an Agent only a few meters away throw a kitchen knife right at her chest. She didn't have time to catch her breath knowing she was too late, that she was about to die.

Then, a cloud of dirt sprayed her and when she opened her eyes and spluttered through the dust, she saw Benji stumble backwards and then collapse on the ground. The knife stuck out of the center of his small chest. His eyes were wide as he lay on the cobbled shore of the lake.

Hunter felt as if the knife had stabbed her – and continued to do so – as she bent down beside Benji's body. Bullets whizzed around her. She looked up at the Agent, who did not bat a single eyelid for the small child he had just killed. She was practically fuming, fire sparking all around her body as she launched a blazing ball of fire at the Agent.

It felt like Sammy dying all over again.

"You killed him!" she shrieked. "You-"

Suddenly there was a male scream like nothing she'd ever heard before, causing her to whirl toward the sound. Mosi was being lifted off the ground and Hunter saw Jet with his hands directed at the floating body. Jet was drawing his hands apart as though cracking open a coconut. Hunter could hear the pain in Mosi's screams and formed a flaming ball of fire to throw at Jet when someone violently pushed her down from behind and she went face-first into the ground. Hunter flipped immediately and saw a woman. She was feral looking and she laughed at Hunter with a crazy gleam in her eyes. Her hair was ratted and her teeth were blackened and broken.

"Hunter the fire girl," she said and laughed again. The harmony of her laugh and Mosi's shrieking made a spine-tingling combination. "I remember you from the caves."

Hunter scrambled to her feet but the woman pounced on her again, cackling loudly in her ear. Hunter set her wrists on fire and grabbed the woman's cheeks, burning her skin, but she didn't seem to care. Her skin melted and yet she kept on laughing.

"Don't feel it," she said as she shook her head in Hunter's hands. "Don't feel it. Don't feel it, ha ha ha!"

She's crazy. Hunter kicked the woman in the stomach. "Get off-"

"Mosi!" someone screeched and from Hunter's left, she felt a spray of blood wash over her like a wave. When she opened her eyes, she saw Mosi's body, torn in half, lying on the shore of the lake just meters from her.

No. Not Mosi.

Jet laughed. Someone nearby was crying, a mournful, wrecked sound that made breaking down and giving up that much harder to resist. But the fight went on and bullets still splayed around her. Hunter had no time to grieve. She only had time for revenge.

Mikayla was busy stopping Joshua from slicing Agents in half with ice stakes. Leaving Joshua to fight hand-to-hand instead of with his powers, Hunter dove for their biggest threat with fire blazing. Jet and Hunter rolled around on the shore of the lake, throwing punches where they could. Hunter blew fire into his face, scorching his hair as he yelped in pain.

"That's for Sammy, you piece of shit!" Hunter screamed.

Before he could use his telekinesis to float her too, Hunter raised her fist and threw it down on his nose, feeling the break just as she had on her first day at ICE.

"That's for Dr. Rosenthal," she growled.

Jet coughed blood from his open mouth, chuckling to himself. "Oh please, that old man was history anyway. I was only doing him a favor."

Infuriated, Hunter brought her knee into Jet's stomach and he puffed air out of his lungs, moaning in pain.

"That's for Mosi. You play with fire, Jet, you're gonna get burned."

"Could you not think of anything more cliché?"

Next second, Jet had knocked her knees out from under her and threw her to the side, sharp rocks pressing into her back.

"Want to know something hilarious? Jack woke up the other day."

Jet held one of her arms down with his foot and the other with his hand. His finger appeared in front of her eyes and started slicing the skin around her neck. Hunter kicked furiously, but it did no good. She clenched her teeth to keep from screaming in pain.

"He was asking for you but you weren't there," he pouted. "He gave in to his dark side and joined Team Evil with me and Dr. Wolfe, isn't that great?"

The fire erupted inside her and all at once, her body was aflame. She gripped Jet's hands as he tried to jump away from her and held on as tight as she could, feeling his flesh burn.

"Jack will *never* be like you," she growled in a low voice that wasn't her own.

Jet screamed and kicked and twisted until one of his hands came free. He flicked his finger and her wrist bent back, forcing her to release him. Hunter ignored the agony of her broken wrist, the fire burning so brightly through her veins that she glowed.

Hunter went to throw a fireball at his face when suddenly, Jet's body seized. His eyes widened. A bubble of blood fell from his mouth and he looked down at his chest where an icicle the size of a carrot protruded from his stomach. Jet's legs crumbled and he fell, revealing Joshua, who stood behind him.

"Thanks," she breathed. Hot blood oozed down her neck from the cut Jet gave her.

"Anytime," he replied.

Hunter looked around, trying to make sense of the chaos. Were they winning? Was it over? Was there a point in fighting anymore?

As an Agent approached her with a raised gun, a voice shouted over the chaos.

"STOP!"

Surprisingly, the Agents did. They looked back to the line of trees that led to the cabin where an Agent whose suit was still unmarked by dirt or blood was emerging, followed by half a dozen strangers dressed in normal clothes.

"The fight is over," said the Agent.

"Says who?" called Mikayla as she lay over Jet's body.

"Says me, you whiney sack of-" The Agent began to shiver, and before Hunter could blink, he was Zac.

"I never thought I'd say this, but it's freaking good to see you!" shouted Marcus from the tree line.

The Agents raised their guns and cocked their hammers. Zac gazed at Mikayla in annoyance.

"Mikayla!" he moaned. "You ruined my act!"

"SHOOT THEM!" screamed Mikayla.

The remaining Agents were slow from the fight, and the new warriors instantly made them nervous. Before they could fire, one of the new women stepped forward, ripped apart her clothes and transformed into a majestic snow leopard, sprinting in a white blur at the closest Agent. At the same time, the short man leapt into the sky and took flight, reaching for a double-headed mutant. She shrieked when he scooped her into the air and dropped her in the lake. The others broke into combat mode. Knives flew, the Agents went down and all of a sudden, Hunter was confident that they were going to survive the fight.

Then she felt a sharp, electric pain in her arm and looked down at her shoulder. A bullet had pierced her skin, opening up a large gash in her arm. She was so distracted by the pain that she didn't hear the roar of an engine until the lake was blinded by light from above. A huge jet like nothing Hunter had ever seen before hovered over them like an alien spaceship trying to abduct them. The few Agents left looked up and started backing away in fear. They shouted 'retreat!' at the mutants. They pulled Mikayla back, but she wouldn't let go of Jet's body. She shrieked and wrenched herself from their arms. They made a desperate decision to leave her and ran back to the shelter of the dark trees, still firing their bullets.

One of the newcomers spotted Ryo sitting on the ground beside the tree where Benji's body lay. Benji was covered in blood.

"Ryo!" the Asian boy shouted.

Ryo whirled, her face a mess of tears. "Mi-kyung!"

They embraced, and Hunter was stuck in a moment of wonder, not sure what to feel. She didn't want to look at the bodies surrounding them.

Mosi and Benji's bodies in particular.

"Hunter!"

She tore her eyes from the massacre of Agents, mutants and her family to see that a ladder had been lowered from the aircraft. Zac was waving at her, urging her to follow them. She didn't know if she trusted where they were going, but it had to be safer than the cabin. She had no choice, not when the Agents were still shooting at her from the tree line.

Hunter ran to Zac. "We can't just leave their bodies here!"

The others were already scrambling up the ladder.

"We don't have time, they could come back with more!"

Hunter was about to follow when she saw Mikayla lying over Jet's body and an idea struck her. She looked up the ladder at the faces staring down at her.

"Ryo!"

The young girl pushed through the crowd. "Yeah?"

"Grab Mikayla!" she yelled.

The jet began to lift off the ground, and Hunter saw out of the corner of her eye that Ryo had appeared on the ground and disappeared a second later. She jumped and grabbed hold of the ladder, looking down at the cabin and the lake where the fire was dying out, thankful the house didn't burn down. At least it would still be there for them when the fight was over.

When she climbed into the jet, the first thing she saw was Joshua's face.

"We can't leave it behind!"

"Leave what behind?"

"Ravenadium!"

Hunter stared at the faces strapping in. The jet was climbing higher into the air. She knew that if Ravenadium was found by any of the Agents, it would be the end of the world.

"Ryo, can you teleport me into Dr. Rosenthal's office?"

She looked exhausted and weakly leant against her brother. "I can try."

"You can do it." She gripped the girl's hand, both of them covered in blood. The jet engine rumbled. "I trust you."

Ryo nodded and then Hunter felt herself teleport through space again. It was a rough landing in the office and she growled when she landed on her sprained wrist and pain shuddered through her body. But she had no time to stop. She reached under the desk for Joshua's briefcase. But as she lifted it from the ground, the clasps came loose and the contents of the briefcase spilled across the floor. She swore furiously, reaching for the first stone she could. It brightened in her hand, rejuvenating her.

"Hunter, we-"

The glass of the window shattered and bullets peppered the room. Hunter and Ryo screamed. Ryo took her free hand and before she could grab anything else they may need, they were in darkness. Hunter gasped, opened her eyes and was back in the jet.

"Take her away, Amelia!" someone yelled. Ryo has passed out and her brother was carrying her away. Hunter was rushed by a handsome man with curly hair into a seat between Will and Joshua and buckled in, the rock still clasped in her hand. She was so numb and exhausted that she couldn't follow the actions of those around her. In less than a few seconds, the jet was at full speed and they were soaring into the night, away from the cabin.

"Did you get it?" Joshua asked.

Hunter held out her hand and smiled at him. "Got it."

Expecting Joshua's eyes to light up, her stomach dropped at his look of utter defeat.

"Hunter, where's the other stone?"

"What do you mean?"

Joshua looked mortified. "There were two."

THIRTY-TWO

he lake was still, silent. Smoke and ash hung in the air. Bodies were scattered across the shore, some charred beyond repair, some simply bleeding out with their eyes wide and empty. A chilly fog crawled over the glassy surface of the lake, creeping toward the cabin and the fire that was dying out.

Jet watched it, half awake, half unconscious. He wanted to get up, but he was afraid of the pain. He knew the ice stake was still buried inside him, but it had missed everything important. It was simply the blood loss that was going to kill him.

Get up, a voice whispered. *You have to live.*

He wasn't sure why. No one cared that he was dead, no one except Mikayla, and more often than not she was just an accessory.

See, Jet didn't feel love like most people. He didn't feel guilt or remorse or kindness either. All he cared about was living, so that he could kill that son of bitch who staked him.

As the fog neared the shore, Jet shakily looked down at the stake jutting out of his stomach. Some of it had melted. It was a cold feeling, a burning cold. He concentrated, gritting his teeth, taking three sharp breaths before holding out his hand and ripping the stake from his stomach where it soared away. He screamed in pain and saw spots in his vision. But the burn was enough to keep him awake.

He felt paralyzed, wondering how he was going to make it to the house, much less back to the new ICE.

There was a scuffling behind him. Someone was talking from a distance. Then there came the unmistakable, high-pitched chuckle of Madam, one of the mutants he'd befriended.

Jet grit his teeth and forced himself to roll over.

"Help ..." he croaked.

Through blurry vision, he saw a shape start to gallop toward him. There were more of them coming out of the trees. It had to be the Agents.

"Ah haaa!" Madam giggled and she fell beside Jet. He made friends with all the mutants – and by friends, he meant that he'd acquired a sort of fan club after bragging to them all that he killed Dr. Rosenthal and he would be leading them to freedom. The mutants were too brain damaged to focus on anything except their anger and didn't think twice about following him. Madam was one of his favorites – if she wasn't completely crazy, he would have looked to her as a mother. "Wakey wakey!" she said and tapped him on the head. Her dark hair fell like a curtain around his face and her breath nearly made him choke.

"Get – off –"

"Is he alive?" asked another voice from beside Madam. Jet looked up and saw Dice's knife fingers glittering in the moonlight. As well as having blades for fingers, Dice was subjected to a brutal experiment in which Dr. Wolfe tried to re-create Zac's ability to change form and instead infected Dice's pigmentation – his entire body was so pale, any exposure to sun would burn him in seconds. He hid in shrouds of black clothing so the only thing Jet ever saw of him were his red eyes and silver knives. He also knew that Dice had experienced brain damage after a fight with Will the night the others escaped.

Madam clicked her long-nailed fingers together. "Staying alive," she said.

Jet felt someone stand over him and he looked up into the face of Agent Bravo – Alpha's second in command.

"Bravo ..." said Jet, "what happened?"

"They escaped in a modernized aircraft. Took Mikayla with them. We're all that's left."

"What?"

Madam began to groan and twitch. She didn't care for Mikayla at all.

"They'll come back," said Bravo. "We saw the fire girl teleport into a room upstairs, so it must have been for something important."

Jet nodded, trying hard to keep his eyes open. "Let's go."

Bravo clicked his finger. He was suddenly being lifted into someone's arms, the pain ripping through his body. It had to be Mouse. He was the largest person Jet had ever seen, so the name seemed to fit. He never spoke a word, and his muscle capacity was unbeatable.

Jet didn't know how in hell he was still living. They hiked through the trees to the door of the cabin, Madam running ahead and singing lyrics that weren't even in English.

The cabin was old and smelled oddly like his last foster home in Kentucky. He could also smell a salty metal and saw a body leaning against the wall beside the staircase. Alpha. Someone had killed him. Beside his body were two more with stab wounds in their chests.

When Bravo saw the bodies of his colleagues, his friends, he swore and lost his cool, swiping his arms over the kitchen bench and sending dishes crashing to the floor.

"Feel the fire, burning bright!" yelled Madam. "Burning, burning, through the night!"

"What are you on about?" asked Bravo.

"She sees something," said Jet. None of the mutants had powers – their abilities were failed experiments. Madam came from a gypsy camp in Georgia where she used to be a fortune teller. She had a natural ability to sense things, and sometimes her ramblings came true.

"If it's fire, I'm getting out of here." A girl in a white dress walked up to Madam and put a hand on her shoulder. The girl was badly burnt on one side of her body – an effect of Hunter's formula failing. She went by her real name – Caitlin. Like Mouse, she rarely said or felt anything.

"Up, up and away …" Madam whispered and pointed at the roof.

Jet understood. She could sense something upstairs. Perhaps it was something to do with their powers, a mutual energy that only those with abilities – failed or not – could sense.

"They were up there earlier looking for something," said Bravo.

"Go with her," he said.

Madam and Bravo disappeared. Caitlin and the girl with two heads they called Twins were whispering to each other and snooping through the lounge room. Jet swore he fell out of consciousness, for they were back within seconds with a briefcase. It was black, leather and modern – not Dr. Rosenthal's. There was an inscription in the gold plate under the handle.

J.H.

"What is it?" he asked.

Bravo lifted the latch on the metal encasing. There was nothing in it. Jet rolled his eyes. "You idiot, that's not-"

"We found this."

The mutants crowded around him. Jet winced, his eyes stinging, until a glowing orange light lit up around them and he gazed in wonder at the stone Madam held in her dirty hand. Jet lifted it with his mind, hovering it before his eyes. The stone turned eerily in the air. He looked for an opening, but saw nothing. Gently and carefully, he raised a finger. And as his finger just barely touched the stone, a shock went through him.

Then a voice came out of the darkness and sent chills through his already cold heart.

Jet ... it said. *You've come home* ...

THIRTY-THREE

Does that make sense, General?"

General Cheng straightened and stared at the map laid out on the table. He met eyes with Dr. Wolfe, seizing him up. Jack could practically here the blood thumping in his body. A war was on the horizon, and he couldn't wait to start destroying things.

"I will need to speak with my associates," said the General, "but I believe we will be able to carry out the mission. As long as you are sure that the President will be at this location on the day and your weapon-" He glanced at Jack through narrowed eyes, "-will be able to distract the defense force long enough to get us into the bunker."

Dr. Wolfe nodded. "I can assure you that this will be one hell of a fight. My men are somewhat … limited these days. I will need as many soldiers as you can muster."

"Already accounted for. We have more men committed to this cause than ever before. I look forward to our next meeting."

General Cheng smiled. He obviously liked the plan. They shook hands, and the soldiers began to move out of the board room, leaving Dr. Wolfe and Jack alone.

The look of bloodlust and evil in Dr. Wolfe's eyes made Jack's whole body tingled. His need to explode, to cause destruction and to feed the darkness was greater than ever.

"When will it happen?"

"A few days," Dr. Wolfe replied. "I'm allowing the General to arrange his attack and converse with his forces. We have another meeting after permission is given."

Jack cracked his neck, feeling the pulse of impatience surge through him. "Permission? I thought he was the General, i.e. the guy who makes the decisions."

Dr. Wolfe gave Jack a knowing smile. "The Chinese are not alone in this attack, Jack. You have no idea how hated your country is. Hopefully, the Agents will have returned from a successful mission, and then there will be no one to stop me."

Jack's thoughts on Hunter had been replaced with a dark hatred that clouded his vision like the haze of a drug. He no longer saw her face, just her red hair. There was no more emotion in his consciousness, therefore no face to remember.

A moment later, there was a knock at the door.

"Sir?" Dr. Hosking poked her frayed head and nosy beak into the room and said in a hollow voice, "the Agents have returned."

Dr. Wolfe jerked toward her. "Were they successful?"

Her face fell. The doctor had such a murderous look in his eyes that Jack thought he would explode as well. It made the darkness excited. He slammed the file down on the desk and stalked past Jack.

He followed.

Before they entered the infirmary, Jack could sense the remnants of a fight in the air. He could smell the blood. Three mutants were thrashing about on their gurneys. Dr. Wolfe was looking for Alpha, but he was nowhere to be seen.

"Sir?"

Jack turned and there stood a well-built man in a suit with a beaky nose and a round face.

"Agent Bravo," said the doctor. "Where is-"

"Dead," said Bravo.

He shot a glance at Jack and then inclined his head as a notion for Dr. Wolfe to follow him. They walked a short distance away so they could not be heard.

In the meantime, Jack walked over to the nearest bed. On it was a pale boy of Jack's age with black hair and slimy features. There was a bandage stained with blood over his stomach. He held onto a briefcase like his life depended on it.

Jack could see evil in the boy's soul. He glared up at him with tired eyes.

"What are you looking at?"

I could snap your body in half like a splinter, said Jack. Then he realized that Jet was probably thinking the same thing. Jet's power was different to his, and yet it had just as much potential.

"That looks like it hurts," said Jack with a smirk.

Jet scoffed.

A moment later, Dr. Wolfe was at his side. "What have you found, Jet?"

"I don't know for sure," he said as he slid the briefcase he held across the bed. Jack curiously leaned over Dr. Wolfe's shoulder. There was an inscription under the handle.

"Joshua Harrison," Dr. Wolfe murmured and a smile spread across his lips.

Something in Jack's mind transported him back to a memory of a dark alleyway and a man who at the time seemed more psychotic than anyone Jack had ever come across. But back then, he hadn't met Dr. Wolfe. Joshua was not a villain at heart.

"Madam found it. We think Hunter tried to go back for it before they escaped in the jet, but she must have missed this one. It looked like nothing at first," said Jet, "but then it spoke to me."

The doctor lifted the case marked with hazard signs and raised a spherical rock. The only odd thing about it was that it looked completely fake.

The doctor was mesmerized.

"Is it speaking to you now?" he asked.

Jet shook his head. "It hasn't said anything since that night."

Dr. Wolfe frowned, stroking a finger down his jaw, and then he turned to Jack.

"Take it," he said.

Jack let the rock fall into his palm.

At first, there was just silence. Jack became so focused on the rock that he didn't know where he was or who he was with. A strange whisper was coming from the stone, and as he listened and peered at it closer, he sensed a pulse inside. There was something living in the stone. Something that felt connected to him.

Jack began to shake. It was not the type of angry quiver he felt before something around him exploded, nor was it dark or evil or consuming. It was a memory, a feeling he'd forgotten.

Jack hated it. He shoved the stone into the doctor's hands.

"It's just a rock," he muttered.

"A rock that Joshua was trying to protect," said Dr. Wolfe. He spun and started to march away from the bed.

"Wait!" yelled Jet. "What about Mikayla? They have her!"

"We can do nothing at this moment but keep searching," he replied. "And you can do nothing but heal. The salves will patch up your wounds."

"But you promise I can make her pay?"

"Make who pay?"

"Hunter," Jet said through his teeth. "She's the reason for all of this. And the Iceman."

"I need them alive."

"But-"

"That's enough!" Dr. Wolfe snapped. Jet's mouth shut.

Jack followed the doctor to the door. He summoned two scientists. Dr. Hosking was one of them. They went across the hall to the laboratory. The doctor was more excited than Jack had ever seen him.

"I need you to analyze this stone. Take a sample with the extractor. Run it against the DNA we have. Try and find a match. Notify me the *moment* you have anything. This substance is highly temperamental and very valuable. Do you understand me?"

Dr. Hosking nodded and started ordering her partners to get to work. The doctor turned to Jack.

"We have what we need," he said with more excitement in his eyes than Jack had ever seen.

"What do you think it is?"

"Power, Jack," he said. "This is power."

THIRTY-FOUR

he cockpit of the jet remained dark and reasonably quiet, except for the sobbing. Hunter looked around at the bloodied faces streaked with tears, a numbness crawling over her. Marcus sat with his head in his hands. He just lost a best friend and a brother. Chantal was lying on a fold-out stretcher, heavily sedated. Hunter wasn't sure what happened to her, but Will said that if they didn't get her medical attention soon, she may be in trouble. Zac sat beside her, his hand hovering over hers as if unsure if she'd notice or not. Ryo was still asleep against what had to be her older brother. Hunter knew that would be easier for her than to be awake with the realization that Benji was dead. Hunter couldn't forget the image of the sweet kid lying on the ground with his eyes open wide and his skull crushed.

They had Mikayla strapped into a seat. She wouldn't stop glaring at Hunter.

At the front of the jet was a young girl flying the plane, two older men and a woman watching the sky. Friends of Zac's, though from where they came, she could not imagine.

Hunter looked to her left at Will cradling Fearne in his arms. He glanced at her, his eyes tired, trying to give her a reassuring look or even a small smile, but it did no good. Hunter's own body was aching, the bullet wound, gash in her neck and sprained wrist providing a good distraction from the pain of grieving. The nurse on board who tended to Chantal's wounds told her it looked like a fracture, but she'd have it x-rayed when they landed.

On her other side was Joshua, sitting rigid and unmoving, just like her. He held the stone in his hand, his blood-covered face filled with worry. She knew he was thinking of the stone she'd left behind and whether or not the Agents found it.

"Should we ask them if we can fly back?" she asked him.

Joshua shook his head so quickly it looked like a twitch. "They won't. They're military trained, I can tell. They take orders from an authority who won't agree to going back."

Hunter stared at the six newcomers. She couldn't see what Joshua could, but then again, he had more experience reading people of this type than she did.

"Do we trust them?"

"They saved our lives. I'd rather be here than back at the cabin waiting for more Agents to come and kill me."

She said nothing.

"It's not your fault, leaving the stone behind. We weren't prepared for an attack."

Hunter nodded. Her thoughts strayed to Jack. Jet had said that he gave in to the darkness. Was he trying to provoke her, or was it true? If Jack really had turned to the other side, and Dr. Wolfe now had Ravenadium … their next battle would be virtually impossible to win.

All of a sudden, someone cleared their throat loudly. The lights flickered on from above and she could see clearer inside the jet. The person who coughed was a handsome man with a slightly awkward smile – considering the circumstances, she didn't hold it against him. He stood behind the pilot's chair.

"Right, uh … we'll be making our descent soon, so you'll need to put your seatbelts on please."

They did as he asked.

"A few housekeeping things quickly. My name is Chevie Barnes. Some of you may remember me as Chevie Pulicover."

There were several gasps. From beside her, Will muttered, "I thought I recognized him."

"Yes, I know, I remember some of your faces from ICE. I'll have more of an opportunity to explain to you how I escaped later, and also a bit about our society. We are called the SSS, or Superhero Support Society as it stands for. We're a safe house for people with powers. I'll give you a debriefing after we get you settled in at the compound so I'm not repeating myself."

They all stared at him, not answering.

"Great, well, we'll have medical checks the moment we land, then we'll get you fed up and rested in your rooms and report later for a meeting. Sound good?"

Again, no one answered. Chevie clapped his hands together and went around to assist everyone in strapping in. It wasn't long before he came to she and Joshua.

"What's that you go there, mate?" he asked, pointing to the stone in Joshua's hands.

Hunter could almost feel the cool chill coming from Joshua's body. "A souvenir," he replied.

Chevie raised his eyebrows and flashed a cheeky smile. "That's a pretty special souvenir Hunter and Ryo risked their lives for, then. What'd you call it? Ravenadium?"

Hunter watched Chevie closely. For a complete stranger, he was quite clued in. She was instantly wary of how much he knew, and she could tell Joshua was just as surprised.

"That's what I said." Joshua put the stone in his pocket and tried to act causal. "Didn't you say we were landing soon?"

"Absolutely. Buckle up," he said and winked as he went to sit down besides the rugged man and his partner.

"I don't like that guy," said Joshua to himself.

"Why, because he's handsome?"

Joshua raised his eyebrows. "Showy, I think he's showy. And he's nosy too. We should be careful."

Hunter wanted to say they couldn't be sure, but she was starting to trust Joshua's intuition. They fastened their seatbelts and prepared for landing in whatever new adventure they were about to embark on.

THIRTY-FIVE

enny had been sitting for hours in the control room, waiting for Zac and the SSS team to return, praying that the mission was successful. But most of all, she hoped she would see Joshua again.

One of the SSS workers had opened up the gigantic hatch windows, displaying a beautiful view of the Nevada desert and hills stretched out under a starry sky. She was alone; Eli had gone off to the Lair, as had most of the others she'd been introduced to. The Captain and his crew were around somewhere. Only she remained to wait for the return.

So when she saw the lights of the jet blink in the distance, her heart started to pound. She sat down at the control desk and picked up a pair of headphones.

"Red Cherry, this is Base, come in."

A crackling came through in her ear and then she heard Amelia's clear tone.

"Base, this is Red Cherry. We're about to make our final descent. We have a very full cockpit, over."

Jenny sighed in relief. But was very full completely full? She just had to be patient.

"Roger that, Red Cherry. Over and out."

She followed the jet as it soared toward the compound, the engine a dull hum in the background. The Captain, Mark and a few others joined her in the communications room. Eli looked wide-eyed and hopeful.

"They made it?" he asked.

Jenny nodded, ringing her hands together as they watched the door. She imagined Joshua leading a group of bloodied and bruised kids, but as the seconds wore on, she began to worry.

"Are you nervous?" she asked Eli.

"Should I be?"

"Hunter may be with them."

Eli stared at the door. "A part of me is scared that all my memories will come flooding back when I see her."

"Why's that?"

"Because it will ... complicate things."

Jenny smiled. "I know you and Amelia have been getting along well lately. But you can't stop real love. If all your memories come back, you'll know that you and Hunter are meant to be."

"You're right. What about you?"

"Me?"

"And Joshua? Is it love?"

For a moment Jenny paused, waiting for an answer to come. Perhaps it was love, but she didn't want to put a label on it. Labels squeeze things into a box they're much too big for. Whatever she and Joshua had, it was complicated and messy and too wonderful to describe.

She was saved from having to answer when the heavy steel doors began to open, and the Impossibles returned.

Ahead of the group was Chevie, not with his usual five-star smile and cheery demeanor. He nodded to her and the Captain, telling them that the mission was successful. Then came Ace, Illya, Koko and Zokani, followed by Yung, who had a young girl wrapped in his arms. She was the time traveler who helped Joshua get Hunter back.

Behind them came a boy of about Eli's age with stocky features holding the hand of a small girl with auburn curls who was dragging her feet, nodding off so much that the boy had to pick her up and carry her over his shoulder. He looked as though he'd lost someone.

At that moment, Dr. Mark saw the girl and cried out, "Imogen!"

"Daddy?" said the girl sleepily and she turned around in the boy's arms. Mark ran to her, practically wrenching her away, and cradled her against him.

Mark's wife joined them and they hugged their long-lost daughter, crying. It brought tears of joy to Jenny's eyes.

Then, Jenny saw Joshua. Her entire body seemed to lift off the ground as she went running to him. The moment she reached Joshua, she threw her arms around his neck and kissed him. He smelled of ashes and blood. She kissed him again and again, tears spilling from her eyes.

"I'm so glad you're alright," she whispered. "I don't know what I would've done if-"

"I'm fine, Jenny. I'm here. And so are you. I had no idea you'd be here."

"I wouldn't want to be anywhere else," she said.

When she broke away, she looked to the doorway and saw Hunter. It felt like years since her student sat on the edge of her hospital bed in New York. Hunter halted, her eyes going wide, looking at Jenny and then at Eli. She was different to the girl from her physics class. Much older, warped by pain and suffering. Broken, yet strong. She started to choke on a sob as her golden eyes swept from Jenny's to Eli's and back again, so shocked he could do nothing but stand there. Then she looked at Joshua.

"How ... h-how ..."

"Hunter, let me explain-"

"They're *alive*?"

"Yes," Jenny said.

There was a war going on in Hunter's mind, everyone could see it. A battle between the fire and her heart, trying to decide whether to be angry or happy that they were standing there in front of her. In the end it seemed that joy overcame the fury and the hurt. She looked at Eli as tears rolled down her face.

"You're *alive*?"

Eli glanced at Jenny uncertainly. There was obviously no recognition in his eyes. "Uh, yeah. I am."

"Hunter," said Jenny. "Eli suffered memory problems when Joshua woke him up from a cryonics state."

"A what?"

"We need to sit down and talk about this," said Joshua in a tired tone. "I am *so* sorry that I didn't tell you."

Hunter wasn't listening to him. She was gazing at Eli in shock. "You don't remember what, exactly?"

Eli rubbed his arm and shrugged. "Uh, nothing, really."

"Nothing. Your whole life?"

"No. Just … you."

It was so silent in the compound that you could have heard a coyote howl from outside the steel walls a thousand miles away.

Hunter nodded, looking down at her wrist that Jenny noticed was quite swollen. Blood dripped from her other arm under a bandage. When she looked back at Eli, she had to force a smile. And then she ran to him and threw her arms around his neck in the same way that Jenny had with Joshua. Eli was uncomfortable, but Hunter didn't care.

"You have no idea how much I missed you," she muttered.

"No, I … I don't. I'm so sorry."

Hunter pulled back, staring into his eyes, and it was at that point when everyone else seemed to snap back to the present, or else decide to leave Hunter, Eli and Joshua alone to sort things out. From the door, a tall boy carrying a girl in his arms saw Hunter with Eli and confusion clouded his eyes.

"Hunter?" he called. "We should get to medical."

Hunter didn't take her eyes off of Eli, but nodded. Chevie started sending everyone to the hospital wing where Mark and another nurse would conduct health checks.

"Hunter!" called Joshua. He was about to run after her when she turned back and held up a hand.

"Don't," she said. Her tone was not angry, just hurt. Deeply hurt. "Later."

The tall boy urged her to the door where the others were going to the hospital. As soon as they left, Amelia went up to Eli and hugged him. They moved off to talk alone.

Joshua turned her toward him.

"Are you okay?" he asked, gently lifting her chin to meet his gaze.

"Am *I* okay?" she huffed a laugh. "How about you? You just battled God knows how many Agents and you had to watch Hunter discover the truth about me and Eli. It's you I should be worried about."

She planted a gentle kiss on his lips and brushed flakes of blood from his cheek.

"Things could be better," he sighed. "Then again, they could be worse."

"Is everyone alive?"

Joshua shook his head. "We lost two, they lost many more."

Jenny stepped into his arms. "I'm sorry."

"Don't worry about it. It's horrible, but at least we got almost everyone out. Only problem is ... we left valuable things behind. I'm going to see if these people will let us go back to retrieve them."

"What valuable things?"

Joshua pulled her away and muttered in a low voice, "Ravenadium. Plus other files I discovered at the cabin."

"Oh. Well I'm sure they'll let you once everyone is settled in. Did Chevie tell you anything about this place?"

Joshua shook his head and started to step back, but suddenly his knees gave way. Jenny caught him and pushed him to a chair beside one of the computer desks. Joshua was holding his hip, and when he pulled his hand back there was blood over his palm and through his suit shirt.

"What happened?" she gaped. "You're hurt. You need to go see Mark."

Joshua shook his head. "I'm fine, it's just a flesh wound. There are people worse off than me."

Jenny wouldn't hear of it. She took his hand and lifted him up. "Don't be a pansy."

Despite being in pain, Joshua laughed.

THIRTY-SIX

Thumped pigs.

That was the very first thing Eli ever spoke to her about. She remembered the moment so clearly. The chatter of the benefit, the clinking champagne glasses, the array of canapés stretched out before her. She remembered picking up the red onion pork appetizer and having Eli stop her, reminding her in that passionate way of his of the cruelty the animal had suffered. He wore a neat tuxedo, his fringe flipped back in a James Dean wave, his tortoise-shell eyes glinting innocently at her behind his glasses. She remembered that night as the beginning of a friendship that turned her life around.

She remembered it. But he did not.

Hunter sat upright on the gurney of the long hospital room, not sure of where she was or who was stitching the cut Jet made on her neck or what the hell she'd just seen in whatever room they called it. She felt as if she were in a dream. The only sane thing she knew right then was that they had escaped the Agents and Will was sitting on the chair beside her.

"You should definitely rest your wrist for a few weeks," said the plump nurse who looked as though she'd seen her fair share of apple pies. Her smile was wide and warm. "But the X-ray came back fine. You're lucky it didn't break. Stay here overnight and we'll check your stitches tomorrow."

"Thanks," said Hunter.

"No problem. I'm going to be in the other room okay?"

"Sure."

The nurse left. They could hear crying in another part of the hospital wing. Somewhere, Chantal was being operated on by Dr. Mark who was said to be the head of the hospital ward at the compound. Joshua had been led in by Miss Smart just a few minutes ago with a nasty flesh wound. Hunter didn't want to see him just yet. She couldn't feel anything but the throb of her wrist and it was good to concentrate on that.

"You okay?" asked Will.

Hunter slid aside on the bed and he shimmied in beside her. They were both dirty and tired, but somehow they stayed awake, staring at the sink on the opposite wall.

"I honestly don't know. What about Fearne?"

"I don't know either. I saw the Agent inject her with something. I think it was just a sedative so that she wouldn't be able to control his mind, but if they were all there to kill us, why wouldn't he just shoot her?"

She shrugged. "Whatever it was, it had no effect on her. She's alive."

"Still … she was hiding something. I could tell by the way she spoke to them."

"That doesn't sound like her at all." Hunter tipped her head to the side and gave him a smile.

Will lifted a hand and gently combed away the curls over her cheeks. She closed her eyes, tiredly reveling in the touch.

"So that's Eli," Will said.

Just the thought made Hunter's heart start to pound. She couldn't believe it. After so long mourning him, after sitting on the floor of room 23 with his frozen body in her arms, how in God's name was it possible?

"That's Eli," she sighed. "He's different though. I could tell straight away he didn't recognize me."

Will looked at her with those eyes she found so comforting. She was grateful that she had Will. It made everything easier to bear.

"It's not fair that you have to go through this after everything that's happened," he said. "To find out that the one you love doesn't-"

"*Loved.*"

Will peered at her questioningly.

"I was heartbroken when I thought Joshua had killed him. I was angry and distracted. That got me thrown into a van and driven to ICE. It was a dark time, and you want to know what brought me out of it?"

He nodded.

"You," she said. "You reminded me that even when I thought I'd given up, I was still fighting. I just needed someone else to tell me that."

"Yeah," Will sighed. "I'm pretty impressive, aren't I?"

Hunter smiled.

Marcus suddenly appeared before her hospital bed. His eyes were bloodshot and watery. It was him they'd heard crying.

"Hey … you guys don't know where I can find some Kleenex in this place, do you?"

Hunter's heart broke for him. She didn't think about how hard it was for him to lose Mosi. In ICE, they were inseparable.

She pointed to the bank of cupboards on the opposite wall. "There's some over there."

"Thanks," he said and drew Kleenexes from the box.

"Hey, I'm really sorry Marcus."

After blowing his nose for a few seconds, he shrugged in that falsely nonchalant way guys do when they're trying to hide their misery. "Don't be. It gives me an excuse to kick even more ass the next time we see Wolfe."

Will and Hunter nodded and Marcus walked off the way he came in. Hunter looked at Will, the two of them held in each other's gaze for a long time. Even though he was immortal, it terrified her to imagine the sight of him being torn apart like Mosi and never put back together again. What if it had been him lying against the tree where they had left Benji's body? What if the Agents had taken him back?

Sensing her fear, Will slipped his hand into hers. It was the first time he'd made a move since the evening they sat on the hill at the cabin and stared out at the setting sun. All it took was a life or death situation for them to stop kidding themselves, for it to be real and not something they should be afraid of. Not wanting to lose the feel of his skin on hers, she held his hand tightly.

Tears began to pour from her eyes. She couldn't stop them. Will rubbed his thumb gently against her skin and she let her head rest on his shoulder as he mumbled that it would all be okay.

THIRTY-SEVEN

Help! Somebody help!"

Hunter snapped awake at the sound of Will's voice. She flipped the rug off her body and wrenched away the curtain. A group of men and women carried a young girl into the hospital wing.

A young girl with blond hair.

Hunter's heart started to beat with the pace of sprinter. They rested Fearne's body on the spare bed. Dr. Mark was there, and Joshua. Will stood beside the bed, holding her hand as she frothed at the mouth. There was something in her veins like a dark, green poison spreading through her body.

"What's happening to her?" shouted Will.

Hunter stood back as though in a dream. She wanted to help, but there was nothing she could do. Others were standing around in panic, including Chevie from the jet.

Dr. Mark held his stethoscope against Fearne's chest and rested a hand on her forehead. "Turn her on her side," he ordered.

Will and Joshua helped. More people crowded around as Fearne started choking.

"Tell me what's happening to her!" Will shouted. Hunter hadn't heard him so panicked since the night she seized in the cabin, and that frightened her more than the distorted scene before her.

Dr. Mark looked at Joshua. "We need to run a rest. Something has poisoned her. Okay, I need everyone out of this room who is not a qualified doctor, a scientist or a patient. Now!"

The crowd cleared. Will refused to leave Fearne's side, so Hunter took his arm and tried to pull him from the room.

"Let them fix her," she said gently.

"No-" He wrenched his arm from hers. "I can fix her, my blood can fix her!"

"Son, until we know what this is, we can't determine a solution. You need to leave and let me do my job," said Mark. A nurse whipped past them. Mark asked her to take a blood sample.

Hunter met Joshua's eyes. *Save her,* she begged him. He understood and gave a curt nod.

"Come on," Hunter urged. At that point, Will let her.

Once they were out in the hall, Will started pacing, clenching his fists. A moment later, he threw a punch into the steel wall, the sound making her jump more than the sickening crunch of his hand.

Will's wrist snapped in half, the bone jutting out like a red iceberg. His face contorted in pain as he pushed the bone back beneath his skin, groaning loudly. The wound started to seal seconds later.

"Did that help?" she asked him.

Will met her eyes. "For a second, yeah."

"Don't worry, they'll make her-"

"What if they don't? Hunter, what if this is the effect of whatever the Agent injected her with?"

Hunter didn't answer. Will sunk down against the wall, cradling his healing wrist. She walked over to him and sat down.

"Don't you think we've been through enough?" he asked her. "After all the suffering in ICE, we had a few *days* of freedom only to lose two of our friends at once? And now Fearne as well?"

Hunter stared at the wall, not wanting to admit how differently they saw things. So much had changed since she left ICE. People had come and gone. A part of her didn't want to accept the death of Mosi and Benji, or the possibility of Fearne's passing, because death was not the end for her. She had just been reunited with her father, her teacher and the love of her life all in the space of a week.

So she did the only thing she could do to comfort him. She took his hand, she held it, and sat with him as he had with her earlier, and every time before that when they needed each other most of all.

THIRTY-EIGHT

Olivia, hand me that tube will you?"

Mark and his wife Olivia – who looked about twenty years younger than her husband – calmly worked on Fearne's body for a solution to her bizarre illness. Only minutes ago, the seizure had stopped. Her body still felt hot. Joshua stood at the foot of the bed with his hand over his mouth. He had his suspicions already and they terrified him.

Memories were bouncing back into his mind. Memories of Liz as she described the surgery with the homeless man. Amidst these suspicions of Fearne's illness was a different kind of panic – that this SSS place had something to do with it all.

Suddenly he was certain something wasn't right. He knew this man, from a different time, a different life.

"Dr. Mark," said Joshua softly, "from New York Downtown hospital."

Mark frowned. "How do you know that?"

"We only met once. I never forget a face though." Joshua peered at Fearne. "You know what's wrong with her, don't you?"

Mark's face went white. "I don't know what you're talking about."

"I knew there was something off about this place," said Joshua. A familiarly cold and dark feeling was spreading through his veins. After everything that happened at the cabin and the way Hunter looked at him after finding out the truth, Joshua had felt his control start to come undone.

The Iceman was emerging from his icy cage once more. If he wasn't careful, he may lose it.

But right then, he didn't care. He stormed up to Mark, grabbing him by the collar and forcing him back against the wall. Olivia gasped in shock. Joshua's fingertips went cool and iced over. He had to admit, he found some pleasure in the look of total fear on Mark's face. The last time he saw the man, he had his disgusting eyes all over Liz the way that hungry men do over beautiful women.

"Tell me everything you know about Feucotetanus."

Mark shot a glance at Olivia. "Could you give us a minute, honey?"

"No," she said.

"Olivia," Mark urged her.

Olivia hesitated, then left the wing. They were alone with Fearne's still body.

Joshua shoved him hard and let go. Mark brushed his coat down and eyed Joshua warily.

"I used to think medicine was black and white," said Mark. "Until a homeless man came into the hospital twenty years ago and that same night, a friend of mine disappeared. A fire killed her husband, but Liz survived. I thought it was strange that she suddenly quit the hospital and left the country, never to return. She was never the type of person to give up helping people, even if her husband died."

"That's because that night changed everything."

Mark's blue eyes suddenly widened. "Joshua ... Joshua *Harrison*?"

"I would say it's good to see you, but it's not."

"Yeah, I was kind of a dick to you."

"You can make up for it by explaining how you found Feucotetanus."

"Feucotetanus." Mark shook his head. "It was *some* drug. I first heard the term when I was studying in the UK. The hospital I worked at was testing a new drug on patients and ... it didn't go well. Said it came from Sweden and they had to send it back. Then it came up on our system because I bought some samples back for my studies and I recognized the formula in the blood of the homeless man. I couldn't believe it. After the fire at Liz's apartment, I started wondering if this drug had anything to do with Liz disappearing. The cops never discovered the drug and closed the case."

"How do you know that?"

"My brother is a detective. Anyway, I found nothing after the laboratory in Sweden was destroyed. I married Olivia and we travelled for a few years. Life got in the way."

"How did you end up here then?"

"Five years ago, our son was killed and Imogen was taken by Agents in the same month. We had nowhere else to go. We knew about Imogen's powers, and we reached out to the SSS. I've been a doctor here ever since."

"Then you know how to save her?"

Mark looked at Fearne. "All I know is that Feucotetanus has poisoned her. If there is some kind of cure for Feucotetanus, I don't know of it."

Joshua ran a hand over his face. He let out a long sigh and said, "I do. I know of a cure."

Mark gazed at him. "What is it?"

"It's called Ravenadium." Joshua reached into his pocket for the stone. "It's-"

He froze. His heart nearly leapt out of his chest. His pocket was empty.

Joshua looked around him. He'd kept the stone in his pocket ever since Hunter gave it to him in the jet.

"It's gone," he said. "The stone is gone."

Mark looked at Joshua and then his expression turned wary. "Is Ravenadium a cure for Feucotetanus?"

Joshua nodded. "If a person has the right genetic code, yes, it is."

Mark groaned. "Chevie ..."

"What?"

"Chevie took it," said Mark. "He's going to try to save his father with it."

Joshua had no time to question how or why that was even possible. He grabbed Mark by the collar again and shook him.

"That stone is the only thing that will save Fearne. *Where is Chevie!?*"

Mark nodded. "Follow me. I'll explain on the way."

THIRTY-NINE

his side of the SSS compound had always been quiet.
Everywhere else was filled with comic book geeks and
soldiers and scientists, and now the new arrivals. No one
came down to Ward E, where they stored the old projects
and things they kept for emergencies.

That was where his father had been for seven months now, on the verge
of death. They were fussing upstairs over some twelve-year-old girl who'd
been poisoned, completely unaware of the life still hanging on the line far
below them.

Chevie stood over the body of his dying father, angry at himself for not
finding the cure.

Until now, that is. He held in his hands a stone Joshua had called
Ravenadium. Joshua didn't see him slip his hand into his pocket in the
chaos of the hospital room and disappear with the stone.

When Hunter went back for Ravenadium, Chevie knew there was
something special about it. Joshua clung to it in the jet and gave Chevie a
look that confirmed his suspicions; this stone was worth risking lives over.
It had to have some kind of power, and that would ultimately help him save
his father.

Alistair once warned Chevie not to use his power for evil. Chevie
listened. It might've taken him a while to accept his responsibility, but when
his father sacrificed himself to give Chevie freedom from ICE, he had to
find a way to repay him.

"I'm going to heal you Dad," he said while he pulled the rolling trolley of instruments under the light and sat down beside his father's twitching body. "This substance will make you better."

Chevie's enhanced intelligence made it easy for him to calculate the most appropriate way to open the stone, extract the substance and inject it into his father's blood. Chevie and Mark had been observing his father's illness over the past few months. When Alistair was let go from ICE for helping Chevie escape, he didn't realize his body had been infected by Feucotetanus. Only it wasn't the same as the homeless man in the hospital, Mark had said. He'd not seen this type of illness before. It had the symptoms of pneumonia, but he'd said Alistair would have been dead by now. He was fighting the illness. Something in his blood was counter-reacting to the poison.

I could be wrong, but this stone has to have something to do with the way we all have powers. Chevie held the stone and looked for some kind of crevice. And as he did, he heard whispers. Whispers that spoke his name. Chills went down his spine. The stone was talking to him, calling out to his soul as though he was connected to it.

Chevie knew he was close. He held the stone, using a tiny drill to pierce a hole in the surface. It was a delicate piece of work, but he had to be quick.

Moments later, someone thumped against the door and when he looked behind him, he saw Joshua and Mark's face in the frosted glass window. He'd disabled the coded panel and locked the door. No one could get in, unless by force.

He pushed harder on the stone.

"Chevie, open this door NOW!" yelled Mark.

"I have to save him!" he shouted back.

"Chevie listen to me," said Joshua, "What you're about to do could have serious consequences. If your father's genetic spiral is closed, his body won't react to the Ravenadium."

"What are you talking about?"

"It only works on certain people with a specific genetic code. Unless I test your father's DNA first, we don't know what this could do to him."

His heart beat faster. *It has to work, he doesn't have long!*

"Plus you're wasting our only-"

Chevie was so panicked that his hands fumbled with the stone and it slipped from his grasp, rolling off the table and onto the ground where it cracked open and spilled liquid lava across the linoleum floor of the hospital room.

Chevie's world stopped. He stared at the bright substance, listening to the strange voice that whispered to him. He suddenly felt as though every hair on his skin was standing up and he was under the control of some form of electricity. The lava bubbled, wiggling back and forth across the ground, looking for something – or someone – to feed on. Chevie was so fascinated that he didn't hear a crackling coming from the door until it burst open in a spray of ice and Mark and Joshua fell into the room. The moment they saw the puddle of lava on the floor, they both froze.

"Chevie, what is that?" asked Mark.

"That's Ravenadium," Joshua whispered. The look on his face told Chevie he'd done something he shouldn't have. But it was too late now.

"I have to save him," said Chevie. He started to reach down with a syringe to extract a sample when suddenly, two things happened.

Joshua shouted "no!" and leapt for Chevie.

And the glowing pool of Ravenadium started to move. It moved so fast that Chevie couldn't catch it. The three of them watched in awe as the snake-like substance crawled up the bed poles and attached itself to the knitted rug that covered Alistair's body. His father stopped twitching the moment Ravenadium touched him. It burned holes in the quilt, seeping into Alistair's skin until he glowed. But it didn't appear to burn him. Chevie held his breath, not knowing whether he should be trying to save his father from whatever the hell this *thing* was, or pray that it was doing its job.

And then, Alistair woke up. Not quietly, either. His eyes burst open. He gasped, his body shooting upright as his hands gripped the railing on his hospital bed.

And right before their eyes, Alistair's withered, tired old body started to change. His gray hair turned to brown, the shade it used to be when Chevie was a boy. His skin gained color, the wrinkles fading away. In just the space of a few seconds, he no longer looked eighty-five, but forty-five. He was Chevie's healthy, strong father again. Tears blurred Chevie's eyes but he was too shocked to move. Dr. Mark swore under his breath and Joshua walked slowly toward Alistair with his eyes wide and expectant.

Alistair smiled, and it made Chevie's heart flip. Not caring that he looked like a blubbering mess, Chevie closed the distance between them and flung his arms around his father.

Alistair laughed, heartily and loudly. "Chev," he said. "It's good to see you, son."

"I thought … I thought I'd lost you forever."

"Not without a fight, m'boy."

Chevie pulled away. He looked into the eyes of the man he hated for disappearing when he was a kid, only to help him escape ICE and start his life again. He couldn't believe that after seven endless months, his father was not only alive, but young and healthy again.

"How do you feel?" asked Joshua.

Alistair turned to him. "Sorry, who are you?"

"Joshua," he replied. "I'm the man who found the substance that cured you."

"I'm not sure I'm cured yet," said Alistair.

"Well … do you feel different?"

"Yeah, I feel alive."

Chevie grinned at his father. When he turned back to Joshua, he could see the anger freezing his cold blue eyes.

"Good for you," spat Joshua, speaking directly to Chevie. "Now we have no chance of saving a little girl from being poisoned."

"What is he talking about Chev?"

At that very second, the Captain and his soldiers appeared inside the room with their guns raised. Chevie looked at Joshua and Mark with a betrayed glare as he lifted his hands.

"What the bloody hell is going on here?" called the Captain.

"Arrest him," said Joshua. "He stole from me the last sample of Ravenadium we have to resurrect his father. Now we can't save a little girl from dying."

Chevie looked at his father. If there was one thing worse than the knowledge that he had, indeed, sentenced a young girl to die, it was the disappointment he knew he would receive from Alistair.

But there was no disappointment on his face. "We do crazy things for the people we love, son. I certainly did. Don't be ashamed of the choices you make. When it comes to family, we do what it takes to stay together. Whatever you did, I'll still be proud of you."

Chevie nodded. "I love you dad."

"Alright, enough," the Captain growled. "Mark, what do you say?"

"Chevie needs to be taken into custody to await a trial from the society, according to our rules."

"Rules I made," said Chevie as two soldiers moved to his side to cuff his hands behind his back. "I built this society!"

"That's no excuse," said Mark.

"Now wait a minute," said Alistair as he made to jump off the bed. One of the soldiers must have taken this as a form of attack and raised his fist to knock him down.

Then, something extraordinary happened. Alistair reacted quicker than any normal human being, taking the soldier's arm and shoving him to the side. Only the soldier – a man built of steel and muscle – did not just stumble backwards. He went soaring across the room into the concrete wall, fell in a heap on the floor and left a decent-sized wedge in his place.

Chevie could not believe his eyes.

"Dad," he muttered. "It worked. You-"

"Have an ability?" Alistair huffed a bewildered laugh. "Didn't see that coming."

FORTY

J ack peered through the lookout room atop the massive hanger where the Chinese aircraft was rolling in. Outside, the rain poured and the wind screamed but he heard nothing behind the glass. He was on his own, told to watch from a room full of computers and old files while Dr. Wolfe met with the General and his men as they marched out of the military aircraft. There were dozens of them. They were all there for war.

Jack didn't care for the Chinese. They saw him not as a person, but as an object of destruction. Though that was what he had become, Jack didn't like to be a possession in their mind. What they didn't realize was that he could crush every one of their bodies with a blink of his eye if he wanted to.

The General and Dr. Wolfe talked in the hanger for a long time, and Jack became bored. It was never a good thing for him to be bored. He let the voices in his mind overpower him, tell him to destroy things, to listen to the darkness.

He started rifling through the filing cabinets in the office. One was filled with papers and printouts of dull things he didn't care about. Another had rows of discs. They were numerically categorized and Jack couldn't figure out the significance, until he saw a name printed on one near the back.

Hunter Harrison – 11/10/2014

That was only a couple of weeks ago. Jack slipped the disc from its case and sat down at one of the desks. During quiet times like this, his body was at normal size, though if he looked at his reflection in the glass he could see black eyes and thick, dark veins pumping through his body. Ironically, that was the darkness. It was a part of him now.

The images on the screen were of the Death Caves where Dr. Wolfe kept Hunter and her friend Will. Jack didn't know why – perhaps they were being punished. She was walking through the door with two guards behind her. She looked different, brighter. Her mouth was moving, and as Jack tried to turn up the volume on the computer screen, she exploded. Fire burned in her hair and she started sprinting toward the camera. Hands stuck out of all of the cells. She reached one and grabbed hold of it. Jack twisted the volume knob.

"He's alive!" she screamed.

"Who's alive?" came the response.

"My dad, Will, my dad is alive!"

Jack frowned. He had no idea what she was talking about, but something in her voice, something about the way she lit up – even with a power restraint – engrossed him. He watched her shout at the Men in White, laugh, smile and jump around as if she'd never been happier. And the fire … it burst from her in crazy sparks, flames twisting around her, and before the guards could draw their tasers, the corridor lit up in light. And it wasn't a fire that burned, it was a fire that freed.

Suddenly, Jack started to become dizzy. He looked away from the bright screen, closed his eyes, and found himself remembering things.

A scream in the distance.

The smell of books.

A pencil.

Smoke, heat, fire …

Hunter.

Jack's eyes flew open. He was back in the quiet control room. The video had ended and the screen was blank. He'd been in some kind of unconsciousness long enough for the computer to move to screen saver mode.

What the hell happened to me?

Jack was so frustrated, not only with the feelings of warmth and longing that had so briefly tried to form inside him again that he lifted the swivel chair he'd been sitting on and threw it against the glass where it shattered to a billion pieces and the chair went soaring down into the hanger below. He huffed and walked across the glass to the edge, looking down into the empty hanger. The Chinese and Dr. Wolfe were gone.

She left you to die ... said the voice in his mind. *She doesn't deserve sympathy or remorse. She deserves pain.*

Whatever had just occurred, he would forget about it. He would forget about Hunter and the fact that she was to blame for his transformation, and he would forget about any connection they had in the past. He was different now, and there was no turning back. In three days' time, he was going to destroy the world. And no memory of a library and a fire was going to stand in his way.

FORTY-ONE

Joshua stormed through the corridors of this bizarre military safe house he'd somehow stumbled into. So much had happened in such a short amount of time, and the anger building inside him was freezing over his heart and making him afraid. He had to stop Fearne from dying. He had to find another way to save her now that their last sample had just been used to give an old man super strength.

He knocked hard on the door that was said to be Ryo's room. She opened up with a sleepy look on her face.

"I need your help," he said.

"I'll take you," she agreed once he'd told her everything. Ryo's normally perky, inquisitive face was sagging and tired, but she was determined to remain strong. "If it'll save Fearne."

Joshua nodded. "Thank you Ryo."

"It has to be quick," she said, taking his hand. "This is dangerous, and a long trip."

"What do you mean?"

"The last time I teleported another person, it was Hunter, and I nearly lost my location. It was lucky I recovered so quickly. I haven't done so much teleporting before. Tonight was also the first time I used my power in battle and ... I wasn't quick enough to save Benji."

Joshua stared at her sadly, taking a moment to pull himself together. "I believe you can do this Ryo. You're one of the strongest people I know, no matter how young you are."

Ryo bit her lip and nodded. "Alright. Hold on."

Joshua hadn't teleported with Ryo before, and it was one of the strangest and most unsettling feelings he'd ever experienced. When he felt the ground beneath his feet and the colors formed actual objects, bile rose in his throat and he ran to the sink in the dark cabin, hurling the contents of his stomach into it.

"Jeez, you're the first person to throw up." Ryo walked to the wall beside the staircase where a pool of blood had started to dry up, and two more were in the entryway. "What happened here?"

Wiping his mouth over, Joshua peered at the empty cabin, hoping they were alone. He noticed a trail of blood coming from the doors leading to the lake. They passed the splat of blood on the wall where someone was clearly shot. The stains matched the story Will told about what happened inside, only there were extra sets of footprints in the blood and darker patterns across the walkway.

"I don't know," said Joshua as he tried hard to fight the motion sickness in his stomach. Blood and bodies he could handle, but rollercoaster rides made him dizzy. "We'd better get out of here quickly. We can't waste time trying to follow blood trails."

"Wait, look-" Something metallic caught Ryo's eye next to the sofa. She scooped up an empty syringe and brought it back to him. He held it carefully, inspecting the canister. At once, he knew that this was what the Agents used to inject Fearne. There were a few drops left, which would allow him to test the liquid and possibly match Ravenadium to the solution if he had the time, and if there was still a sample left.

I might actually be able to save her.

Joshua ran up the stairs with Ryo on his heels and threw open the door to the office. Immediately, his heart leapt into his chest.

It was a complete mess. There was blood smeared over the furniture and on the papers and files Joshua had sorted through.

Ryo gasped. "It wasn't like this when we left it! Hunter dropped the briefcase and it …"

Joshua fell to his knees and patted around under the desk.

"Did you see any more stones?"

Ryo gripped her hair and shook her head. "I ... I don't remember, I think something rolled over toward the bookshelf but I didn't think it was important-"

"It's not here. The last stone, it's not here." He moved to the desk and rifled through the papers. "All of the files are gone as well."

"How?"

Joshua threw books from the shelves in search of anything that could resemble a clue or an answer but found nothing. Someone had been in there. Someone who wasn't one of them.

"Agents. They took the one thing that was going to save Fearne's life, and if it's Dr. Wolfe who has it now ... we just handed him the most powerful weapon in the universe."

FORTY-TWO

I t had been a very long night, but Joshua couldn't sleep. He and Ryo returned safely to the SSS compound, after which Ryo passed out and he let her angry brother take care of her. Joshua took the empty canister down to the hospital and Mark led him to a lab of sorts where he could run tests on it. It was lucky they had lots of resources and equipment there, or Joshua wouldn't have been able to try.

Joshua didn't know much about creating cures for poison, and it pained him to admit it. The only person he knew who might be able to help was someone he never wanted to speak to again.

But if there was a chance he could save Fearne, he'd do anything.

Mark told Joshua that they arrested both Alistair and Chevie and put them in containment where Mikayla was locked up. Alistair felt guilty about what he did to the soldier and didn't want to fight them, but Chevie was less enthusiastic. Regardless, they were both detained and Joshua asked a member of the SSS where he could find them. There were so many corridors within the compound that Joshua's head spun. Carrying a microscope, a laptop and anything else he could, he went into the containment ward and asked the security guard to let him in to see Chevie.

Joshua felt himself become cold at the sight of the man sitting on the ground in his cell. It was a well-furnished room, unlike those at ICE. Chevie looked up with a smile on his face.

"Can I help you?" he asked.

Joshua snorted and put his equipment down on the desk. "I don't know, can you?"

"I know it may seem like I'm this … Prince Charming character, but looks can be deceiving. I know a lot about a lot of things. It's kind of my power."

"Oh really? I thought your power was fucking everyone over for your own selfish reasons."

Chevie chuckled. "You'd know all about that, wouldn't you Joshua?"

For a moment, Joshua looked away from his microscope and stared at Chevie. He used to think he was good at reading people. Most of them are either good or evil, and those in between hadn't decided where to turn to just yet. But Chevie was different. He knew more than he let on, but for everyone else he put on a show and pretended to wear his heart on his sleeve. How much did he really know?

But despite being furious with Chevie, Joshua suddenly realized he was right. If anyone knew the reason behind Chevie's actions, it was Joshua. Chevie did everything he could to save his father, his *family*, even if it meant sacrificing someone else. Joshua had sacrificed Jenny, Eli and Jack to keep Hunter's secret.

That didn't stop him from being angry.

"You don't know what people will think of you when they find out," said Joshua. "They'll never forgive you."

Chevie nodded. "I know. That's why my father and I are leaving tomorrow."

"You're escaping your own compound?" He shook his head. "I don't think I've ever known a more cowardly act."

"You don't need me and my father here to remind you of what you lost. I'll stay for the funeral, but after that they'll likely put me on trial. I personally don't believe we deserve a trial. I did what I had to do, and it worked. I thought I'd be allowed at least some sympathy after I practically created this place, but I guess I'm not as valued as I thought. I have no other choice."

"We don't get to quit," said Joshua. "If you make a mistake, you do everything you can to make things right. You earn your forgiveness. I learned that the hard way."

Chevie looked pained for just a moment, then he got to his feet and brushed away the dust from his hands. "You're not here to interrogate me, are you?"

"Wow, you really are intelligent," spat Joshua.

"I want to help you try to save Fearne. It's the least I can do."

He tapped the microscope and wiped his hand over his face. "Go nuts."

Chevie sat down at the desk and leant his eye on the nozzle, twisting the dial and gazing into the lens for only three seconds before flipping open the laptop and quickly typing up a formula. A list of possible analysis began to upload on the side of the screen. "This poison is definitely a toxin, derived from a bacteria ..."

"Feucotetanus?"

Chevie shook his head. "I thought so at first, but it's not the same symptoms. I believe it's a form of poison mixed with Feucotetanus. That makes it deadly. You may be able to fight the bacteria-"

"Tried that. The poison kills the antidote."

"And it has already spread through her cells. I'll keep looking, but ... we may already be too late."

Joshua watched him type, wondering how he stayed close to sane after what he'd just done. Joshua went mad with guilt, but he was so casual. He stared at Chevie, not realizing exactly how bitter his expression was until Chevie glanced at him and managed to smile sadly.

"My dad once told me that I was chosen to have powers and that what I do with my life either honors that choice or destroys it. And when I was released, I was so messed up that I ran away and used my power to become one of the best poker players in the country. But it never filled the hole inside me. I was empty, and I couldn't escape the guilt of how I had disappointed my father." He chuckled to himself. "Amelia reminded me that whatever I did in the past, whatever circumstances I blamed myself for, I can always start a new page. It doesn't mean that the past becomes erased, it just means that we get to write a newer, better version of our lives. And before I found the SSS, I realized that I had to start using my powers not only to help people, but to help my father."

"That's a touching story," said Joshua. "But it doesn't save Fearne."

"That's my point," he grinned. "Whether we save lives or destroy them, we were chosen for a reason. May as well stop blaming ourselves for not being perfect and just keep fighting."

Chevie continued to work and Joshua watched him feeling his eyes slowly start to droop closed. He didn't want to be alone and unconscious with Chevie – still unable to trust him – but the night's events were drowning him in exhaustion and sure enough, he couldn't stay awake anymore.

While Chevie sat bent over the microscope, he fell into a dream.

Joshua found himself sitting in a green field surrounded by trees. In the distance he thought he saw a collection of camper vans and soft music, a pillar of smoke rising into the beautiful blue sky splattered with clouds above him.

"I was born here," said a voice. He looked down and saw Fearne. She lay beside him on the grass in a pale-pink dress, her hair tied back with a ribbon, the sun glittering in her green eyes.

"Fearne," said Joshua. "This is a dream?"

She nodded.

"And you're …"

"Dying? Yeah. I'm sorry to put you through this, to put everyone through it. I just knew it was safer this way. My power is more dangerous than Dr. Wolfe himself and one day, I could go under like you or Hunter or Jack and … I may never come out."

"You can fight it. I'll teach you."

She smiled and shook her head. "I'm sorry Joshua. I can't take that risk. Please don't tell Hunter or Will that I let the Agents inject me, that I didn't fight my power like you and Hunter did. Will, of all people, would be heartbroken."

Joshua nodded. He could take the blame for it, Will already hated him.

"No, do *not* take the blame for this," she said in such a forceful tone that he couldn't resist nodding. Even in the dream she could read his mind. "This isn't your fault. Stop beating yourself up for everything bad that happens and start forgiving yourself."

Joshua's throat started to clog up. He looked down at Fearne and wished he knew her better, wished he helped them escape from ICE earlier, wished he did everything he could to save them. But she was right. The hardest part about all of this was forgiving himself and, like Chevie said, to keep fighting. He couldn't believe the man actually made sense.

"You really don't trust him," she stated.

"Do you think I should?"

Fearne pursed her lips and said, "I think you should try and see both sides. What Chevie did to save his father was both selfish and sacrificial. We all make choices to save those we love, and sometimes those choices affect others. Yours did." Fearne smiled and let her head flop back, closing her eyes. "I miss this place. I miss the smell of the meadow and the campfire. I miss my mother calling out to me and braiding my hair with flowers and singing and dancing."

"You didn't deserve imprisonment, Fearne. You were too young, you had too much potential."

"I was needed somewhere else," she said happily. "But I'm not needed anymore."

"You will always be needed," he said. "Especially with Will. You were there for him when I wasn't. You're his family."

"He has a new family now. And he has Hunter. Will only ever opened up to me, but … the moment he saw Hunter I knew, without having to read his mind, that she was the one for him." She gazed out at the meadow, tears in her eyes. It broke his heart. "Do me one last favor?"

Joshua couldn't do anything but nod.

"Just … be there for Hunter. Don't lose yourself to the Iceman because you're trying to protect her, you'll only get yourself killed. What she needs now, more than anything, is a father."

Joshua thought of the promise he made to Liz and how he had lived his life by it. He wasn't sure he could let that go and just be a father to her.

Fearne grinned. "You always *were*, Joshua. Since the day she was born, you were there for her. No one else was. Just you. You have to believe in yourself."

"I'll do my best," he said.

"Thank you. Oh, and … make sure Will knows that I love him. One day he'll understand that what I did was the right thing. But until then, make sure he knows I love him to the moon and back. Tell him that."

"Absolutely. I promise."

Joshua felt the grass in his fingers and the peacefulness in the air, watching the way the wind rippled through Fearne's hair and her little cheeks flush with warmth.

"Please stay with me until it's over?" she asked.

"I'll probably get sunburnt soon."

Fearne giggled. "Not in my dream."

They relaxed in the meadow, pretending reality was non-existent and the sun and summer breeze was all there was in the world until Joshua could feel her fading and when he looked to his left, she was gone.

FORTY-THREE

Joshua approached them what felt like only minutes later to deliver the verdict. Hunter and Will woke up stiff from leaning over Fearne's now still body and stood, waiting like parents in a hospital for news that their child was alive.

Joshua looked as if he hadn't slept for a week. His shirt was still covered in blood and he slumped, not his usual OCD self. Hunter tried to forget about their earlier conversation; there was still a lot to talk about without the current drama to deal with.

"What is it?" she asked.

He motioned for them to follow him outside into the corridor. "It's a toxin," he said and ran a hand through his hair. "A rare one. It doesn't give her long to live, and it's designed with only one cure."

Will's face went white. "M-me, I'm the cure."

Joshua frowned. "I'm sorry Will, I don't think your blood is-"

"Bullshit," he hissed. "My blood will heal everything!"

"Not in this case," said Joshua.

"What? Why?"

He let out a sigh. "The toxin was derived from Feucotetanus."

"How-"

"The only answer to curing Fearne's disease is with Ravenadium. But … we don't have a sample."

Hunter frowned. "What happened to the one I found?"

"It's gone. Chevie stole it and used it to bring his father back to life."

Hunter and Will were so shocked that they didn't move, standing there like statues. And then, at almost the exact same time, they started to get extremely angry. Hunter's body pulsed a bright, orange glow and Will's muscles clenched as he breathed heavily. Joshua forced the air to cool so that they would both relax, but it did no good.

"He did *what*?" Hunter hissed.

"I don't care who he is," said Will through his teeth, "I'm going to kill him."

Joshua raised his hands. "We can be angry at him all we want, but that won't bring her back."

"She's not dead yet," Will growled.

"Can we go to the cabin to see if the sample is still there?"

"Already did," said Joshua. "It's gone."

Hunter looked suddenly dizzy and leant against the wall. She put her head in her hands. "Dr. Wolfe has Ravenadium?"

Joshua nodded.

"Holy shit, we're all dead."

"Wait," said Will, "why is this stuff the cure to Fearne's sickness?"

"Hunter, you know what happened when Feucotetanus fused with Ravenadium?" asked Joshua.

"It created my powers, and yours."

"Correct. I thought that by dosing her with straight Ravenadium, it would heal her by boosting her powers and killing the infection in her system. It would be a risk, but the only safe option we have. Giving Fearne *Will's* blood will fuse with this new toxin and Fearne's already unique formula for her abilities. It would take me years to research the effects, and we don't have the time."

"Then we do it anyway," said Will. "If you don't have a cure for her, then there's nothing else for us to do. We have to save her!"

Joshua tried again to explain the repercussions, but Will only yelled louder and nothing Joshua said or did could calm him until –

"Stop!"

They turned to Hunter, whose palms were on fire. As soon as they paused, she pulled the flame back inside her skin and sighed.

"Dr. Wolfe would rather her be dead than an asset to us. He did this so that we couldn't use her. She was the most powerful weapon we had."

"*Have*," Will spat and shoved Joshua in the shoulder as he passed, stalking back into the hospital wing.

"He's going to do anything he can to save her," said Hunter. "You should at least let him try."

Joshua turned and put his back to the wall. He was exhausted. "I can't fix her. Trust me ... it's over."

Hunter didn't much want to talk to Joshua anymore. A part of her – the fire and its fury – wanted to scream at him for keeping the secret of Eli and Miss Smart from her for so long, for not telling her that the former love of her life was actually alive. Her skin started to glow the more she let the anger get to her. But then she looked down at the broken man before her and it reminded her of the warehouse.

I walked away from him once. I won't do it again. He's put too much at risk for me this time.

So Hunter sat down beside Joshua, just as she had done with Will.

"We both came back from our powers overcoming us," said Joshua. "But Fearne's power is so damaging and so dangerous, that in the wrong hands, she could be the end of the world. She knows it."

"But ... I beat the fire. I learned to control it. Why can't Fearne be the same?"

Joshua almost smiled. "Because she doesn't *want* to, Hunter. She can't risk the consequences. I don't know anyone in this lifetime who would rather give up their chance at happiness at the chance that she could be a poison in this world. That is truly brave."

Hunter lowered her head and tears spilled from her eyes. Fearne was a true hero. But Will could never know that she had given her life for it.

"I'm so sorry that I didn't tell you about Eli and Jenny."

Hunter raised an eyebrow at him. "Jenny?"

His cheeks filled with color. "She ... she prefers Jenny. It's a beautiful name."

For a moment, Hunter couldn't believe it. She'd never seen Joshua act this way.

"Wow, not the forty-three-year-old virgin anymore, eh?"

Joshua smiled, his pale eyes glistening with something she hadn't ever seen in them before. It was a completely new Joshua.

"Oh my God," she whispered. "You love her."

"I … I don't know. I've never felt this way before about a woman. Except … except Liz."

Hunter put a hand over Joshua's, the strange feeling of ice beneath her fingers like a familiar smell or a memory.

"I want to forgive you Joshua," she said. "But I need you to promise me that we don't have to go through this again."

He nodded, sniffed and met her eyes. "I'll try my hardest. You should know by now that I'm not a perfect man."

"Neither am I. A woman, that is."

He chuckled.

"I know you've done everything you can for Fearne."

"I wish it were enough. But there's nothing more I can do. You should go back to your bed and rest."

Hunter wasn't yet ready to accept that there was no hope left. It was the hardest thing she'd ever had to do.

"You should rest too," she said. "You've done all you can, and it's more than any of us."

"No, I have more work to do." He winced as he stood up, holding his hip. Hunter made to help him, but he smiled down at her "Don't worry about me."

Hunter nodded and went into the hospital wing. Will was standing beside Fearne's bed. He had a syringe in his hand and was trying to find the vein in his arm.

Hunter rushed forward. "Will, what are you doing?!"

"I'm saving her."

"You can't-" He and Hunter wrestled with the syringe as she tried to pull it away from him. "Didn't you hear what Joshua said?!"

Will shoved her away so hard that she skidded back against the bank of cupboards and knocked her head on the handle. She stopped, her mouth open. She gazed at Will, on the verge of losing his sanity. They say that men become monsters when those they love are in danger of dying. This could easily be said for Joshua. But Will was not a monster, just broken and desperate to hold on to the girl who was there for him all his life.

"In ICE, Dr. Wolfe used Mikayla's blood to stop my power from working," he said. "If her power works in my system, then my power will work in Fearne's. If she's going to d-" He grit his teeth and couldn't bring himself to say the word. "I have *nothing* left to lose."

She stayed silent for a moment. There was no changing his mind unless she forced him to stop, and he may never forgive her for that. Her only option was to help him.

Hunter strode forward and turned on the second monitor for her bed beside Fearne's. "You're doing it wrong," she said. "You need to be monitored just in case your blood reacts to hers. And you suck at finding the vein."

Will let her fix it to a catheter and inject the needle, his eyes never leaving Fearne. But as soon as she asked him to sit back and let the transfusion take place, he grabbed Hunter's hand.

"Thank you," he said. It broke her heart to hear the quiver of fear in his voice that he may actually lose her. "She'll pull through this. I know she will."

Fearne was asleep, her skin paler than snow and the black veins pumping through her blood as they consumed her.

Hunter couldn't look at them anymore. She said goodnight, crawled into her bed on the other side of the curtain and tried to ignore the sound of Will's sobs as they cut into her heart.

FORTY-FOUR

Will didn't really sleep. Every time his eyes drooped shut, he forced them open again. Every time he heard voices, he jumped and turned to her body, praying it was Fearne speaking to him. But it was only a nurse on her night shift checking the injured.

The transfusion hadn't worked. Will tore the needle from his arm and threw it to the ground, ignoring the gash he'd opened up and the fact that Joshua was right. He didn't understand. She should have healed.

Fearne's hand was cold. He held onto her tiny fingers, her delicate skin so soft and frail, her eyes unwavering. She took a shallow breath in.

Tears rolled freely down his cheeks as he stared at her peaceful face.

"Fearne?" he said. His voice broke. "Fearne, p-please open your eyes. *Please.*"

She didn't move.

Eyes closed, he prayed that she would reach out to him in his dreams, just one last time, to speak again in that warm, pure voice inside his mind.

And for a moment, he thought she did.

"*You'll be okay …*"

The echo of her voice was hauntingly soft, weak and about to disappear. Will looked up at her through blurry eyes.

"Fearne?"

"*I love you, Will …*"

He looked up at the heart rate monitor and saw the ECG lines spike with the slow beat of her heart until suddenly, the line was straight and her heart stopped beating.

She breathed out for the last time, and Will stared at her peaceful face for what could have been minutes, not wanting to believe she was gone.

No one came running. They didn't try to save her, there was no CPR or anything. Her end was inevitable. They knew it. Somewhere deep inside him, even before he stuck a needle in his own arm to try and save her with his blood, he knew that everyone had given up on Fearne.

Even Fearne herself.

Will broke down. He pressed his head against her chest and cried silently so as not to wake Hunter. He wasn't willing to part with her hand.

Eventually, though, he decided he needed to be away from her body. He couldn't comprehend the fact that he would never hear her laugh or feel her frail arms wrap around his neck and hold him or tell him something wise that only she would say or smile and light up her green eyes with joy and wonder. He couldn't.

So he went looking for her in the only place he knew how.

It felt like a dream, walking through the compound. It was very early in the morning and the corridors reminded him of ICE, only foreign and never-ending. Knowing they were on a mountainside, he went upstairs to find the surface. On Ward A, he walked to the end of a low-roofed concrete corridor where there was an exit sign and a hatch leading up. There were no warning signs or coded doors. It was so strange to be free.

As Will shoved the hatch and climbed up into daylight, he came face to face with the second most amazing view he'd ever seen. It was some kind of desert – a picture he'd only seen in Dr. Rosenthal's books. There were orange, rocky mountains all around them and rolling hills stretched far and wide. The sun was about to make its appearance soon, and Will was just in time to witness it.

But he was not there to see the sun. He was there to see Fearne.

It was a tricky climb down the dusty path to the edge of the cliff the compound was built beneath. The view didn't particularly matter to Will – it was the dangerous edges he searched for. After heading down the slope and over a challenging mound, he found a clear spot on the edge of a drop that had to be over twenty meters. That would certainly hurt, but not enough to kill him instantly if he landed right. That was what he wanted.

Will gazed out at the valley, feeling the wind flow through his hair, trying not to think of what he left behind in the hospital wing and focus on what he knew was coming.

Pain.

I have to see her. This is the only way.

"Hey!"

Will started. His feet slipped on the loose dirt and he whipped around.

There were four people watching him at the top of the mound. On the far right with her hand outstretched was a girl in a plaid shirt and jeans, pink and purple streaks in her blond hair. Beside her was another girl with hair in ragged clumps twisted around in a thick ponytail. She wore loose, layered clothing that made her look like a tent, her face long like a horse. The two boys were similar in their style but opposite in their looks. One was large with a beard shaved only on his chin and very pale, freckly skin. The other was thin with glasses and dark hair, hunched over as though he spent too much time peering at a computer screen.

Will couldn't understand what they were doing outside so early, let alone interrupting him.

"What the hell are you doing?" the first girl shouted.

Will looked down at the cliff and back at the group, not knowing how to answer.

"You'll kill yourself," she replied and started to slide down the hill toward him.

Stunned, Will backed away from the cliff. "Get back!"

"No, are you crazy, you'll-"

"Heal myself? Yeah."

The girl stopped sliding. One of the guys said, "sick!" and Will dropped his arms.

"Oh," she said. "You're Will."

It should have unnerved him that she knew his name, but he didn't care. "Could you leave me alone? I'm kind of dealing with a lot here."

He thought they would listen to him and heard shuffling on the dirt. But all of a sudden, the girl was next to him, holding out her hand.

"I'm Ella," she said. "Nice to meet you."

Will slowly and cautiously shook her hand, conscious of the fact that they were still dangerously close to the edge.

"So why are you jumping if you can't kill yourself?"

Will closed his eyes, willing himself not to cry.

"Come on, I really like stories," she smiled.

"I'm about to lose the closest thing I ever had to family. But when I feel pain, I get to see her, so I've decided to jump so that she can take me to paradise and I'll be with her until the pain ends. Then I'll do it all again."

Ella frowned suddenly and shot a glance back at the group.

"So you should probably leave now," he said. "This won't be pretty."

Ella didn't move. She tucked her hair behind her ear to keep it out of the wind. "It's okay, I've seen all this before in a lame vampire novel. You miss someone and the only way to see their face is to do something reckless and jump off a cliff. It always ends with the guy taking their shirt off, revealing fake abs and a lot of chest h... uh, forget I said that." She waved her hands, not glancing at the perplexed look on Will's face. "But that's not real life. You have to face real life, because when you do, you'll find it's easier than the pain you go through when you figure out you're imagining things. Real life hurts, but it hurts more when you lie to yourself."

Will stared at her. "Who are you guys?"

"We're SSS members," she said. "And we're really excited to see you guys. Apart from Zac, it's been a while since we've met others with superpowers and ... well, it's been a huge journey for you and the others. We're eager to hear all about it."

Snorting, Will shook his head and stared at the sun that had just appeared atop the horizon. It was blindingly beautiful, a glowing orange ball lighting up the day. "It's not a pleasant story, I can assure you that."

"They never are," she said. "But ... I don't think there's anything more heroic than people who chose to be heroes even when they have the option not to. Just because you were given powers, doesn't mean you have to use them. There are more people out there with abilities that hide in the shadows, but you guys ... you're not afraid. I think that's brave."

Will was in too much of an emotional and desperate state to thank her for her words. All he needed was to see Fearne again. So he simply twitched a smile and said, "you have a lot more to learn about us."

Then he stepped over the edge.

FORTY-FIVE

The ground came up to meet Will and he braced himself for the impact, but it did not come from where he thought it would. Something clamped around his waist, and instead of hitting the ground, he started to soar back up into the air again.

Will's eyes opened.

He was flying.

"What the-"

"You're an idiot!" said the guy with his arms around him. His accent was distinctly Spanish and he had short-shaved hair and scratchy clothing. Will wriggled from his arms, but he'd already dropped him at the top of the cliff where Ella and the others were still standing.

Will scrambled to his feet and turned to jump from the cliff again, but suddenly the flying man was there, shoving him back.

"Stay away from me," said Will. "I don't need you to save me."

"No," he said, "You just need someone to snap you out of this suicide phase."

"Zokani, don't-"

Will felt some kind of force inside him take over, and next thing he knew, he was throwing his fist into Zokani's jaw. His head snapped to the side. Someone behind him gasped. Zokani touched his chin gently and then looked back at Will with a glare that could have burned holes in him.

"Fine," he snapped and stepped aside with his arm outstretched. "You want to be a coward and not face your grief? Go ahead."

Will's shoulders shook with anger. He couldn't comprehend where this rage had come from or why he was taking it out on a stranger. But he couldn't be around them. He *needed* to see Fearne.

So for the second time that day, he jumped.

But not once did he see her. He saw a shape, a white shape, but couldn't make out her face. Pain spliced through his legs as they snapped in half. The crack of his bones was almost as loud as his scream. His body tumbled to the side and he rolled in the orange dirt. He coughed, tasting metal and salt in his mouth, and when he looked up at the cliff he'd jumped from, Ella and her friends were no longer peering over the edge. They must've grown tired of his act, just as Zokani had.

On his fifth try, Will looked around for Fearne, his vision blurry from the pain. He saw dried bushes and mounds of dirt, an arch between two more cliff faces and a slope down the way that dropped over more cliff edges.

He groaned into the dirt, clenching his muscles, confused as to why Fearne did not appear. Where the hell was she to pull him into a better place, away from the pain? How could he live without seeing her again?

Will couldn't take it. "Fearne!" he screamed at the mountain, her name echoing throughout the valley. "*FEARNE!!*"

His frustration grew as his legs healed together again. He threw his fist into the dirt, not hard enough for it to break, the tears building up in his throat until he was heaving wretched sobs, rocking back and forth. He was alone, and he would never see her again, no matter how much pain he went through.

He sat there staring at the valley for a long time until he decided he needed to burn off some frustration. After climbing up the mound to the hatch and entering the cool compound, he didn't even go back to his room to shower.

He went straight to Chevie.

He passed two SSS members who gave him startled looks and pointed hesitantly to the stairs when he asked them where Chevie's room was. Ward B, they told him. He was released from containment that morning. Something about good faith. Will thanked them and stalked down the stairs until he found Chevie's room. As he waited for him to open the door, he felt jittery and ready for a fight.

Chevie's door opened and Will pounced on him. Before Chevie could recover himself, they were rolling on the floor, grabbing each other's shirts and throwing wild punches. Will was angry and Chevie was just trying to defend himself. Will managed to get in a few hits before suddenly, he was being lifted off the ground.

Will looked to his left, his feet swinging above the floor, and saw an older man with very pronounced muscles clenching the back of his shirt. Will was so shocked that he stopped kicking. Chevie rolled over and ran around his studded leather sofa, his hands raised.

"Please, Will, let me explain-"

"Put me down!" Will yelled. "Who the hell are you?"

"I'm Alistair, Chevie's dad." He gently dropped Will, who stepped back and shoved his shirt straight. "And you need to stop hitting my son."

Will nodded. "Right. Okay. So you're the man who's alive because this wanker stole Joshua's Ravenadium and used it to bring you back to life when we needed it to save Fearne? And now you have what, super strength?"

"Hey, I didn't ask for this."

"Dad, I can handle it," said Chevie. "Could you please just give us a minute? I'll meet you at your room."

Nodding, Alistair walked away, closing the door behind him. Chevie and Will circled the sofa. Will didn't even pay attention to the details of the room, brightened by the open window displaying a view of the valley. He clenched his fists, ready for more blood to be shed. "I didn't have a choice, okay. You would have done the same thing!"

"No, I wouldn't, because I know the consequences of when people do selfish things. *Other* people get hurt."

Chevie's arms dropped. "Look, I'm not gonna say I regret what I did. He saved my life – I had to return the favor. Plus, he's the only family I've got."

Will scoffed. "Right, because your family loved you. You dad risked his life for you. Mine threw me to Wolfe and walked away. Fearne was the *only* person who believed in me, who mattered to me, for *fifteen* years growing up in ICE. And now she's … she's …"

Will broke down again. The pain was too fresh, and it would not heal like he was used to. He dropped down on the sofa and put his head in his hands.

He could hear Chevie rummaging around in his cupboards. Next thing Will knew, there was a glass with some kind of toxic liquid held under his face.

"I know how to take it all away." Chevie's expression was apologetic and genuine. Will knew he should hate the guy and keep trying to throttle him, but he wanted more than that to get rid of the agony of his loss. He took the glass and sniffed it. It made him cough.

Chevie smiled. "First drink, eh?"

Will nodded.

"Then let me introduce you to the ever so potent Mr. Johnnie Walker."

"Is it strong?" asked Will.

"Don't worry," said Chevie and he skulled his glass in three mouthfuls, wincing. "It tastes better after a few. And besides, we Brits gotta stick together. Drink up."

Will stared at the glass and shook his head. *If it makes it go away.*

He dropped the glass on the table, picked up the bottle and skulled it.

"Uh-" said Chevie, "-I don't think you should."

He lowered the bottle half way through. "It's not going to last long – I bet you alcohol doesn't even affect me."

"We'll see," Chevie smiled.

FORTY-SIX

Hunter woke up after a terrible nightmare. She was walking through the corridors of the death caves, everything empty, the doors flung wide open, freeing the shadows to attack her. As soon as she started running, she could hear a girl screaming. It sounded like Fearne. The faster she ran toward the door to freedom, the louder the screams became until her ears were burning and she tripped on the stone floor, waking up with a start.

She was in a dark room a little bit like a cell, only more furnished. Everything was cream and dark gray. Her blanket was red, the bed relatively soft. There were various clothes hanging in the closet. Was this her room or someone else's?

Then she remembered – she'd already been down to breakfast that morning. The Captain even ran a meeting to explain who the SSS was and that they were going to take the jet back to the cabin to retrieve the bodies of those they'd lost. Something about the FBI was mentioned. She talked to Miss Smart, too. She recounted the events of the past several months in which she woke up in the lab, discovered Eli had lost his memories, barely escaped the Agents, travelled the country with Eli and Joshua, saw a completely different side to him and fell in love. It was all a blur to Hunter. By the time she'd finished trying to eat breakfast, she was tired again. Miss Smart led her to a spare room and she fell asleep again, not feeling the throb of the flesh wounds in her arm and neck and her broken wrist.

No longer wanting to be alone, she decided to find Will. He wasn't there when she woke up in the hospital. Neither was Fearne's body. While she walked around the compound, she tried to get used to the thought that she would never again hear Fearne's voice in her mind. Her thoughts were empty, like a house with no furniture. She couldn't imagine what Will was feeling.

Eventually, Hunter found a girl who said she had seen Will go into Chevie's room. This made Hunter panic. She asked for directions and ran up the stairs to Ward B. Just as she was about to knock, the door opened and Chevie exited his room looking grim.

Forgetting that Chevie was responsible for stealing their only sample of Ravenadium, Hunter said, "have you seen Will?"

Chevie nodded and flicked his finger toward the door. The corner of his lip was cracked and swollen. "He's in my study. We were havin' a drink or thir'ee but I leff 'im alone."

Chevie stumbled against the wall and laughed to himself, making Hunter worry. Will had never had a drop of alcohol in his life.

"Can I see him?"

Chevie nodded. "I'm … gonna go pack so you … look arfer him, 'kay?"

"Pack?"

"Oh yeah," he smiled, "everyone hates me now coz I saved my dad an all so … may as well bugger off."

Coward, though Hunter. She nodded. "Sure."

Chevie slumped into the corridor and Hunter warily entered his study. Inside was a large room filled with the kind of taste you'd expect of a wealthy older man; a pool table, a rich mahogany desk facing a window displaying a view of the afternoon sun. Studded leather armchairs and glass coffee tables. It was the stuff Joshua used to dream about.

And on one of the sofas sat Will with a glass of what had to be scotch in his hand, three empty bottles on the table. His clothes were covered in orange dirt and blood stains and his eyes were peeling shut. It looked like he hadn't slept at all. Hunter remembered the day he walked into the breakfast hall, carried by the guards, a tortured soul with nothing left to live for.

Somehow … this was worse.

Hunter walked over and sat beside him, the sofa puffing out air. Will started, turned to look at her and nearly dropped his glass.

"Bloody hell," he grumbled. "I thought you were a fire truck."

Hunter blinked in surprise, too shocked to laugh. "Are you actually drunk?" She could smell the scotch on his breath and his eyes were struggling to stay open. "How much have you had?"

"Jusssssss … you know wha'? I'm not sure. Thiss bottle comes from England. Hey!" He raised a hand. "Guess wha'? Both me an Chev come from East London, did you know tha'?"

"No, I-"

"Chev said I could 'ave as much as I want. So I will."

"Um, it was probably not a great idea to have so much on your-"

He pushed her away when she tried to take the glass from him. His movements were sloppy and he swayed toward her. "No! It helps Hunter."

"Yeah, for like an hour and then you have a horrible hangover and life hasn't changed."

"Not me, I'll just heal up an' be rain as righ'," he chuckled.

What? Hunter released the glass and it slipped from his fingers, spilling scotch across the plush red carpet.

"Whoopsie," said Will with a chuckle.

"Okay, I think you've had enough. You need to sober up before the funeral-"

"No no no *no*. No. Nnnnno. I'm not going."

Hunter gripped his shoulders and peered into his sleepy face. "What do you mean, you're not going?"

"I'm not. I don't need to say goodbye, I already-" *hiccup,* "-said it."

"It's what they'd want Will. Benji, Mosi and … Fearne."

Will's eyes filled up with tears, and in a sudden outburst, he jumped to his feet with a near-empty bottle of scotch and threw it against the bookcase. It smashed and sprayed glass over the floor.

"I said I DON'T WANT TO GO!" He screamed at her. "I don't want to because *I can't,* Hunter! I can't lose her, she means *everything to me!!*"

"You're not the only one she meant something to," said Hunter gently, trying to calm him. To see him so hurt was worse than knowing Fearne was gone.

"You don't understand, I …" He gripped his long hair, his chest heaving as tears rolled down his cheeks. "She was … only one who saw me for who I really am. Who came out of nowhere and lit up my darkness with this … light. And the light never wen' out. Not until now."

Hunter approached him, slowly so as not to startle him. She put a hand on his shoulder to steady him as the rest of his body leaned against the bookshelf. He breathed so heavily as she tucked his hair behind his ears, flinching at the touch, his eyes flickering with uncertainty.

She remembered what Fearne once said to her about moving on when she was consumed with grief. *You can never truly move on until you've said goodbye.*

"I know what it's like to lose someone I loved with every part of me." She held him steady, consumed by his gaze, her heart pounding for reasons she did not understand. "But you know what? The love they give you will never leave. *Fearne* will never leave you. Remember that, okay?"

Will nodded, focusing so intently on the curls that splayed out over her shoulder.

"I know that you'll miss her," she said. "But after everything we've been through in this life that keeps hammering us around like we're nothing, I'm going to choose to be thankful for the people I'm with. And the most important person is you."

Though he was under the influence of strong spirits, she could see the warmth and understanding in the glow of his shadowed, haunting eyes. In that moment it was just the two of them, two broken people trying to battle life together. Hunter tried to keep her heart from thumping out of her chest as he moved closer. His footing suddenly became strong and sure. With both hands he cupped her face. His thumbs stroked her cheeks. Then, as gently as he could muster and with a feather-light touch he brushed his lips against hers. The kiss sparked a new blaze within her of a longing so strong, she was left breathless and dizzy.

Apparently it left him dizzy also, for at that moment Will's legs caved in and his body slumped against hers, his face pressed into her chest.

"Will?" She gripped the shelf of books for support but he was heavier than she could handle and her wrist was throbbing from the weight of him. "Will, please stand up."

A part of him responded to her and his feet moved, one after the other.

"Okay, let's get you to your room."

Their rooms were only one floor up, and as she dragged him along, they passed two random older women giving them stunned looks.

"He's okay," she said as she punched the up button on the elevator.

Will's long legs were bent awkwardly as she hauled him into his room and onto the bed. His head hit the wall hard and she winced, thankful that he could heal himself.

Hunter hoisted his legs onto the bed and lifted the quilt over his body, ignoring the fact that he was still covered in dirt.

Suddenly, Will reached out to grasp her hand and she froze. She looked into his sleepy face and took a mental picture, knowing she would never see Will so vulnerable and sweet.

He mumbled something and she had to lean down closer to hear.

"What?"

"I have a secret," he said.

"What's that?"

"I want to go … to paradise … with you."

Hunter flashed back to her dark cell in the Death Caves. He wanted paradise more than freedom. What did paradise mean exactly?

If anything were ever more beautiful than the sincerity and love in his words, Hunter would search the world to find it.

"One day," she replied. "I promise."

He fell asleep with a smile on his lips.

FORTY-SEVEN

he view from the jagged mountain on top of the compound was more beautiful than anything Hunter had ever seen. The colors of pink and orange across the sky as the sun crept closer to the horizon were spread out before them. A warm breeze danced over the large group of people who stood before the three bodies of the lost, wrapped in white sheets and lying down atop a pile of stones.

Hunter looked to her left at those she'd met in ICE – injured or not, they were all there. On her right were Jenny and Joshua, arm in arm, and Eli and his new friend Amelia holding hands. Oddly enough, it did not bother her. They had each found new love. Behind them was the Captain and every other member of the SSS, stretched out across the toothed mounds. Too many to count.

Will was there. He slept for a few hours, showered and came out for the funeral, not hungover in the slightest but still drowning in depression. She was proud of him for being there.

One of the SSS members – a girl called Ella, who was apparently a writer and a blogger – volunteered to read a passage she'd written to open the funeral. Hunter and the others had no problem with it; even though these people didn't know who the dead were, they still respected them.

Ella stood before the bodies with a crumpled piece of paper in her gloved hands. Her hair swept across her face. She cleared her throat and spoke clearly.

"There are many things a hero is. Loyal. Honorable. Courageous. A light. Sometimes they are victorious, facing monsters like fear with their swords held high. Sometimes they fail, but they learn to get up and keep fighting because no one else is brave enough. But always ... they are there for those in need. We cannot all live forever. But their sacrifice will not be forgotten.

"I don't know much about life or death, but I know that in between we do the best we can to be remembered. The world did not know who they were, but we did. So we will remember Benji. We will remember Mosi. And we will remember Fearne. We will remember our fallen heroes."

Ella hung her head, folded up her words and turned around, touching the paper to her chest. Hunter was entranced as the girl she did not know wedged her personal goodbye at Fearne's feet between two stones where it fluttered in the breeze. Then she walked back into the crowd.

Ryo stepped forward, a tattered copy of *Peter Pan* in her hands. She placed it carefully beside Benji's head, her shoulder's shaking.

"To die," she said, "would be an awfully big adventure."

Hunter's heart ached. Tears swarmed in her eyes as Ryo ran back to her brother's arms.

Marcus approached Mosi's body, also covered in a white sheet so no one could see how torn apart he was. Hunter hated seeing Marcus so distraught. He put a hand on Mosi's chest and closed his eyes.

"I never had much of a brother but ... you were all I could have asked for. Goodbye, brother."

He walked back to the crowd, hunched and broken.

Will was gazing at Fearne's body, his brow furrowed. Hunter wasn't sure if he was going to say anything, so she reached for him and squeezed his hand. He gave her a nod.

The walk to Fearne's body felt like a mile. The wind blew against her left side, the sun nearly gone.

She took a deep breath and spoke so everyone could hear her. "Fearne once told me that ... we can never truly move on until we have said goodbye. And today we say goodbye to Benji Givens, a boy who once never believed in himself. But in the face of danger, Benji didn't back down. We say goodbye to Mosi Sofano, who was strong and hard on the outside, but had the softest heart any of us had ever known. And we say goodbye to F-Fearne Matherson. She thought of others above herself, she always knew exactly what to say and-" Hunter met Will's tear-filled eyes and said, "she lit a light in our darkness that could not be diminished. We say goodbye to three beautiful people today and hope that we will never forget the blessing they were in each of our lives. They were ... they *are* ... a light in the darkness."

Hunter clenched her fists, proud that she didn't break down. She turned her back on the crowd and stood before Fearne's body in the middle pile, the valley below her. It was the hardest fire she'd ever had to light. With one breath, she raised her hands and the three bodies burst into flames. From the back of the crowd there were gasps of surprise - some of them had never seen her power in action. The three fires burned and the bodies melted and Hunter held the fire but she couldn't for very long. Tears were flooding from her eyes and she found herself sobbing as she stared into the bright flames.

Then a hand was upon her shoulder. She looked behind her to see Will, his face a mix of sorrow and release. Hunter dropped her hands and curled into his chest where he wrapped his arms around her and they cried together. She didn't know for how long, but when she pulled away, the fire had died and the ashes of those she loved blew away, carried across the valley and into the orange glow of the setting sun.

– PART 4 –

A LIGHT IN THE DARKNESS

Forty-Eight

fter the funeral, word got around that there was some kind of movie marathon happening in the Lair, and Ella and her friends were already setting it up. The others wanted a distraction from their grief.

Marcus followed.

He always followed. Never said much, unless it was a sarcastic comment back at one of Zac's stupid jokes. Or something obvious that no one else was brave enough to voice.

Mosi always said less than he did. Marcus watched Mosi sometimes, the way his white eyes surveyed the situation, calculating it. Fearne had once said that Mosi's mind was one of the most beautiful and tortured places she'd ever visited. Marcus often wished he could sneak a peek at it.

He walked behind the others who were just as silent as he was, in their own thoughts. The SSS members – some he'd met at breakfast that morning but could not connect with – were trying to lighten the mood with their excitement in showing the new crowd their favorite superhero movies. Usually Marcus would have been ecstatic to sit in front of a television again, and even more excited to touch a computer, but today he didn't feel anything but sadness. It just didn't feel right without Benji, Fearne and his best friend Mosi.

Sometimes Zac joked that Marcus and Mosi were secretly in love. It had often come across Marcus's mind. He didn't understand their friendship, because he never fully understood Mosi. He was always a mystery and perhaps that's what drew Marcus to him. There were moments while they fought in the fitness room at ICE where they both paused, locked in each other's gaze, Marcus trying to read his thoughts but never cracking his hard exterior. And of course, Mosi hardly said a word.

Now the world felt empty, and no amount of movie education the SSS fans could give him would fill that hole.

"Hey."

Marcus snapped back to reality, realizing he was staring at one of the SSS members he hadn't met yet. He was in his mid-twenties, surely. Spanish or Latina with very dark skin, but not as dark as Mosi's. His hair was shaved short, his jaw lined with black stubble, his eyes careful and conniving. He wore thick clothes despite the heat of their location, his elbows on his legs, peering at Marcus curiously.

"What?" Marcus snapped.

"I think they're having trouble starting the movie," he said and cocked his head to the right.

Marcus looked up. Three of the comic book geeks he'd met that morning were arguing over which cable was missing. Marcus used to hang out with these types. He was often regarded as a god in their mind, his talent with technology blowing their *Superman* socks off. He sighed and sat back, not wanting to use his power anymore.

"They'll fix it," he said.

The guy moved closer to him, making Marcus frown. "You see, I don't think they will." Then he pulled a coaxial cable from his pocket, giving Marcus a sideways smirk. "I just like messing with them."

"You should probably meet Zac then. Messing with people is his specialty."

He looked at Zac and grimaced. "I hate that kid. He annoys the shit out of me."

Marcus breathed a laugh and held out his hand. "I'm Marcus."

"Zokani."

Marcus nodded. "Interesting name."

"I'm from Peru. I don't even think the name is native, but I like it."

"Uh-huh." They watched the three geeks turn the television upside down while the girls shouted at them to switch cables and everyone was growing increasingly frustrated.

"So what's your power?"

Zokani raised an eyebrow at him. "How'd you know?"

"You're different from them. A bit like me, actually."

"I can fly," said Zokani as he ripped the cable from his pocket and threw it at Peetee, who jumped in fright. "You may need this, putty."

Peetee glared at him but didn't say a word. Marcus distinctly noticed that Zokani was a bit of a dick and reminded him of his brother, but then that made him think of ICE, which again reminded him of Mosi and he needed a new distraction.

Fortunately, Zac was his answer.

"Why don't we all just get drunk and play 'Never Have I Ever'?" he shouted to the group.

Imogen and Ryo – the only small children left at the compound, were spending time with their family. Marcus then realized that getting drunk sounded like a pretty good idea until they finally got the movie playing.

Marcus retreated back into his world of sadness, conscious of Zokani's eyes still on him. A girl who looked very similar to Zokani flipped over the sofa and introduced herself as Koko, his sister. Marcus met many more faces as the movie played and tried to forget about Mosi and the others that died, focusing on the story playing out on the screen. But a guy with razor sharp blades coming out of his knuckles and a stupid haircut wasn't enough to make him forget how much he missed his friend.

So he went walking. The SSS compound was huge, with multiple levels, many locked doors and giant, empty rooms. After walking around for almost half an hour, Marcus stumbled upon the unmistakable sound of someone boxing and halted in his tracks.

He peered into a room decked out with gym gear. A boxing ring stood under floodlights in the corner. Mats were stacked beside it. Three punching bags – new ones, not like the tattered old bag they had at ICE – were being used by soldiers. And over on the other side, he spotted Ryo and her brother Yung dressed in black and white martial arts uniforms.

Ryo very rarely participated in their workouts at ICE, but Marcus knew she had been trained before. She also neglected to mention that her brother's superpower was martial arts itself. Marcus watched them from the doorway, amazed at his speed as he challenged his sister, blocking every one of her jabs and unafraid to knock her to the floor. But Ryo had a secret of her own. Every time her brother grew brave enough to strike her, she vanished and appeared behind him, looping her leg around his, prepared to knock him to the ground. But Yung never fell and, like a cobra, lashed out at her before she could trip him up.

This was how their fight went on, and the soldiers boxing on the other mats were soon engrossed in their dance. Marcus's heart ached, wishing Mosi were there to watch them too.

"You can come in," said a man to his left who was unstrapping his wrists. He had an Australian accent, a ripped body and was dripping in sweat. "We don't charge for an audience."

Marcus didn't answer, but stalked inside all the same.

Suddenly the man threw out his arm and stopped him. "There's a catch though," he added. There was a gleam in his eyes that Marcus recognized; the blissful gleam of adrenaline and a good, pumping fight.

"What's that?"

The guy handed him the straps. "There are no audiences. If you're here, you're here to join in."

Marcus surveyed Ryo and Yung once more and felt his heart start to pound in excited anticipation. *This* is exactly what he needed. He took the gloves.

"Sounds good to me."

"I'm Ace," he said. "Welcome to the Ring."

FORTY-NINE

Hunter didn't feel like being around a big group of people, so she walked upstairs to her room after the funeral, showered for the second time that day, changed and climbed into the bed, listening to the humming of the pipes and the clank of footsteps on the metal outside. It was lonely and she missed the sounds of the forest at the cabin. It was almost like being in a cell again.

There, she was alone with her thoughts. And suddenly, without warning, she was sobbing for Fearne. She didn't hide it or try to toughen herself up. She didn't have to be a hero for anyone when she was by herself. Alone she was Hunter – a girl with too much responsibility and a power greater than her comprehension who lost a sister and a friend and was about to face the greatest battle of her life. It was all so much that she felt as if her head would explode.

A while later, after she'd washed her face in the bathroom and curled up in her bed again, there was a knock on her door.

Perfect timing, she thought as she opened the door to Will. He stood there in sweatpants and a white T-shirt, clean again, his hair damp and his eyes bagged with purple rings just like hers. He looked at her through furrowed brows.

"Hi," he said.

"Hey." She gave him a small smile.

"I wanted to uh … apologize for the way I acted today. And I brought a peace offering." From behind him, he pulled a box of matches and some old candles. "If it's not too weird, I just thought it would take us back to the good old days."

She smiled. "This is probably the most normal thing in our lives at the moment. Come in."

Hunter stepped aside and Will walked into her room. She took the candles and placed them on the shelf beside her bed, where she lit them. He sat down on the edge of the bed, his hands gripping his knees. Hunter placed herself next to him, bending one leg.

"I shouldn't have put you through that, and I shouldn't have shouted either."

"You were upset," she said. "I would've done the same thing. In fact, I probably would have set the room on fire."

Will's smile tipped to the side, but it only lasted a fraction of a second. They sat for a moment in dead silence. Hunter wanted to comfort him or make another joke or change the subject – and she wanted to do it all at once. It was strange how simpler things used to be in the guard's quarters of ICE, not just in their circumstances but in their relationship too.

A second longer and she couldn't take it.

"Will, I don't know if you remember, but earlier you-"

"Hunter." Her name on his lips silenced her immediately. He turned his gaze to hers and she was not only lost for words but lost for breath. "Whatever I said and whatever I say from now on, I need you to know something."

She waited, her heart pounding, feeling the heat of the fire coursing through her body. The candles flickered in response to her anticipation.

"I spent my entire life thinking that I would die alone and never experience these … feelings. And after everything that's happened since I met you, my life has transformed. You brought comfort. You brought joy. You brought chaos too, but let's not get into that."

Hunter sniffed a laugh and tucked her hair behind her ears.

"But more importantly, you opened my eyes to the world again. I started to have faith that I was going to live past twenty-one. That I wouldn't be alone until the day I took my last breath. Fearne-" He swallowed a sob and a tear rolled down Hunter's cheek. She quickly brushed it away, not wanting him to see her tears. "She brought me out of the darkness and showed me the light but you … you showed me a *fire*. I'd never have had the courage to face a raging dinosaur if I didn't have faith that you'd save me. I'd never have followed anyone else back to the Death Caves, even though I knew it was a suicide mission. And I'd never have run toward your scream in the bathroom, knowing what I was getting myself into, if I didn't feel anything for you."

Her throat was suddenly dry, her heart thumping with emotions.

"Will …"

"If there is anything I have learnt in my abysmal life, it's that I can't be afraid anymore. I can't take anything for granted or hide my feelings or wait to be healed. Life is too short and too precious for regret."

Hunter bit her lip. She couldn't describe the warmth inside her and if he had said anything more, she would have been overcome by love. Perhaps it was the gloom of the day that made her so desperate for his affection or to feel close to him in every way. And among the many things *she* learned in life, it was that no human love was perfect, but it could never be wasted.

"And Fearne wouldn't have wanted us to wait another minute." Will's eyes filled with tears at that, and he wiped them away. She could see frustration forming in his eyes – the kind of anger that only grief controlled.

"Will, it's okay, you can –"

He didn't listen to her and got to his feet, stormed over to the wall and threw his fist into it, the same way he had last night. He punched the wall three more times before Hunter ran to him and squeezed his shoulders.

"Will, stop! It won't bring her back, okay? Just stop it!"

"When?" he yelled. "When does it get easier? When will this pain go away?" He shrugged her off and sat on the edge of the bed again with his hands clenching his hair. She stood in front of him, holding back her own tears. "I don't know how to deal with this, Hunter. Knives and drills and bullets I can handle, but death …"

"Death is the worst kind of pain," she murmured. She slowly dropped to her knees in front of him, taking his hands and pulling them away from his face. "But you are not alone, Will. I'm here for you. I know what it's like to lose your other half. It hurts, and it doesn't get better, not until you stand up to your grief and move on."

His eyes bore into hers, sweeping back and forth with such intensity that her heart wanted to leap from her chest.

"What was it you said before?" she murmured and placed her hands on his cheeks. "That life is too short and too precious for regret."

Something burst to life in Will's soul. He placed his hands around her waist and hoisted her onto the bed with a force so strong and powerful, it lit the fire inside her with a potent fuel. When he had her lying beneath him on the bed, he brushed a stray lock of hair away from her lips and then he claimed her mouth with his.

Their lips moved in a desperate dance, their limbs entangled and their bodies burning. It was so wonderfully passionate that Hunter forgot to keep control of the fire. But that didn't matter. Will was not Eli, he could not be burned by her flame. And even if he could, he didn't complain one bit.

Soon she began to notice things about him that she hadn't thought much of before. Things like the stubble that lined his jaw, becoming thicker as it grew closer to his ears. Or the fact that he smelled like dirt mixed with soap in a strangely rugged sense. Things like how big he was when he guided her onto the pillow of the bed and towered over her, making her feel more protected than she'd ever felt in her life. Her thoughts strayed to Eli for just a brief second when she recalled the last time she was in such a passionate embrace, but then she felt like laughing. Her love for Eli was not the same as her love for Will because of how much she'd changed and experienced and endured.

And Will was … more. So much more.

For someone who hadn't ever expressed this hunger in a romantic sense, he somehow knew exactly how to make her toes tingle. He held himself above her, pressing down only slightly to keep her trapped beneath him. He buried his face in her hair and kissed a line down her neck, making goosebumps appear on her skin. He dipped over the strap of her tank top and kissed the bump of her shoulder. At that point, Hunter's inhibitions went completely haywire and she grabbed his neck in a vice-tight grip and pulled him back against her mouth. Their lips clashed together, the taste of mint lingering on his teeth as their tongues touched shyly and disappeared again. She gripped his T-shirt, pulling upward until he gave up and yanked it over his own head. She gazed up at his sculpted chest and lightly tanned skin that looked golden in the dim light from the candles. There were no scars on his chest, only the one down the side of his cheek, so faded now it was hardly noticeable.

Will couldn't be away from her lips any longer and cupped her head with one hand. Will's kisses were delicate even when forceful and she felt weak after each movement.

"I could kiss you … all night," he murmured against the side of her mouth.

Hunter opened her eyes and they fluttered in surprise at how close Will's were. "I'd happily kiss you all night," she replied with a smile as she ran the tip of her finger along the line of his jaw and marveled at the sparkle in his doe-brown eyes. "You help me forget the world."

They were lost to each other from that moment onward. Hunter remembered clothes being torn from their bodies. She remembered how strong he was and how beautifully seductive his eyes were as they captured her and made her insides burn with desire. In the glow of the candlelight, she never looked away from his gaze as he took her completely, in a way that she'd never imagined possible. After everything they'd been through together, she had waited for this moment, to be entangled with him in both a physical and spiritual sense, to be intimately close to him and to know that he loved her. Losing members of their family or being betrayed by Joshua again or knowing that the world was about to end now that Dr. Wolfe had Ravenadium was a distant worry, overpowered by comfort and passion and safety.

She knew, without a doubt, that Will was the man her soul had searched for all her life. It was an electric connection unlike what she had with Eli. Eli was fragile, Will could not be burned. Eli was her opposite, Will had been through every hardship she had, and more. Perhaps she knew the very moment that he came to her rescue in the bathroom of ICE. It was only a matter of time before they let their responsibilities go and realized that the only thing that ever mattered was that they be happy, and happy together.

Will kissed her delicately when it was over and settled in beside her with his back against the cool wall of her room. Hunter twisted sideways, spreading her injured arm over his heaving chest and pulled the sheet over them with her other hand.

"Will … I'm sorry, but I have to ask. You mentioned paradise this morning when you were …"

"Heavily intoxicated?"

She tilted her head and smiled at him. "What did you mean by paradise?"

Will stared up at the ceiling. His thumb traced invisible circles on her skin, making her tingle all over. "For some people, paradise means heaven. A place where there are no fears or cares. I wanted heaven in ICE, and I wanted release. For a long time I dreamed of being dead. And then when I met you ... my perspective of paradise changed. I saw it as a place, anywhere in the world, where you were there with me. A place where we don't have to hurt. A place where no one could separate us and we were happy. That is the paradise I want."

Speechless, the only thing Hunter could do to promise that was kiss him again and pray they would find happiness soon.

"I wish I could end this. I wish we didn't have to worry about Dr. Wolfe or Jet or even Jack anymore. I want paradise too."

"We're getting close," he whispered.

She tilted her head up and frowned. "I'm pretty sure this is as close as we can get."

He chuckled, his smile spreading and sending her heart into a frenzy again. "No, you silly goose. To paradise."

"Oh. Yeah. Paradise."

Hunter closed her eyes. Will's body rose and fell with each breath and if she listened to it carefully, she could forget everything and lie with him.

FIFTY

Hunter and Will slept soundly and wholly in each other's arms for the first time since their return from ICE. Perhaps they were simply overtired, or maybe it was the comfort of another person that made sleep seem less frightening. Either way, they woke up and said good morning to each other, deciding first that what they needed was some breakfast and some coffee. Then they could figure out what to do next.

Not only were they facing the biggest threat to mankind the world had ever known, what with Dr. Wolfe having Ravenadium in his possession, but now Hunter had the issue of Will on her shoulders and what stage their relationship had moved up to after sleeping together.

Things were much simpler in Physics class.

Will mentioned nothing while they walked down to the kitchen, his hand holding hers as though that were the most natural thing in the world and he hadn't freaked out over her touch just a few days ago on the hill in Seattle. She would normally psycho-analyze his behavior like any human being, but circumstances were different to normal life and frankly … she just didn't care.

They found the breakfast hall occupied by only a few SSS members that she wasn't familiar with just yet. She and Will walked to the coffee pot and Will decided to fetch some toast. As Hunter was stirring a sugar into her black coffee she felt the presence of someone behind her and – thinking it was Will – raised the coffees and turned to see Eli.

Shock caused her to drop both Styrofoam cups and splash coffee all over her legs and the grates of the floor.

"Oh shit," she muttered.

"S-sorry," he said and bent down to pick up the cup. "I didn't mean to scare you."

A few of the SSS members stared at them from a table nearby, but otherwise left them alone to clean up. Hunter took some napkins from the coffee table and dabbed at her jeans and shoes.

"It's okay, it's my fault."

"Want me to grab you another coffee?" he asked.

Hunter straightened up and looked at Eli directly in the eye for the first time since they came face to face the night she arrived. In a split second, she was able to come to the conclusion that when Joshua woke Eli up from cryonics state, not only did he not remember her, but his personality had changed as well. She noticed that he was much more confident than he used to be. He didn't look down as much. There wasn't the same innocence in his turtle-green eyes. He wasn't the same Eli she knew, therefore he wasn't the same Eli she fell in love with.

That made it easier to deal with any guilt of sleeping with Will when – technically – she had never broken up with Eli. It wasn't a conversation she really wanted to delve into the morning after.

"It's okay, I'll make it." She took the cup from him and turned her back to fill it.

"Hey, uh." Eli lifted a cup from the stack. "I was wondering if we could talk."

"Is there really anything we need to discuss?"

"I'm not sure, to be honest."

He reached over her to pour milk into his coffee. Hunter watched him check the bottle first before deciding not to add it. He put the carton down with a sigh and didn't see her smirking.

At that moment, Will walked up to the two of them with a plate of eggs, bacon and toast, looking as though he wanted to turn right around and walk out of the room.

"Am I interrupting something?"

"No, not at all." She held out an arm and pointed to a nearby bench.

242

The three of them swung their legs over the chairs and sat down facing each other. Will slid Hunter's plate under her nose and she shot him a sideways thanks.

Will didn't say a word, slowly eating his way through their delicious breakfast. Hunter blushed every time her thoughts strayed to last night. Then she looked at Eli and blushed even more, not knowing whether she should be feeling guilty or comfortable. He certainly didn't look comfortable, and she could understand why. He was sitting at a table with someone he couldn't remember losing his virginity to who was clearly now seeing someone else because she thought he was dead when really, he wasn't.

"Okay," he finally said, "seriously, I'm just going to lay it out on the table."

Will and Hunter listened intently.

"Your friends kind of filled me in yesterday as to what's going on. And this," he waved his hands in a circle, indicating to the three of them, "isn't going to be one of those despised love triangles like in *Twilight* or whatever. In some fucked up universe, this could all be worked through over months of competition and heartbreak, but I just don't see us having the time or the energy. We might have been in love once, Hunter, but … I'll never love you like Will does. I'm sorry."

Hunter was so shocked at Eli's blunt honesty that she sat there with her mouth open. Will was either about to laugh or barf, for he decided to take his breakfast elsewhere.

"I'll leave you two to catch up," he said with a sideways smirk at Hunter. "Nice to meet you Eli."

Eli muttered something that made his voice break and Hunter looked down at her breakfast, hoping the bacon rashes would wrap themselves around her neck and choke her so she could pretend this was all a dream and wake up with Will again. It had been a while since she'd prayed for suicide by breakfast.

"Um," said Eli eventually, "so I feel like we should at least get some things out in the open."

"Like?"

"Like Jack."

Instantly, her heart dropped and she wanted to leave. He could see it in her eyes, for he held up a hand in protest. "Just at least explain to me what happened to him."

She felt she owed him the truth, considering Jack was his closest friend. It didn't feel good to be speaking about Jack the way she thought it would, because it forced memories she'd shoved away to breach the surface. The coffee distracted her with its strength and so she went and made another one as she finished the story.

"I did everything I could to bring him back but ... I had no other choice."

"Because he's possessed now? By this dark power? Why aren't all of you possessed?"

Hunter shrugged. "That's a question not even Joshua can answer. Perhaps Jack's past is too dark, or he isn't strong enough to fight the voice inside him. He doesn't have support like I did; he has Dr. Wolfe breathing down his neck."

"Okay. I understand a little better now." Eli looked down at his cup and frowned. "I really hope it's not hard for you to be sitting here talking to me, what with ..." Eli glanced behind him, but Will was gone. "I mean uh ..." For a moment, Hunter saw some of the old Eli. The Eli she knew, lost in his memories. "I might have changed, but I can't imagine what you went through when you thought I was dead. Especially in a place as awful as ICE must have been."

Hunter sipped her coffee, remembering the nightmares of Eli lying coated in ice as Joshua stood in the shadows and chuckled. It seemed like the world was ending, but compared to her problems now, they were so small. Now she dreamed of a maniac and Fearne dying and feeling so cold and alone. Except last night. Last night she dreamed of soft sand and the rhythm of the ocean waves on the shore and glorious sunlight. Paradise.

"Maybe one day I'll be able to sort through my feelings on the matter of ... you and me." She stared at his eyes through those square glasses. "But right now, I'm up to my nose in responsibility. I have a bad guy to catch, friends to mourn for, relationships to fix and a world to save."

"That's a lot to have on your shoulders."

She nodded and sipped her coffee. "Tell me about it."

Eli hesitated before speaking in a quizzical manner. "Hunter, why do you think it's up to you to handle all of this 'hero' stuff?"

"I don't."

Eli smiled. "Yeah, you do."

Feeling hot in the face, Hunter crossed her arms. "Prove it."

"Okay. I heard that you led those kids out of ICE."

"Uh, yeah and then I ran back in which was the stupidest mistake I have ever made."

"But why'd you do it?"

"To save-" She shut her mouth the instant the words formed in her mind. *Damn, he's right.*

Eli looked quite pleased with himself. "And you stopped Mikayla at the cabin, right?"

"How'd you know that?"

"I've been catching up. Most people wouldn't have taken a risk like that, but you did."

"I sort of knew I could overpower her though. I did it once before in ICE."

"But you see my point right?"

"I do. But does that make it wrong?"

For a moment, he stared at his cup as he pinched the edges with his fingernails, making crescent-shaped marks in the Styrofoam. "I don't think it's wrong, I think it's your nature. I used to ask questions about you. Jenny only knew you briefly and all she had to say was that you impulsively act a hero. In the school fire. In the restaurant fire. With Jack in the warehouse. Joshua says you've grown up, but you were always a hero."

Hunter was touched. Now that she thought about it, he was right. It was once all about figuring out her past and trying to be a normal teenager with a fire in her veins that played havoc with her hormones and made her into the worst possible human to be around.

But now …

Selflessness led you back to these caves, Dr. Rosenthal had said. *Qualities of a true hero. And heroes have no time for themselves.*

"You really think I'm a hero?" she asked.

Eli tipped his glasses further up his nose and said, "A hero is an ordinary individual who finds the strength to persevere and endure in spite of overwhelming circumstances."

Hunter felt a giggle bubble out of her mouth.

"What?"

"That's a quote from *Superman*, right?"

Eli's cheeks filled with color. "I thought maybe you hadn't seen it."

"You made me watch it," she said. "But you see Eli, I'm not an ordinary individual. I actually *have* powers."

Eli gave her a quirky smile as he stood up and slipped out of the bench.

"So did Superman," he replied and walked away.

FIFTY-ONE

Hunter remained in the cafeteria until the crowd started filing in. She was so focused on her thoughts of Dr. Wolfe and Will and Eli and everything else that had overcomplicated her life that she didn't see Ella sit down opposite her until she was clicking her finger in front of her face and giving Hunter a fright.

"Hey!" she exclaimed, her energy too much for so early in the morning. "Earth to Hunter."

Hunter smiled. "Sorry. I'm a deep thinker."

"I can tell. How'd you sleep?"

Instantly, blush started to creep into her cheeks again. "Uh, not bad."

"My sleep was *horrible*," she moaned. Despite Ella being overly enthusiastic, Hunter very much liked the girl. She was kind and quite extraordinary, and obviously loved by everyone at the SSS. "But anyway, I have a couple of people who really want to meet you." She turned to the table nearby and waved at some people. Eagerly, they climbed out of their table and made their way toward her.

Despite her exhaustion, Hunter still found the energy to be incredibly shocked by the three people who were smiling and waving at her as they approached. The first was a large man with a weirdly-shaped beard. The second was a scrawny man with red hair. And the third was a girl of about sixteen whose eyes sparkled at the sight of her.

"Kate?" Hunter gaped.

She nodded. "I never did get to thank you for saving my life at the restaurant so … thank you."

Hunter couldn't help herself. She swung out of the bench and wrapped her arms around Kate. The young girl seemed surprised. When she pulled away, she looked at the two men and almost laughed.

"You were there in the alleyway too – you helped pull us out of the building!"

"Oh my God," said the red-head. "She remembers us Peetee."

"I think I'm going to faint," said Peetee.

Hunter laughed. "How did you get here?"

"We knew you had a power," said Kate. "I mean, there was no way you could have saved me without your power. I was padlocked in the freezer."

"Yeah, and plus your skin was glowing when you came out with Kate," said Peetee. "Me and Andy couldn't stop talking about it for weeks."

"So we three got together," said Andy. "And then Peetee found the SSS website and we decided … to hell with it. We joined."

"You changed my life," said Kate. "I'd be dead if it weren't for you, and I've waited this long to thank you for it."

Hunter felt tears brim in her eyes. She looked at Ella, who gave her a proud wink. *I don't get to see this side of being a hero very often,* she thought. *It's kind of nice.*

They sat down at the table as Hunter asked them to tell her more about their adventures since the restaurant fire in New York, happy to hear another story for a change. Others joined their table and by the time Ryo entered, all of Ella's friends were sitting with her.

"Look what I found," said Ryo as she placed a sketchbook on the table beside Hunter. "You won't believe what's in it."

Hunter put down her coffee – fourth cup that morning – and turned the cover. Inside were pages filled with sketches. Sketches of superheroes.

"Oh my God," she muttered. "Did one of you guys do this?"

Ella and her friends peered at the sketchbook, frowning.

"It's not ours," said Ella.

"That's because I found it at the cabin."

"Whose is it?"

Before Ryo even answered, Hunter's eyes noticed the signature at the bottom corner of the drawings and felt her heart break in half.

"Benji," she whispered.

Zac and Marcus joined the table then. Zac snatched the book and started looking through it with Marcus peering over his shoulder. She should have cared that they were, in some sense, reading Benji's private thoughts, but somehow it felt right to show it to the world.

"Are you serious?" Zac exclaimed.

"Careful!" Ryo tried to pull it away from him but he held on tight. "Don't rip the pages."

"Relax, jeez. I can't believe little Benji drew these."

"He gave us names too?" Marcus gasped.

Zac's eyes went wide and he scanned through the book to find his own sketch. When he did, his face fell. Hunter saw a black suit with silver streaks running from the shoulder to the hip bone. There was a name scribbled along the side.

"Two-face?!" Zac exclaimed.

Every single person at the table burst out laughing. Even the SSS members thought the name was stupid.

"Something funny?" asked Jenny as she and Joshua joined the table meeting.

"We're looking at Benji's sketchbook," said Ryo. "He gave us all names and costumes!"

At that, there was a sudden screeching sound and all of the people in the cafeteria started to crowd around the sketchbook. Most of them were artists and designers themselves, or so she'd heard Ella say over her shoulder. They were intrigued by the book.

"Where's mine?" asked Marcus.

"Here," said Joshua and he turned the book around. Marcus' sketch was majestic, surrounded by bolts of lightning. It was titled 'Static'.

"Static," said Marcus with a nod of approval.

"That's a sick name," said a bearded guy who'd appeared behind Joshua.

"He called me Time Warp," said Ryo. "I like it."

A few of the newcomers nodded and voiced their agreements. Hunter couldn't get used to all of their faces.

"Your costume design is really great," said Ella who was sitting beside Zac. Her girlfriend Dakota was leaning over her shoulder. "It wouldn't be hard to make."

"There's one for Fearne," said Zac, his voice almost a whisper. "He didn't have a name for her, but her picture is beautiful."

At that moment, another member joined them. Hunter looked up in time to see Will's face go pale as he saw over Zac's other shoulder the pencil sketch of Fearne in a suit, a cape flowing out behind her, hair in ringed pigtails, sunlight beaming down on her. Her eyes were closed and a peaceful smile lit up the page as other faces surrounded her, portraying the power of her mind.

"Can I see that?" he asked, his voice thick.

Everyone was silent as Zac handed Will the book. He blinked a few too many times. He was handling himself incredibly well, considering.

Then suddenly, Will burst out laughing as he flipped the book around and showed everyone Zac's picture.

"He called you 'Two-Face'?"

The crowd roared with laughter again, their laughter filling the room and echoing throughout the cafeteria. It felt wonderful to laugh as a group – even though some of them were missing, they felt fuller than they had in days.

Jenny and Joshua, with assistance from some of the SSS members, started bringing over coffee and tea and breakfast. Everyone talked loudly, making new friends. Hunter introduced Will to Ella's friends Peetee and Andy, and her girlfriend Dakota, but apparently they'd already met yesterday morning. Will said he'd explain later. Joshua was particularly interested to hear about Kate's involvement in the restaurant fire. Hunter gave him a warning look.

She also met Koko who could turn invisible and Zokani who could fly. Aside from the two of them, and Yung and Illya, there were no other people at the SSS with powers. One guy claimed to be able to skull an entire bottle of milk in ten seconds, but the others only laughed at him.

Apparently their 'fanclub' was a mix of social media experts, comic book creators, critics, and all-round lovers of superheroes. Their enthusiasm and friendliness was uplifting. Hunter couldn't remember a time when she was surrounded by so many people so eager to meet her. It was hard to remember her life before she inherited powers and went to school and had hardly any friends. She liked all of the SSS members immediately and, in spite of yesterday's events, she felt slightly cheerful for the first time.

"So where's my costume?" asked Chantal. She hadn't been able to walk without a crutch since the stab in her side, and it was the first time Hunter had seen her looking fresh. Zac slid her the book.

"Don't get too excited; it doesn't have high heels or anything."

Chantal rolled her eyes and stared down at her sketch.

"Siren," she said with a slow nod. "It has a ring to it."

"There's one of Joshua too," said Zac. "You're the Iceman."

Hunter watched a smile play over Joshua's face at the irony. "Of course."

They found Mosi's picture and Benji also drew one for himself. He wanted to be called Bullet, and he'd named Mosi Aftershock.

"I still need a name though," said Zac over the top of the excitement.

"Oo! Oo! How about Shifty?" said Ella.

"No."

"I still like Two-Face," said Marcus and several of them chuckled.

"Nah," said Zac thoughtfully. "It's gotta be something more epic. I was thinking – get ready for this …" He held his arms up and paused for dramatic effect before proclaiming, "Lord of the Faces!"

Laughter rung throughout the room as Peetee stared at Zac in awe. "That's brilliant. I love it."

Chantal threw out her hand and said, "Oh *please* call yourself that. I'd piss myself laughing if I saw a newscaster say 'The Lord of the Faces was seen today buying a hotdog off the street'."

"No," said Zac. "The report will read 'Lord of the Faces wins Sexiest man of the year for the thirtieth time'."

"Yeah, because you'll cheat," said Marcus.

"Hey." Jenny frowned as she flipped through the sketchbook. "Will and Hunter don't have names."

"Do we really need them?" asked Will.

"Yes, and fast." Zac chewed on his toast. "They've gotta put names to all our faces when they see us on the news. And we'll have to do a special press release–"

"What makes you think we'll be on the news so soon?" asked Joshua.

Zac shrugged. "We should be prepared for these things in case they happen, right? And we should really get costumes made."

Chantal scoffed. "Who's going to make all our costumes?"

"We will!" Ella exclaimed. "And by 'we', I mean our design team. We just need to ask the Captain to help us get the materials for it. It would be a lot easier with Chevie, but he left, so …"

"Wait, you think you can actually make these suits?" asked Zac. Hunter hadn't seen him so enthused about anything in a long time. "I mean, you'll have to design special ones for Hunter and Marcus, and Joshua too."

Ella nodded. "There's plenty of people with the right skill set here. I'm sure we can work something out. We may need some assistance though — I'm afraid we're not too scientifically gifted."

At that moment, everyone turned to Joshua. He froze with his cup halfway to his lips, staring at the faces. He shot a look at Hunter and she raised her eyebrows as if to say *well, you wanted to make it up to me. Here's your chance.*

Joshua sighed. He looked mentally exhausted, but he still agreed to help. "I'll see what I can do, though I can't promise anything overnight."

Zac whooped loudly and there were murmurs of excitement around the table. Ella took the sketchbook and started voicing her ideas to the SSS members around them. They left to go brainstorm in private.

"So guys," Zac said to Hunter and Will directly. "Names."

"Will could be … Mr. Invincible?" said Ryo.

"Molecular Man!" Chantal exclaimed.

"The Crab?" Everyone stared at Zac with mouths agape. "What, they can grow back their limbs!"

"We are *not* calling him that," Hunter snapped. She caught Will's crooked smile and felt hot again. *Jeez, I can't even look at him without swooning anymore. What is wrong with me?*

"I think you should call him the Immortal," said Joshua. Everyone turned to stare at him amazedly. He simply shrugged and said, "Dr. Rosenthal called you that when you were a boy."

Will's jaw clicked. He looked down at his hands on the table. "I remember."

"I like the Immortal," said Hunter. "After all, that makes you the most powerful person in this group."

"She's right," said Ryo. "It's perfect for you."

"The Immortal!" Zac shouted loudly and both Marcus and Jenny jumped in surprise. "Last but not least … Hunter."

"I already have a name."

"And what would that be?"

As she said the word, she was thankful it did not hurt to remember the morning she spent with Eli. The memory was so pure and uncomplicated, and a part of her was happy that no one else in the world would ever see it apart from her. It felt special and beautiful. And she would never have any other name but —

"Rouge."

Silence fell around the group. Everyone seemed to sense there was a story behind the name.

"I like it," said Will. "It suits you."

"Thank you." To have her name officially made known to everyone filled some distant hole inside her that she never knew was empty.

"We need to name everyone else too. What about the Bushwhackers?" asked Zac.

Ryo elbowed him. "Don't be so racist."

"That's not racist!"

"Shh!" hissed Marcus, but it was too late. Ryo moved aside and there stood Ace and Illya themselves looking less than pleased at being talked about.

Zac swallowed nervously and gave them a wave. In a high-pitched voice, he said, "G'day!"

Hunter and some of the older ones dropped their heads, trying not to laugh. Ace crossed his arms under his enormous pecks and stared down at Zac.

"We were just uh … discussing names for us. Superhero names."

"We're not superheroes," said Ace. "So just call us who we are."

"Well that just makes it easier for people to find you," said Zac. "How about Captain Australia!"

No sooner had Zac opened his mouth did Ace whip from inside his leather jacket a knife that looked bigger than Hunter's forearm and stabbed it through the top of the plastic table. Everyone gasped and froze. Ace leant toward Zac slowly and said through a snarl, "We're not here for your superhero parade, kid. Next time I hear you mention that word, I'll knock your teeth into next Tuesday, ya got me?"

Zac nodded fervently, sweat starting to seep from his brow. Ace ripped his knife from the table, leaving a large slit, and he and Illya walked away from the group to the cafeteria line.

They relaxed at the table and giggled at Zac's reaction. He didn't look at all amused and started awkwardly excusing himself.

"Where are you going?" asked Chantal.

"To shower," he said. "I think I just shat myself."

FIFTY-TWO

It was late the next evening when Will felt he couldn't sleep. It had been happening rather a lot lately. He would finally relax with Hunter curled up against his body, her breathing even, when an overwhelming sadness and the need to get his mind off things would take over. The Lair was often a place he could find distractions, but tonight he wanted something different.

He found himself walking to the kitchen to perhaps make a cup of tea. The SSS was quiet, the emergency lighting on, and it was eerily freeing, as though he was walking through a dream.

When he came to the cafeteria and passed through the door to the communal kitchen that everyone has access too, he was surprised to hear a shuffling sound in one of the back aisles where the food was kept. He crept along the linoleum floors, his heart starting to pick up pace, until he recognized the sounds.

Someone was making out behind the fridge. He could see golden-blond hair and hear disturbing noises. Praying it wasn't one of the SSS members he'd only just been introduced to, Will decided he'd better not interrupt and turned to leave.

That was conveniently when his clumsy left foot caught on one of the wheelie tables and a metal bowl skidded across the floor, spilling cooking utensils with a noise loud enough to wake the dead. When he looked up, he saw Chantal, hair in disarray, her arms wrapped around a body he didn't recognize. But whoever he was, he was quite handsome, with a strong physique, structured jaw and rippling muscles through his half-open plaid shirt. They both gaped at Will.

"Spying, are we Willy?" asked the boy and he transformed back into Zac.

Will was so embarrassed, his cheeks were flaming. "I – I'm sorry, I didn't know who you –"

"Yeah," snapped Chantal, "that's because he's not *himself*."

"Hey," said Zac defensively. "What's that supposed to mean?"

"It means," she growled as she zipped up her sweater. "That I shouldn't have to make out with a stranger when I know that's not who you are!"

"I am my true self, I just have lots of faces."

Chantal ran a hand through her hair and Will sensed some tension in the air. He had no idea this was going on, let alone that they were already fighting. *I really need to pull my head out of my ass and focus on my friends a little more.*

"I'm uh … I'm really happy for you guys," he said, "but I'm just gonna go back to –"

"I want to know what you think, Will," said Chantal as she crossed her arms. "Should Zac change bodies whenever he feels like it, or for the sake of sex?"

"Look at me, Chantal," Zac said, and for the first time Will heard real sadness in his voice. "Why would someone like you be with a chubby, oily-haired loser like me?"

Chantal rolled her eyes. It took her a long time to answer. Then she said, "because you have a good heart. I know you use humor as a disguise more than your many faces. And I know that you don't tell the truth about what your true self looks like because you're afraid for people to see the real you." She turned to him and looked at him lovingly. "But I see the real you. I always have. And I want you to be happy in your *own* skin, not someone else's."

Zac twisted his ankle awkwardly. Will felt trapped in the moment, as though he were watching another movie with the SSS members. This was a bloody good distraction.

Zac opened his mouth to retort with something sarcastic, but Chantal knew it was coming and silenced him with a kiss. She leapt like a lioness onto his body, pressed against the side of the fridge. They became, yet again, entwined with each other. Will couldn't help but smile as he awkwardly excused himself, no longer hungry, and went back to Hunter's room to find her twisted in their sheets with one knee bent up and her hair flowing out around the pillow. It didn't take much for Will to tip over the edge with her anymore, but he knew he couldn't wake her for sex – they'd both been sleeping periodically these days, and it was too selfish to deprive one another of it. As soon as he had slipped in beside her, she mumbled something sleepily and then snuggled up against him, one hand splayed over his chest and her eyelashes fluttering on his shoulder. He kept thinking of Zac and Chantal and how they had to fight, just like everyone else, to find love and sustain it.

Will watched Hunter sleep for a while longer. Despite all the horrible things he'd endured and the loss he'd suffered, Will thanked God for the blessing he'd sent in the beautiful girl he held in his arms.

FIFTY-THREE

An emergency meeting was called late that evening. It seemed as though urgent matters had been postponed after the battle so the people of ICE and the SSS could come together and mourn their losses. Hunter enjoyed getting to know the members and being around her friends again, because she realized that their time together could be shorter than she anticipated and she wanted to make the most of it. But the Captain was right – there were strategies to discuss, and that was why only those from ICE, those with powers and the Captain's tech team and advisors were present that night.

It was with dinner in their bellies and eyes dried from tears that they congregated in the communications room, alert and ready for the news.

"Right, we're all here now because despite having suffered a great loss, it is time to focus on the crisis at hand," said the Captain. "You-" He pointed in the general direction of Hunter and the group, "-know this Dr. Wolfe character. You also know the threat. We-" He threw out his arms, "-are your support and your resources. Anything you need to take down this asshole, you got it."

They smiled in thanks.

"Alright," the Captain continued. "We're at a point now where things have become serious. And not just serious; personal. It's time to make a strategy."

Around the slightly empty room, there were murmurs of agreement.

"We have several very real threats: Dr. Wolfe, his institution, his army of Agents and mutants – of whom we do not have numbers – and this Destructo villain character."

"Jack," said Hunter and Eli together. She couldn't hear them call him Destructo when they hadn't seen him destroy anything. To she and Eli, he was and always would be Jack.

"Yes," the Captain shrugged. "Whatever. Point is, we may have numbers and weaponry here, but we don't know the doctor's limits, nor do we know his plans, which brings us to the second issue: The prisoner."

The Captain clicked a button on his remote and a recording of a room somewhere in the compound showed a high camera angle view of Mikayla huddled in the corner on the screen.

Hunter was ashamed to admit she'd forgotten about her completely. It was on a whim that she decided Mikayla would be a valuable insight into Dr. Wolfe's plans, but then she did nothing to interrogate her.

"Has she said anything to anyone?" asked Joshua.

"She hasn't said a word. Hasn't answered any of our questions. Obviously she thinks we're going to kill her even if she reveals the doctor's plans."

"She probably doesn't know them," said Marcus. "Trust me, she's my brother's girlfriend and I know her better than anyone here. Dr. Wolfe wouldn't reveal his world domination schemes to someone of her profile."

"Which is?" asked the Captain.

"A weapon," said Hunter. "That's all she is to him."

"All she was," said Marcus as he turned his gaze to her. "Until you stopped her."

"Yeah, how *did* you stop her?" asked Ryo.

Hunter looked around at them, then to Joshua. They'd discussed this at the cabin, but it hadn't been spoken aloud to the group.

Joshua explained how her powers were stronger because she was conceived of Ravenadium and Feucotetanus. She looked at the faces in the room and found that her friends were staring at her differently. She didn't realize how the truth of her origin would set her apart from the others. It made her feel like she was being put on a pedestal.

"Ravenadium was the key to saving Fearne's life, but unfortunately, the last sample I had was stolen from the cabin the night of the attack. And Jet's body was missing also."

"Holy shit on a stick," Zac gaped.

"What? I thought he died!" exclaimed Marcus.

"His body vanished. It would have been easy for the Agents to return to find out if anyone was alive and steal anything they could. But only Jet would know its true value. He must have taken the other sample Hunter left behind when she and Ryo went back."

"Why the hell didn't you tell us you had something so valuable kept in a *briefcase* in an unlocked office," said Marcus. "We could have protected it!"

Suddenly, Joshua was being bombarded by questions and accusations. The supposed plan of action had been ignored, and there was shouting and raising of hands and too much noise for Hunter to handle. They were all angry and hurt over what had happened and scared of what was to come. She found herself staring at Will and how utterly broken he appeared as he sat in an office chair at the back of the group. His thoughts were not even present.

A sharp whistle blew over the noise and they fell quiet to see the Captain step forward.

"Enough!" he shouted. "There's no time for technicalities. We have a very real threat on our hands and we need a strategy. Which brings us to our next issue."

Up on the screen, a news report started playing. A blond reporter by the name of Catherine Sherman with a beautiful face stood before the FBI building in DC where an American flag waved in the background. The report was titled 'HEROES IN OUR MIDST'. Instantly, Hunter felt her stomach drop.

"After the announcement just last week from the Federal Bureau of Investigation stating that there are 'altered DNA' humans living among us, we have been given exclusive footage of these heroes in action."

The reporter disappeared and a new video played. It was clearly recorded on an iPhone or similar, because the quality was unclear and everything was dark. Static sounds blared through the speakers. A male voice was bleeped out and then suddenly, there was an explosion of fire and he screamed and stumbled. "Holy *bleep*!" he exclaimed. The camera steadied, and then they saw images of themselves on the lake behind the cabin, squaring off against the Agents and mutants. The fight was messier than she remembered and the camera didn't hold for very long before a tree nearby was hit by a bolt of Marcus's electricity and the cameraman dropped his phone.

The camera flicked back to the blond reporter. "This footage goes in conjunction with a fearsome rescue back in March this year at a New York restaurant, where a red-headed heroine much like the fire-wielding girl caught on camera only recently went into a burning building and came out with a girl who had been trapped inside." Two images of Hunter, side by side, frozen in blurry action at the cabin and outside the burning building filled the screen. She couldn't look away from them and didn't want to see the faces of the others staring at her. "Sources inside the FBI have confirmed that other powers do exist and that these people are the future heroes of our country. Fire wielders, technopaths and shape shifters are just some of many abilities that really do exist. Could this be the birth of a new generation of superheroes with unique abilities? Thanks John."

Newsreader John Crown appeared at a desk back in the studio, smiling in anticipation. "Thanks Cathy, and we have just heard now that police and FBI officials have investigated the sight of this so-called 'battle' but have found no leads as to who participated and if any were injured. Our inside source also confirms that the FBI's plans to hunt down the dangerous geneticist Dr. Winston Wolfe have come to an end when they raided his supposed institution in Yellowstone National Park, but found no possible leads as to his accomplice's location."

The report cut off.

"Fortunately for us," said the Captain, "when we returned to collect the bodies we were able to clean up the mess." He turned to Zac and glared at him. "We have you to thank for spilling the word 'hero' to this reporter, do we not?"

Zac pretended to be very interested in the ceiling for as long as he could avoid their attention.

"You told someone about us?" Chantal growled.

"Okay, *fine*. I spilled coffee on her at the FBI building and we got to talking. I had no idea she was a reporter, I thought she was an intern or something. And I wasn't flirting!" he added quickly.

"We know," said Amelia. "We had you wired, remember?"

Zac's jaw clicked. "So the media knows we're not just 'altered DNA' people but that we have superpowers. So the fuck what?"

"It's just not what we need right now," said Joshua.

"Hey, what was with that burning building thing Hunter?" asked Zac, if only to turn the blame on someone else.

"It was a stupid mistake I made when I didn't know how to use my powers and what to do with them. And it got me thrown in ICE, so I'm sorry. Do we have any leads as to what the FBI found at ICE? Was it definitely empty?"

"Marcus?" asked the Captain.

Marcus stood up from his stool. Hunter only just noticed that he had on a wireless headset and his eyes were bloodshot, his hair in disarray. She figured he'd be back on the computer immediately. He was their most valuable asset into tracking the FBI network.

"No new progress on more Impossibles. The FBI have come up with nothing and, in my opinion, they're looking pretty damn stupid right now."

Most of them nodded in agreement.

"However, since the FBI finally cracked my security system, they found ICE's location and raided it. There's been a sudden spike in security across the nation. ICE was empty."

Their reaction was less than dramatic. By this stage, they were expecting Dr. Wolfe to run.

"Wolfe wiped everything that would connect to his past, his current projects and where he ran to. I looked through all of their documented evidence and came up with nothing. The government have taken precautions and secured all nuclear weaponry with new access codes and military-grade security. They've also sent the President to a secret location for extra protection and locked up the Pentagon and the Whitehouse. All control now belongs to the Cabinet Members and their advisories. Whatever Dr. Wolfe has planned for world domination, it's going to be a ton more difficult to take control of our country with all this extra security."

"But we're not worried about the Embassy, are we?" asked Hunter. "We're worried about Ravenadium."

"We should be worried about both," said Joshua.

Zac moaned. "That's too much to worry about! Can't we just have like … one big battle and get it over with?"

Everyone looked at Zac as though he was stupid.

"Are you absolutely positive the FBI found nothing at ICE?" asked Chantal. "If Dr. Wolfe has Ravenadium, he could have created someone like me, who could have told the FBI that they saw nothing just like what I did when they came to our cabin."

Marcus shrugged. "It's possible. There wasn't any proof that ICE was empty in their files, just reports filled out by forensics."

"Why don't we blow up the mountain, just in case?" Koko suggested.

Everyone looked at her as if she were insane.

"What, like with bombs?"

"No, Zac, with rainbows," spat Marcus.

"We can't," said Hunter. "Jack and Alfie may still be inside."

"So could Dr. Wolfe," said Zokani. "And isn't he the person we're trying to destroy?"

"It's too risky."

"As opposed to risking the safety of our planet," said Koko.

"Ryo could teleport inside," said Chantal, "to see if it's empty?"

"Oh, sure, send me in again."

"Alright look," the Captain took a step closer to the center of their group. "As much as I don't want to admit it, blowing up ICE is the best idea we've come up with. But the issue is we don't have that kind of weaponry in our kitchen, and we don't have the time to get it. There has to be another way to catch Wolfe sooner."

They all stood deep in thought, and Hunter nervously tapped her fingernails on the bar.

"Okay," said Hunter finally. "Until we come up with something, the only thing we can do right now is to talk to Mikayla. Maybe she'll listen to me."

"Why, because her power can't affect yours?" said Marcus. For some reason she registered a bitter tone in his voice and the fire flared up, anger becoming her favorite emotion all of a sudden.

"Do you have some kind of *problem* with me talking to your psycho brother's girlfriend, Marcus?" She pushed herself away from the bars so she could walk down to the bottom level.

Marcus registered the same bitterness in her tone and ripped off his headset, standing up. "Actually, I have a *problem* with the fact that you suddenly think you're better than all of us because you were a freak even *before* you could breathe."

Electricity sparked from the tips of his fingers and behind him, all of the computer screens started to flash and the lights flickered. Hunter set her palms on fire and that was when everyone seemed to register what was going on and started shouting at them.

"That's enough!"

Hunter only had eyes for Marcus, the both of them consumed by anger, but not until Will stepped between them and held up his hands did she realize how childish she was being.

"There's no use fighting, save it for Wolfe." He stared with fierce eyes and instantly, the fire calmed. "Hunter, you should talk to Mikayla."

"Yeah, maybe she'll spill to someone who doesn't have a dick," Zac shouted.

"The Immortal is right," said the Captain with a nod at Will. "Hunter, talk to the prisoner." He handed her a key-card. "She's locked in the second containment room in Ward D. Marcus, get back to the computers and keep an eye on the FBI's progress. See if you can pinpoint where they're keeping the President and where their weaponry is being controlled from. If we know where the control is, we know where Dr. Wolfe will target to take over the country. I want my tech team online searching for any sign of Dr. Wolfe's whereabouts and any clues into his past. We'll take shifts through the night. The rest of you need to get some rest. Does anyone have questions?"

Zac's hand shot up. "Can people actually cry underwater?"

Those from ICE groaned, especially Marcus who slapped his forehead. The Captain looked as if he had heard wrong.

"I beg your pardon?"

"Don't listen to him, he's being an annoying."

Zac was snickering to himself. The Captain grumbled a dismissal. Marcus shot one last tainted look at Hunter and sat down behind the desk. Will reached out a hand and she took it.

"Thanks," she muttered. "I needed that."

"Be careful with Mikayla," he said. "You're on the fringe of your emotions right now."

"You think?"

"But you're stronger than she is." Will squeezed her hand and gazed down at her fiercely. "Remember what's at stake."

Hunter nodded. "I know."

With that, she marched out of the room and didn't look at any of the faces that watched her leave.

FIFTY-FOUR

knock on the door made Dr. Wolfe's anger build. He was overtired, had been working with sleepless nights and was so close to a breakthrough that the idea of dealing with another human being's problems made steam ooze from his ears.

The door handle creaked. "Dr. Wolfe?"

He let out a long breath of air and told himself to be calm. When he turned, he found Jamison at the door.

"What is it?" he asked through his teeth.

"Sir, Dr. Hosking is here to see you. She says her team has discovered the substance's origin."

Dr. Wolfe's eyes sprung wide open and he whirled, instantly interested. "Bring them in, now!"

He turned back to the brightly lit operating table where tubes were running down around his feet and the body of a young girl lay asleep. He looked down at her with longing. He wanted so badly for this experiment to be a success. And with the added bonus of pure Ravenadium, he was confident it would be.

Footsteps approached him and he turned to see Dr. Hosking and her two associates that he didn't care to learn the names of. Dr. Hosking held a tablet out to Dr. Wolfe with graphs and maps.

"Dr. Wolfe, we were able to match the rock-type with a specific area in Cuba, as described by you, and we came up with only one possible mountain." She leaned forward and enlarged the screen. "This one. It's outside La Marca Del Portillo, and according to our research it is twenty miles wide. Not only that, but it's a volcano."

"A volcano?" Dr. Wolfe rubbed the gray whiskers on his chin. "Well, that makes sense."

"How we get *into* the volcano and find samples remains a mystery. It'd take a team of volcanologists days to find a safe entry."

"I'll take care of that," said Dr. Wolfe. He needed someone who knew the mountain to be their guide. That was another part of his plan. "Would you like to know what I have come up with?"

"Yes," said Dr. Hosking. She and the other two scientists stared warily down at the girl lying on the table.

"The research that was collected by the Agents, written by our late friend and associate Dr. Rosenthal, proved that when combined with a particular chemical, the power of Ravenadium alters DNA, giving a person whatever ability is in relation to the conjoining chemical. For example, one dose of Ravenadium plus a liquid solution of, say, titanium, could create an ability to transform oneself into an entirely metallic physique, impenetrable and undefeatable."

"Kind of like Colossus?" said one of the scientists.

Dr. Wolfe turned himself toward the man, who looked to be in his mid-thirties, and gave him a curious look.

"I beg your pardon?"

The scientist looked suddenly terrified. "You know … Colossus? From the *X-men* comics? He has-"

"What's your name?"

"S-Simon, Simon Carter, sir."

Dr. Wolfe nodded thoughtfully, enjoying watching the color drain out of Simon's face.

"Dr. Carter, do you understand what this substance will mean for my company, for my future experiments?"

"Well," Simon pointed to the body of the girl. "If you have Ravenadium, w-which you do … all you have to do is invent a formula that will combine a specific chemical and the power of Ravenadium – being mindful of the effects it will have on the body and other factors … and you'll have yourself a brand new, genetically enhanced human with powers."

Dr. Wolfe bent over the body of the girl and turned her head toward him very gently. She was fast asleep, still dirty from living in the Death Caves. The side of her face was burnt from the doctor's experiments with Hunter's powers. The other mutants called her Caitlin.

"What it means, Dr. Carter, is that I do not need to search the globe for children with superpowers. I always chose children because their bodies change so rapidly at such a young age and it's easier to see the growth of their cells. But now … I no longer need those with abilities, and I no longer need humans with which to experiment. I can create my own."

The three scientists looked at him in horror.

Dr. Wolfe leaned over Caitlin's body and very gently whispered her name.

Caitlin's eyelashes fluttered. The heart rate monitor started to pick up pace. And after a few seconds, the young girl opened her eyes.

"Dr. Wolfe," she said.

"Hello my dear," he smiled. "How are you feeling?"

Her eyes roamed the room. "I feel … dizzy."

"What can you hear?"

Caitlin's eyes rested on his, staring at him in a familiar manner. She was reading his mind, his soul, just as Fearne had.

"I hear your thoughts," she said.

From behind him, Dr. Hosking gasped.

"What are my thoughts saying, Caitlin?"

Caitlin frowned, focusing with calm fascination. "You're thinking of Fearne."

For the first time since he handed Alpha the syringe filled with poison, Dr. Wolfe felt as if the guilt had been lifted from his shoulders. He had succeeded. He had created a brand new Fearne.

"Yes, sweet child," he murmured and ran a hand down her bumpy, scarred skin. "You're absolutely right." Dr. Wolfe turned back to his associates with a large grin on his face. "In order to create more genetically enhanced children, I'm going to need a large supply of Ravenadium. That is why I decided to join with the Chinese Embassy, so that while they are trying to gain control of the USA's nuclear weaponry system and the entire country through the White House, distracting the media and the FBI from scouring the globe for my whereabouts, I will be taking a little trip to Cuba."

"Dr. Wolfe, what if the Chinese are successful?"

He let out a low chuckle. "We do not need to worry about that. Dr. Hosking, what is more terrifying than an enemy who wants to unleash war on your country and have the means to do so?"

She shrugged, as did her co-workers.

"It's someone who can stop them," he said. "Jack is more powerful than ever. And once I have my hands on enough Ravenadium to create my own army, the Chinese, the Americans, even the little band of superheroes all over the news cannot stop me. I will be the most powerful man on the planet, and nobody will ever see me coming."

The three scientists gazed at him in awe.

"What do you want us to do?"

He tapped the metal table with his long fingernails. "I will need a volunteer to come with me to Cuba to extract the samples. I need my Agents prepped to travel with me as well, and I need a team to assist the Chinese soldiers with their mission. Have they found the new location of the President?"

"Yes sir," said Dr. Hosking. "We overheard the Korean hackers say that the President is hiding out in an abandoned army base in Louisiana. They've set up an emergency bunker for terrorist attacks such as this, figuring we have the means to break apart the White House. They thought their network was secure, but using Marcus's security system, the techs belonging to the Korean team hacked into it and discovered the location."

"We heard all this from them," added the other scientist.

"Very nice," said Dr. Wolfe. "You three would make excellent undercover agents if you weren't geniuses."

Simon's goofy face lit up, but Dr. Hosking never accepted any compliments. Her expression did not change.

"Dr. Wolfe?" asked Caitlin.

He turned to her, instantly worried. "Yes? Are you alright?"

"I was just wondering ... how can I hear her thoughts?"

Dr. Wolfe looked at Dr. Hosking, who pursed her lips as if she could stop Caitlin from reading her mind.

"It is a combination of a beautiful young girl's blood and a very precious substance called Ravenadium."

"No," she frowned at Dr. Hosking. "Not her voice."

"Whose voice do you mean?"

Caitlin grinned. "The voice of the girl you call Fearne."

267

FIFTY-FIVE

After the chaotic discussion in the communications room, Joshua needed air. He needed cold air, but that apparently wasn't the season outside in the Nevada desert where the sun was at its quarterly mark and the air was warm even with the breeze. Still, it was peaceful and quiet and that was exactly what he'd searched for.

"So you and Miss Smart, huh?"

Joshua nearly jumped out of skin, turning to see that Hunter had found him on the cliffs nearby the hatch of the compound sealed into the mountain. Over to the right, down the way on a ledge, was where they cremated the three dead children.

Hunter skidded down the slope and sat next to him.

"This is not a comfortable subject for me," said Joshua if he had to be honest.

Hunter sniffed. "It's never been a comfortable subject. You still do that thing where you blush and your eyes go all squinty."

"Well ... it's sunny out here."

Her hair hadn't looked so clean and healthy since the first few months she had her powers. It helped to be happy and free again, to let the fire roam.

"A lot's changed since we were last together Joshua. *A lot.*"

"I know."

"So whatever is happening between you and Miss Smart, I'm going to choose to be okay with it."

He raised an eyebrow at her. "You are?"

"Yep." She nodded her head firmly. "Things are crazy right now and if you can find love in all this chaos ... well, you deserve to have someone."

Joshua felt more guilt seep from his soul again. "Hunter, I am so sorry about Eli. And about Jenny. In fact I'm sorry for every wrong I ever did you. I shouldn't have been so strict on you when you first discovered your powers, I shouldn't have kept secrets from you or tried to stop you from seeing Eli. I'm sorry that all this time I never told you how much I truly love you."

Hunter gazed at him, her golden eyes swimming with a smile of wonder. "You have no idea how good it is to hear you sat that."

Joshua lowered his head and breathed a laugh. A relieved laugh.

"I'm sorry too," she said to the valley. "I'm sorry that I was such a whiney, moody, impatient, self-centered, angsty teenager last year. I thought that I deserved better than you, that I *was* better than you. But I had a lot to learn about humility. And about being a hero."

"Doesn't look like it now," he said. "You're more of a hero than I ever was."

"Not really," she smiled. "You were a hero every day Joshua. Every day when you made me breakfast and you burnt the toast." He sniffed a laugh, shaking his head. "Or when you came to my piano practice when I was seven years old and that fat woman with the 80s haircut kept begging for you to ask her out until you-"

"Told her I was a homosexual?" They laughed so hard that real tears formed in Joshua's eyes. "I never wanted to show up to that rehearsal hall ever again!"

"I know!" she grinned. "But you did. I never noticed how much you cared about me. You were there every day to pick me up from school. And I couldn't even stay for your entire university benefit without running off with some boy I just met."

Joshua sighed. "We could sit here and compare our mistakes Hunter, but the truth is we're both broken people. And we're going to keep making mistakes."

"I guess being away from you put things into perspective for me. And life will never be the same again, you know?"

"You're right. Did you have any luck with Mikayla?"

"Sort of. I'm getting Zac and Marcus to talk to her later and see if they can get anything from her. She told me Dr. Wolfe is apparently working with the Chinese and Korean government. Obviously they want to settle some score with our country and he's using them as a distraction while he goes after the real prize."

"Ravenadium," Joshua nodded thoughtfully. "So there'll either be a fight between us and whatever threat there is to the President, or there'll be a fight with Dr. Wolfe, his Agents and those crazed mutants he let loose."

"Question is; do we have enough strength in numbers?"

"We have our team, the new 'Impossibles', the SSS soldiers and whoever else wants to volunteer, and I'm sure the FBI will lend us a SWAT team or some SEALs even." Joshua shook his head. "Ultimately, I think our best bet is to wait for the doctor to make his move. We can't waste any more time discussing strategies."

"Well it's better than doing nothing, right? I mean for so long I was in ICE feeling like I was doing nothing, letting Dr. Wolfe get away with so much torture and not being able to do a thing about it. It was so *hard* to have so much power inside me and yet feel so much fear for a mortal man."

Joshua nodded. "But you have to remember what's important. Which reminds me-" He reached into his pocket and pulled out a silver chain with a Chinese symbol attached to it. It was the necklace she left with Eli the night of prom. The necklace her mother made for her. "We're all human." She bent her head and lifted the red curls that blew around her face so he could clip the necklace together. "You can have a power and still be scared. But the true heroes are the ones who have courage, even when they have no power at all."

Her eyes glowed as she looked into his face, a rush of thankfulness washing over him like the desert wind. He should savor this moment of being alone with her. They were endless when the two of them lived alone in New York. But everything was different now. She was different.

"I'm proud of you," he said. "Your parents would be too."

Hunter leaned forward and wrapped her arms around his neck. The smell of her hair pressed against his cheek and the strangeness of fire touching his skin in an uncomfortable warmth was no bother to him anymore. Just to be near her, alive, was blessing enough for a man who did not deserve such happiness.

FIFTY-SIX

Hunter walked into the Ring the next morning hoping to get an early workout before everyone else decided to wake up. She flicked the light switch on, watching the fluorescents blink awake and walked over to the lockers full of gym gear. As she was strapping her wrists, she heard the door creak. When she looked up, Will was stalking toward her in the same clothes he slept in.

"Did I wake you up?" she asked.

He shook his head, following her lead and strapping his own wrists. His hair fell in his eyes and as he dragged his fingers through it, Hunter bit her lip. *Don't ever let him cut his hair.* "I felt you get out of the bed and figured you'd be here. I thought it was a good idea."

She gave him a smile which he didn't return. He was still suffering from the loss of Fearne – unable to move on as fast as the others. That girl had been a part of his life for six long years. Not just a part of it, but his whole world.

He picked up the pads and helped her into her gloves. They moved onto the mat and started with some quick, successive jabs and hooks. Hunter was much fitter after being out of ICE for a couple of weeks, as was Will. Her wrist was still a little sore from the battle at the cabin, so she went easy on her left hooks. Thankfully, the bullet that grazed her arm wasn't too deep either.

They switched after twenty minutes and Hunter held the pads up for Will as he jabbed. She watched his eyes, so stern and focused. Then she was thinking about what Mikayla had said yesterday.

"Mikayla told me what the guards were doing to you in ICE."

Her words broke his concentration. He shot her a bitter look and then shrugged, picking up the pace. "It wasn't – anything important. I didn't want to worry you."

"Are you kidding?" Her arms burned from the pain of holding up the pads. "They tortured you for *fun,* Will, and you didn't tell me about it because it's not important?"

Will stopped. "Can we just forget about it Hunter? I think we have a bit more to deal with at the moment without bringing up the past."

Hunter dropped her arms. "If I had've known-"

"You wouldn't have been able to do a goddamn thing about it, now please, can you just drop it? And put your arms up again."

Hunter gave him a look of defiance and crossed her arms. The pads made it awkward to hold the position. She saw the corner of his mouth twitch in a smile.

"I don't think so. If I knew, I'd have been a *lot* more lethal with Jet at the cabin. He would've known a whole new meaning of the word 'burned'."

Will's frown turned into a beautiful crooked smile and he closed the distance between them, wrapping his arms around her. The pads were so big that she couldn't pull out of them and stood there with her arms crossed, her cheek pressed against his damp, toned chest. She closed her eyes and imagined Will, strung up and beaten until he couldn't stay awake any longer and the fire began to burst inside her, so much so that there was a sizzling sound and Will jumped away from her with a yell. His skin was pink and her arms were on fire.

"Oops. Sorry," she murmured. Then she realized that she'd burned a hole in her pads. Ripping them off and shoving them to the ground, Hunter sat down, buried her head in her hands and sighed loudly. She heard Will sit beside her and felt his arm around her back. She was probably still hotter than a stovetop, but he didn't care. Hunter looked up at him in surprise.

"I won't keep things from you again," he said.

The fire dimmed, simmered by his loving gaze just like her heart.

"You'd better not," she smiled.

He leaned over and pressed a soft kiss to her lips, moving harder and gripping the back of her neck to keep her there. She still couldn't believe he'd never had this kind of physical relationship before now. He was incredibly good at everything they did.

When he pulled away, she saw pain in his eyes.

"Are you … okay now? About Fearne?"

Will's fingers brushed across her skin, his other hand reaching for hers and playing with her frail fingers. There was a flash of darkness in his soul that she noticed, and it worried her. Will was not the greatest at hiding his emotions, but he was good at deflecting the subject.

"It's not easy but … you make it better."

"Aw," she grinned. "You're just a big softie, aren't you?"

Will sniffed a laugh. Then his arm scooped around her neck and he pulled her into a headlock.

"Ow – Will!"

He laughed loudly, shoving her body to the ground. "Gotcha!"

"Get off!"

He slapped the ground, shouting "One! Two! Three!" and released her. "I am the champion!" he yelled at the empty room with two hands raised in triumph.

Quick as a flash, Hunter slipped her leg around his knees and yanked him to the ground where she jumped on top of his body and pinned his arms down. Will's smile was so bright and full of amusement that she couldn't help but kiss him. Her kiss was hungry and passionate and their sweaty bodies out in full view of anyone to walk in and witness them made it that much more appealing. But when they broke away, they were still alone.

As they were unstrapping and putting their gear in the lockers – or in Hunter's case, the trash – Will turned to her with a smile on his face.

"Look what I found," he said and held up a half-empty packet of cigarettes.

Hunter's mouth dropped open. "No way!"

"Should we, for old time's sake?"

"Absolutely."

After looking around for any smoke alarms, they decided to hide in the back corner where the mats were stacked up. With their feet dangling over the edge of the blue mats, Hunter lit the cigarette and they shared a moment together like they used to in the guard's quarters, talking about nothing important, because everything important in their lives involved death and destruction, and they weren't in the mood for that. They found an old tape player with the *Dirty Dancing* soundtrack inside, and Hunter felt it was her duty to show Will how to do the lift in the final dance. She scowled when he chickened out as she sprinted at him, and Will's impersonation of a prim and proper ballerina had her in hysterics. They laughed together, pretending they were the only two in the world, and 80s romance movies and smoking rebelliously in the gym was everything that consumed them apart from the love they had for each other.

When the soldiers entered the Ring to train, Hunter and Will reluctantly snapped back to reality, but that morning was more wonderful than any they'd ever had because for a moment, just a moment, they existed without a care, together and in love.

FIFTY-SEVEN

I t happened two days later.

Hunter was on her way to the communications room for an update on the outside world when the alarms sounded. Her heart skipped a beat and she froze like a deer in the headlights.

Those sirens.

They reminded her of ICE. She was about to scream when suddenly someone came up behind her and took her hand.

"Hunter, are you alright?" asked Will.

His worried face distracted her for a moment. "Y-yeah, I'm okay."

"Come on, we need to get to the communications room," said Zac as he whipped past them.

"What's going on?" asked Will.

"I dunno, but everyone's going this way."

They hurried up the stairs and joined the crowds of people filing into the communications room. Marcus sat at the computer system – he'd been working for days on a way to track down Dr. Wolfe's Chinese connections and monitor the UN. Ryo and her brother were with him to translate. Other SSS members were standing around the platform above their heads, peering down. More were seated against the back wall, at the computer hubs and the control units and standing around with coffees in their hands, a handful in army uniforms. The Captain's soldiers. Hunter hadn't ever seen all of them there at once. She guessed there were about thirty of them.

The Captain stood at the head of the room. Images of news reports flashed across the screen behind his head.

"Attention, everyone, we have breaking news," the Captain announced. "The war we've all been anticipating has apparently begun without us knowing."

Whispers and cries of shock erupted throughout the room.

The Captain continued in his booming voice. "Right now, the White House is under attack."

"What?" several people shrieked.

"Is Obama still alive?" asked Zac loudly.

"He isn't in the White House anymore, Zac," said Marcus with a sigh. "Remember? They moved him, along with all their other military shit to the secret facility."

"Right, the Area 51 in Louisiana?"

"Exactly."

"So then … the Chinese don't know the President has been moved?" asked Zac.

"We're not sure. It happened only fifteen minutes ago. A squadron of Chinese soldiers invaded the White House, and from what it looks like-" The Captain clicked a controller operating the screen. He froze the image of a large, horribly familiar figure on the steps of the White House, explosions all around him as someone opened fire. It didn't appear to be hurting him. "Your Destructo is there as well."

Hunter put a hand over her mouth and stared at the screen.

Jack.

"Oh no," she muttered so only Will could hear her. "Dr. Wolfe got through to him. He's completely lost control."

The Captain resumed the playback and they watched Jack – Destructo – surge back down the steps toward a SWAT vehicle that had parked on the lawn. He froze – still under heavy gunfire – raised his clenched fists and then threw them down on the lawn.

All at once, the camera shook and there was a thunderous rumble that echoed through the communications room. Crowds of people screamed. The SWAT trucks were blown backwards, along with everyone around them.

Then Jack turned and ran back, disappearing into the White House foyer.

The Captain turned off the playback. "After discovering the secret location of the new bunker, we've been tracking its data usage and communications. Slater, what can you tell us?"

Marcus stood up from the back computer hub and puffed his chest up, looking pleased to be so valuable to the team.

"The wire transfers between ICE and China were coming from a facility in Suzhou, which has one of the fastest growing economies in the country and a seriously scorching power consumption. They were protected by a security algorithm that would normally take at least three months to crack, but I was able to work my magic." He nodded and raised his eyebrows proudly. From Hunter's right, she heard Zac cough 'nerd'. "I did some research and found out that the area is owned by a line of royalty called the Jochis, whose heir ended in 1227. But the *facility* is military. Some guy named General Psi Chang runs it."

"Psi Chang?" asked the Captain. "Never heard of him."

"Okay, well as Mikayla told Hunter, Wolfe and Chang are working together to take down the American Embassy. It looks to me like they know about the secret bunker, because from my thermal imaging scans, I can see that there's only one team of Chinese soldiers inside the White House and Destructo. That's not enough to take down the entire special forces, plus whoever else they send in."

"So they're already at the base?" asked Chantal.

"Not yet," said the Captain, "but they will be any second. We have to get to the army camp before they destroy it. Destructo is only a distraction for the media and the authority."

"But we have to stop him," said Marcus. "The guy could destroy thousands of innocent lives. There won't be any civilians at this army camp to protect, so the White House should be top priority."

"Marcus is right," said Joshua. "Jack is our biggest threat. He must be stopped."

"With what?" asked The Captain. "Nothing military will take down Destructo."

"His name is Jack!" Eli shouted.

"*Jack*," spat the Captain. "Whatever. How do we fight him?"

"We don't," said Hunter. "I'll talk to him."

Every eye turned to her in absolute surprise. Eli's mouth was hanging open.

"Are you crazy?" Marcus exclaimed.

"Yeah, are you?" asked Will beside her.

"Look I *know* him. I think maybe I can get through to him."

Joshua shook his head. "Hunter, that's absurd."

"No, it's not. You know as well as I do that the only thing standing in the way of Jack's soul and total destruction is the darkness in his mind, the voice in the back of his head. Dr. Wolfe brought it out, maybe I can suppress it. Maybe I can cure him. And while I stop Jack, you guys need to fly to the army base and save the President and the country, because let's face it – losing that battle would be way worse than Jack killing a bunch of people. You'll need every man you can muster."

For a moment, everyone stood there in stunned silence. Or perhaps they were all considering their options. Some didn't look convinced – the Captain, Eli and the soldiers, for instance – but others trusted Hunter's judgment. After all, only she and Eli knew Jack well enough to get through to him.

The Captain let out a long sigh and surveyed Hunter through his bushy, gray eyebrows. "Looks like it may be wise to keep you on Destructo duty, Miss Harrison. We'll send you with a defense team to the White House in our smaller jet – Amelia, you'll fly that one."

"But Dad-"

"That's an order."

Amelia lowered her head and Eli slipped his hand into hers, squeezing it. For a moment, Hunter remembered when Eli's father used to order him around as well. Perhaps that was one thing the two of them had in common.

"Once you've taken down the threat, get in contact with the Red Cherry and get to Louisiana as fast as you can."

"Wouldn't it be easier for me to pick her up?" asked Ryo. "It'll take a lot less time."

"We need you at your full strength," said Joshua. "You may not be able to handle all the teleporting."

Ryo glared at Joshua but didn't rebut.

"The rest of us will fly to the army base and take down the Chinese before they can gain control of our nuclear weaponry. I'm also willing to bet there'll be Dr. Wolfe's assassins – the Agents, you call them?"

They nodded.

"Don't forget the mutants!" shouted Ella, and then she slunk back, almost embarrassed that she'd spoken.

Hunter shuddered. She'd rather take on the Agents than the mutants. They freaked her out.

"But hold on ... what about Dr. Wolfe?" asked Ryo. "He's the guy with the ultimate power in his hand, where will he be?"

"We don't have time to worry about killing him," said the Captain. "We'll take down Wolfe another day, when there isn't a direct threat to our country."

Some of them were a little wary of the Captain's priorities, but Hunter didn't argue. She and Joshua exchanged glances, both knowing where Dr. Wolfe would be at that very moment. It was too hard, however, to fit a flight to Cuba into their battle agenda.

"Alright, is everyone good with the plan?"

Murmurs of agreement bubbled throughout the room. The Captain crossed his arms and stared them all down.

"I've faced many battles in my day serving as a sergeant," he said. "And I've seen men fall and not get up again."

"That's encouraging," Marcus mumbled.

"*Men*, Slater," he said with a point of his finger. "I've never served alongside children before. I don't know what lies in store for us at that army base, but I know that when we step out of that jet, I will not be surrounded by *just* soldiers. I will be surrounded by heroes. Because after everything you've all been through, to be suiting up and going into battle at your age with no training is heroic in itself. Brave men will die today. But heroes ... heroes live on." He looked directly at Hunter with a smile in his eyes. "They are a fire that will never burn out."

"A light in the darkness," said Will, remembering Fearne.

And then, from all around the room, there were murmurs from the SSS members as they raised their fists into the air. "A light in the darkness," they whispered. Hunter looked at their hopeful faces, for the first time truly thankful for their support.

"Suit up, Impossibles," shouted the Captain. "Meet in the hanger in ten minutes."

As the Captain continued to shout orders at the SSS members who handled the communication between the jet and the compound, there was chaos everywhere. Hunter felt her heart beating like a hummingbird's wings in her chest as Will pulled her away from the chaotic area. The SSS members stayed clear of them so they could run to their rooms and gather whatever it was they needed.

Hunter had never dressed so quickly in her life. Her suit had been finished that morning and the tests were successful. She stared in her bedroom mirror at the suit of black and crimson fabric that Ella and her designers had made. There were beautiful flames engraved along her wrists and ankles and a large flame reaching from her torso to her neck. With her wild, red hair she looked fiercer than ever.

Suddenly, Hunter couldn't help but feel like she was in a great, big, unbelievably weird dream.

I'm in a badass superhero suit about to go and fight my deranged high school friend at the White House. When did this become my life?

She had no time to think about the press who would eat this up, no time to feel terrified that she would be doing this alone and no time to remember what it felt like to run into a burning restaurant or face the unknown. She could only remember what Dr. Rosenthal had told her in the letter he wrote:

You must all face you future as heroes in this world. You are not just children anymore; you are warriors.

Someone rapped on her door and she yanked it open. Will stood there, his suit colors of black, dark blue and tinges of gray. The suit fitted him to a tee, accentuating every muscle of his body. His eyes rolled over her suit and instantly, his mouth dropped.

"Phwoar … you uh-"

"Yeah, you too."

Will's mouth spread into a grin. His smile still melted her, but she had no time to marvel over him. She went to push past Will and head for the jet when he shoved her back inside the room and slammed the door shut behind them.

"Wh-"

His lips pressed against hers and silenced the words in her mouth. Hunter momentarily lost herself when they both softened and she had wrapped her hands around his firm biceps, his fingers gently scratching the line of hair beneath her neck that sent shivers of ecstasy down her spine. The feel of their silky suits pressed together was thrilling.

She moaned against his lips, wanting more of him, but he smiled and pulled away with one last gentle peck, his hands still cupping her face.

"I was going to say that I'm coming with you to the White House," he began and when she opened her mouth to object, he covered her lips. "But I *know* you won't let me. There hasn't been a moment of our time together where I haven't tried to save you Hunter, and vice versa, and I understand that this is one mission we must fight apart, but ... it's okay. I know you'll save Jack. I know you'll survive this, and not because you have an 'eternal flame' or some bullshit like that. I know you'll come back to me-" His doe-brown eyes bore into hers, large fingers tracing a line down her cheek. "Because if there's anyone who can pull someone out of the darkness and remind them of what love is, it's you."

"I hope so." She gripped his hands tight.

"And whatever happens today there's something I have to say."

"What?"

He gave her a crooked smile. "I'll tell you when it's over."

Hunter threw her fist into his arm. He jokingly frowned and made out that she'd hurt him. "You can't do that to me, what if-"

Once more, he grabbed her chin and kissed her passionately. She wanted to push him away but his kiss was too intoxicating and the fire roared for him.

"That's not fair," she said.

He laughed. "Race you to the hanger!"

Despite being frustrated, Hunter couldn't help but smile at the child-like happiness in his eyes as he sprinted to the stairs. It reminded her of Fearne.

As she closed her door, she prayed his belief in her would be enough, so that when it was all over and he said the words he so desperately wanted to keep, she could say hers.

"I love you," she whispered under her breath.

Then she ran after him.

FIFTY-EIGHT

For the first time since Jenny's life had turned completely upside down, she didn't know where to stand. Everyone around her was busy doing something, and yet she didn't have a place to be or a job to do or anything at all to prepare for. Joshua and the Captain were talking in hushed tones, Eli had run off after Amelia to say his goodbyes, all of those with superpowers were out of the room and all of the SSS had a job to do except those that Jenny heard someone refer to as the 'fans'. They were standing around talking to each other excitedly about how the fight would go down and who could create the best comic book. For a moment she remained fascinated by their conversation, bewildered that this was the world she was a part of now. A superhero compound. A terrorist attack. A threat to the world.

And she couldn't do a goddamn thing about it.

She heard yelling from behind her and turned to see the Captain stalking away from the front platform with Dr. Mark in his wake.

"You cannot make her go!" he yelled. "She's only *six*!!"

"Yes, and she has one of the most defensive powers in our arsenal," said the Captain. "Imogen may be a child, but she can protect herself from whatever they throw at her."

"And if she can't? Captain, I know you run this place and I know that you took Olivia and I in on your good graces, but I have done *nothing* to deserve this and neither has Imogen!"

"Hey." Joshua interrupted, raising his arms and standing between them. "Mark, she's not a baby anymore. She's been through a hell of a lot worse. I understand your need to protect her, believe me, but there are more important things here."

Mark looked like he wanted to rebut, but he thought it best not to. For a moment, Jenny felt sorry for him and made a note to ask Joshua to keep an eye on Immi for Mark. He didn't deserve to watch his long-lost daughter die. Even the thought brought tears to Jenny's eyes. She couldn't stop it. She couldn't do anything.

Joshua saw the look on her face and hurried over to her. "What's wrong?"

"I'm *useless*."

Joshua spat out a laugh as if that were the most preposterous thing she'd ever said.

"Well it's true," she snapped.

His shoulders fell. "Jenny, you're not useless. You're just not use*ful* at this point in time."

"They're the same fucking thing, Joshua!"

Several people close to them turned to stare at her. Joshua pinched the bridge of his nose. Jenny suddenly realized how completely childish she was being in light of current circumstances. Joshua had somewhere else to be right now.

"Look, I'm sorry. Just tell me what I can do to help."

Joshua stared at her for a second longer than he needed to, and then he placed a hand on the back of her head, pulled it toward him and kissed her passionately. As per usual, his kiss sent cold shivers of pleasure down her spine.

"Be here when I return?" he whispered against her lips.

She smiled. "You got it."

"And rub my feet?"

"I-" Jenny shut her mouth when she realized what he'd said. "You don't like me doing that."

"I'll put up with it for your sake," he said with false sincerity. Jenny started laughing and he planted one last extra-long kiss on her lips. He must've been worried for her, because she felt the chill of his power seep into her skin from the tips of his fingers. She shivered, causing him to lurch away.

"I'm sorry," he moaned. "Sometimes I can't-"

"It's okay," she assured him with a smile. "The cold never bothered me anyway."

"I love you," he smiled. "I'll see you soon."

"You'd better. Good luck."

Joshua nodded and kissed her for the last time before running to the exit.

FIFTTY-NINE

The hanger was packed with soldiers loading weapons in the jet that was going to transport them to the army base. Joshua had suited up – only because they went to so much trouble making it for him – even though he felt ridiculous in such a skin-tight suit with silver shards of ice artistically crafted along his arms and chest. And the mask was uncomfortably sticky around his eyes. But the others were wearing their suits too and it almost made Joshua happy in light of such a gloomy situation.

Boy, if Leo and Liz could see me now ... they'd probably die of laughter.

"Woah," said someone from behind him and Joshua turned to see an extremely attractive male strolling confidently up to him in a tight-fitting suit. His was red and silver, with the letters 'LF' across the chest area like lightning bolts. "Looking good there, popsicle."

"Who are *you?*"

The man raised an eyebrow at him. "Do you even have to ask?"

"Put that gorgeous body away, Zachary," said Chantal as she joined them on the platform. Her suit was so well-designed, she may as well have picked out the fabric herself. It was black and hot-pink, her leather boots stretching up to her knees, the heel at least two-and-a-half inches high. Joshua had heard she had to compromise with the designers who suggested she wear flats, not eleven-inch heels. She wouldn't dream of it. Her golden hair flowed in luscious curls down her back. Zac's mouth fell to the floor.

"Fuck – me," he whispered.

"Maybe later," Chantal winked.

Immediately, Zac changed back to his normal self. He shot Joshua a goofy sideways smirk before galloping after Chantal onto the jet.

Just before Joshua braced himself to follow them, he noticed a suspicious figure trying to appear casual as he slunk toward the hanger on the right where the smaller jet was, the one that Hunter was taking to DC. Joshua marched up to the figure, grabbed him by the shoulder and shoved him against the wall.

"Just *what* do you think you're doing?"

Eli stuttered, "I'm g-going with Hunter!"

Joshua sighed. "No you're not, you're staying right here."

"Hey." Eli shoved him away, surprising Joshua with his forcefulness. "You've got no right to tell me what to do. If I want to go on that plane you can't stop me."

"Want a bet?" Joshua formed an icicle in his palm. "It's too dangerous for you, and you won't be able to do a single thing to protect yourself from someone like Jack."

Eli scowled and straightened his jacket. "I know, I'm not an *idiot*."

The Captain ordered everyone to their jets and the rest of the soldiers marched up the ramp.

Joshua wasn't sure why, but he stepped away from Eli. He knew how hard it would be to stand around in the compound waiting for the fight to be over. And at least if Eli was there, he may be of some use when it came to getting through to Jack.

"Fine," said Joshua. "Stay out of trouble."

Eli didn't smile in thanks like Joshua hoped. But his eyes were grateful, and there was a moment that mended between them, something Joshua had irresponsibly avoided since they split up at the cabin. Now was as good a time as any to mend things.

"Good luck," he muttered and slipped between two crates and into the other hanger.

As Joshua walked back to the ramp where the Captain was assisting with the final crate, Hunter and Will appeared, both in their suits. Joshua's heart started pounding. He didn't want her to fight Jack by herself. Even if he believed she could succeed, it went against everything he'd lived his life by.

Protect her, Joshua.

How could he protect her if they were in different states? Hunter kissed Will goodbye – a sight he hadn't quite gotten used to yet – and approached Joshua.

"You look after yourself, okay?" he said.

Hunter looked up into his eyes and bit her lip. Either she had nothing to say or she didn't want to say it, but all she did was wrap her arms around his neck and hug him.

"I'll see you soon," she said.

"I'm counting on it."

"Oh-" She pulled something out of her pocket and folded it into his hands. "I found this, I thought you'd like it. To take the stress away." She gave him a wink and then made her way over to Amelia, who was waiting to take her to the second jet.

Joshua waved, finding it harder to say goodbye to her than it would be to face the enemy. But something told him he'd see her again.

Joshua gripped the armrests of the jet as they took off into the bright sun. His thoughts were momentarily distracted by the rocky takeoff, but once they were clear of a few thousand feet, the Captain unclipped his seatbelt and walked over to Marcus, who was stationed at the control desk near the cockpit.

As Joshua looked around, he felt his stomach sink. Their numbers were still limited, even with the soldiers. Could they fight a bunch of Chinese assassins, Agents and mutants without losing anyone again?

After a long moment, the Captain stepped back and stood before the hanger.

"Marcus has just unlocked the schematics of the underground army base." Marcus lowered a screen in front of the cockpit that was larger than Joshua's TV back home. The screen showed a 3D model of the army base. "We'll land in this area, a mile away from the base, and enter in through the hanger."

"Um question?" asked Zac.

"Only if it's relevant," growled the Captain.

"Won't the army or Secret Service or whoever is guarding the president just … mistake us for the enemy and try to kill us?"

A few others mumbled their agreement and voiced their concerns. The Captain crossed his arms.

"I agree with you Zac – it'll be difficult to even land in a secure property without raising questions, even if this jet has invisible capabilities. Which is why I made a few calls with the Unites States Armed Forces and an old friend of mine. They know we're coming."

"How did you convince them?"

"I didn't," said the Captain. "He did."

With that, he gave Marcus a nod and up on the screen, a video message played.

"Hello everyone," said Chevie. He sat in a dark, heavily guarded room filled with military equipment. The feed was fuzzy and his voice cut out a couple of times, but he at least looked well. "I'm here with Secretary Sage and the army ready to take down our attackers. They made their move unexpectedly, and we have already lost a lot of men. We're waiting for you so we can attack. The President is in their custody, but we have it on good authority that they will not kill him unless directly threatened. I guess we're going to have to threaten them anyway if we want to save this country. I'm sorry for being such a jackass, and for leaving so suddenly. But I'm back, and I'm here to help. We both are."

Chevie's father Alistair came into the frame and gave a hesitant wave.

"The Secret Service and the army are your back up. You'd better get here in a hurry – they won't wait for long."

The feed cut with a snap and the jet was shocked by Chevie's sudden turnaround and the news that they may not be as screwed as they all thought.

"So," said the Captain. "It's going to be a messy fight, but we have the nation's best to back us up. We can win this, I believe we can."

It was a two hour flight in the jet to Louisiana. Joshua distracted himself with general wonderments, such as how Chevie managed to build a jet that could reach up to two-thousand kilometers per hour all on his own.

The Captain encouraged them to rest, but they were all too nervous. Zac, Chantal and Marcus were trying to lighten the mood by talking about something Joshua only just caught the beginning of.

"Do you guys think Alfie will be there?" asked Chantal. "We don't even know if he's still alive."

"That'd be a shit storm," said Marcus.

"Oh man," said Zac, "I hope he's there. I mean he can't be dead, he's a freaking dinosaur."

"And all the other dinosaurs, what happened to them?" Marcus said sarcastically.

Most other people were paired together, trying to fuse a battle plan in their minds, all of them not really sure as to how it all would work out. A heated argument had started at the back of the plane on his side. Illya and Ace were talking loudly to each other.

"What's going on?" asked Joshua.

"Its' nothing," said Ace in his hoarse tone.

"Are you sure? Because you sound like you really don't want to be here."

"You Americans think you're capable of anything, don't you? You never look at the consequences, never consider the wars you may cause. Why do you think it's always America being targeted for destruction?"

"Because we have the greatest range of nuclear weaponry in the world and a fuck-ton of people who support us," said Marcus.

"And our President is black!" shouted Zac.

Everyone looked at him in astonishment.

"Sorry," he said.

"Illya is right," said Zokani, and his sister nodded in agreement. "Are we really prepared for what we're facing here?"

"We're protecting our country," said Joshua. "We're showing the world that we can be heroes and that we'll die trying. We can't be fully prepared for this, but at least we're doing *something*."

"No," said Ace, "you're fighting fire with fire."

"Actually, Hunter is fighting with fire for us," said Marcus. "I don't see either of you taking a jet on your own to take down a guy who can blow apart your mind without blinking. She's the bravest of us all, and the two of you sit there thinking you're better than her!"

"Not better," said Illya, "Smarter."

"Well you're either with us or – as the Captain suggested – you can jump off this plane. Maybe you'll land on your feet," Chantal snarled at Illya.

She and Ace locked gazes. After a moment in which they hardly moved, Illya nodded.

"We'll fight," she sighed. "But we're staying out of all your patriotic crap."

"That's fine," said Joshua. "But if this were Australia being attacked, I wouldn't be going in with my tail between my legs."

Illya raised her eyebrows, a sly smile crossing her long, red lips. "I'll be holding you to that, *Iceman*."

With the argument settled, everyone went back to their whispering and plan-making. But none of it stopped Joshua from worrying about Hunter. He couldn't take the pressure. He needed some way to relieve it all.

He reached into the small zip pocket of his superhero suit and took out the tiny snow globe Hunter had given him. He couldn't even see what was inside it with the dim light of the cabin, but when he shook it, the snow glimmered and reminded him of when Hunter was a young child and Joshua took her to *Toys R Us* around Christmas time. He expected her to beg him for a Barbie Beach House, but instead, she found a snow globe. And she would not let it go. Her golden eyes watched as the snow swirled around in the globe with child-like amazement. He gladly bought it for her, and another one the year after. Eventually she grew tired of them, but Joshua didn't stop collecting. They reminded him of the young, innocent Hunter that he had raised alone. She never knew the truth about the snow globes, but he was happy to keep that secret. Just like he was content to let her go, knowing she may not survive this fight, because they had made their peace.

He watched the snow swirl in the tiny glass ball and waited for it to begin.

SIXTY

It was a strange flight to DC. The jet they took was much older and smaller than the Red Cherry. Amelia could fly well, and the eight soldiers that sat in the cargo hold behind the cockpit remained silent. Hunter was allowed to ride shotgun with Amelia and rather enjoyed the view as they soared between white clouds into wide open spaces.

She didn't like the silence though. It freed her thoughts to imagine horrible scenarios of how the rest of the day would pan out. She imagined pain and war and death, but she prayed for victory.

"You know," said Amelia after about half an hour of no words. "I often find that the best way to get rid of nerves is to pump myself up with some great music."

Hunter turned to her. "What do you suggest?"

"I dunno. *Starship.* Some *ACDC.* Maybe a bit of Beyoncé."

Hunter snorted a laugh. "Those are some very specific tastes."

"They all have their meanings."

Hunter smiled and said nothing as Amelia flicked a switch above her head and music started playing. Hunter only recognized the song because of an album that played almost on repeat at the cabin while they cooked dinner.

"*Sleep when I'm dead?*"

Amelia nodded along with the beat, her hair falling in her eyes as she pretended to play an air guitar to Bon Jovi. The plane dipped and everyone jumped in fright as she grabbed the wheel, laughing at the shocked look on Hunter's face.

There was a crash from behind them and when Hunter spun around, she saw that the dip in the plane had caused a crate to fall off a stack against the back wall. Someone else fell with it. Eli stumbled to his feet and smoothed down his jacket as the entire plane stared at him. Somehow he'd snuck onto the jet *and* kept out of sight for half of the trip.

"Eli!" Hunter shouted as she unclipped her seatbelt and jogged to the back of the plane where he was trying to scoop up the heavy crate and pile it on the other stack. Some of the soldiers were snickering, not doing a thing to help him. "What the hell are you doing here?"

"I'm – saving – Jack –"

He was struggling so much that Hunter rolled her eyes and helped him replace the crate.

"You're the biggest idiot I've ever known."

"It's too late now. I'm coming. And I'm not going to sit on the plane either, I'm going to try and talk to Jack."

"Eli, that's stupid. You'll get–"

"Killed?" he snorted. "Don't talk to me like Joshua, you can't tell me what to do. If I want to try and save my best friend, my *only* friend, who's going to stop me?"

"Jack will, probably."

Eli's mouth dropped open.

"Come on. You know what Joshua's like when he loses it to the Iceman! Jack is a hundred times worse, so you being there isn't gonna do a thing to bring him back. I'm sorry, but you're just putting yourself at risk."

Eli shook his head slowly. "Everyone's right about you Hunter. You *do* think you're invincible."

She blinked in surprise. This certainly wasn't the Eli she once loved. Perhaps it was a good thing he didn't remember her. She stepped back from him, conscious of the eyes of every soldier in the aircraft – and probably Amelia's – boring into her back.

"I'm not gonna tie you to the jet. You can do what you want. But you're wrong. I know I'm not invincible. Which is why I'm asking you to stay here, because chances are I *won't* be able to save you when Jack tries to tear your head off."

"We'll see," said Eli. Then he sat down in one of the empty seats and strapped in. Some of the soldiers were following her with their eyes as she stalked back to the co-pilot's seat. Amelia shot a glance at her.

"That was kind of rude," she said. "He just wants to save his friend."

"I would've thought you'd thank me for trying to stop him committing suicide."

Amelia switched on auto-pilot and unclipped her seatbelt.

"You know, Hunter," she said with a small smile. "It's not your responsibility to save everyone. Regardless of whether or not we have powers, we're all allowed to be heroes."

Hunter left to go speak to Eli, and when she peered over her shoulder, she saw Amelia wrap her arms around his neck. Hunter's stomach clenched in knots. Her love for Will was strong, but the memory of Eli still burned in her heart. She couldn't bear to watch him die again, which was partly why she had to be so honest.

"You asked me once who I think you are," she overheard Amelia say to him. "Do you remember?"

"Yes," he replied.

"Well, power or no power, I think you're a hero. You should save your friend."

Hunter turned back to the sky and bit her lip. To encourage a loved one to walk into the line of fire because that's what he wants to do is braver than she wanted to admit. *I couldn't do that, I couldn't willingly let anyone I care about face danger. What does that make me? A hero? Or just a selfish human being?*

Yes, Eli had the freedom to make his own choices, but he didn't know the kind of pain she went through when he was killed. She was going to the White House to save a friend, not to watch one die.

SIXTY-ONE

The jet was cleared for landing on the Ellipse park. Hunter had no time to prepare herself before the ramp was lowered and half a dozen army officials carrying loaded weapons and other men and women in suits marched up the ramp with stern-looking faces. Leading the way were two FBI agents; Barry Sanders and his superior, Special Agent Fitzpatrick. The moment Barry met her eyes, he smiled and nodded. Hunter nodded back. It was surreal knowing that just last year, he was having beers with Joshua in her kitchen. Now they were fighting a war together.

From outside in the distance, Hunter could hear screams and explosions.

"Officer on deck!" someone shouted and the soldiers already on the jet stood sharply to attention. She hurriedly unclipped her seatbelt and stood up, only Amelia behind her. Eli kept himself concealed, trying to appear completely invisible.

A very tall man with broad shoulders and a gruff expression wearing a military uniform with a lot of badges marched toward her. His boots made a loud *thunk* on the metal grating. He looked around, raised his eyebrows and shook his head.

"Captain Mackintosh, you son of a bitch," he muttered to himself and shoved his hat under his arm. "So this is it?"

"General Rogers," said Amelia and she saluted him. "I'm Captain Mackintosh's daughter, Amelia. I assume my father contacted you about the situation?"

"Indeed," said General Rogers. "I half expected more of an army, but I trust the Captain's judgment." He turned his attention to Hunter. "You're the fire girl, yes?"

"Hunter," she said and shook his hand.

"This is my team. They're here to escort you directly to the building. We aren't authorized to arm you, but I presume you have a weapon suitable for this mission?"

"Yes," she lied. "I do."

"Right, well let's move out then. We don't have time to lose; this monster has already taken down two of my squadrons."

"His name is Jack," said Eli loudly.

The entire group turned to him. Bravely, Eli stepped into the light with his chin up.

General Rogers looked fit to blow. "Who in God's name are you?"

Hunter was beyond amazed at how tall Eli stood against this military figure. Simply standing up to his father brought on an asthma attack, and now he was a completely different person. A person she admired for his courage and his faith in Jack.

"That *monster* is my best friend. I'm going to save him."

The General chuckled under his breath. "Hunter," he said to her. "I don't know much about your kind and how it is you came to be … how you are." Hunter's eyebrows shot up at his bluntness. "But whoever that is in my President's house, he has killed over thirty of my men within the last hour. He is dangerous, deadly and works for the devil. He is not your *friend-*" he sneered at Eli, "-any longer. If you want to save this country, you will take him out. We cannot fight this. You're our only hope."

Hunter looked up into his harsh face, thankful that she knew something he didn't. She was going to stop Jack. But she was not going to destroy him.

"Yes sir," she said with a sparkle in her eye.

"Good."

"Once this mission is complete," said Fitzpatrick, "there will be a team out the front of the White House, including the Chairman of the Joint Chiefs, Mr. David Meyer. You will report to General Rogers and he will transport you back to this jet. Understood?"

Hunter nodded, even though she didn't care who the Chairman was or whether or not he'd be waiting outside.

"I don't have time to prepare you for what you're about to face," said the General. "My men have trained for years for these kinds of missions. So my only advice to you is to keep your eyes on the target and don't give up until you can't breathe in anymore."

Hunter nodded, her heart rate thumping.

"Good luck Hunter," said Barry.

"Thanks."

"Let's move."

The escorts grouped, gathering their weaponry. Hunter heard Amelia whisper to Eli. She didn't hear what she said, but when Hunter looked over her shoulder as she was urged down the ramp, she saw Eli remain on the jet. Amelia had convinced him to stay. *He must really like her,* she thought.

The moment they were on solid, damp ground she forgot all about Eli and focused on one thing only; Jack.

The smell of fresh air filled her lungs, the scent of dirt and smoke and gunpowder still remaining. Hunter heard explosions and felt her heart leap.

They ran across the grass, the soldier's weaponry clicking in their arms. She caught the eye of a soldier directly on her left. He was huge, his jaw square, his muscles bulging through his uniform. Did he know what he, too, was getting himself into?

"You okay?" he muttered to her in a deep voice.

"Just a little nervous," she replied. "How do you do it, how do you go to war not knowing if you're going to make it out alive?"

"To protect my country," he replied. "So that my wife and baby girl have a house to live in and a roof over their heads."

Hunter nodded. *There are many different kinds of heroes in the world,* she thought.

She tried to make everything peripheral and focus on the White House where she knew Jack would be but there was too much going on in her mind, too many emotions ruled by the fear in her heart. She focused on the fire for comfort and ran.

It wasn't long before they made it across the road where barricades and police cars blocked the traffic. There were people off to the sidelines, some not noticing them and others pointing. They didn't know who she was, thankfully, but Hunter didn't doubt that after tonight, they would remember her.

Then suddenly, there it was. Giant and beautiful. For a moment she paused to admire it. Joshua took her to Washington when she was thirteen. She didn't appreciate it much back then, but even with smoke around it, the house still projected elegant history all on its own.

The plan was to sneak through the back and make a surprise entrance. Hunter ran in the center of her protection, the memory of the map completely lost inside her head. There was too much else to think about. She didn't focus on what entrance they came through or where Jack was supposed to be. She didn't notice any of the artwork or pay attention to the damage.

Not until suddenly, there was gunfire. Someone had seen Jack. Hunter covered her head from the ear-piercing noise, afraid like a child as a terrible rumble shook the ground and it sounded as if the roof were caving in. A huge chunk of sandstone hit her left leg and she groaned in pain. A soldier screamed and when she looked up, a body landed beside her. He'd been flung at her, blood across the left side of his face, his eyes wide open. Dead. Another scream came and a soldier pushed her forward. It was the one she'd spoken with before.

"Keep moving," he growled. "Don't think about the dead."

Hunter stumbled into the entrance of the White House where a giant room was spread before her with two staircases on either side and a chandelier bigger than a car above her head. Dust from the explosions settled and she saw him.

He stood on the other side of the foyer on top of a fallen pillar, the size of two men fused together, his chest bare, spidery veins littering his body. In his eyes she saw nothing, no relief to see her, no hope at all of humanity. Just darkness.

It really did take over him.

"Jack," she breathed. "What happened to you?"

SIXTY-TWO

r. Secretary," said Captain Mackintosh as he strolled forward and shook the man's hand.

The Red Cherry touched down outside the rural army base nestled between two hills and surrounded by greenery. The air smelled fresh from rain. As promised, the squadron of army officials and soldiers were there to meet them. Chevie and his father Alistair were there as well.

"Hi everyone," said Chevie rather reluctantly. The SSS members ignored him.

"Captain Mackintosh," said the Secretary of Defense as he strolled forward and shook his hand. "It's been a while."

"Indeed it has."

"Now, in any normal circumstance, all of this-" He gestured to the plane and what was going on outside of it. "Would go very differently. But we all know what's at stake here and quite frankly ... none of my methods have been successful in eliminating the threat."

The Captain nodded. "Sir, I have firm faith in my men. We will handle the situation and have the President and all of our defense systems safe and sound, I can assure you of that."

The Secretary looked around at each of their faces. He frowned when his eyes rested upon those of them in superhero suits.

"What's this?"

"These are our ... special fighters," said the Captain.

Joshua immediately wanted to barf. *That's a pretty loose term for it.*

"They're kids, Mackintosh."

The Captain's face became harsh. "With all due respect, would I send in a bunch of kids to save our country, Mr. Secretary, if I didn't think they were prepared to fight?"

He didn't seem to have an argument for that. "Alright, well we have an escort to take you directly into the hanger. And Washington?"

"Already on it."

"Good," he nodded.

"Do we have any communication with the bunker, sir?"

"All communication is down," he said grimly. "Which means that the enemy has already infiltrated the bunker. We have very limited time."

"Is the President alive?" asked Zac loudly.

The Secretary, at this point, cleared his throat. "We know the President was inside the bunker and we do not know his condition. The enemy has not made contact."

"Captain?" came Marcus's voice from the computer. "You're gonna want to see this."

Everyone spun around as Marcus pulled up the imaging from a camera he'd managed to hack. It showed a long room with dozens of computer panels and many men inside. In the corner sat a group of men and women tied in a messy bundle. One of them was unmistakably the President, alive.

There were sighs of relief from the crowd.

"How the hell did you do that?" asked the Secretary.

Marcus shrugged. "It was cake. I just had to rewire the-"

"Good work Slater," said the Captain proudly.

"Can we speak to them?"

Marcus touched a button on the wall. He turned to the Secretary and nodded. "Go ahead."

"This is Secretary Sage of the President's cabinet." The men and women inside the bunker turned and looked around as if wondering where the voice came from. Some of them started typing madly on their computers.

"Let me try and get some of their faces up on screen," said Marcus.

The camera zoomed in on the Chinese and Korean men inside the bunker and matched their identities through facial recognition through the Red Cherry's database. At once, he found the General.

"Psi Chang," said the Secretary loudly and a short, fat man turned around with a fearless, smug smile on his face. "I wondered when you'd be causing trouble in our country again."

"It's good to see you're finally here to fight, Mr. Secretary. Are you prepared for what you're walking into?"

The Secretary pursed his lips and was obviously trying to stop himself from mouthing off to the enemy for fear they'd do something irrational and kill the President. But he couldn't stop himself.

"You bet your ass we're prepared," he snarled. "Stay where you are, we're coming to get you."

The screen went blank and the Secretary stood up. He addressed them all clearly in a loud voice.

"Our mission is simple – get in, kill as many of these sons of bitches as you can, get the President and our men out of the bunker and back to this jet. We have snipers stationed at every possible range outside the facility. If anyone comes out, they're authorized to shoot. That means that *none* of you are to leave the base until every last one of those fuckers is dead. Am I understood?"

There were nods and the soldiers saluted. Joshua glanced down at Imogen who was holding on to Chantal's arm, looking pale. He felt instantly guilty about taking a six-year-old into a war zone, but there wasn't an alternative option.

"Who's ready?"

Joshua flinched at the loud jeers and cries from the soldiers. He stayed with those he knew as they were led down the ramp into the daylight. There were low trees everywhere and a dirt track that snaked down the way toward the army base entrance.

Joshua didn't feel afraid for himself as they came near the doors to the hanger and the soldiers scuttled with raised guns to the entrance. He was only afraid for the younger ones, who didn't look very brave.

"Hey," he said to Ryo, Imogen, Zac, Chantal and Marcus. Zokani had taken off into the air – it was the first time he'd seen the guy fly. Koko vanished as well. Ace, Illya, Chevie and his father were waiting nearby. "You're all going to be fine," he said to the young ones.

"How do you know?" asked Imogen.

"Because," he said. "I have faith. And I promise, once this is over, you'll never have to fear Dr. Wolfe or ICE or the Agents ever again. Now, I need you all to put on your masks and pretend they're your shield. These bad guys can't kill you when you have your masks on. You all have superpowers, remember? You're heroes. And at the end of the day, who wins? Evil?"

"Nuh-uh," Imogen smiled, her yellow and black mask sticking to her face. "Good wins!"

"Exactly," he said. "Good always wins. Ready?"

They nodded.

He put his hand into the center of their huddle. The younger ones eagerly placed their hand on his. Marcus, Chantal and Zac smiled almost comically and reached in.

"For those we've lost," said Joshua. "And those we left behind."

They pressed their hands down with a determined nod and then split apart. Zac muttered "Break!" because of course, he couldn't help it. Joshua heard him turn to Marcus and say, "Wait, what am I doing again?"

Marcus rolled his eyes at him. "Try not to get killed."

There was a sound of stone grinding and when they looked down, the bunker doors were opening. The soldiers signaled for entry and they ran down the dirt slope and into the bunker.

Instantly, there was gunfire. Joshua's heart leapt into his chest. The bunker was huge, an old war aircraft to the left and dusty equipment and crates to the right. Straight ahead of them, Chinese soldiers were firing at their soldiers. Two soldiers on his left went down. Imogen threw up a force field against them. Once the bullets couldn't penetrate her force field, the gunfire ceased.

Through the clear haze, Joshua could see only half a dozen Chinese soldiers. The rest were Agents and mutants, jumping from all directions in their ragged clothing.

"Marcus," said the Captain in a low tone. "Once we can get a clear opening, I need you to go with my left team to the control room to power down the bunker."

He nodded.

"The rest of us will need to take out these men if we want to go deeper."

"Yes sir," they nodded.

At that moment, something hit the ground beside the soldiers near to Joshua and he looked down to see a black, egg-shaped object.

Joshua's heart stopped.

"GRENADE!" he screamed.

Everyone dove for cover. Imogen spun and threw out her hands just as the grenade exploded.

Bright, white light obliterated around them. Joshua was thrown backwards. He hit a soldier and then went flying into a nearby crate.

His ears rung. Everything around him was still clear, so nothing had been destroyed. He stumbled to his feet and found Imogen lying on the floor around a stain of black smoke. He didn't know if she was alive or if the force had killed her.

The bodies of several soldiers were burnt and crisp on the ground. Not a meter from them was Koko's disfigured body. She'd been killed by the blast. Joshua's heart sunk, but he didn't have time to care, for it was then that the real fight began.

They were suddenly rained upon by gunfire. One soldier went down. They only had a dozen left, including the military officials who had joined them. Imogen could no longer protect them from the bullets.

The soldiers opened fire from behind anything they could protect themselves from. The sun was blazing through the bunker door behind him. He saw the soldiers shield Marcus toward a door on the far right, but their path was blocked by Agents. The soldiers attacked with their weapons but Marcus attacked with brute force, not electricity. His combat skills were more impressive than some of the men Joshua had trained with. He took down two Agents at a time and the soldiers shot the other.

A mutant was running at him. He was terrifying to look at and far more pale than Joshua had ever been, which was definitely a surprise because Joshua often compared the paleness of his skin to that of a piece of paper or a stick of chalk. The mutant's red eyes bore down on him and suddenly, he had whipped out his knives – or were they his fingers? – and was waving them in Joshua's face.

Joshua backed up a few steps, ducked under his right hook and threw a punch to the slasher's gut. He doubled over but sliced a large gash in Joshua's leg at the same time, causing him to stumble back with a yelp.

"Iceman, Iceman," the mutant chanted as he put one hand on Joshua's chest and pushed him to the side wall. The fight was in full-force before him, but he could only see the red eyes of the mutant who had him cornered. "Iceman wants some Dice, does he?"

Joshua didn't know what this man used to be like before he was mutated in one of Dr. Wolfe's sick experiments, and if the situation were any different, maybe he'd try to save him. But like himself, when his power warped his mind and there was no stopping him, Joshua would have wanted someone to put him down too.

"I'm sorry Dice," said Joshua. With a breath of air he formed an icicle and was about to drive it through the man's heart when he felt a sting in his neck. A raspy voice whispered in his ear as unconsciousness came over him.

"You're needed elsewhere, Iceman."

SIXTY-THREE

I changed."

Jack puffed his chest out, as though he were proud of this fact. In the White House, Hunter could hear nothing. All of the soldiers were either dead or keeping very still and watching her. Outside, there were sirens and screams from the public.

"I found my true purpose," he continued, gazing out the window and envisioning his transformation.

"To be a monster?" she said. "No, that's not your purpose Jack. You wanted to be a hero like in your comic books."

"They're fiction, Hunter. True power doesn't come from being a hero. Being a hero means you get stepped on for doing the right thing, you get criticized for trying to do good deeds and you get squashed by people like *me*."

Jack began to stroll toward her. Hunter found her feet rooted to the spot. Before she knew it, he was right in front of her and suddenly, Jack swung his oversized fist and it collided with her rib cage. She huffed out air and went skidding along the dusty ground of the foyer. Jack stomped over her and grabbed a hold of her hair.

"Come here," he snarled and wrenched her to her feet.

Suddenly, there was gunfire. Jack's body twitched violently and he dropped her, turning around to face the shooter. When Hunter looked up off the dusty ground, she saw the soldier she'd spoken with before, his rifle aimed at Jack.

No, Hunter thought. Images of his wife and daughter filled her mind, even if she had no idea what they looked like.

"Leave the lady alone," he growled. "Don't make me blow your head off your shoulders."

"Run!" Hunter called out to him.

She heard Jack chuckle so darkly, it gave her shivers. He raised his hands as if in surrender, and as he did, the soldier dropped his gun. His entire body started to quiver. Hunter had seen this before, deep in the Death Caves.

"We'll see whose head explodes first, won't we?"

A moment later, the soldier's head exploded. His body flopped over a slab of metal.

Hunter lowered her head and tried to stop herself from crying.

Jack crouched down beside her. "Don't cry Hunter," he said and gripped a fistful of her hair, wrenching her head back so he could look into her tear-stained face. "He's not the first soldier to die for his country tonight, and he won't be the last. Now what were you saying about heroes?"

"I was saying," she breathed, "that it's not too late to be one."

"Let her go Jack!"

Both of them turned and saw Eli stepping over the dust-shadowed debris. With her head tipped back and his hand around her throat, Hunter found it hard to see if Jack had recognized his childhood friend. Eli certainly couldn't recognize him. He was slowly making his way toward them with his hands raised and his eyes filled with sadness.

No, not him too.

Jack chuckled under his breath and muttered, "this will be fun." Then he threw Hunter hard on the ground. She felt as if her hip had cracked.

Jack stalked to Eli. "Hey, buddy!"

"Jack," said Eli in a cautious voice. "C-could you like ... stop being a dick for a little while?"

Jack laughed. "And why would I do that?"

Hunter pushed herself to her feet, shaking. Jack had his back to her and she waved at Eli to run. *Please, don't hurt him Jack!*

"Because you're killing people, bro. You're not with it, and if you let me I'll help you get on your feet again."

Jack was so close to him, he could reach out and snap his neck. Hunter knew the only way to save Eli was to make him run.

"Eli, please get out of here! He's dangerous and unstable and he'll *kill you!*"

"Aww," said Jack as he looked back at her with pouty lips and the devil's eyes. "You guys are all re-united again, are you? Hey, how was the prom? I never got to ask you on account of ... well, what happened at the warehouse with Hunter's psycho guardian. Want to know where I spent my prom night?" With that, he reached out quicker than lightning and wrapped his huge hand around Eli's neck. "In a fucking freezer," he growled and picked Eli off his feet and launched him across the room.

Hunter screamed.

She was torn between running after Eli to see if he was hurt – and by the sound of the crack his body made as it fell against the wall, she didn't want to know – or attacking Jack. So full of emotions, Hunter did nothing as Jack turned on her next. Before he could throw a punch, she took hold of his thick wrist and forced the fire into his hands. It would have melted any normal human being, but there was something impenetrable about Jack's skin.

"I want to know-" He raised her up above him and held her by the neck. Hunter kept a grip on his arms to support herself, but she couldn't breathe properly. "Why you never came back for me."

"I did – come back," she gasped. Spots were dancing in her vision.

"LIAR!"

Hunter felt him tense up and then she was airborne. She hit the ground on her side, her hip jarring painfully and her head knocking against a cracked stone. Hot blood seeped from a cut on her lower skull. She coughed, turned over and saw Jack's body quiver with rage. He turned toward the front door of the White House and took two deep breaths before screaming loudly and throwing his fist into the ground, just as he'd done on the news report. The impact was so strong that the entire front wall cracked. The sound was deafening. Hunter watched in horror as it tipped outwards, coming down with a horrible bang on all the bodies of the dead lying on the steps outside.

As the dust cleared, Hunter could see the entire front garden of the White House. Every person who had their faces pressed against the gate could now see the fight between she and Jack. Onlookers, Federal agents, policemen, news crews, cameras. The world. She knew it would be just like the burning restaurant or the cabin, only now the fate of the country rested on her shoulders. What would happen if she couldn't beat Jack? What hope or belief in heroes would people have if she could not triumph over evil?

Hunter had already been on the news, and she couldn't hide the color of her hair so the mask was useless. She ripped it away from her eyes and dragged herself to her feet.

"I'm not lying, Jack," she said.

"Some friend you are," he growled. "I never did *anything* to you, and you took all of your little ICE friends and went skipping off to La La Land and *left me there.*"

"I didn't," she said, trying to be firm and make him believe, but her voice was too shaky. "I swear to God Jack, I c-came back to get you but Dr. Wolfe locked me up and-"

"He locked me up too. But you still got out. And you rescued Will, right?"

"I never forgot you," she said as honestly as she could. "I kept hoping you were alive, and when I saw you in the Death Caves and Dr. Rosenthal shot you, I was so afraid to leave you there. Even though you were in a coma I s-still came back for you!"

"I don't believe you," he said. "I don't believe you ever cared about me. *Ever.*"

Hunter looked up into Jack's demonic eyes, so consumed by hatred and darkness and evil that there was nothing, no sign of him at all. He really had become Destructo.

But if Hunter had learned anything about controlling the darkness in her, it was that light is always somewhere, even buried deep inside. There was still light in Jack. He could be saved from the darkness.

She just had to be brave.

Hunter pushed herself up onto her elbows and buried her fears. There was no time to be afraid. It was only Jack. It was only the guy who asked her for a pencil in the library, who discovered her powers before anyone else, who used to tell her with such innocence in his eyes that he wanted to be like her someday. It was only Jack.

"You're stronger than this darkness," she said to him in a voice she hoped was fierce. "You can beat it, I know you can."

Jack's hand reached out and grabbed a fistful of her hair, wrenching her head back.

"What did you say?" he growled.

She gazed up into his eyes, clenching her teeth from the agony, refusing to back down. So she didn't have enough power to match even his little finger. So she was weak and tired and emotionally drained, and she'd only been there for an hour. She had no other choice. For the sake of those she loved and for the sake of Jack, she had to do this.

"Think of … Clare."

Jack's squinted eyes softened for just a millisecond. Even through her blurry vision, she saw a glimmer of humanity pass through them like a reflection of light in the black waters of the abyss. It was all Hunter needed to confirm that the Jack she used to know was still alive.

"She needs you, Jack."

Jack's grip on her throat strengthened. She saw spots in her vision. Death was creeping toward her. She was going under.

"She loves you."

Something happened in Jack's eyes. They softened, fading from black and manic to the kind, teddy-bear brown they used to be. The poisonous veins started to dissipate and his body began to shrink.

Then, Jack let go.

SIXTY-FOUR

ill hated leaving Hunter behind. He hated not being able to protect her and he prayed, even as he fought in the hanger alongside his fellow heroes and the military soldiers who kept behind the planes and the crates, that Hunter would remain safe.

He'd been hit by a bullet in the thigh, but it was slowly digging itself out of his skin. Another had just popped out of his left bicep. He tried to take them for the others, but in the panic after the grenade took Imogen down, they scattered for shelter and became separated.

Will ignored the burning bullet holes in his body and charged forward, clumsily taking on an Agent who was a far better opponent than he. Reminding himself to get Joshua or Marcus to teach him the techniques of combat when this was over, he swung hard punches where he saw the opportunity, and when the Agent took out a knife and stabbed it into Will's stomach, he cringed and then smiled. The Agent's eyes widened as Will grabbed the hilt of the knife, drew it out of his flesh and – quicker than he expected – drove it into the Agent's chest.

"Sorry mate," he muttered. "I'm Immortal."

The Agent's body crumpled to the floor. Will spun and surveyed the fight.

Imogen had gained consciousness and was throwing her force fields at anyone who needed them. The soldiers had killed most of the Chinese, leaving only the Agents and four mutants. Behind him, Zokani swooped in and attacked an Agent who was firing consistently at Ryo. She kept appearing and disappearing in different parts of the room to confuse them. One Agent in particular seemed determined to take her out and kept shooting in her direction as soon as he saw Ryo appear. Suddenly, Ryo blinked in front of another Agent that had just knocked Chevie to the ground. Before the first Agent could figure out Ryo's next move, he pulled the trigger, Ryo disappeared, and the bullet ripped through the second Agent's chest. His colleague was so shocked that he dropped the gun. Ryo teleported right to it, whipped around on her knees and shot him in the heart.

Chevie climbed weakly to his feet and thanked her before turning to help his father – who didn't look like he needed help at all. Alistair and a mutant who was twice the size of Will were street fighting on the other side of the room, breaking crates and throwing large objects at each other. They were growing dangerously close to the door of the hanger, and when Alistair realized this, he saw his opportunity. With a force Will could not describe, Alistair spun a roundhouse kick and the mutant's huge body soared back at least four meters into plain sight of the snipers. In less than three seconds, he was ripped apart by bullets and lay unmoving on the dirt path.

Yung was using his martial arts power to fight three Chinese men at once, moving faster than Will could comprehend. Suddenly, a high-pitched cry startled him and he whirled to see a mutant woman launch herself at him. She was feral and large and cackled as they rolled around on the dusty hanger floor.

"Pretty boy," she cooed. "Pretty pre-"

Will threw her off him. She had blood dripping from her arm but she didn't cradle it. Her ankle was bent at an odd angle. Will frowned. Did Dr. Wolfe re-create his power or just cut off her ability to feel pain?

The woman leapt at him again and Will threw a right hook at her jaw. He didn't realize how powerful the punch really was until the woman fell and didn't get up.

"CHANTAL!"

Out of the corner of his eye, through a blur of bullets, Will saw Chantal tip gracefully to the floor, almost in slow motion. Her head hit the concrete, her blond hair spilling out around her, empty eyes staring right at him with a bullet hole in the middle of her forehead.

Will felt a stab through his heart worse than any weapon. Zac ran to her, dropping to his knees, scooping her head up into his hands and crying for her to come back.

"Chantal," he whispered.

Will saw what looked like a black panther zoom past him and throw itself at a nearby Agent. It had to be Illya. The piercing roar echoed in his mind – as did the sight of an Agent having his throat torn out by the panther's jaws.

A heavy bang sounded and Will whipped around to see two-dozen soldiers spill from the door they were supposed to take once the hanger was clear. Behind them was a group of Men in White – one of them being Jamison. Their bullets soared through the air. One hit Imogen in her chest.

It reminded him so powerfully of Fearne that he froze amidst the battle, bullets tearing into his skin. He did not feel them, only the agony of watching death take more of his family. He tripped backwards over a body. When he looked down, he saw Ace lying at his feet with his neck broken and slash marks across his face.

It was all too much.

"NO!" someone screamed and Illya fell beside Ace's body, making Will feel sick as she held his face in her hands just as Zac did with Chantal. With Ace's head clenched against her chest and her eyes like murderous, green floodlights, Illya looked at Will with a face so torn apart by agony that he felt almost guilty he didn't stand up for her on the plane. She was right: they were all led to the slaughter.

Will couldn't take the bloodshed. All around him, his friends were dying. It felt as though they came so prepared, with their superhero suits and their new ambitions and the Captain and his men to back them up. Now, as gunfire rained upon them, he didn't see any of them making it out of the hanger alive, let alone with the President.

"Ryo!" Will called out. "You need to get into the bunker!"

"What?" she yelled at him as she and her brother fought the only remaining Agent, a mutant and three Men in White. At the same time, Will was suddenly attacked by a guard and a Chinese soldier.

"You're our only hope of stopping them." He punched the guard in the stomach and threw him into the soldier, satisfied to be returning some of the hits he took from them at ICE. "Run to the bunker when you get the chance!"

"What if-"

Ryo was knocked down by Jamison and he paused to grin maliciously at Will before throwing his foot into Ryo's stomach. Yung yelled ferociously and dove on Jamison, wrapping his arms around the man's neck and, quicker than lightning, Jamison's head snapped to the right and he fell on the floor. Two Chinese men jumped on Yung and he was in a fight again. Will took down the guard, but wasn't ready for the soldier. And more were running toward him.

We need a miracle.

A terrifying girl with two heads came out from behind the wing of the plane. The sight was so unnatural and terrifying that Will remained frozen, almost curious as to what they were going to do to him. He wished he didn't find out, for they reached with long, skinny arms and fingers and opened their mouths, ready to bite into his flesh. Will scrambled for freedom and gripped their hair, wondering if this was what zombies looked like when they were at their most ravenous, and when he rolled over to try and escape, his hands closed around a gun. He spun onto his back, raised the weapon and fired twice, both shots hitting them between the eyes. The adrenaline passed and Will's hands shook as he dropped the gun.

Then, something truly strange started happening. The ground rumbled. Everything around him shivered as though they were being struck by an earthquake. Those remaining – even the Chinese soldiers – froze in wait of what Will knew somewhere in his conscience was coming.

And then came the roar that turned his blood to ice.

"You've got to be kidding-"

A deafening explosion interrupted Zac and suddenly, the entire left wall of the hanger caved in. Cement and debris rained down upon them. Everyone still alive dove for cover, several of them screamed, and as Will lifted his head from behind a giant slab of cement, he saw the head of a T-rex protrude from the dusty hole.

"Alfie!" shouted Zac excitedly, seeing the dinosaur's return as something positive while Will did not. All it did was make it harder for them to fight without worrying about getting stepped on.

But then he looked back to where Ryo had been lying seconds before and saw that she was gone. She must have finally teleported to the bunker.

I have to help her.

At that stage, only he, Illya and Zac were left. The soldiers were dead. The Captain and the rest of their team were dead. Will hadn't seen every death and therefore didn't know how someone like Alistair or Zokani had been killed, but what he had managed to witness was a devastating nightmare.

Ignoring the bodies strewn under the rubble and the sound of the dinosaur roaring and stomping around, Will grabbed Illya from her husband's body and yelled out to Zac, who was staring up at Alfie like some beacon of hope.

"Let's go," said Will, "we have to get to the bunker!"

"I'm so happy to see him! Look at that magnificent beast!" Zac yelled and held out his arms. Losing Chantal must have flipped his crazy switch. At that stage, Alfie spotted him and started to charge, making Zac's face transform instantly into terror. "AHH!" he screamed and the three of them sprinted to the door.

The ground shook so much that it was hard to keep his footing. When Will looked behind him, he saw the huge body of the T-Rex with his gaping jaw descend upon them and shoved Zac through the door after Illya. A second later, the dinosaur's teeth were slashing at the doorway and the walls cracked as he chomped, trying to catch them in his mouth. A few more head-buts and he'd be through.

A long, lit corridor stretched before them, pipes dripping through the ceiling. Will knew that the bunker was only one floor down through a steel door. He had no idea how they were going to get inside. He could only hope that Ryo had managed to teleport there, or Marcus had shut down whatever the Chinese were trying to take control of.

"You guys have to go!" shouted Illya. "I'll stay and stop the dinosaur!"

"Are you nuts?" said Will.

"He'll kill us all, just GO!"

"Can you turn into a dinosaur too?" asked Zac with eyes wide.

"I can try."

Will nodded. "Thank you."

"Good luck!"

As they sprinted away, getting closer and closer to the stairs at the end of the corridor, they were suddenly skidding to a halt as three Chinese soldiers appeared through a closed door on the left, guns raised and pointed at them both. Will stepped in front of Zac, his heart pounding.

One soldier opened fire. Will felt the sting as a bullet hit his chest, only it wasn't a bullet at all. It was some kind of dart. He lost all feeling in his legs and then his torso and finally his upper body. His legs caved. He fell to the ground but didn't feel the pain.

"Hey, get away from my Willy!" shouted Zac. If this were any other circumstance, Will would have found that funny. But that was just Zac – making a joke even when he knew he was about to die.

He heard gunfire and saw Zac crumple awkwardly beside him. But unlike Will, Zac was shot with real bullets. A pool of blood spread around his chest. Zac's face gazed at him, almost with a smile on his lips, and did not transform into his original body like Will thought he would. Perhaps that's because this goofy, mousey-haired kid *was* the real Zac, and he had been all along.

"Yippe … kiyay … mother …"

Zac's eyes drooped closed, and he was gone.

Will wanted to say goodbye but his mouth wouldn't move. A single tear rolled from his eyes as the soldiers crowded around his body and lifted him up. Darkness came over him but he could still hear. There must've been something covering his head. The soldiers carried him through several doors, muttering to each other in Chinese. He heard the word 'Wolfe' and his insides cringed.

No, he thought. *They're taking me back.*

SIXTY-FIVE

Hunter gasped for breath as she lay on the scratchy, marble floor. She looked up at Jack as he gripped his head and roared, as though there was something trying to tear its way out of his chest. He stormed to the opposite side of the room and started smashing apart giant wads of concrete from the staircase. The ground shook violently from the force. He was growing dangerously close to Eli's body, a body she didn't know was alive or not.

"Jack!" she shouted and a searing pain tore through her chest. "Stop it!"

"*You did this!*" he thundered and collapsed on the ground, rolling in the debris and causing gashes to open on his skin. Hunter didn't know how she did it, but she must have had some energy still reserved inside her. She pushed herself to her quaking feet and stumbled to him. Unafraid, she bent over his writhing body and the moment her hands touched his shoulders, he flipped and gazed up at her. "Hunter, I'm so sorry!"

Her heart broke at the look in his eyes. The darkness was starting to wear off, but it was putting up a damn good fight.

Hunter didn't know much about demon possession or exorcisms, but she imagined it was something like this. When she was 'possessed' in the warehouse, it was the rain that pulled her back to reality and flushed away the fire. It was the thought of her mother's words and her memory of Eli. She had to bring back strong memories for him and help him fight the fire. The darkness.

"Don't let it turn you into a monster!" she begged him. He was straining against it, the black veins flickering on and off under his skin. She started panicking, wondering how she could draw the real Jack out. "You have too many people who love you! Clare needs you, she's alone. And Eli, h-he wants his best friend back, don't you want that? And I need you to remind me of when things used to be so normal and simple and … I can't just let you fall into the hands of this darkness forever because it was my fault it consumed you in the first place. I'm so *so* sorry. Please, Jack, fight it for the people that *love* you!"

Jack was heaving, but the more Hunter shouted in his ear as he lay on his stomach, his fists clenched hard, the more his breathing decreased. Hunter's tears were dripping onto his huge arms. She wished she could draw out all the darkness, all the hate and regret and anger and evil possessing him and put it all on herself. But this was *his* battle.

"Fight it," she whispered, gently stroking his shoulder. She kept whispering, watching his clenched muscles slowly unclench, watching the darkness fade away. It was working. The darkness was slowly releasing its evil clutch on her friend.

And then from behind them there came a loud, very obvious clapping.

Hunter turned.

Jet was slowly approaching them. Each footstep made crunches on the gravel. He limped from the still healing stab-wound in his stomach, but didn't let it show on his face. He'd lost a lot of his confident snark, and now it looked like he was running on pure, psychotic rage.

The fire burned white-hot inside Hunter. She kept hearing the sound of Mosi's body as Jet ripped it apart from the inside. Hunter could only imagine how much he wanted to do the same to her for taking Mikayla.

"Is there something I can help you with?" she said to Jet in the most casual manner she could muster.

"Actually, I think he's still struggling a little bit." Jet peered around her and frowned.

Jack glared up at Jet, breathing hard through his nose. He was still in a battle with the darkness, wanting to stand beside Hunter, but something was holding him back. Perhaps it was just Jet's presence that reminded Jack of ICE and what had trapped him there.

"See, I don't think he'll ever change, Hunter. People like us will forever have darkness in us, a darkness that we can't tame."

"No, you're a special case," Hunter spat and lit her palms on fire. "Jack is different. He can-"

A hand snatched her ankle and wrenched her feet out from under her. She went crashing to the ground, the air knocked out of her lungs. She turned over weakly and looked up into the darkness as it swam in Jack's eyes again.

"Jack no," she breathed.

Jet was laughing. "You think a little pep talk is going to get him to release the most powerful evil inside his soul? You're stupider than I thought. I told you, it can't be tamed!"

Jack reached down and grabbed Hunter by the collar of her suit. He lifted her off her feet, dangling her above the ground.

He's going to kill me.

"I'm afraid that the war is not over yet," said Jet. "But your fight is. Unless-"

"Unless what?"

"Unless you tell me where you're keeping Mikayla."

Hunter felt like laughing. She didn't think Jet was capable of any feelings, of any longing for Mikayla at all.

Even if she did tell him – which would risk the entire operation and every life at the SSS compound – he would kill her anyway.

Hunter stared down into Jack's menacing eyes. If Jet was capable of feelings, surely Jack was too. She'd seen it. He fought the darkness. Something brought him back, now she needed something more powerful to overcome it.

"I'm waiting!" shouted Jet.

"You'll have – to kill – me first."

"I won't have to kill you," he laughed. "Jack my little puppy here will do it for me!"

Something in his tone made Jack suddenly stop and realize that's exactly what he was – Jet's puppy, used as a torture device. Still with his hands around her neck, Jack lifted his other hand and pointed it at Jet.

Jet's face fell. "Wh-what are you doing?"

Jack clenched his fist. Jet's body twitched violently and his arms wrapped themselves around his stomach. His eyes grew wide. He looked like he wanted to throw up. His muscles started to seize and his skin paled.

Then, his torso exploded. Blood splattered all over the two of them. Jet's body was shredded in half as though something had ripped him apart like the leg of chicken.

Even though Jet was the spawn of the devil, the way he died would never be erased from her mind. It certainly wouldn't have missed the eyes of the public and news crews who captured it on tape.

But Hunter had other things to worry about.

"Jack, please-"

"No more games," he growled. "This ends now."

You're right. It ends now.

Hunter didn't think twice about what she did next. There was no other alternative, no more ideas in her disoriented mind, only a need to save Jack and everyone else affected by his power. She couldn't if she was dead.

So Hunter pulled her hands away from Jack's wrists that still clenched her collar and placed them on his cheeks. Jack's eyes followed her hands and, for a moment, he was frozen in shock. Almost in slow motion, Hunter pulled his face toward her, the pressure on her throat becoming hard to ignore, and with as much passion and love as she could muster so that he could *feel* it, she kissed him.

The fire blazed in her. The kiss made everything in her world pause. And even though she did not love Jack the way she had loved Eli and now loved Will, there was a strong connection between them that she'd never realized was there before. And it was warmth at its most vulnerable, warmth that drowned his darkness like sunlight through the cracks of a very dark and lonely place.

When she broke away, Jack was Jack again. Just like that. The black veins faded completely. His body shrunk again and his soul peered through at her, as if waking up from a very long sleep. He released her, looking horrified at himself.

"Hunter-" he began in a soft tone drowned in guilt. Hunter was so stunned that it worked, she found herself speechless. She could only throw her arms around his neck and thank Will's higher power God that Jack had defeated his demon.

"You did it," she half whispered, half sobbed.

"*You* did it," he said. "I couldn't have done this without you. I can't-"

Hunter seized up and suddenly, she was being hoisted into the air like a rag doll, wrenched from Jack's arms.

"Hunter!"

Pain tore through her body. She was dizzy and didn't know what was happening. Fire spurted from her hands and blasted against the walls of the White House. She screamed so loudly that she could hear nothing else.

Then she looked across the room and saw one of the soldiers stalking to them with his arm raised. He was covered in dust from the explosion, limping on his right leg. Hunter was so confused she could hardly speak.

"You bitch!" he shouted at her.

"Let her go!" screamed Jack.

"You ruined *EVERYTHING!*"

Then the soldier quivered and shook and screamed and suddenly, he was Mikayla.

"How the hell-" Hunter stopped herself when she saw Jack's body start to ripple in rage again. "Jack, NO!"

He turned to her. There was darkness in his eyes once more. He had to leave.

"Run Jack," she said.

The warehouse flashed in her mind, only this time it wasn't because she had to face Mikayla that she needed him to leave, it was because she didn't think she had the strength to pull him from the darkness again.

But Jack wouldn't hear it. "Not this time Hunter," he said. "I won't lose control. I promise. I won't let myself hurt you again."

"Jack, she'll kill-"

Mikayla screamed and waved her arm at Jack, whose body fell sideways and his head hit a slab of concrete. Jack tried to get up again but she held him down.

"You don't know what you just did," she snarled. "Jet was the only person in my life I cared about. YOU DESTROYED THE MAN I LOVE!"

Jack looked at her but did not move. Either he didn't want to let the darkness take over or he just couldn't get up.

Then, his eyes widened. He choked on air, his hands scraping the stone he was pressed against as if that would help him breathe. And just like Jet, Jack's body seized up and blood started to bubble from his mouth.

"Feel that?" Mikayla smiled as she twisted her hand. "That's your spine stabbing your lungs over and over."

"NO!" Hunter screamed, tears blinding her eyes. "Mikayla, STOP!"

But she didn't. And a second later, Jack's mouth opened and a great clump of red burst from his throat. It spilled down his chest and he lay against the slab of concrete with his eyes open wide.

SIXTY-SIX

Hunter couldn't take it anymore. Too many people were dying horrible deaths around her. She started sobbing uncontrollably, the way a mother sobs when her baby dies in her arms or a child cries when they lose their parent in a crowd. The pain she had felt for so many months took control of her happiness. And the fire, the consuming fire that was always there, did not burn anymore.

Mikayla turned to her. With the telekinesis power she must have stolen from Jet, she lifted Hunter off the ground once more. Only this time, Hunter didn't fight her. She didn't feel the burn of her throat closing as Mikayla took away her air supply. She didn't care anymore.

"What's the matter?" Mikayla called. "Too tired? Too weak? Not gonna pretend to be a hero anymore?"

"No," Hunter whispered through her clenched throat. "I'm not a hero. I never was and I never will be."

"You're right. Because you're about to die."

There was silence around her. Maybe it was just in Hunter's head. Maybe the thought of dying brought peace to her mind. This was too hard. She'd had powers for only a year. Before that, there was no responsibility on her shoulders. No one to save, no lives to protect, no person to be but her own arrogant, teenage self.

She looked away from Mikayla's demonic face to the front lawn of the White House where bodies were strewn across the chaotic grounds. Beyond

321

the turmoil, there was a crowd. Policemen with their guns raised behind their cars and flashing lights. Paramedics waiting to run in and collect the injured when it was safe. Crowds of pedestrians and onlookers who could be family members of those brave men who were dead on the lawn or could just be itching to get a glimpse of the heroes they saw on the television. Heroes they may even idolize.

All those people had courage just standing there. Either that, or they stood by waiting to *see* courage in action. Her courage.

Can I do this?

Mikayla's telekinetic grip tightened on her throat as the world started to fade. It would be so easy to meet a peaceful death. Her soul was tired and weary, starved of hope and drowned in grief. The feat seemed unimaginably hard.

But what about Joshua? What about Will? What about my friends who may need me at the army base? What about the SSS who inspire us, who support us, who believe in us? What about the President, the nation, the world?

What about those who fell before me so that I could reach this moment? Mom. Sammy. Dr. Rosenthal. Benji. Mosi. Fearne. Jack. Would I be honoring them in giving up?

Inside her soul, the fire started to flicker to life. It wasn't because it ever left. It would never leave. Neither would that still, small voice in her mind that came from not her mother as she'd always imagined, no. The voice was always the fires. Her soul. Her own.

You're not alone.

Somewhere in her heart, a new kind of courage bloomed. And it was not anger, or evil, or a need for revenge. It was a consuming fire, built from a powerful feeling of love for those she still had and would always be there for.

The grip on her throat loosened. In Mikayla's eyes she saw the reflection of something bright, a light coming from her own eyes. But she couldn't feel it, because all she knew was that the fire was awake again.

Then something even greater happened. The sound of cheers started to rise from the crowd. Hunter felt the fire grow, bloom, blaze, spark and ignite until suddenly, Mikayla staggered back and Hunter dropped to the ground. But she was not tired anymore. She stood steadily on her feet. She stared at Mikayla, the cries of courage coming from those standing bravely nearby.

"It's over, Mikayla," she growled. "Back down."

"Never," she said. And with that, Mikayla raised her hands and fire burst from them.

Hunter realized then that somehow, Mikayla had figured out how to mimic her powers. When Hunter visited her in the containment room, that feeling as she grabbed her ankle was the girl taking her fire. She did the same with Jet, Marcus and Zac in order to escape the SSS. All this power was making her weak. The burst of fire she threw hit Hunter with nothing but a small pinch, weak and messy. She didn't know how to control it, and the anger of Ravenadium had already taken over her.

But Hunter knew she was stronger.

"Mikayla, you've take on too much power. You're going to kill yourself."

Mikayla screamed and threw another ball, but all it did was allow her to draw more fire in. It felt different and foreign coming from someone so filled with hatred.

The crowd was chanting something now. Mikayla's eyes kept darting to them. She was panicking. Using her telekinesis, she knocked Hunter sideways and she crashed into a slanted piece of sandstone. Mikayla stood over her, grinning.

"I have all the power now," she snarled, sparks coming from her fingers as though the fire and electricity were going hand in hand. "And nothing-"

At that point, something inside Mikayla's body began to change. She twitched. Her hands went to her head. She was looking down at Hunter in confusion.

"What's happening?"

Hunter didn't know.

Mikayla started screaming. "Get it out! Get it out of my HEAD!"

"Get *what* out?"

She didn't stop screaming. Her skin started shivering as though she were shape-shifting. All around Hunter, bursts of static were popping and walls were crumbling. Mikayla's veins glowed orange, then blue, then orange again.

Hunter understood. The power was becoming too much. She scrambled to her feet and grabbed Mikayla's wrist, feeling the pulse of her skin thump faster than the sound of running feet. She wanted to help, but there was no stopping it.

Mikayla's body seized and then, in one mighty scream that burst Hunter's eardrums, Mikayla exploded. The force sent Hunter flying back ten feet. When she turned around, she saw the most horrible sight. In a combination of all her stolen powers, her body started to melt, contract and shatter all at once. Fire, force and blood blasted her. There was a horrible splat and all that remained of her body was a pile of slimy skin, red goo and smoke.

Hunter was so shocked that she remained still, staring at the pile. Her body ached – the adrenaline of the epiphany moment fading – and when she eventually did get up, she felt like someone had run over her with a train.

But she'd done it. She'd won the battle and saved hundreds of lives, even at the cost of a close friend. She paused for a moment, if not to catch her breath and slow her racing heart, then at least to give herself a small pat on the back for not giving up. For fighting with every last ounce of energy she had.

Mom and Dad would be proud, said the fire. *Joshua would be proud too.*

But now, someone else needed her. She stumbled across the wreckage and bloodied bodies to Eli. As she fell to her knees beside him, she was struck with a memory. Room 23. She couldn't stop thinking about the night of prom, the night he died, the night he lost his memory, the night her world fell apart.

"Please d-don't be dead." She pressed two fingers under his throat and waited.

A pulse.

Hunter smiled in relief. She couldn't bear to lose him again. She had no strength to carry him, and she had to tell the authority that it was safe to recover the bodies. So she leaned down and kissed Eli's cheek, then she got to her feet once more.

Her attention was diverted to the crowd outside. She moved her legs through the ruins and down the cracked staircase, around the pile of bodies to the lawn. The sun was almost set over the city skyscrapers, casting bright orange light across the sky. She stood, by herself, before the faces staring at her in awe and said nothing. It was the most surreal moment of her life.

She thought back to the restaurant fire and never imagined she'd be there, fully visible before the crowd. Her life had changed. Her friends were dead and people were going to put it on the television or write it in a comic, but they would never know the pain.

Hunter felt an urge to break down, but thankfully, her life had made her strong. Their support gave her courage. She could break down later, but for now, there was still work to be done. She needed to find the General and whoever was waiting for her to figure out how she was going to get to the army base, or at least contact them and find out if they were successful in preventing the terrorist attack, and then try and stop Dr. Wolfe from finding Ravenadium if he hadn't already.

As she approached the gate, the crowds around her started to clap. The applause grew, people cheering and screaming, lifting her spirit. It was a strange, strange sight.

As soon as she reached the crowd, she was bombarded by paramedics trying to get her into the back of an ambulance while the police forced onlookers and news crews to back away. All the faces and cameras trying to catch even a glimpse of her were too much to handle. Thankfully, Hunter was numb to it.

Amelia rushed out of the crowd. "Where is he?" she shouted.

Hunter waved at the White House. "He's alive."

Amelia snapped at a team of paramedics who carried a stretcher into the war zone. Hunter remembered a day when it would have been her fretting and crying over Eli's body. How things had changed.

The paramedic who was in charge of her asked her to look him in the eye. It was a simple command so she did it, and found it easy to focus on one thing. He had beautiful eyes, startlingly blue with long eyelashes, thick hair and a movie-star smile. She hadn't realized someone was already cleaning up her scrapes and another was slipping a gas mask over her face. She started to feel a little calmer.

"What's your name?" the paramedic asked.

"Hunter."

"Where are you, Hunter?"

"In an ambulance outside the White House."

"How do you feel?"

"Sore."

He smirked amusedly and put a hand on her shoulder. She found herself hypnotized, as though she had nothing more to think about than going with him to the hospital.

"Hey," he said. "You did an incredible thing out there. I've never known anyone braver."

She nodded. Just as he was telling her to lie her head back and relax while they took care of everything, someone angry shouted through the crowd and suddenly, General Rogers was there with another official-looking man she assumed was the Chairman of the Joint Chiefs – military advisor to the President.

"Hunter!" he shouted. "Thank God she's alive!"

The paramedic opened his mouth to remind him to keep his voice quiet, but he was silenced immediately.

"Shut up or I'll have you fired!" General Rogers sat down on the paramedic stool beside the bed. The Chairman joined them. "Hunter, David Meyer, David Meyer ... the woman who took down our enemy single-handedly."

Hunter ignored the compliment and gave the Chairman a quick nod, forcing herself to sit up and instantly incurring a splitting headache. "Have you heard from the others?"

"It's a mess," said the Chairman. He had a soothing, kind face that reminded Hunter of Dr. Rosenthal. "We need to get you back there *now*. We've lost contact with your team and we don't know who is alive and who isn't. In terms of our men ... they're all lost."

Hunter's stomach did flips. "How is that possible?"

General Rogers glanced at the faces peering in on them. The paramedic in particular was giving him furious eyes. He jumped up and closed the ambulance doors, assuring them he wouldn't be long.

When he turned to her, he had a radio in his hands. He clicked the side button and said, "Ambulance on the driveway, in the center."

Hunter frowned for only a second before there was a *whoosh* of air and suddenly, Ryo appeared inside the ambulance.

Hunter leapt up from the bed and removed the mask, throwing her arms around the girl. Ryo hugged her so tight that Hunter felt pain shoot up her back, but she didn't care. Ryo was alive and that was enough.

"Ryo! You're okay!"

"So are you," she sniffed. "Did you just see Eli being carried into an ambulance?"

"Yeah, he snuck onboard the jet and nearly got himself killed." Hunter stared into Ryo's eyes. They were saddened beyond compare, the kind of look a child has when their parents are ripped from their arms. Ryo had worlds of wisdom in her mind, but her heart was still young and she must have seen something truly horrible to look so dejected.

"Hunter … we lost."

"Wh-what do you mean?"

"I mean everyone is dead."

Hunter gazed at her. "Everyone?"

She nodded.

"That's not possible. Are you sure?"

"No," she said, trying to hold back tears. She explained the fight from the very beginning up until Alfie arriving.

"What about Joshua? And Will?"

Ryo shrugged. "I didn't see their bodies, but Joshua disappeared before things got really nasty. And something weird happened. They didn't kill Will, they *took* him."

Hunter felt as if someone had shattered every bone in her body. "*What?*"

"Zac and Will were the only ones left. I went back for them after I couldn't get into the bunker; there was something blocking me from teleporting inside. When I went to find Marcus, he … he …" She couldn't finish the sentence without breaking down. "I went back to get help and that's when more soldiers came out of nowhere. I hid and saw them kill Zac, but they dragged Will away."

Hunter's mind reeled, not only with the news that just about everyone she loved was dead, but that Will was not. He had been taken. She understood why they might have taken Marcus, but why Will?

It was suddenly so obvious. Dr. Wolfe didn't care who won or who lost the battle at the army base, or even there at the White House. He only cared about getting what he wanted: Ravenadium. The reason he took Will – and perhaps Joshua as well – had to be because they mattered to her. And he knew she'd come after him, so they were once again his leverage.

I have to get to the volcano.

"Ryo," she said. "I need you to teleport me somewhere."

"The army base?" she asked.

"No. Cuba."

Ryo, General Rogers and Chairman Meyer gaped at her.

"Hunter," began the Chairman, "we are in the middle of a-"

"I know where Dr. Wolfe is. He has Will and he probably has Joshua. He's going to get Ravenadium, and I have to stop him."

"What's Ravenadium, and how is it more important than stopping a terrorist attack?"

"You don't want to find out," she told the Chairman. "Regardless of what is going on at the army base and whoever is still alive, this is far more important."

Ryo looked at the Chairman.

"I don't know," he murmured. "Is it wise?"

"I know we look like kids to you Mr. Chairman," she said. "But I know this man. He wouldn't have gone to such lengths as this if he didn't have a greater agenda. He's more dangerous than the Chinese army taking control of your weaponry. Hell, he's *behind* this entire operation. If you give me the chance to stop him, I don't care what you say about us after that. I don't care what the media or the public or the authority does to us, just let me stop him. Please."

Chairman Meyer was clearly taken off guard by the tone of her voice, or perhaps the pleading, desperate look in her eyes. Part of Hunter was only thinking of Joshua and Will, the two most important people in her life, maybe even secretly hoping her father was there too, because if she had already lost everyone else she cared about, she was going to do all she could to save those left. Everything was at stake. He had to see that.

"Do it," he said after a moment, ignoring General Rogers' look of utter shock. "Catch this fucker before it's too late."

Ryo nodded a little uncertainly. "Where am I teleporting you exactly?"

Hunter hurriedly explained the location as specifically as she remembered and prayed it hadn't changed. She knew the smell, knew the structure of the shack and everything in it. It was only a matter of trusting Ryo to take her there.

"Can you do this?" she asked.

The young girl pursed her lips. She took Hunter's hand firmly, just like in her cell at the Death Caves. "What have we got to lose?"

Hunter looked at the Chairman. "I'll stop him," she said. "If it's the last thing I do."

"God be with you, Hunter," he replied.

"I'm sorry about the White House too."

He smiled. "Insurance will cover it."

"Right. Let's go."

"Remember," Ryo urged and her small, stern face was the last thing Hunter saw. "*Don't let go.*"

They vanished.

SIXTY-SEVEN

When Hunter stepped out of the void of bright colors and tightness, she opened her eyes and found herself standing in front of the shack. It was the strangest thing to be back in the home she was born into such a very long time ago. It was surrounded by tropical trees and animals hiding out of sight and the sound of waves crashing just a few steps behind her like a soothing lullaby. In light of everything that had just happened, Hunter allowed herself a moment to pretend she was dreaming, that she didn't have to worry about reality, that she could be young and free of problems again. That this was her paradise.

But there was a great responsibility on her shoulders and she couldn't have peace until that responsibility was upheld.

"This is where you were born?" asked Ryo from beside her.

Hunter looked away from the shack down at the small girl. A line of blood was falling from her nose very slowly. Hunter lifted her sleeve and wiped it.

"Are you okay?"

"Yeah," she shrugged. "That's where you're going? That's where Dr. Wolfe is?"

Hunter followed her gaze. Joshua never allowed her near the volcano. Every time she begged him, he told her that it was too dangerous. She felt drawn to it. She even found herself walking toward the volcano in an almost dream state. Now she understood why. A part of her had already heard the whisper.

Come ...

"Yeah, or he will be soon." She looked down at her. "You should get back. Go to the army base and try as hard as you can to stall the Chinese until more help arrives. But don't put yourself in too much danger and don't overuse your powers. That's what happened to Mikayla."

"Mikayla?"

Hunter nodded and explained Mikayla's escape plan.

"We can become so consumed by power that we forget to focus on the most important thing."

Ryo looked up at her quizzically.

"Love," said Hunter.

"It's funny," she said, "that we were chosen for this."

"I guess it is."

"It just makes me wonder why, of all the seven billion people in the world, it was me who was given this power. I wasn't at all equipped or prepared for it. Yet I find myself in this situation and I have so much potential to change things."

"I think we were chosen *because* we weren't equipped or prepared." Hunter stared at the shack, wondering how different her life would be if she or Joshua never had powers. But she didn't have to wonder, because it would never change.

"All our actions have consequences and are a part of this huge story that somebody wrote," said Ryo. "I think that somebody knew what he was doing though."

"You think? Even though whoever he is let Benji, Mosi and Fearne die? Let everyone else die tonight?"

Ryo didn't flinch at the thought, and Hunter admired her bravery. "Maybe it's because we can't see a reason for it until the war is won. We can't explain how or why, but when we get to the end, it will all make sense."

"I hope so," Hunter said and she reached down and hugged Ryo. "You should get back."

The young girl nodded. "Good luck."

Hunter blinked and she was gone and the shack stood before her, old and worn down by the sun and the tropical storms but still holding some value in her heart. She decided to search the shack first to find any sign of a trail Joshua may have mapped out.

When she entered the old house, she had an overwhelming sense of nostalgia, remembering the eight months she and Joshua lived there together. When Joshua brought her to the shack at age eight, he left her alone to do whatever she pleased. She saw no photographs, but there was always something womanly around. A pot of wilted flowers on the kitchen windowsill. Seashells in the bathroom. Trinkets in the living area that her mother had made out of the copper wire, the same wire used to make the symbol of fire that hung around her neck. They made Hunter smile and wish she knew her.

Now, everything looked different. Gloomy. As though this were another person's life she was remembering.

Hunter had to brush the moment under the metaphorical rug and run through the house to the back shed where Joshua used to keep all his research and equipment. He'd only taken her once for a tour and told her never to go back in, for everything was dangerous. Curiosity sparked inside her as she pushed open the creaking tin door and found herself in a small space with one side cluttered by junky mechanical equipment and a large workbench, and the other side covered in shelving and paperwork. The moment Hunter swung the door behind her, she felt instantly as though someone was watching her. A chill went up her spine.

She went to the right where a faded geographical map of the volcano was spread across the desk. There were stains on the work, making the lines bleed into each other. She started opening other rolls of paper, panic bubbling inside her stomach. What if Dr. Wolfe had already hurt Will or Joshua? What if they were dead and he'd found a way to Ravenadium, and by the time she found him it was too late?

She was so consumed by her fears that she didn't notice a figure creep toward her from the other side of the shed until he was right behind her and had tapped her on the shoulder.

Hunter screamed and whirled, and there stood her father.

She was so shocked that she couldn't control her limbs, and next thing she knew, her arms had flung themselves around his neck.

"Woah," he said and slowly embraced her. The feeling felt disjointed. "Sorry I scared ya."

Hunter pulled away and stared at him in disbelief. "How did you ... what are you ... h-how-"

"I used my ninja skills," he said and raised his eyebrows, overly pleased with himself. "No, I actually don't know. I woke up on the beach yesterday and found myself here."

Hunter frowned at him. Was this some kind of trap? Was Dr. Wolfe waiting for her to arrive so he could tempt her with her father and then destroy them both?

"That makes no sense."

"I know," Leo shrugged. "I think he's trying to get me to remember how to find the rock I brought home. Pretty smart, I guess. But I have no idea how long I've been here for. I feel like I'm on an episode of *Survivor*, only ... it's just me."

"So do you remember everything now? About what happened to you?"

"Of course! I never forgot," he winked at her. "I was faking it."

Hunter peered at her father curiously. The nostalgia completely surpassed his ability to see the danger they were in. She wondered if maybe he was a little loopy. *Makes sense, he was in a coma for twenty-odd years.*

"So you don't know if Dr. Wolfe is here yet? You haven't heard a plane or anything?"

"A plane?" Leo frowned and hummed a long, low note. "Nope. Haven't heard one."

There's no way they could be here yet if they're flying, they had to pick up Will and Joshua and then it'll be another two hour flight in a really fast jet.

"Well if Joshua is leading the party to find the stone, where would they be going?"

"The caves, probably. We studied the activity when we arrived and figured out which parts were researchable. We discovered some vents that are still geothermally active and recorded the pattern. The gas that blows out of the holes is basically fire. Do you want to go grab a coffee while we wait? There's still some inside."

Hunter made a face at him.

"What?" he said.

"Dr. Wolfe is on his way *right now* and you want to go inside and make coffee?"

"Good point." They tromped to the back door of the shack. "So the doc wants the stone – he gave it some weird name ..."

"Ravenadium," said Hunter as she closed the shack door behind her and peered through the window. Leo went into the kitchen as casually as if this were his own house – which technically, it still was – and filled the kettle up with water. Then he turned on the gas and looked at Hunter expectantly. She frowned. "What?"

Leo wiped a hand over his mouth and laughed under his breath. "Joshua. I can't believe he raised you. I can't believe …" He shook his head. "What was it like, growing up with him?"

"Leo … uh, Dad." Hunter rolled her eyes to the ceiling and sighed. It was more difficult figuring *that* out than it was to battle evil. "Dr. Wolfe has Joshua and he wants samples of Ravenadium. How would he get it?"

"He'd need to navigate his way to the caves, go inside, avoid the vents and extract the stones," said Leo and he stirred his coffee quickly before dumping the spoon in the sink. "You didn't want one, did you?"

"No. It's that simple? How far are they?"

"About an hour's hike. You have to walk along the beach before going into the forest. I have all the coordinates written down in the shed."

"Do you think Joshua will take Dr. Wolfe straight there, or will he come here first?"

Leo sipped his coffee again and shrugged. "My best guess is Joshua will direct the plane to land on the shore down the end of the beach and then make the rest of the hike to the caves on foot."

Hunter stared Leo in the eye, her mind ticking away. If he were to land on the beach, they would see the plane and know they'd arrived. There was no more time to lose. Hunter grabbed her father's wrist and he sloshed coffee over the bench.

"Hey-"

"We have to go, we have to make it to the caves before they do!"

"Okay," he nodded. "We'll need some supplies then."

"What supplies?"

"A compass." Leo hurried past her and out the back door into the shed again where he scrounged through the paperwork for tools, stuffing them in an old Indiana Jones satchel hanging on the back of the door. Hunter caught sight of a decent-sized pocket knife on one of the shelves and slipped it into the belt around her superhero suit, just in case. Leo riffled through the papers and came up with a rough, scribbled map that resembled one you would find in a child's toy chest leading from the shack to the volcano caves. "And of course, the trusty map."

Hunter couldn't believe her ears. How could he be so enthused at a time like this? The more cheerful and optimistic he became, the more she worried about Will and whether he was hurt, or Joshua and whether he had given Dr. Wolfe the key to the end of the world yet.

"Is that all we need?" she asked.

"I think so."

She nodded, her throat tight, and marched to the door.

"Hunter, wait."

She turned back to him.

"Yeah?"

"Uh … I just want you to know I'm proud of you. The fact that you're here means that you're brave. It was a quality your mother always had." He smiled. "She used to say that when there is nothing else, there is always-"

"-faith to cling onto," they finished together.

Leo's golden eyes sparkled. "She'd be proud too."

Hunter felt her throat clench painfully. "Thanks."

"You're welcome. Now hurry up and go get Joshua."

"What? You're not coming with me?"

Leo threw her the satchel. "Nope," he said. "This one's all you."

Hunter stared at him, completely confused. He grinned, the kind of grin that made it seem like he was waiting for her to figure out the end of the story.

And even though she'd already been through hell tonight, Hunter's mind was still able to put together the final pieces of the puzzle.

"You're not real, are you?" she breathed.

Leo clicked his mouth and winked at her.

"But in ICE-"

"That wasn't me, Hunter. I couldn't have survived the fire – I was dead before your mother left me. I'm sorry Dr. Wolfe filled you with false hope, but if you think about it, you really needed the pick-me-up in that awful place. It helped you find the fire again and keep fighting."

"How did I-" She held up the satchel, beyond confused. The past twenty minutes were a conversation between her and … herself?

"You always knew where to go – Joshua told you when you were young. It was just fun for me to narrate it." He grinned goofily at her.

Hunter felt like crying again. "But … I need you."

"You don't need me. And you never did. Joshua didn't ask to be your father, but he never did anything better than care for and protect you. The greatest thing a father can do for their child is to love them, and Joshua's love for you runs deeper than any power that could have overcome him."

Hunter nodded. "I guess I always knew that."

"Well, you *are* talking to a figment of your imagination, so …"

She breathed a laugh. "Okay. I should be going."

"Good luck," said Leo. "Tell Joshua I say hi."

Hunter frowned as she turned her back on her father, not sure whether she'd see him again or if it were just in heightened times of emotion, also making a mental note to sort through her schizophrenic mind and kick out all of the imaginary figures and voices she had. The fire was a big enough personality to deal with, let alone her mother and her father's voices.

And as she left the shack, a strange sensation of comfort spilled into her heart, as if reminding her yet again that she was not alone.

SIXTY-EIGHT

Will opened his eyes to the sound of an engine dying. He could smell fuel and the fresh breeze of something salty blew across his right side. The drug they injected in him had faded and finally, he could feel his body again.

He blinked through the blurriness and found himself inside a plane, the door just behind his shoulder wide open with a ramp folding down onto a sandy beach. He looked around and saw five Agents, a scientist he knew as Simon packing a kit and Dr. Wolfe standing directly in front of him.

"You're awake," he said and tapped Will's cheek. "Good, we have to walk now."

Will stared up at the man responsible for ruining his life and counted him lucky that his hands were tied. It didn't stop him though. The moment an Agent unlatched his seatbelt, Will lurched forward with his hands tied behind his back, intent on bowling Dr. Wolfe to the ground. The Agent only just managed to yank him back against the wall of the plane.

"You son of a bitch, you-"

Will stopped dead when he felt the weight of something heavy around his stomach. He looked down and saw that a belt with several pouches was attached to him. And inside the pouches were bags of dark liquid.

Blood.

A tube ran up the inside of his arm. Will couldn't feel the sting but he sensed a thickness in his veins. He knew that sensation.

"What's in me?" he demanded of Dr. Wolfe.

"You should know by now," said Dr. Wolfe, "that I like to take precautions. You have an unfair advantage and … with Mikayla's blood in your system, you're no threat to me."

Will's heart began to pound. It was then that he noticed that in the seat on his left was Joshua, slowly waking up. Blood coated his thigh and there was a decent-sized gash in his skin. He moaned and opened his eyes, peering up at Will and then gazing at Dr. Wolfe in horror.

"Hello Joshua," said Dr. Wolfe. "It's been a while."

"Not long enough," Joshua growled.

What is happening? Will thought.

"Where are we?" asked Joshua.

The doctor didn't feel the need to keep them informed. The Agent took Will's right arm and shoved him to the door.

But as he ducked under the doorway and started down the ramp, he nearly went head over heels after being so distracted by the sight around him, a sight he'd been dreaming of since the day he was born.

Paradise.

In ICE, the older ones used to speak of paradise as an island just like this. Crystal-clear waters. A forest of greenery on the right. Pearly-white beaches. Everything was just as warm and just as beautiful as he imagined. Were it not for the thought of Mikayla's blood pumping through his system, Will would have allowed himself a smile.

The sand made him unsteady. He'd never felt anything like it. The air was sticky and immediately he became hot in his superhero suit. The shore ran all the way along the bay, further than he could make out. Behind the plane that had landed awkwardly on the beach, there was only a rocky face that blocked the rest of the shoreline.

The waves crashed in a soothing rhythm that lifted Will's spirits and in the trees. It was magical.

Joshua looked more stoic than ever, his eyes continuously darting behind him at the large hill in the forest and then over Will's shoulder at the coast. There was something in his eyes …

And then suddenly, he knew. They were near the shack. It was hidden in the trees somewhere, the place that Hunter told him about long ago in the guard's quarters. The mountain had to be the volcano, where Ravenadium originally came from.

They were there for Ravenadium.

But why did Dr. Wolfe need *him*?

"Alright Harrison," said Dr. Wolfe. He looked very out of place, still in a lab coat over gray pants, his sleeves rolled up to his bony elbows. His skin was as pale and ghostly as the sand beneath their feet. "Since I have neither the time nor the patience to figure out how to get into this volcano so I can extract enough samples of Ravenadium for my experiments, why don't you do me a favor and show me the quick route so we can get this over with?"

Joshua stared at the doctor and then turned to the mountain. Was he trying to remember how to reach the part of the volcano where he and Hunter's dad found the rock samples? Or was he trying to think of a way to escape?

"Tick tock, Harrison, we don't have all day."

Joshua nodded his head at the rock face. "It's this way."

The Agent behind Will shoved him in the right shoulder blade and he stumbled forward through the sand, the blood packs sloshing around in his belt. Joshua limped the way and the rest of them followed.

"Why am I here?" Will whispered to Joshua as they hiked.

Joshua shot a sideways glance at him. "Leverage," he said.

It wasn't long before Will started to feel the heat. Perhaps it was the effect of Mikayla's blood pumping through his system, or he just wasn't used to the humidity of the location. Although he loved the feeling of the sun shining through the trees of the jungle they were hiking through after leaving the beach behind, he had never been in such a climate.

When Will imagined paradise, he didn't expect to be a prisoner again, and only there for the purpose of leverage in case Hunter came to the rescue. Which she would. And then what? Would Dr. Wolfe kill him? Would Hunter do what she did last time and choose to risk his life rather than give Dr. Wolfe what he wants? All the questions buzzing around in his mind kept him sidetracked from reality.

They stopped at a small clearing with a rock pile for a drink. The Agent fed him only a few mouthfuls of water and did the same for Joshua, whose face was paler than usual from the blood he'd already lost. Then Simon switched his blood bag for a fresh one. Sweat dripped down Will's face but he couldn't wipe his eyes because his hands were still bound behind him.

"How much further?" asked Dr. Wolfe. He was looking far worse than Joshua and the Agents, who had ditched their blazers and ties at the plane.

The scientist named Simon looked as though he belonged in this climate; dark skinned, possibly of Mexican or Latina heritage. He took it all in his stride, as most scientists under Dr. Wolfe's instruction would.

"This is the halfway mark," said Joshua. But his eyes, again, were somewhere else. He was looking at the ground in front of him. Dr. Wolfe was too distracted by the heat to notice that Joshua was carefully inspecting the tracks before them. Had somebody already been there? "We should be at the caves soon."

"So these caves were the ones you found the stones in?"

"Yes," said Joshua. "We should keep moving."

Even though Dr. Wolfe didn't look largely pleased by that, he followed anyway.

After what felt like hours, Joshua finally took them down a narrow path lined on the left side by a giant rock face, trees planted close together, their roots almost tripping him up as he walked. He ducked under a low-hanging branch and they came face to face with the mouth of a cave in the shape of an upside-down 'V'. Inside, there was a faint glow of fire.

Will's heart started to pound. Something in his mind was whispering to him, urging him into the mouth of the cave. Was it the living stone, or was it just dehydration?

For a moment, all nine of them stood outside the mouth of the cave. Dr. Wolfe was trying to make up his mind as to how to go about getting the samples. Something was holding him back.

Bravo cleared his throat and Dr. Wolfe turned to him.

"Sir, is there something we can do to … move this process along?" he asked.

"Oh yes," said Dr. Wolfe. "By all means, go on inside."

"Are you sure this isn't a trap?" asked the Agent holding Joshua.

"Charlie," Bravo scolded him.

"Well, I'm just putting it out there." Charlie's hair had started to come out of the small bun he kept it in at the nape of his neck. He was quite fit, but short and obviously a loud mouth. "It doesn't even look safe, how can you prove it?"

"I can prove it."

The voice came from behind Will. A wave of red hair danced through the line of trees and, a second later, Hunter appeared on a rock to their right, beautiful like a goddess, her face full of anger and a burning desire for revenge as she leapt gracefully from the rock onto the path directly between their group and the entrance to the cave.

The Agents drew their guns, but Dr. Wolfe whipped up a hand for them to hold their fire.

Hunter met eyes with Will and instantly, relief blew through him. She had survived the fight with Jack and somehow made it to the caves before they did. Despite having visible bruises and blood stains on her body, she was still standing tall, ready – like him – to end this fight for good. Her golden eyes smiled at him, and he smiled back.

Joshua staggered toward Hunter, but Agent Charlie wrenched him back. "You're alive!"

"Hunter," said Dr. Wolfe with a smile. "What a pleasant ... well I was going to say surprise, but I was counting on you showing up."

He drew his own gun at that stage, took two steps forward and rested the tip against the back of Joshua's head. "Let's not make this a long and drawling process. I know what I came for and you're in my way. So I will put a bullet in Joshua's head, and then I will put a bullet in *your* head Hunter and ... well, there's a cell with your name written on it in my new institution, William."

At the thought, Will felt like vomiting.

"Unless I get what I want, of course."

"Dr. Wolfe," said Joshua. "You and I both know that the only person who can go in that cave and come out with the right stone is me."

"Who said anything about you coming out," Dr. Wolfe said with a smile.

For a second, Will swore he felt the ground beneath him rumble. And then behind Hunter, a bright light blared inside the cave and disappeared.

Will glanced at the doctor and his men, noticing, too, their shock. Hunter stood proud and strong, her veins glowing like snakes of fire.

It's the volcano, Will thought with a smile. *She's bringing it to life.*

SIXTY-NINE

It was a miracle, in Hunter's opinion, that she could be standing so composed when behind her, there was a force stronger than her will to live drawing her back. It was not the gentle whisper she heard when she arrived at the shack, nor the voice of what she thought was her mother.

It was an unbearable, unshakable grip on her heart that felt as if it could physically drag her backwards. She would have, if Dr. Wolfe didn't have a gun at Joshua's head.

"What are you going to do then?" asked Joshua – obviously trying to distract Dr. Wolfe from Hunter's instability.

"I need *you* to come with Simon and I inside the caves – along with Bravo as protection – and Will and Hunter will remain here with my Agents. We will extract samples of Ravenadium, exit the caves, and then I will release you. It's that simple."

"You cannot take him in there," Hunter snarled. "I know what you'll do to him once you have what you want."

Dr. Wolfe gazed at her with his oyster eyes. She had run over this moment for at least an hour before she heard them coming. Dr. Wolfe would use all the leverage he had to gain power. Even Hunter's life was at risk standing between him and the mouth of the volcano. But Joshua, he needed. Only until he had Ravenadium, that is.

"I can't go in there alone, Hunter," said Dr. Wolfe, as though this were a diplomatic discussion and not a matter of life and death. "If I do, you'll only awaken the volcano and make it swallow me whole."

So he did sense the fire. It was so eager to drag the doctor into its depths and destroy him. She would have brought the lava right out of the cave, had it not been for Joshua and Will.

"Take me," said Joshua.

"No!"

"I swear I won't do anything to harm you, Dr. Wolfe. How can I when you have all these weapons and hostages, ones I care about?" He inclined his head at Will. "It's why you brought us here, isn't it?"

The doctor raised his eyebrows and nodded in agreement. "You have a point." He shoved Joshua in the back and he stumbled toward Hunter and the cave. She stepped aside. The scientist and Agent Bravo scuttled after him. "I'll be back with samples. Charlie, Agents; make sure you hold tight to those guns and don't let either of them out of your sight. You hear me?"

The men nodded. Hunter saw Agent Charlie put a gun to Will's head. He didn't falter, staring at Hunter with a look of calm defiance. That was when Hunter noticed the blood bags. Her mouth dropped open.

"Please Dr. Wolfe," she begged him. "Don't do this. What if Joshua melts?"

"I won't melt," said Joshua, though he didn't seem so sure of it. Ignoring Dr. Wolfe's protests, he marched up to her, his pale eyes consuming her. She wrapped her arms around him, not even caring that he couldn't hug her back. The comforting feeling of his cold body against hers, that nearness and connection with the man who was there for her from the moment she was born, made the fire stir in fear. With his forehead pressed against hers, he murmured, "I have faith. But even if I *do* burn, it's okay. I will not let him have the fire."

Hunter clenched him tightly. She didn't want to say a goodbye, because that made the possibility of losing him that much more real.

"I love you, Joshua."

"I love you too."

Joshua was pulled away by Dr. Wolfe, the gun once more against his head, but he did not leave her gaze as they marched into the volcano cave.

Her heart pounded. It was one of the hardest things she'd ever had to do. She looked back at Will and felt tears of frustration come to her eyes. She couldn't stand there. What if Dr. Wolfe did something horrible inside the volcano? What if Joshua burned the instant they entered?

This is wrong. I should be in there. Hunter couldn't decide if that was the fire talking or her own conscience. Either way, it was right.

An Agent was suddenly beside her with a gun to her neck. He wrenched her back from the opening of the cave to the shade of the trees where the others were gathered. Four Agents, she and Will.

"Are you alright?" asked Will.

She nodded to him as the Agent tied her hands together with a flexi-cuff. *Stupid idiot.* They also took the knife she had in the belt of her superhero suit. "Are you?"

"I'm fine. I'm sorry I got caught. I'm sorry Joshua got caught as well. It was unexpected."

"A lot of it was. I didn't expect that it would all end here."

"How did you get here so fast?"

"Ryo," she said. "I defeated Jack. I was going to go back with Ryo to the army base but-"

"Everyone is dead," said Will.

Hunter couldn't bring herself to say anything. It was too soon to accept that they were gone. She held back tears and nodded.

The Agent behind them snickered. "What did you expect? Your stupid team of so-called superheroes have no *real* power. Can't you see you were outnumbered from the very beginning?"

Hunter was very tempted to turn around and burn his eyes out with her fingers. She shot a quick sideways glance at Will. He was warning her to keep her cool.

"I think that's enough talking," said Charlie. To make his point clear, he cocked the hammer on his gun and moved it to Will's temple.

Hunter's brain ticked. Will could not get shot. It changed everything. Hunter was willing to bet that if she acted fast enough, she could avoid a fatal wound. But with Will completely restricted and Joshua at the mercy of Dr. Wolfe, her choices were limited.

She weighed ideas in her mind, but her thoughts kept turning to the heat beneath her feet. She could *feel* the mountain, feel the power of Ravenadium beneath her, the birthplace of her powers, the very soul of her being. It was right there, waiting for her to use it.

Somewhere inside her, Hunter felt the presence of the fire tell her to trust it. And so she did. She let go of the fear and breathed from it courage, taking one last look at Will, telling him it would be alright. And then she closed her eyes and drew the fire from within.

– PART 5 –

THE FIRE WITHIN

SEVENTY

Ryo peeled her eyes open and found herself in her bedroom at the SSS compound rather than back in the chaos of the army base.

She frowned at the silence. "Huh." It had happened before; she tried to teleport to one location and ended up in another. Bending space was so difficult, and sometimes her thoughts were not completely in it. But this time felt different.

She turned around, expecting someone to be in the room, but she was alone. And her superhero suit hung over the mirror on the wall. Ryo looked down and a sinking feeling settled inside her stomach. She was wearing the clothes she'd had on earlier that day, before they went to Louisiana.

"Oh no." Heart pounding, she ran to her bedside table and picked up her watch with fumbling fingers. One of the SSS members gave it to her to keep track of time, just as a joke.

It read 5pm.

Ryo's stomach flipped. "I've gone back in time."

She stared at her superhero suit in absolute horror. The last time she went back, she changed the history of her family and everyone they influenced. Her brother Yung never let her forget it. He blamed her for their sister's death, and in time she understood why. Changing the future meant changing life as it should be.

But suddenly, without her permission, her body had moved itself back in time.

Ryo believed wholeheartedly that everything happens for a reason. Just a minute ago, she was standing under a canopy of palm trees talking to Hunter about this exact situation.

We can't explain how or why, but when we get to the end of the war it will all make sense.

She reached out and touched the silky, thin material of the beautiful suit Ella had made for her. The shimmering, dark colors reminded her of the flashes she saw whilst travelling through space. Suddenly, she was slipping off her clothes and zipping up the suit, gazing at herself in the mirror.

The weight of responsibility fell heavily on her shoulders. She knew what she had to do. The author of her story placed her very carefully in this moment, and now it was time to change things. To save them all.

A plan fell into place inside her mind as though someone had slipped it in there. She was thankful not to feel weak from so much teleporting through space – now time, as well – and was suddenly strengthened by the excitement pumping through her blood. Ryo understood her duty to bring them all back. And maybe, even, to win the war.

First order of business ...

"Mikayla," she said aloud.

Ryo closed her eyes and pictured the containment room. In a second, she felt the weight of gravity lift and then yank her back again. She opened her eyes in the corridor outside Mikayla's cell.

Ryo needed to find a way to keep Mikayla inside the room, and if she already had Jet, Hunter, Marcus and Zac's power – which Hunter told her she did – then it would be nearly impossible for her not to get out. Knowing this, Ryo snuck into the next room which was like a storage cupboard filled with office supplies and some random weapons. Of the many weapons, they kept a container of tranquilizer fluid with syringes in the cupboard. Zac had told her so.

Ryo inserted a reasonable dose that would keep Mikayla under for at least a few hours and then teleported directly into her room. For a moment, Mikayla gazed at her in surprise, then came to the quick conclusion that Ryo's power would be the best of all to steal.

"Hey Ryo," she smiled, doing well to keep her demeanor casual and not give away her escape plan. "What's up?"

"Oh nothing much," said Ryo.

"Nice suit. What's it made of?"

Ryo glanced down at her arm and pretended to look thoughtful when she knew that Mikayla was three strides away from her. Mikayla took the bait, but before she could reach out and touch her skin, Ryo – quick as a flash – thrust the syringe into Mikayla's neck and pressed on the plunger. Even though Mikayla had drawn her teleportation into her body, Ryo still had excellent reflexes. The girl went out like a light.

She dragged Mikayla into the corner and tipped her over, making it look like she was asleep. Then Ryo went to the hanger.

The Captain's men were loading the Red Cherry and Joshua and Zac were standing near her, talking. Chantal strolled past them in her ridiculously high heels.

Moments later, Hunter walked toward her. "Hey," she smiled. "Good luck."

Ryo was struck suddenly with a wave of tears. She knew what Hunter was about to go through, and she couldn't stop it. That part of time was out of her hands. It pained her, but Hunter was stronger than any of them. If there was one thing Ryo knew for sure, it was that Hunter would walk away from this war with her head held high, no matter who she left behind. That was the type of fearless, courageous leader she had become.

Throwing her arms around Hunter's waist, Ryo muttered, "be strong, okay?"

Hunter sniffed, stroked her silky black hair and chuckled. "Coming from you? We'll all be fine."

"I know. Oh, and by the way, I saw Eli sneak onto your jet just before. You'd better kick him out – he'll get killed."

Hunter's eyes went dark. "I will. Thanks Ryo."

They parted ways and Ryo boarded the Red Cherry, taking her seat beside Yung. She was shocked to feel the stab of pain as she looked at each of their faces. Chantal, a bullet through her skull. Imogen, knocked to the ground and bleeding out. Her brother Yung, crushed under concrete. Zac's smiling face devoid of humor in a pool of his own blood.

They all didn't know the horrible fate they were about to meet.

"Are you okay?" her brother muttered to her in their language.

She turned to him. His eyes displayed an understanding only they shared. He knew something was wrong.

"Did you *see*?"

Yung referred to their term for her travels in time. Though they were not frequent, it had happened once before. Ryo shook her head. He could not know. But he would know, eventually. Until then, it was her burden to bear.

The flight was exactly as she remembered. She kept thinking about how she was going to save them all, trying to calculate the exact time in which to act. It was harder than she imagined; even though it was a habit of hers to remember specific times of events, this was much more difficult because the situation they faced was still something of a blur. At least she knew that Hunter would most definitely arrive in Washington first, because her jet was smaller and faster than theirs.

When they touched down outside the base and the Secretary of Defense met with them on deck, Marcus tapped into the security system and brought up the camera showing the inside of the room.

This time, Ryo really paid attention. She didn't feel afraid to teleport directly into the bunker, but there was something blocking her last time – a telepathic force that she'd never encountered.

Now she was given a second chance to figure out why, and it became obvious the moment she opened her eyes a little wider.

Beside the President and his group of colleagues huddled in the corner, Ryo could see a figure standing up against the wall that she remembered from the cabin. A girl in a white dress who had been badly burnt in one of the doctor's experiments. Ryo watched her interactions with General Chang closely. She passed gazes with the President as well, but never once said a word.

It quickly became obvious that this girl had a telepathic power, and the General was using her to get the nuclear codes directly from the President's mind. It wouldn't be more than an hour before their country was in serious trouble.

Dr. Wolfe must've figured out how to use Ravenadium. He created an Impossible. He created Fearne.

This made their situation that much more desperate. Instantly, Ryo's mind kicked into action. She was ready. She accepted the challenge and she marched down the ramp into the entrance with names bouncing around in her mind. Names of those she was going to save.

When the soldiers opened up the bunker and faced the enemy, she remembered first the grenade.

Ryo saw them launch it before anyone else did and teleported to the place where it was going to land, catching the grenade in her hand. They stared at her in utter shock. She could have thrown the grenade back at the Agents – who were equally taken aback by her quick movements – but instead, she disappeared and reappeared before the lower level door, dropping it in front of the sealed entrance and teleporting back to the hanger. It would have been easy for Marcus to crack the security system, but that would have taken time and this was much quicker. Now there was a clear path down the staircase to the bunker door where the Chinese were keeping the President. From beneath her feet, she felt the vibration and knew the door had been cracked.

Marcus sprinted to the door that would lead to the communications room. Ryo looked down at her watch. In thirteen minutes, Marcus was going to be attacked. She had to remember that. Timing was everything.

In order to even the fight, Ryo decided to take all of the weapons first.

One thing that suddenly became apparent to her now that she had travelled back in time was the possibility of freezing time. She'd never done it before, but now was as good as ever to test her abilities. With an unbelievable amount of concentration, Ryo retreated into the Zen place she had found before teleporting and told her mind to freeze time. And when she opened her eyes, things had changed.

She hadn't stopped time, but it wasn't moving at normal speed. It was slow motion, so slow that she could count to three and Yung on her left hadn't finished blinking.

Grinning, Ryo burst into action. She had to be wary of the hot bullets floating through the air as she ran from Chinese soldier to Agent, snatching their weaponry and anything else she could find that may hurt her friends. When her hands were full, she shoved the weaponry inside an empty crate stacked up against the back wall. No one would look there. Time sped up the moment she asked it to, and in at least five seconds, the soldiers fired their guns and half the Chinese men and Agents were dead on the floor.

The mutants looked terrified. When one of them launched itself at Zac, Zokani soared forward in flight, hoisted her squirming body up and threw her into the wall, circling back and landing on the ground. One of the mutant's was attacked by an invisible blade that sliced across its neck. Koko appeared behind the body. There was an abnormally large man who somehow could not be killed by bullets, but when Chantal stepped in front of him and met his eyes, he was under her spell and surrendered in tears.

The rest were killed with the soldier's guns and fought in combat. Ryo was dizzy from freezing time and lost focus for a moment when an Agent tried to tackle her. Yung swooped in and gracefully hooked his leg over the Agent's shoulder, wrapping his arms around his neck and snapping it clean to the side. When Ryo gained her footing, she realized that Joshua had been taken. Soon, Will would be too. *You can't save everyone,* said a voice in her mind.

And then there was a pause, a moment of peace. Everyone looked at each other proudly, as though they didn't expect it to be so easy.

You all have no idea, thought Ryo.

Next to arrive were the second squadron of Men in White and Chinese soldiers. In the first battle, more than half of their American soldiers had been killed, but the Captain remained alive.

Now, it was time to save Marcus.

Ryo had faith that her team could handle the rest of the attack, and so she vanished just as the second squad was coming through the door and teleported straight to the control room she'd seen through Marcus's security cameras on the plane.

Banks of computers surrounded her. It was only small, but there was room enough to comfortably fit the five of them – Marcus, three soldiers and Ryo.

"Ryo?" Marcus frowned. "What-"

Ryo's attention was forced to the screens. They showed every angle of the bunker on the right side, the hanger where a battle still raged on the other.

She clicked her fingers at the soldiers. "They need your help down there."

"But our orders are-"

"This order came from the Captain, now MOVE!"

Without a second thought, the three of them marched to the door and were gone in seconds.

Marcus' eyebrows shot up to the line of his black hair. "What the hell are you doing?"

Ryo bent over the screens to listen to the audio. She understood the language of the many soldiers and their leader General Chang, but they were not all Chinese.

Some, in fact, were Korean. North Korean.

Yung had filled her in over the past few days while they spent time together at the SSS on the situation in North Korea and the treaty made with the Chinese government. Together, they had the power to exterminate the United States using electromagnetic pulse technology, essentially destroying the electronic equipment that this country, and all others, relied on. It was common knowledge among her people, and would soon become common knowledge within the US. But if the Chinese and the Koreans had the power to exterminate America *outside* the country itself, why then were they attacking the core of its government system?

Whatever they were doing, she didn't have time to question it.

"What have you found out?" she asked.

Marcus pointed to the girl in the white dress. "She's a telepath. Dr. Wolfe must've created her using Fearne's formula and the Ravenadium he stole from Joshua. That's why he didn't care when he killed Fearne."

Ryo glanced at her watch. *How am I going to get inside if she can block my mind from concentrating? I could teleport into the wall if she tells my mind to do so.*

"Did the bomb destroy the door?"

"That was you?" Marcus gaped. "I heard this bang and-"

The rumbling started. Then came the roar. Marcus's face went pale – he already knew who it was. And the cameras in the corner displayed the gruesome sight of Alfie the dinosaur bursting through the wall, ready to destroy them.

"Holy f-"

The door of the communications room flew open and two Chinese men stood ready to raise their rifles and fire. Ryo smiled. *Right on time.*

Of all the weapons Ryo had taken from the guards, there was only one she kept for herself. One of the Chinese soldiers had it sitting inside his pocket, glinting at her as though tempting her.

Ryo knew the men were about to burst through the door because she saw the timestamp frozen on the cameras when they shot Marcus the first time and his power froze the screens. So even before the soldiers had raised their rifles, Ryo flicked the two Chinese throwing stars straight into the soldier's necks. They sliced cleanly through their flesh and killed them quickly.

She turned back to Marcus without a single breath.

"Holy f-" he began again.

"Can you open the bunker?"

Marcus gaped like a drowning fish.

"Marcus!"

"Y-yeah, uh ..." He turned back to the screens and stabbed commands on the keyboard. "I was going to shut down the power altogether, but they might hurt the president if they considered us a threat. So I switched the security footage. They don't know we've infiltrated the base. Their techs set up an algorithm to hide their plans, but I was about to crack it when you came in. Give me a minute, then I'll-"

Ryo didn't hear the end of it. She teleported back to the hanger and stood beside the cluster of horrified heroes being backed into the corner as Alfie swung his massive tail and crept curiously closer to them.

They shot a glance at her perplexedly.

But Ryo was beaming. They were all alive. The Men in White were dead. She didn't care how they did it, it was enough that only a dinosaur stood between them and reaching the bunker.

"Niiiice dinosaur," murmured Zac. Chantal elbowed him.

"Shh! He could think we're human and try to eat us!"

"He knows we're human, you idiot," Zac snapped back with minimal lip movement.

"Where's Marcus when you need him?" asked Chantal.

"Where's Will when you need him?"

The group looked around. Will had vanished too and none of them knew how or why, except Ryo. The dinosaur started sniffing the bodies on the ground. It was as if he avoided having to face them.

"What do we do?" asked Chevie.

"Let me take care of it," said Illya and she stepped away from the group.

"No-"

"Ace." She turned to him and gave him a reassuring smile. It was the first time Ryo had seen her look happy, and her beauty took Ryo's breath away. "I need to do my part. These guys saved our lives." She looked at the rest of the group. "I was wrong about all of you. You're not stupid, you're brave. Besides ... it's just old Rexy."

With that she turned, bent her body inward and began to change. They all expected she'd transform into something like an elephant or a dragon, but instead Illya's body shrunk down in her leather clothes, and out of the hole in her jacket came a rabbit.

"Bugs Bunny?" Zac gaped. "She turned into *Bugs Bunny*?"

Alfie caught sight of Illya as she started hopping over the bodies and suddenly became very agitated. He roared deafeningly and chomped down hard, trying to catch the rabbit in his oversized jaw. She just dodged him and sprinted outside into the forest.

Alfie became consumed by Illya and ran after her. The moment he was out in the open of the forest, the snipers attacked. The gunfire would not hurt Alfie, but at least it drew him away from the army base, leaving the rest of them to gaze in bewilderment at the sight they had just witnessed.

"Dinosaur chases rabbit around the Louisiana countryside," said Zac as he shook his head disbelievingly. "Now *that's* gonna be a headline."

Suddenly, Ryo remembered Hunter. She had to get to the White House and teleport her to the shack before it was too late, or she may never find her. Ryo glanced at her watch. She still had a little bit of time. *Wait, no I don't. Hunter doesn't have to fight Mikayla now. She only needs to rescue Jack.*

"Listen up guys," she said loudly and clicked her fingers at the group. "Marcus has figured out a way to get into the bunker and disable their security. I need to go help Hunter–"

"Why?" asked Zac.

"I'll explain later. It's up to you guys to get the President out and kill General Chang. Be careful – there's a telepath in there. Take her out first. I'll be back as soon as I can."

Before she could disappear, little Imogen raised her hand. She had blood running down the side of her face. She was only six years younger than Ryo, but it felt like they were worlds apart.

"But we need you," she murmured. "How do you know we'll win?"

She brushed a tear away from the little girl's cheek and caught a proud look in her brother's eyes. "Because," she winked. "Good always wins."

Ryo closed her eyes and they were gone.

SEVENTY-ONE

When Ryo arrived at the White House – directly beside the ambulance she knew Hunter would either be in already or be taken to soon – she felt the crowd jump back in shock as soon as she materialized. Ryo ignored them, too anxious of what had occurred while she was at the army base. As happy as she was to be able to turn back time again, she wasn't sure she'd get another chance. She had to be extremely careful.

Ryo stalked up to the nearest policeman.

"Where's General Rogers?"

The policeman had clearly not seen her apparition and looked her up and down. "Get back in the crowd kid, it's dangerous-"

At that moment, the people outside stopped cheering. Ryo's heart leapt. She ran to the front of the crowd.

There, she saw Hunter. Battered and bruised, she came out of the White House building and limped toward the crowd.

And beside her, there was a boy. He was her height, with dark hair and slumped shoulders. He had his arm around Hunter. It had to be Jack.

It was such a surreal sight. Hunter – though weakened by the battle – did not look defeated. She was so beautiful, a hero inside and out. Jack was no longer the dark figure Hunter described him to be. He was saddened and crushed with guilt as he leant against Hunter and they walked to the crowd, out of the smoke and dust.

As Ryo tried to stop the tears from spilling out of her eyes, someone pushed through the mob of people. She heard a police officer ask him to step back, but he shouted "that's my best friend!" and then Eli broke through the crowd. He sprinted to Jack, who looked up and smiled so wide, a burst of joy went through Ryo. They nearly knocked each other over with their embrace. The crowd began to cheer. Hunter stared at the two boys in tears until they opened their arms and wrapped her in a hug too. Hunter, Jack and Eli, re-united once again.

Ryo liked to think she had a hand in saving Jack's life – and Mikayla's, as well – and that made it special. She didn't care that Jet was dead.

The crowd stopped cheering for Hunter and were now hissing at Jack. Ryo had to jump over the bodies thronging around her. "It's Destructo," people were saying. Ryo saw someone throw something at Jack.

"Hey back off!" Hunter shouted at them, but they weren't listening, they were shouting at him, cursing. And why wouldn't they? He'd just destroyed their White House.

The police and national security were trying to tear Jack away from Hunter and place him under arrest when Ryo finally reached her.

"Ryo?" Hunter frowned. "What happened at the army base?"

"It's all under control," she said. "But I need you to come with me. There's something you have to do. I'm so sorry, but you must leave Jack here."

"I can't," she said. "They're arresting him and I have to stop them!"

Ryo caught Jack's eyes. They were so filled with regret. He let the policemen wrench his hands behind his back. They weren't gentle with him either. Jack was thrown to the gravel and cuffed tightly.

Hunter shoved a policeman. "What the hell are you doing to him?!"

General Rogers suddenly appeared beside them. "We're doing what needs to be done. This boy has killed hundreds of our men and destroyed our nation's capital. No matter what you say, Miss Harrison, he is in our care now and-"

"He's *unstable*," she growled. "If you treat him like that, you could push him over the edge again!"

General Rogers glanced at Jack uncertainly. One of the officers with a mean smirk was holding him down, squeezing his face against the pavement.

Ryo hadn't thought this part through. Jack had killed *so* many people. He had demolished the White House, putting the entire country in danger. Even though he looked innocent now, no one could deny his actions. In fact, there was proof.

The police surrounded Jack, their guns raised, fear on their faces. Jack let them secure him roughly, gazing at the crowd who looked down on him in loathing. He did not fight back, taking it on his shoulders.

"Go Hunter," he said to her. "I deserve whatever punishment they have for me."

"No," she replied in a tired voice, "you don't. You were acting on Dr. Wolfe's orders and a slave to the darkness, they just don't understand-"

"And they won't." Jack gave her a sad smile as the officers dragged him to his feet. Two SWAT soldiers joined them, their guns pointed at Jack's head. "Not until they see me surrender." He nodded at the officer beside him, who glanced at General Rogers for permission. Ryo saw that he looked not only angry, but nervous. She would be, too, if she was arresting someone as dangerous as Jack.

"Where are you taking him?" asked Hunter.

"Somewhere secure," said the General. "We'll take care of it Hunter, don't worry."

Eli had somehow been excluded from the private arrest, but suddenly broke through the police barricade again and ran to Hunter's side. "What the hell are they doing?"

"They're taking him away," said Hunter with tears in her eyes.

"But Jack, you-"

"Don't worry about me," he said. The policemen lifted him to the right and shoved him toward the back of a SWAT vehicle where six armed guards climbed in after him. "You have more people to save!"

Tears spilled out of Hunter's eyes. Ryo gently touched her arm. "I know it's hard. But there is no one stronger than you."

"You said that," she murmured angrily. "But I don't feel strong right now."

Ryo was about to take her hand when suddenly, the Chairman of the Joint Chiefs appeared beside them.

"It's over," he said dejectedly, out of breath. "The President is dead."

Some of the policemen close-by heard the statement and before they could stop it, the news spread like wildfire and people were screaming.

Ryo stood, dumbfounded.

"No. What happened?!"

"We received a live broadcast from the bunker at the army base. General Chang shot the President because ... because they knew we were trying to hack their network and stop them from gaining technological control. They were never bluffing."

Ryo shook her head. "No, we were going to save him-"

"You couldn't," General Rogers spat. "You were too late."

Hunter looked down at Ryo, who felt the weight of his words fall on her shoulders.

You're too late.

Ryo didn't know what happened then, but suddenly, the world disappeared. Her body was teleporting without her consent. Was it taking her to the army base? Would she find her brother, Zac, Chantal and everyone else dead? Was it the telepath who created this disaster, or the General himself?

But Ryo did not re-surface in the army base. Instead, she opened her eyes to her room at the SSS.

And it was 5pm.

SEVENTY-TWO

It occurred to Ryo as she zipped up her superhero suit for the third time that night that no matter what she changed in the past, someone would always suffer in the future. People were going to die, and she couldn't keep going back to try and stop it. That was against nature.

But Ryo was not controlling this. Some unknown force was sending her back to this same moment so she could try again. Just like re-starting a computer game, Ryo had experienced enough to know how to make it better.

And she did know. She knew exactly what she had to do.

It would only end if she stopped the telepath. Ryo didn't know anything about the young girl, except that she was in the Death Caves when Ryo rescued Hunter, she had burns across her body, and she was now equipped with Fearne's power. Which meant that the only way to stop her was either to become immune to mind control or take away her power altogether.

And who could take away her power?

Damn, Ryo sighed. *I so enjoyed tranquilizing her.*

Ryo found Mikayla in the exact same position she had what felt like only ten minutes ago. This time she didn't try to be nice.

"I need your help."

Mikayla snorted. "Please, why would I help you?"

Ryo wasted no time. "Because otherwise, both you and Jet will die tonight."

Her face when blank, pale as a ghost. "Wh-what?"

"You and Jet will-"

"Oh come on Ryo," she scoffed in an utterly false show of confidence. "This is just some ploy, isn't it? A trick to mess with my head so I won't-"

"Steal Hunter, Zac and Marcus's power, pretend to be a soldier, sneak onto the jet and follow Hunter to the White House to kill her?"

Mikayla's mouth dropped open.

"Yeah," said Ryo, "I've already been there and it doesn't end well."

Her arms flopped to her side. "Oh, right, okay. And I'm supposed to believe you?"

Isn't what I said proof enough? "Do you really want to take that risk?"

"Uh, yup."

Ryo rolled her eyes. "Okay, well *before* you do that and make a complete idiot of yourself until all the powers you took on destroy you, I need you to come with us to the army base."

"Oh, you need me now?"

"That's what I just said." *Can I please hit her now?* "Mikayla, can you do this for us? I promise that once we defeat Dr. Wolfe – a man who didn't care about you at all, by the way – and we stop Hunter from killing Jet, I will get the SSS to release you."

Mikayla crossed her arms. The two of them never really got along – in fact they never talked at all – but Mikayla came to the conclusion very quickly that Ryo could easily stop her from escaping the SSS, and this way, she could be free and Jet would still be alive.

Sure enough, Mikayla rolled her eyes heavily and agreed. "Fine, what do I have to do?"

"Wait here."

"What? Why?"

Ryo shook her head. "No time to explain, and you can't take any more powers. You'll explode if you do."

Mikayla scoffed.

"Stay right here, okay? The fate of our country depends on you."

Just before Ryo disappeared, she saw a look of pride flash across Mikayla's face.

The only thing Ryo now had to change was Jet. As she went back to the hanger to find Hunter, she tried to think about how it would alter her fight with Jack. Surely it would cut the time in half? Ryo knew almost nothing about their fight other than what Hunter had mentioned earlier. If there was a way for them to not kill Jet and still defeat the darkness in Jack, Ryo was sure Hunter would know.

But Ryo couldn't tell Hunter, because then Hunter would want her to change the future and stop Dr. Wolfe from taking Will and Joshua.

Man, this power sucks.

Ryo looked down at her clock, calculating Hunter's arrival time at the White House with how long it would be before Jet arrived. *It's going to be messy.* She glanced up at the tin roof. *If I muck this up, you'll send me back, right?*

There was no answer. Ryo almost smiled.

Right. Faith.

Ryo's eyes hardly left her watch during the flight. It was about fifteen minutes until they arrived at the army base when she sensed the urge to disappear. Ryo gripped the syringe in her hand as she told her brother she was going to the bathroom, and then she disappeared.

Inside the White House, all Ryo could hear was silence. She'd miraculously teleported into the upstairs bedroom – President Lincoln's, she believed – and when there was a sudden rumbling sound, she knew she'd arrived on time. Ryo sprinted down the corridor, not trusting herself to teleport into the lobby where Hunter and Jack had walked from. Besides, there was blood dripping down her nose now from so much time and space travel.

Please God let Jet be alive! Ryo shook her head in disbelief as she ran, baffled that those words became a prayer in her mind.

She came to the top of a giant marble staircase, and when she peered around the wall, she saw them.

Destructo – Jack's demonic side – was towering over Hunter as she slid backwards in fear. Ryo's heart started to pound, her admiration for Hunter strengthening. She couldn't imagine facing such a beastly looking monster, especially one she used to actually care about. If Ryo hadn't seen the normal Jack and remembered his sacrifice, she might have tried to kill him instead.

But Jet was her priority, and from her vantage point at the top of the stairs, she saw him hiding in the shadow of a doorway on the opposite side, watching the fight with intensity. Ryo's smile widened.

I've got you, you son of a bitch.

After a deep breath, Ryo vanished and appeared just behind Jet, slipped the needle into the side of his throat and pressed down on the plunger. Hunter and Jack were so consumed by each other that they heard and saw nothing.

Ryo dragged Jet's limp body into the first room she could find and then paused for a moment to catch her breath, surprised at her own agility. There was a strength inside her that she never knew she had. Smiling, Ryo looked at her watch. She'd have to be back in at least ten minutes to take Hunter to Cuba, then go back to the army base before the Chinese soldiers could kill Marcus, and then go to the SSS to pick up Mikayla so she could help them defeat General Chang and save the President.

God, help me get through this, she thought. Then she vanished.

SEVENTY-THREE

You've got to be kidding me," was the reaction that everyone in the small control room at the army base had when Ryo brought Mikayla back. The fight in the hanger was won. Joshua and Will were most likely with Hunter, who had hopefully defeated Dr. Wolfe by now and was on her way home. They had paused for a moment in the shelter of the control room, aside from Ace who went to rescue Illya from Alfie the still-raging dinosaur, and the Captain, who went back for more men to raid the bunker.

"She wants to help," said Ryo. Her brother was holding her against him and dabbing at the blood dripping from her nose. Her head felt heavy and light at the same time.

Mikayla didn't say a word, knowing that Ryo couldn't spill her secret of having gone back in time. Though Ryo herself didn't know how they hadn't already figured it out.

"How can *she* help us?" Chantal scoffed.

"Yeah, I think we're doing a fine job on our own," Zac crossed his arms.

If only you knew, thought Ryo.

"There's a telepath in that room," said Ryo. "Mikayla can shut off her power before she knows what's hit her. Then we can go in and take down the General and the rest of his army. They'll know we're onto them in no time at all, and the President could get hurt if we're not careful."

"Oh," said Chevie in a remarkably cheerful tone. "Alright then, good to have you on board Mikayla."

366

The rest of them glared at him.

"What?"

Suddenly, static came through on the dead guard's walkie-talkie from the corner of the room and a voice in Korean barked out a question. Hurriedly, Marcus yanked the radio from his belt and handed it to Yung.

"Tell him all is clear," said Ryo.

Yung nodded and muttered a reply over the radio. They waited anxiously for the General to report back, watching him on the screen. He glanced at his advisor standing beside him – a male who was much shorter than the rest of them. Then he gave a short reply and Yung's face softened.

They all breathed a sigh of relief.

"We need to make ... a plan," said Ryo.

Zac's hand shot up. "Oo! I've got it! I'll pretend to be one of them-" He indicated to one of the Korean soldiers leaning against the wall with a slit throat, "-and I'll go into the bunker, then while I distract them, all of you guys can sneak in and take them out."

"It won't be that easy, they know you can shape shift. You have to take Mikayla," said Ryo.

Zac frowned at her as he transformed into the soldier. "What, as my escort? I don't think you're this guy's type Mikayla, sorry."

Mikayla rolled her eyes and changed into the other dead soldier.

"You sneaky little fox," said Zac. "You took my power!"

"Argue later," snapped Chevie. "Ryo's plan is perfect. That way, you and Mikayla can distract the telepath. How will we stop those fifteen other soldiers with powerful weaponry though?"

Korean-Zac wrapped his arms around Imogen – who looked a little displeased about being in the soldier's embrace.

"Leave it to Immi," said Zac with a grin.

"Actually," said Koko, "I can take anyone into the bunker without being seen if they hold my hand."

"Kinky," said Zac with a raise of his eyebrows.

"I'll be able to shut down the power directly and stop their hack if I can touch their systems," said Marcus.

"How long will that take you?" asked Zac.

"About a minute. Can you distract them for that long?"

"I can try," he said with a shrug.

Koko nodded. "I'll take you, Marcus. And I'll take Imogen as well so she's protected."

"Sounds like a plan!" said Chevie with a clap of his hand.

Ryo smiled and tilted her head to the side. "Go for it."

Zac and Mikayla almost turned and left when Chevie barked out, "Wait! What are you two idiots doing, you can't walk around in a superhero suit and a gray prison uniform!"

The two Korean men looked down at themselves and were instantly sheepish. With the help of Marcus and Chantal, they stripped the soldiers and slipped on their uniforms. Zac's name badge read 'Hu', and Mikayla's read 'Lee'. Zac looked high as a kite, picking up the soldier's semi-automatic and swinging it around.

"Be careful!" Chantal hissed.

Nodding, Mikayla and Zac headed the group that ran from the room to the downstairs area. Koko took Marcus and Imogen's hand and they disappeared with the blink of an eye. Chevie brought up the cameras from all the screens that Marcus had edited to look blank so that whatever the Chinese were accessing from inside the bunker was blank as well.

"Okay," said Chevie, "they should be there in a few seconds …"

That was the last thing Ryo heard before she passed out.

SEVENTY-FOUR

I t was a little hard for Zac to believe that he was standing next to Mikayla in a Chinese body about to casually enter a military bunker to stop a terrorist attack and save the President.

I mean ... it's Mikayla.

Zac glanced at her hesitantly as they made the march toward the bunker door.

"What?" she hissed. "Stop looking at me like that."

"Do you speak Chinese?"

"Do I *look* like I speak Chinese?"

"I always thought you were part Asian."

"I'm Italian," she growled.

Zac rolled his eyes. "Let's just get this over with. You take out the Fearne clone and I'll handle the rest."

Mikayla didn't look like she trusted his plan-making skills, but it was too late to take it back.

A large part of Zac felt absolutely no fear at the thought of a murderous clan of Chinese and Korean assassins/soldiers waiting in the room ahead. While someone else would normally see the absurdity of what they were doing and otherwise run screaming for the hills, Zac couldn't contain his excitement.

When they came to the bunker door, they saw that their only way in was to crack the coded keypad filled with numbers and complicated algorithms that made Zac's head swirl. He really wasn't technical. At all.

"We didn't think this through," Mikayla muttered.

Suddenly, there was a whisper in Zac's ear and he jumped around to see the empty corridor behind him.

"Who's there?"

"It's me, dumbass," said Marcus's voice. He started tapping on the screen to force the door open. After a long moment, they started to grate apart.

Zac and Mikayla marched into the bunker. It was exactly as it seemed from the cameras, only smaller. There was a bank of computers against the far wall, something you'd imagine in an old-school call center. The equipment looked ancient. This was definitely not the President's first choice as a back-up safe house.

There were, in total, eleven Chinese soldiers – or Korean, he couldn't tell – including General Chang and his advisor. To their left were the hostages: three men in suits, a woman and the President himself. They were all sitting against the wall with their hands tied. Zac resisted the urge to salute him.

The General and all his men turned to the two of them looking confused, suspicious and ready to murder all at once. The bunker doors grinded shut behind them. Zac saw Korean-Mikayla put her hands behind her back and creep toward the creepy-looking girl in the white dress who stood beside the hostages. The General was on the lower level of the room at the head of the communications desk where he presumed the nerdy hacking was taking place. If it hadn't already. That was where Marcus, Koko and Imogen would be heading so that Marcus could stop the viral terrorist attack.

The General barked something in Chinese and the tension in the air was so thick, Zac felt breathless. But then he remembered what he'd always learnt whenever he became somebody else – if he didn't embrace his character and give it everything he had, they would never believe him. Confidence convinces people. It wasn't just about acting the person, it was about *being* the person.

Zac straightened his coat compulsively and – without speaking a single word – he strolled away from the bunker doors and down the steps to the power dashboard.

The soldiers raised their guns and pointed them at him.

Shit, thought Zac as he froze on the spot. *They've got me.*

Again, the General shouted at him, and this time it felt like something final. Clearly he trusted Hu enough not to shoot him straight away, which gave Zac some time to distract them.

Problem was, he only knew one form of distraction aside from his ability to change form. If it didn't work, at least he had the opportunity to test it out before he died. He cleared his throat, took a deep breath and started to sing.

"Imagine there's no country … it isn't hard to do. Nothing to kill or die for, and no religion too." Holding their attention – very tentatively – Zac started to sway and click at the same time. "Imagine all the people … living life in peace–" Zac took a deep breath and steeled himself for the high note of the chorus when the General snapped a sharp word and silenced him.

Then the young girl in the white dress spoke aloud and he knew it was over.

"He's one of them," she said. Her tone of voice was exactly like Fearne's; dreamy and breathless. "The song is a distraction."

"And a damn good one!" Zac yelled.

The General gave him a terrifying smile and raised his arm to signal open fire.

Zac threw up his hand as if to protect himself, ready for the pain, waiting for death, but … death never came. The gunfire roared. Tentatively, he opened his eyes and there was a sparkling wall before him, bullets slamming against it like glass that would not shatter. Zac grinned, amazed at the sight before him, when suddenly, it was gone.

Imogen stood beside him with a cute smirk on her lips.

One of the Chinese women at the computer started shouting at the General and all of a sudden, the screens were flashing. She stepped back from her chair and knocked someone over. That someone was Koko and she and Marcus were wrenched apart, severing their invisibility and revealing them both. The soldiers aimed their guns at them and they were surrounded.

The soldiers were waiting for a command from the General. He seemed taken aback, which confused Zac. If he were planning a terrorist attack with the *help* of superheroes, wouldn't he bank on *other* superheroes trying to stop him?

That's where copycat Fearne must have come in. The General turned to her as though expecting her to take control of their minds. He relied on her. But the girl in the white dress was not looking at the General. She was watching Asian Mikayla.

And suddenly, his hands went up in flames. His body transformed back into Mikayla and marched at the Fearne clone, who screamed and cowered beside the President. Clearly her fear of fire was derived of the torture Dr. Wolfe put her through.

"Games up, General," said Zac.

The General merely laughed at him. The soldier near the President aimed a gun at his head.

"It's not over yet," said the General. The soldier cocked the hammer of his gun, and at the exact same time, the other soldiers with their weapons aimed at he and Imogen cocked theirs too. Imogen panicked. She couldn't shield every one of them individually.

"Stop what you're doing and put your hands up."

A voice – a sweet, melodic voice – came over the speaker system and Zac's body went weak with relief. Everyone in the room dropped their weapons and put their hands up. Even the President and his men lifted their hands – still bound together.

The General happily raised his hands, however, just moments before Chantal's command sounded over the radio, his assistant had activated something in the security system and suddenly, the room was filled with sirens and flashing lights that told Zac something very, very bad had just happened.

"What is that?!" screamed Mikayla with her hands over her ears.

"That's the sound," the General said gleefully in clear English, "of your country being blown apart!"

"You're freaking *in* our country!" Zac yelled back.

The soldiers then decided that their mission had ended. One by one, they picked up their handguns, pressed them against their temples and fired. Zac watched in horror as soldier after soldier fell dead on the ground. All but the General.

"You're too late," sneered the man. "Phase one is complete. Now, you will all perish. We have won."

"But you're forgetting one thing, General."

The voice came from the bunker door and Chantal appeared with Yung and Ryo. The young time traveler looked tired and weary, but the strength in her voice was enough to make Zac proud.

The General snorted. "What's that?"

"Evil does not win."

Ryo and Yung split apart and that was when a huge, lethal-looking black panther leapt through the air with a hair-raising screech and landed on the General with its jaw clamping down on his head. The last thing they heard was the General's screams before Illya tore out his throat.

Marcus leapt from the ground and practically fell on the desk with his hands tapping furiously at the touch screens. The rest of them crowded around him, staring at the countdown on the monitor that was coming up to ten seconds.

"I'm guessing that's not the countdown for *One Direction*'s new album, right?"

"Not helping, Zac!" said Chantal.

Marcus's fingers blurred across the dashboard of dials and keyboards. The clock read nine seconds.

"Marcus?" said Ryo nervously. "Now would be the time to use that power you were given!"

"Come on, nerd power!" yelled Zac.

"Marcus!" Chantal squealed as the clock hit five seconds.

Marcus turned to them with a crooked smirk. "I'm just screwing with you guys," he chuckled. His hand came down on a red button and the bank of computers – the entire room, in fact, exploded with electric sparks. They ducked down for cover as a message in green appeared along the giant screen reading 'SYSTEMS DE-ACTIVATED'.

"Piece of cake," he smiled.

It took them all a moment to realize that they had done it: they had won. And then they were turning to each other with grins like Christmas morning spread across their faces, eyes glistening in relief, so happy to be alive and together and victorious.

Cheers and whoops of joy rang throughout the room. Zac felt as if the moment needed another classic song of which he could actually belt out, loudly and perhaps in a microphone. But all he needed was the wonderfully passionate kiss Chantal gave him after she flung her arms around his neck. The kiss was so powerful, his knees grew weak and it took him a few seconds before he was able to wrap his arms around her, soon realizing that he was not himself but a Chinese man. He shifted back and when Chantal pulled away, she gave him an even bigger smile.

"Don't ever change," she whispered.

"I can't promise anything," he winked.

Someone cleared their throat and they turned to the men and women who were now free of their bonds and standing on two feet. The President fixed his tie and gave their team a very serious look. Zac felt as if that look were directed at him and lowered his head. He'd nearly gotten the President killed.

"I've met a lot of heroes in my time as President," he said to them. "But none had ever stood before the enemy and *sang* a John Lennon classic with such ... finesse."

Zac raised his head and saw that the President was smiling. He couldn't help the gigantic grin that spread across his face.

"Thank you," said the President. "For being brave and for saving us. For saving *America*."

And then he raised his hand and saluted them.

SEVENTY-FIVE

Joshua remembered the day he and Leo found the cave. He was young, a bit of a dreamer but not as adventurous as his best friend and partner Leo Phillips. It had been a long and strenuous journey to find the volcano, and back then the mouth of the cave had been covered in rocks and shaded by the rainforest trees. It was a miracle they stumbled upon it. Leo had hired a device from one of the local geologists that measured spikes in volcanic activity, and Joshua had followed him there.

"Look Joshua!" Leo said gleefully as he pointed to the screen of his thermometer. His rich curls were stuck to his forehead, the loose beige shirt he wore drenched in sweat. "Can you see that, it's on eighty nine!"

"Uh huh." Joshua swatted flies away from his face. It was covered by a ganza cloth attached to his wide-brimmed hat and still the flies managed to get under it. Every part of him was hot and he had only half a bottle of water left. "It's because we're on a volcano, Leo."

"No, the guy said when it goes above seventy, we've struck gold!"

Joshua didn't understand Leo's fascination with the volcano. Their expedition was purely to come up with as many different types of igneous rocks they could find. But their trip had been extended courtesy of Leo and his obsessive need to discover greatness. Joshua wasn't sure whether the volcano was really extinct – which they were certain of when they arrived – and that it had erupted in the past thousand years, or that there was something strange going on. Leo spontaneously bought the shack with some money he'd earned through college years ago – the owner was happy to get rid of it – and said he was going to come back in a month to explore the volcano in more depth. This was after they'd found the cave.

At first, Joshua didn't want to go inside. It made him nervous to think that there was live magma inside. And Leo was suspicious of volcanic vents. He was far too young to die.

Leo had been pulling rocks away from the mouth of the cave for half an hour when finally, he found an entryway.

"Are you sure you want to go in there?" asked Joshua as he swatted at the flies with a banana leaf. "I mean, it could be really dangerous."

Leo turned to him, his golden eyes more alive than ever. "Joshua," he said, "what if we find something wonderful in there?"

Leo had a kind of charisma that other people flocked toward. Sometimes Joshua didn't know why they were friends in the first place. Leo kept him alive and reminded him of what it was to live in the real world rather than through a microscope. That was what made his presence so contagious. "What if this changes our lives?" he continued. "I mean ... don't you ever think about finding a substance so amazing that it could cure cancer? Or make you rich enough to never have to work again? You could just travel and keep exploring and ... and Liz and I could start a family-"

"Leo, those are *your* dreams!" Joshua moaned.

Leo stood up straight, looking like Indiana Jones in the rays of sunshine that filtered down through the trees.

"And what are your dreams, Joshua?"

Twenty years later, Joshua stood inside the entrance to the cave and felt a pain in his chest. He never had dreams like Leo. He never thought about his future.

He thought about Hunter's.

About which classes she needed to take in school. About which college she would go to. About whether or not she would be happy if she found out about her powers, and how to make her life as normal as possible when she got them. He thought about her future with Eli, and then he thought about Will. He accepted that they were in love and he was happy for her to be with him, because Joshua knew he would always stand by her, just like Hunter said he would.

His dream had always been for her to be safe. And he was okay with going into the caves with Wolfe, knowing that he would never come out, because he had done well for Hunter. It might not be completely his doing, but one way or another, she was a hero because he made her so.

Dr. Wolfe's gun between his shoulder blades bought Joshua back to the present. Inside, the volcano caves hadn't changed. There was a narrow path in which they both had to duck under that led down a few meters before opening up into a large cavern. On the left was a lake the size of a house pool filled with bubbling, molten lava. Joshua winced at the heat that struck his body. It wasn't agreeing with him at all. The day that he and Leo explored the volcano, they had to take regular breaks from the heat and even then, they were burnt for days afterwards.

The doctor started to cough behind Joshua, but he did not move the weapon. Joshua skittered down the jagged path into the lower chamber where there were spherical stones imbedded in the right wall. They glowed bright red, shelved in perfect symmetry the way one might align photographs on a wall. Beautiful, as Joshua remembered.

The doctor's mouth hung open at the sight of them. "Incredible," he said. "It's like they were purposefully placed there. Marvelous."

Joshua couldn't agree more. But it soon became obvious to the doctor as he stood well back from the wall of Ravenadium stones that they needed to be pried from their place in the wall. He turned to Joshua.

"How do we do it?"

Joshua shrugged. "Ask your fancy scientist."

Before Simon could interject, Dr. Wolfe rolled his eyes. "Joshua, may I remind you that I could have Hunter killed if you so much as try to cross me?"

"And may I remind you, Dr. Wolfe, that this is my mountain. You should have been more careful stepping inside someone else's territory."

With moves much quicker than he expected to use in such extreme heat, Joshua snapped the flexi-cuffs around his wrists. They were weakened from the temperature. He whipped out a hand and struck the Agent in the jugular, cutting off his air supply, then threw a sharp haymaker into the Agent's jaw, knocking him out and possibly snapping his neck. The Agent stumbled back a step, dangerously close to the edge of the lava lake. All Joshua needed to do was finish him with a roundhouse kick and the Agent tumbled into the pool of lava at his feet.

Joshua turned back to the doctor and his scientist, who were gazing at him, completely gob-smacked.

Dr. Wolfe raised the gun and pointed it at Joshua. "No more games, Joshua. Simon, go over there and take one of those stones. I don't have all day."

Simon gazed at him in fear. "I ... I ... I ..."

"Well go on, you blubbering idiot!"

Simon started toward the wall. Dr. Wolfe trained the gun on Joshua, but his attention was on Simon. So was Joshua's, waiting.

And then, just as the scientist stepped within arm's reach of the stones, his foot knocked the trip wire Joshua had set up the last time he was in the volcano caves. He knew that the world wasn't safe with Ravenadium in the hands of men. If anyone tried to take the stones –

The trip wire set off a detonator he'd buried in the ground at the entrance to the cave. Miraculously, the wire was still connected. Simon and Dr. Wolfe knew it was too late and suddenly, there was an explosion in the entrance. The rocks started to cave in, covering the exit.

The explosion caused Dr. Wolfe to fire his gun. The rockslide crushed Simon, who stood closest to the entrance beside the wall, smothered before he could dive to safety. Dr. Wolfe and Joshua were thrown backwards, then there was nothing but silence.

Joshua covered his head as he lay on the ground. When the stones stopped falling and all he could see around him was dirt and dust in the air, he rolled over and saw that Dr. Wolfe sat beside the wall of glowing stones looking at the entrance in horror.

Pain came from a wound in Joshua's stomach. He looked down to see a dark stain spreading through his suit, slowly bleeding him out.

"What did you-"

"Now, Dr. Wolfe," Joshua coughed. "It's over."

SEVENTY-SIX

When the ground started to shake around them, Hunter saw that as her opportunity to make a move. There were four Agents, each of them with their guns raised and pointed at them both. When they were surprised by the earthquake, Hunter burned through the cuffs, lifted her hands and concentrated hard.

She had learned the limits of her powers, but it seemed that there, in the presence of the very power that made her, she was strongest. She didn't know if it would work, but like Joshua, she had faith.

Seconds later, all four Agents gasped and threw their guns to the ground. The weapons were bright orange as though they'd been drowning in fire. Hunter smiled and whirled around to face the four of them.

It all happened so quickly.

The Agent next to Will drew a knife. Hunter couldn't save him – the other three Agents were about to force an attack on her. Will twisted just as the Agent went to stab him and managed to catch the knife between his bound hands. She was sure the knife sliced his hand open, but at least he was free, and as he drove his foot into the Agent's chest, he tore Mikayla's blood bags from his waist and threw them on the dirt.

The three Agents had knives out too, and they were circling her, trying to determine what angle would be the best attack. She only smirked at them. For men who once haunted her nightmares, they were suddenly nothing compared to the fight she'd just survived at the White House.

The first Agent charged and Hunter easily dismissed his attack with a quick jab to his gut. Bent on one knee, she ripped the knife from his hand and drove it into his lower spine. The second Agent tried to stab her also, but she dodged his blow by a hair's width. Leaping to her feet, she threw a fireball into the Agent's face. While he was distracted, she scooped one of the guns from the ground and fired two shots into the third Agent's chest. She turned to the second Agent whose face had started to sprout nasty blisters and was about to fire when Will stopped her.

"Hunter, don't!"

She turned. His eyes distracted her, and the face she loved so much gazed at her pleadingly. Why? Why shouldn't she shoot this man who would have killed her if she didn't attack? A man who took children from their homes and threw them in ICE? Hunter looked down at the two Agents she'd killed and the third Will had knocked out, then she turned her eyes upon the last. She recognized him. He was there the night they took her outside the schoolyard with a packet of cigarettes in hand. It seemed like so long ago.

But if they hadn't, she would not have met Will. She wouldn't have more friends than she'd ever had. And she wouldn't have a purpose. For that, she was thankful.

"Kill me," he sneered.

Hunter shook her head and dropped the gun. "You're not worth it."

"Hunter, the entrance!"

At that, she raised her head and turned to the cave entrance that had been blocked by stones. "Joshua," she breathed. Forgetting about the Agent, she ran to the wall of rocks with Will on her heels. "He's trapped in there!"

Desperately, she started clawing at the stones.

"Hunter," said Will. "Hunter! You can't get in there."

"Don't tell me I can't!" she yelled back. "He trapped himself with Dr. Wolfe so that he can't have Ravenadium."

"Then perhaps it's a good thing that they can't ever get out."

"No, I have to get him out, and then I have to kill that son of a bitch!"

Will took Hunter's arm and stopped her from heaving at the giant rocks. "I'm sorry Hunter."

"No, I have to-"

"He's gone."

The rumbling beneath her feet began again. Hunter looked behind them to see that the Agent had fled. He sensed the danger, felt the awakening of the volcano. Hunter stared at the rock wall stopping her from reaching Joshua. The volcano was rising, feeling her pain, her desperation. She could sense the unimaginable heat inside it.

Don't hurt him, she begged it. *Please, don't let him be dead.*

"I can't leave him."

"Even after everything he did to you, after Eli?"

Hunter heaved at a rock. "I used to think he could never give me – what my real parents could. But he gave me *more* than I could ever need." No matter how much she tried, the stones wouldn't move an inch. "And even when I didn't know it, he showed me what it means to love someone so much that you would do anything for them. I just can't let him die!" She was scratching at the rocks with so much force that the skin of her fingers was shredding.

"Hunter, stop!" Will grabbed her wrists and forced her away from the wall.

"No!" She wrenched away from him and dove on the rocks, pulling harder than her body could muster.

Will's arms wrapped around her again. This time he didn't let her go. He dragged her, kicking and screaming, across the dirt until –

BOOM!

The volcano errupted. From outside, the force was so great that Hunter and Will tumbled head over heels and rolled to the tree line. They kept rolling, their backs colliding with trees so powerfully that the wind was knocked out of them. When Hunter stopped rolling, she coughed dizzily and turned to see lava seeping between the rocks of the cave entrance way up the hill.

SEVENTY-SEVEN

Joshua and the doctor stared at each other as the river of lava bubbled beside them. Joshua didn't think his life would end by gunshot wound, alone in a volcano with Dr. Wolfe. But it didn't matter, because as far as he could tell, the world was safe for now.

"It's not over." Dr. Wolfe shook his head. "My legend will live on, my company will never stop researching your genetics and Jack will continue to destroy the world."

"Hunter cured Jack," said Joshua through gritted teeth, knowing Hunter would not be there if she hadn't defeated him. He could feel the blood seeping through his wound and the life slowly draining from him. "He is no longer consumed by the darkness."

For a moment, the doctor was stunned. As if he needed to hide anything from the man he was going to die with. "But the world will never be the same," he sneered. "The public knows about you now. They know that you're more dangerous than you are heroes, and they will never trust you."

"You're forgetting that it doesn't matter who is a hero and who is not. All that matters is that we plant hope in people's minds. Encourage them to keep fighting."

"You're delirious," said the doctor. He stumbled against the heat of the lava and fell to the dirty floor just feet from Joshua, who could not get up. Sweat was pouring from his face. He felt as if he were melting.

"Not at all," said Joshua. "I'm just a *person*, Dr. Wolfe, a single person on this earth filled with billions of other people just trying to find their purpose in life."

"So you're just going to let yourself die. In here?"

"I may have powers, but I'm not invincible. You look at all the other men like you." He spat the words as though they tasted bitter. "How many of them tried to become momentary kings or gods or powerful leaders in a lifetime that lasted a fraction of history? You are delusional to think that your selfish quest to gain power is anything but a meager, limited, *human* speck on history's page." Pain throbbed through his body but he forced himself to go on. "You are *one* man on a giant planet in a universe full of wonders, and in fifty years' time, you will no longer be here to appreciate it.

"I am sorry, Dr. Wolfe, that you wasted your life fighting a war with yourself. But if there is one thing worth fighting for, it's for a life that helps others understand how privileged we are to be happy, to be special and to be free. You don't understand. And you never will."

Dr. Wolfe didn't say a word. It was as if he suddenly realized that he truly did have nothing to live for. He would not be leaving the volcano with the bounteous supply of Ravenadium he dreamed of. He had nothing but evil and there was no turning back, no starting over.

Dr. Wolfe looked Joshua in the eye, and through the haze of smoke Joshua thought he saw a sad smile on his lips.

"Until next time, Joshua," he muttered.

Then Dr. Wolfe climbed weakly to his feet and walked away. Joshua was so disoriented, his body overheating, his vision blurry and contaminated by the burning haze that he could not see where the doctor had disappeared to.

They say your life flashes before your eyes when you know you're about to die. But it wasn't Joshua's life that he remembered. It was Hunter's. Nothing before that ever mattered. Joshua remembered taking Hunter home from the hospital, how daunting it was to be a single father, how she filled his loneliness and distracted him from grief. He remembered the day the principal called him saying Hunter had started a fire in her grade one classroom. He remembered how proud he was to have her stand in the crowd of university lecturers and other important people, to see her wave and smile and cheer for him. He remembered her laughter in his lab when she tormented him with fire, not knowing exactly how much it scared him.

But he did not fear the fire any longer. The peace that overcame him was a peace that *came* from the fire.

Joshua stared at the empty cave. Either he was already dead and having a strange dream, or the heat was making him hallucinate, for from the lava lake he saw two figures arise. They took the unmistakable form of Leo and Liz, locked hand in hand, their eyes glowing brightly and their bodies encased in flames. They smiled at him.

"I did what you … asked …" he whispered.

You did more, said Liz in an eerily dreamy voice. *You loved her.*

Leo stared down at him proudly, making Joshua feel more at peace than he'd ever been before. As Liz's smile grew wider, she extended a bright, fiery hand.

I'm taking you home, she said.

Joshua reached for her, clasped her hand and held it tighter than he clung to life itself.

Then, everything was gone.

SEVENTY-EIGHT

The scream that came from her mouth was so angry and broken that it didn't feel like hers. Will took hold of her again as the ground cracked. Beside them, two trees crashed in on each other. She heard him tell her to run, saw the panic in his eyes and felt his hand wrench her to her feet. Then suddenly she was sprinting from the caves, focusing on her footing as they fled down the mountainside.

She and Will ran for their lives as the ground continued to quake and the volcano roared at them. Hunter didn't think of anything else but putting one quivering foot in front of the other and Will's tight grip on her hand. Twice they tripped on roots and rocks and Hunter's battered and bruised body could hardly get up, but Will picked her up and they ran further to escape the volcano. Suddenly, they broke through the trees and onto the shore of the beach.

Hunter collapsed on her knees. She couldn't catch her breath. Things were quieter there, the rumbling of the volcano background noise now. She turned around and saw an ash cloud climbing slowly into the baby-blue sky.

The volcano had taken him. Joshua had been killed by fire. She never thought it would happen this way. He was gone.

Will sat beside her. He took her hand and put his arm around her as she sobbed, just as she'd done when he lost Fearne. The last time she felt so torn apart by grief was when the young girl died.

She buried her head against his chest, clenched his arm and whispered, "don't ever leave me."

Will kissed her hair and held her tightly, rocking her back and forth. "Never," he said.

They remained on the shore until Hunter felt it safe to open her eyes to the real world. After time, she became soothed by the gentle crash of the waves on the shore. She tried to pretend that she and Will were alone and everything they'd been through that day was a dream. But it wasn't. Joshua was dead.

Eventually, dark clouds moved over them and thunder rolled across the mountains in the background. They realized they had to get back to the others to find out what happened, but the plane that Will and Dr. Wolfe arrived on had vanished. The Agent Hunter didn't kill must have fled in it. They decided to take shelter inside the shack and figure out what to do next.

They crunched over palm tree branches and ducked under vines until they came to the clearing in front of the shack. For the second time that day, Hunter stared at the house with a sense of what used to be. She'd lost her entire family. Her mother at birth. Her father, whom she thought had been resurrected but turned out to just be a figment of her delirious imagination and her desperation for someone to cling to, someone to shelter her.

And Joshua. He protected her from the start. He loved her unconditionally. He was the father she never knew she had.

A fresh wave of tears swept over her and she curled up against Will just feet away from the porch, feeling his arms wrap her tightly in a comforting embrace. Thunder clapped and the heavens opened up to a heavy shower of tropical rain. Hunter looked up at the downpour. The water washed away her tears, taking her back to the warehouse when it rained upon her and reminded her of what she needed to fight for.

For love.

Will started to laugh in wonder of the heavy drops of warm water. His child-like glee made her realize that she needed to be thankful she still had someone to love, so she leaned in to kiss him. Hunter never thought she'd get to kiss him in the rain, and what better time to do it than –

"Hey!"

The shout came from the porch. Hunter and Will broke apart and whipped around.

"I'm gone five minutes and you're already fornicating on my property!"

Hunter couldn't believe her eyes. Through the rain she saw a distorted image of a man with glacier-blue eyes standing under the porch.

It couldn't be.

Hunter away from the rain and up the steps of the shack. And there he was, leaning on Ryo with his hand over a bleeding wound in his stomach, alive.

"Joshua," she breathed and threw her arms around him. "How-"

"I couldn't do it," said Ryo. "I couldn't leave it up to fate."

Hunter gazed down at the girl in wonder. "You came back for us?"

"Of course," she said with a mischievous smirk. "What use is my power if I can't save lives? Besides ... the world can't live without this creep."

Hunter laughed and hugged Ryo, her hand still in Joshua's and Will by her side. If they hadn't managed to save the country, it didn't matter. She still had the two most important people in her life.

When she broke apart, Will held his hand out to Joshua. Weakly, he shook it. "I'm glad you're okay," said Will.

Joshua nodded. "Thank you."

"What happened at the base?" asked Will.

After the way they left it, Hunter didn't want to know. But Ryo merely smiled. "It's a pretty epic story. We're meeting back at the SSS compound to celebrate our win."

"We did it? The world isn't in danger anymore?"

Ryo smiled. "Well, not for now at least."

"Come on," said Joshua with a smile. "Let's go home."

"Wait, I just have to do something first." With that, Hunter took Will by the hand and pulled him back down the porch. She turned in the pouring rain, lifted her hands and pressed them against his cheeks. "How's this for paradise," she said with a loving smile.

Then, they kissed.

EPILOGUE

I'm right here," said Hunter with her arm wrapped around Will's body, pressed against him to keep away from the chill of the winter air. "You can do this."

They stood together on the doorstep of a very large London home, grand and historic, more of a castle than a mansion. Every window was lit, warmth radiating from the stone walls draped in overhanging vines. With snow covering every tree and sloping lawn around them, it was hard to keep the heat inside. But somehow the ancient house stood tall against the winter winds.

Hunter and Will stared at the brown oak door under the light of the porch lamps, a Christmas wreath adorning it, and listened to the footsteps that approached after Will rang the doorbell. With a lump in her throat, Hunter squeezed Will's gloved hand and held her breath.

The door swung open to a glowing entryway complete with a coatrack, a long carpet runner and a woman wearing a white turtle-neck sweater and slimming black pants. She held a mug in one hand. Her hair was blond and curled to perfection, her face flushed in surprise. The moment she saw Will, her hand released the door and rested over her heart.

"Oh … my …"

Will didn't move. Hunter had never seen him so stiff and rigid, and she knew enough about him by now to understand his fear. This house, this woman … it was just like Hunter returning to the shack, only there were no fond memories here.

It took a lot to convince Will to return to his home in London. After the White House rescue and their defeat of Dr. Wolfe, everything took a drastic turn for the better.

The world was taken by surprise after the public announcement of superheroes. Hunter, Will and all the others became celebrities. It was too much for some of them, who preferred to keep their identities a secret. Hunter and Will moved to the shack to keep away from the paparazzi, and because it was their paradise. The rest of them officially joined the SSS, which became their center of operations for any other cases that begged for the help of the world's first superheroes.

The Chinese and Korean soldiers and officials were ordered back to their country and matters were taken into the parliament's hands to keep them away. But even if they made plans to attack, it wouldn't be hard to stop them. Not with Jack on their side.

After a long and grueling trial, the authorities were able to overlook Jack's crimes if he agreed to undergo a year of observation at a special facility that studied human genetics – the right way – and he couldn't have been more grateful. After everything he'd caused, he was happy not to be executed. The public saw the soft, innocent side of Jack who presented his case with heart-warming apologies and his story of being overpowered by darkness and a madman. They couldn't say no. He was then moved to the facility called GENE Corp in upstate New York, where he was often visited by Clare.

Those who *were* arrested included Jet. After being found in the White House quite unconscious, he was marked by the SSS as 'highly dangerous' and taken to GENE Corp, only they had to sedate and secure him before deciding what to do with him long-tem. Mikayla wasn't allowed anywhere near Jet, which of course sent her into a furious frenzy and destroyed half the building, until the SSS was notified and Hunter and the others came to the rescue. Both of them are now under heavy observation.

From the wreckage of the army base, several Men in White and mutants were rescued. One of them included Jamison, who miraculously survived being trampled by Alfie. After recovering in a highly monitored hospital, they, too, were put up for a delayed trial and held in custody.

That left Alfie the dinosaur. With help from Marcus, Alfie was detained and turned into his normal self again. But he was unstable and sick in the head. Sadly, Alfie was put in a coma until geneticists could find a way to either reverse his power or psychologically condition him not to turn when he was angry. Until then, he was also moved to GENE Corp for further analysis.

Eli took Amelia back to New York to reunite with his father and fix whatever issues they had to start with. Jenny became a lecturer at Colombia University and assisted Eli part time with the opening of his own marine research and activist center, of which the SSS was always happy to fund. Joshua bought back his old apartment and Jenny moved in immediately. They often flew to Cuba to visit Hunter and Will, sharing stories of their lives and news from the SSS, because Will and Hunter preferred to stay away from telecommunications and just be with each other.

Others like Ryo, Chantal, Zac and Marcus went on their own adventures, but were always there for special occasions. Will's twenty–first birthday was a celebration to be remembered when Chantal convinced the local circus to perform a private show for them and Zac thought it would be funny to disguise himself as one of the clowns and sneak backstage to let all the monkeys loose on Seattle. It took them three days to find all of the animals and bring them back. The FBI rained hell upon them, reminding them of the agreement they made after the war never to use their powers unless in a crisis, otherwise they would be under arrest.

Holidays like Christmas and New Year's, where everyone would gather at the cabin with their families, were Hunter's favorite times of the year. She looked forward to campfires and hearing all of the mischief and adventures they were having across the globe. It was in those times that they missed Fearne, Mosi and Benji the most.

There were some challenges ahead of them. It seemed that the birth of superheroes brought with it doubt in society's mind. They were, as Joshua and Dr. Wolfe had warned them all, blamed for the horrible acts that were committed around the world and their inability to stop them. But they accepted it and understood that a world who believed in evil had to also believe in good, and they would try their hardest to do good for those who judged them. Humans, as Will said, need a higher power to blame because they themselves aren't strong enough to face their own sins.

It was easier to forget about the world when Hunter and Will lived in paradise. They would walk the small coast between the shack and the rock cliff and the path that lead to the volcano caves, where Hunter had sealed the entrance in a wall of solid magma so that no one could abuse the power of Ravenadium ever again. She knew she could not stop those that were hidden around the world; more people were coming forth with superpowers, joining the growing number of SSS members. The society was now the most successful rising organization in the world.

Sometimes they would swim in the ocean, sometimes they would laze about and stare at the wide, blue sky. When it rained, they would sit out on the porch in the humid air and listen to it, talking of the future and what it had in store for them. Hunter simply liked to be close to the mountain, feeling like a part of her existed in it. It was a soothing voice in her mind, a gentle warmth in her soul.

"This is definitely paradise," said Will, his tired, loving eyes happier and more peaceful than they'd ever been before.

And now, after seventeen years of bad memories of a home he was cast away from and parents who considered him a freak, Will couldn't speak or even smile at his mother. She remained speechless also.

"Who is it Rose?" called a sharp, masculine voice from the room down the hall and Will's entire body flinched. "I'm in the middle of-"

A man appeared beside Rose. He wore a business suit with a pinstriped blue tie, suspenders and shiny black shoes. His hair was graying on the side and his eyes like brown beetles glimmered at them both. Judging from the white sheen of sweat on Will's handsome face, this had to be his father. They were incredibly different from each other. While Will was tall and muscular and had strong, dark features and warm eyes, his father was just a head shorter with slim bones and an unevenly shaped upper lip that twitched the moment he laid eyes on Will. His mother – though beautiful and elegant as Hunter imagined her to be – remained completely shocked.

For a moment, nothing was said. The snow swirled around them as they stood on the doorstep, and everyone but Hunter was pale. Not knowing how this reunion would pan out, Hunter half wished she wore warmer socks.

When Hunter first saw Joshua after everything he'd done to destroy her, there was so much hatred in her mind that it was hard to keep the fire at bay. But she knew that forgiveness was the only way to solve their problems, and she was thankful that she did.

Will, however, had a childhood worse than anything she could have imagined. It was because his family deserted him that he was stuck in ICE for the majority of his life. Even now, a year after the White House incident and the public announcement the President made about the Impossibles, his family still had not made an effort to seek forgiveness or even apologize for their actions. If it were Hunter, she would have at least thrown a punch or set their Christmas tree on fire.

But Will was better than that. He gripped her hand tighter and cleared his throat.

"Mother, Father," he nodded at each of them. Rose made a small squeak in the back of her throat. "I'd like you to meet Hunter."

She looked up into his eyes as he smiled down at her, as if to say 'I don't care that they don't love me, they better love you'. She'd never been more proud of him.

"Hi," she said to the two of them, following his lead, joining in the game. Apparently Will found it easier to pretend that he knew his parents better than anyone and was simply bringing home a date. It didn't matter that he hadn't spoken to them in over seventeen years, nor that they were possibly the most disgusting people Hunter had ever known for doing such a thing to their son, because they were *his* parents, and it was better to forgive and forget than to hold on to resentment. "You have an absolutely lovely home," she added.

"Uh-" Rose stuttered. "We uh-"

"Saw you on the television," his father grumbled. "What a bloody mess *that* was."

"Elliot-" Rose snapped in a sharp tone. Will's father shut his mouth and puffed up his chest as Rose turned back to them, and for the first time, she actually gave Will a smile. It lit up her entire face, making her more radiant than she'd already been. It was a smile just like Will's. "William ..." Just his name was spoken with a thousand apologies and more sadness and love than a name could ever carry. "Hannah has made a lovely roast for dinner," she said through tears. "Would you both like to come inside?"

Will let out a long breath of air and nodded. "Yes," he said, "I mean ... we would like that."

It was one of the happiest moments of Hunter's life. To see Will forgive his family so quickly, and for his mother to welcome him back in such a perfect way was well worth the time it took for Will's father to come around. Hunter could see the pain and guilt in his eyes, however silent he remained throughout the brief tour of the house.

As dinner was being served, there was a rumbling from the grand staircase and suddenly, two young girls appeared. They wore beautiful dresses and bows in their hair, the most cliché example of proper English girls Hunter had ever seen. Shyly, they approached the dinner table and sat down opposite Hunter and Will.

"Will, these are your ... sisters," said Rose, again with tears in her eyes. "This is Emily–" The older one, who was at least fourteen, flicked her curly brown hair over her shoulder and smiled. "-And that's Eva."

"I'm eight," said Eva proudly and her blond hair as perfect as her mother's bounced into her eyes.

The look on Will's face made Hunter's heart melt. Under the table, she gripped his hand for support, just like he always did, and he twitched back.

"Emily," he breathed. "Eva. It's ... wonderful to meet you."

"Who is he Mummy?" asked Emily.

"He's your brother." Rose's voice broke at the end of her words. She looked at Elliot with sparkling eyes and for a moment, Hunter thought she saw him blink away a tear.

There was silence at the table. Will had never looked so overjoyed, not since Fearne passed away. The fact that he now had two little girls to love again was more than either of them could have asked for.

"You've got *reeeally* nice hair!" Eva shouted at Hunter and broke the silence. Laughter burst from their mouths, and they didn't stop, especially when Eva couldn't understand why they were laughing so hard and started to cackle madly, giving all of them an excuse to cry and laugh at the same time. Will stared at his father, who didn't look like he had ever laughed, and needed no more words to pass between them. Elliot nodded, raised a glass and grumbled out grace. He clearly wanted to apologize but his pride remained his strongest emotion. Yet the fact that his heart was softening made all the difference in the world.

During dinner, the housekeeper Hannah ran out from the kitchen and carried on like a mad woman, planting kisses all over Will's face and pulling him into a vice-tight hug. After she ran to make Will's favorite dessert, the little girls laughed at the lipstick smudges all over his face and his messy hair, which Hunter smoothed down lovingly.

At the table, Will and Hunter talked about the rescue at the White House, to which Emily and Eva listened intently. Eventually they couldn't contain their enthusiasm, saying they had posters in their rooms of 'Time Warp' and

'Static' and 'Rouge', even though the posters were only images of actors. For just last month, there was a movie released about the attack on the White House and the Army Base. They had all sat down at the SSS compound to watch it and laugh at how ridiculous and far-fetched it was. Except for Zac, who would not let anyone play him in a movie and insisted he be in it. They only agreed because of the publicity, however Hunter and the others were quite impressed with his performance. So was he.

"I always like Rogue the best," said Eva.

"Eva, it's *Rooouge*, not Rogue," said Emily matter-of-factly. "Can't you *read?*"

Hunter giggled at Emily. "A lot of people say that, it's okay."

Eva and Emily asked Hunter to show them her fire power. Elliot seemed reluctant and Hunter assured the girls there would be plenty of time in the future for them to see it.

"You must come back for Christmas dinner," said Rose. "We're having a party Christmas Eve and a family get-together the following day."

"Pleeeeease come!" Eva begged.

Will glanced at Hunter, who smiled in encouragement. "We'd like that."

"Actually," said Hunter, "we came here to invite *you* to a party."

Rose raised her eyebrows in excitement. "Oh?"

"Yes," said Will. "Our wedding."

Both Rose and Elliot looked as if they had been slapped in the face. Rose composed herself quickly and leapt from her seat in excitement, kissing both of them on their cheeks. The young girls clapped and cheered and Elliot rubbed his forehead and exclaimed, "you're getting *married!?*"

"Yay!" said Eva. "Yay!"

"Can I be a bridesmaid?" yelled Emily. "Please please *please!*"

"Girls, enough," said Rose. "I'm sure they haven't even figured out where the wedding will be yet."

Hunter and Will glanced at each other. They had considered the cabin, but the details were not concrete just yet.

"We wanted to extend an invitation," said Will, "and we hope you can make it."

Rose and the two girls looked at Elliot for his approval. His beady eyes swept over the two of them, not entirely certain what to say. Finally, he released a sigh and grumbled, "Only if there's good scotch provided at the reception." And he lowered his empty glass, reminding Hunter of the day of the funeral in which Will became intoxicated and told her he wanted to live with her in paradise, the same words he said when he bent down on one knee at the top of the hill they used to run to at the cabin with a view of Seattle stretched before them and a magnificent sunset and asked her to marry him. It was the beginning of a life she never imagined and a future she could not see.

The hard part may not be over. In fact their journey as heroes had only just begun. But it was like Dr. Rosenthal had said – it's about time they rested.

INTERVIEW WITH THE AUTHOR

Questions from Wattpad fans

WHAT WAS THE ORIGINAL PLOT OF THE ROUGE SERIES? - crazycookieheart

Originally, the second, third and fourth chapter of *Rouge* (about Liz and Joshua) did not exist. I felt like their story ended too quickly and I needed to open up their world a little more. *Embers & Ice* change a lot as well. ICE used to be an institution like Professor X's school for the gifted, run by Dr. Rosenthal. The kids used to go to classes (yep, Math included). But I felt it too similar to *X-men*, so I re-invented it the classic way and turned ICE into a horror show.

WHAT EFFECT DID THE SERIES HAVE ON YOU AS A PERSON? – BookMagic09

It's been a huge part of my life for the last three years. I've certainly grown as a writer, and it's pushed me to open my eyes to what's out there for writers. I don't think I'd ever have gotten this far if I hid behind my story. It's also been my escape from the struggles of daily life. I often lived through Hunter, comparing my circumstances to hers, and it helped me realize that I could be *way* worse off than I am. Hunter's growth is very similar to mine. How she matured, learned to be grateful for what she had and stepped up as a leader and a role model. A hero.

DO YOUR CHARACTERS REPRESENT ASPECTS OF PEOPLE YOU KNOW? – greencat1999

Actually, not really. It's more situations that are representative of my life. I wrote *Embers & Ice* while I was living in Canada over the winter. There are parts of Will and Hunter's relationship that reflect circumstances I found myself in. Hunter is certainly deeply ingrained in my mind. The parental aspect between her and Joshua is also representative of my own relationship with my parents in some ways, but I try not to draw too much from my real life, otherwise it's not an escape for me.

ARE THERE ANY OTHER INSTALLMENTS WITH SUPERHEROES IN THEM? – sawantrachana

At the moment, I want to take a break from the series to write about something else. But I know I will never let go of this story, and I have plans to perhaps write a spin-off with other characters like Marcus or Zac.

IF YOU COULD HAVE ONE POWER, WHAT WOULD IT BE? - african_queen_454

I think I'd take Chantal's power, because it would make life so much easier. Or Ryo's power. To go back in time has always been a dream of mine, and I often find myself wishing there was more time in the day to write.

WHAT IS YOUR FAVORITE CHAPTER AND/OR SECTION OF CONSUMING FIRE? WHAT WAS MOST FUN TO WRITE? – Hylla_Ramirez_

My favorite moments are always the epic ones. I loved writing the scene with Hunter, Jack, Jet and Mikayla at the White House. It was iconic for Hunter, and her connection with Jack is so strong that she pulled him out of the darkness. The moments between she and Joshua were particularly special, and I enjoyed watching their relationship grow. I also loved writing the scenes between she and Will, and the rollercoaster they go through before they finally admit they're perfect for each other and in love. I like the funny moments too, especially the ones with Zac. There's just so much I enjoy about writing this series.

HOW LONG DOES IT TAKE YOU TO WRITE A CHAPTER? - DragonPop

That depends on how much of the chapter is already in my head. If I get into a zone, it can take me an hour. Sometimes, though, I get stuck and spend days on one chapter. I usually force myself to finish the chapter if I can, even if it's horrible, so that I can pick up on a fresh page the next time I sit down to write.

WHO WAS YOUR BIGGEST INSPIRATION? - olivianorcutt

Easy. Hands down, J.K Rowling. If I'm stuck for inspiration, I watch the documentary *Magic Beyond Words*. That moment when her sister says, "If this is what you want to do, do it. Write. What have you got to lose?" always makes me jump from my seat and straight onto my laptop.

HOW DO YOU STAY SO INSPIRED AND DEDICATED TO A STORY THAT YOU JUST CAN'T STOP WRITING? - nyx_the_great

I suppose the only way to describe it is an addiction. It's just something I have to keep working on. And I love going back over what I've written – it inspires me to keep writing more when I read the story so far, and in my head I get ideas about what will come next and then the story continues. It's habit. Besides, I can't start something and not finish it. I want to know how it ends.

For more on the Rouge series, head to:

http://www.wattpad.com/user/IsabellaModra
http://www.isabellamodra.com/
https://www.facebook.com/RougeNovel
https://www.goodreads.com/author/show/7153840.Isabella_Modra

www.ingramcontent.com/pod-product-compliance
Lightning Source LLC
Chambersburg PA
CBHW051517250626
47156CB00001B/124